EMPIRE HIGH Forever

IVY SMOAK

ISBN: 978-1-942381-69-3

2024 First Edition

To me.

Because if there's one thing I learned on this journey, I need to always be true to myself and the story I set out to write.

CHAPTER 1

Friday

Matt

I could have stared at Brooklyn tied up in bed for a lifetime. Completely at my mercy. *But no.* Nigel had to go and ruin it.

"And if I ever catch you looking at my fiancée like that ever again, we're going to have a big problem." I let go of Nigel, depositing him back into the prom section of Club Onyx.

"But I was just trying to keep you and the lovely mademoiselle safe, Master Matthew."

"From what? We're in the middle of a private club." I started to walk away, but Nigel was hot on my tail. I spun around.

He froze, pressing his back against the wall.

If he was trying to blend in, he was failing. I glared at him and kept walking. But I heard his footsteps behind me. Was he trying to get punched? "Seriously, stop it. Stay right there."

Nigel froze in the middle of the hallway mid-step. "Like this?"

I ignored him and kept going. Luckily this time I didn't hear him following me. I opened up the door with the symbol of a masquerade mask and stared at the empty bed.

What the hell? "Brooklyn?" I called and looked around the room.

But she didn't respond.

I walked around the bed, but no one was there.

"Brooklyn?!" I said again and turned in a circle. My heart started racing as I faced the empty bed again.

I'd left her naked. Tied up. Alone.

Fuck.

I sprinted out of the room. "Nigel!"

"Yes?" His voice was faint in the distance.

"Where are you?"

"You told me not to move!"

I ran toward where I'd told him to stop following me.

He was still frozen mid-step.

"Where the hell is Brooklyn?"

"In the room with the masquerade mask."

Did he think I was dense? "I know where she's supposed to be. But she's missing."

Nigel's eyes grew round. "Well, I'd know where she was if you'd let me keep watching. Alas, my duties were tooketh away."

I hated everything he'd just said. "Do you have cameras in this hall? To see where she went?" But I had this sick feeling in my stomach that Brooklyn didn't just up and leave. Why would she? We'd been having the night of our lives. And…how could she? She'd been tied up.

"She was bound," Nigel said. "Which means something sinister is afoot. Luckily I'm always packing." He pulled a gun out from the back waistband of his tuxedo.

"Jesus, what the fuck are you doing?"

"Saving the day, Master Matthew. Someone must have kidnapped her!"

Oh. Wait. Kidnapped. I laughed as relief filled my chest. *Of course.*

"This isn't funny! Mistress Brooklyn is in danger!"

"She's not," I said. "It's just Rob. He told me he wanted to recreate our homecoming where Brooklyn got kidnapped and James saved the day. Only this time…I'd save the day." I shook my head. I'd specifically told Rob not to do that. And I didn't love the fact that he'd fake kidnapped my fiancée while she was completely naked. "I'll go find them."

Nigel nodded. "I'll search the room and bring up the security feed. You beat the shit out of Robert!" He sprinted off with his gun.

I was glad it was me rather than Nigel going to talk to Rob. Nigel might have shot him. I laughed again as I walked out of the Club Onyx hallway and back to the dance. I'd been so amped up, I'd let my imagination run wild. Of course Brooklyn was fine. I'd only left the room for a minute or so.

But then I saw Rob dancing with Daphne in the middle of the dance floor. Brooklyn was nowhere in sight. My heart started beating funny in my chest again. I pushed my way through the crowd until I reached them. "Where's Brooklyn?"

Rob shrugged and kept dancing. "I don't know. I haven't seen her in like an hour. What have the two of you been up to?" He winked at me.

"This isn't funny. Where is she?"

He lowered his eyebrows. "I just told you. I haven't seen her."

"Cut the shit, Rob. You said you were going to fake kidnap her..."

"And you told me not to. So I didn't. We went with your proposal idea instead..."

I grabbed him by the lapels of his tux.

"What the hell are you doing?" Daphne said. She grabbed my arm but I shrugged her off.

"Where. The. Fuck. Is. Brooklyn?"

"Are you high?" Rob said and shoved my chest, but I didn't even flinch.

I tightened my grip.

Rob sighed. "I was really trying *not* to recreate homecoming. Please don't make me throat punch you, man. I'm too old for this shit. How am I supposed to explain a black eye to my daughter?"

"Both of you, stop." Daphne grabbed Rob's arm this time.

But I wasn't letting go. Not until Rob stopped whatever stupid prank he was pulling. He always did this shit. He made pranks too big. Or way too small to even notice. I knew this was the first one. But it wasn't fucking funny.

"Not again," James groaned and pushed the two of us apart. "What the fuck, Matt?"

"He..." I pointed at Rob. But Rob looked genuinely clueless. And I knew Rob. He'd have an evil glint in his eye if he was in the middle of a scheme.

Rob ran his hands down his lapels. "Matt's lost his mind again."

I didn't know what he meant by *again*. But I felt my mind scrambling. "You didn't fake kidnap Brooklyn?" I asked, even though I already knew the answer. I didn't even pay attention to his response. I ran my fingers through my hair and turned in a circle. "Then where..." My throat felt tight. *Fuck*. I couldn't have a panic attack right now.

Breathe. If this wasn't a fake kidnapping, it meant it was a real kidnapping. I'd promised Brooklyn I'd protect her. I'd promised. *I can't breathe*.

James grabbed my shoulders and made me face him. "Let's split up and look for her, okay? Where did you last see her?"

I shook my head. "Mr. Pruitt."

"Her dad is here?"

I shook my head again. *No. Well, maybe.* All I knew was that if Brooklyn was in trouble, Mr. Pruitt was the one to blame. "This has to be related to her dad. I… I gotta go." All I could picture was walking into Mr. Pruitt's apartment 16 years ago and being told Brooklyn was dead. Tears started welling in the corners of my eyes. *Not again. Fucking breathe.*

James kept his hands on my shoulders. "Last time Brooklyn disappeared, we weren't there to help you. This time we are. Penny, go find Mason and Bee so they can help too. Daphne, get the lights turned up and make an announcement. Rob, go find Tanner."

Penny and Daphne darted off. But Rob stayed put.

"Seriously?" Rob said. "*That's* the task you give me? Psh Tanner. He probably took her. He's up to something shady, I'm telling you."

"Then I'll find Tanner," James said. "You stay with Matt." James ran off to go look for Tanner.

The music cut off and the lights turned on. Daphne tapped the microphone and asked if anyone had seen Brooklyn.

What if she's dead? What if I lose her again? I can't breathe.

Rob looked around, trying to spot Brooklyn in the crowd. "Is this a bad time to mention that if you'd let me fake kidnap Brooklyn then she probably wouldn't be real kidnapped right now?"

I bent forward gasping for air. *Fuck.*

"Hey," Rob said and put his hand on my back. "Take a deep breath."

"I…"

"Don't talk, man. Just breathe."

His voice was oddly soothing.

I took a deep breath. And then another. I couldn't afford to lose my shit right now. Brooklyn needed me.

Rob patted my back. "What would you and Sanders do without me?"

"I can't lose her again."

"You won't. Like James said. You've got all of us this time. We're not going to let anything happen to her."

But it already had. I stood up straight. The panic had settled in my chest, and now all I could feel was this sense of doom. *I can't live without her.*

James, Tanner, and Nigel all ran up to us. Quickly followed by Penny, Mason, and Bee.

"Nigel caught me up on everything," Tanner said. "Weapon them."

"Yes, Master." Nigel pulled out a suitcase from behind his back and popped open the lid. It was filled with guns. He lifted one up and tossed it at me.

I dodged to the side. "Would you stop throwing around firearms?"

Nigel looked horrified. "Why did you not catch it? You're supposed to be good at American football! And it's loaded. You could have hurt someone."

Me? "We don't need guns. We need to go see Mr. Pruitt."

Tanner shook his head. "Mr. Pruitt has nothing to do with this. He'd never hurt Brooklyn again."

"And how the hell would you know that?"

"Because we had a dinner..." his voice trailed off. "It's not important. All you need to know is that he didn't put that bomb in Brooklyn's car. And he's not responsible for this either. He'd never hurt her. Trust me."

Never hurt her? He'd fucking stolen her kidney and ruined my life.

"We don't trust you," Rob said. "That's the whole problem, man bun. Get lost. Matt's real friends can handle this."

Tanner sighed. "Do I look like I have a man bun, Young Robert?"

"Stop it," I said. "Both of you. I know it was Mr. Pruitt."

"Shouldn't we call the police?" Mason asked.

"I don't know if that's the best idea if the mafia is involved," Tanner said.

Yeah, probably not.

"And we don't want them poking around in here, scaring off potential lovers. Besides, it wasn't Mr. Pruitt. She was taken from one of the rooms. You have to be a member to even get access to this floor. Which Mr. Pruitt is not. And even if he did infiltrate somehow, he'd need the key. It had to be a member of Club Onyx."

"Then one of his hitmen must be a member here."

"None of his wet workers are club members either. I specifically checked. I wanted Brooklyn to be safe."

Well, great job with that. "Then it's someone he just hired. Specifically for this."

"I really don't think..."

"I don't care what you think right now, Tanner! Brooklyn is in danger. That's all I care about. And I'm going to get to the bottom of it by talking to Mr. Pruitt."

"Okay," he said. "But I'm worried we're wasting time."

I pulled out my phone and called Mr. Pruitt. It went straight to voicemail. *Son of a bitch.* "We need to go there. Now."

"Why?" Nigel asked.

"Were you not listening to anything I just said? Even if Mr. Pruitt didn't take her, it doesn't mean it wasn't someone with the mob. Poppy. Mrs. Pruitt. Fuck." I had no idea which one of those was worse.

Nigel sighed like I was boring him. "A big, beefy man took her. Not a sexy woman or an old lady."

I did not love the fact that Nigel thought Poppy was sexy. "What man? You got the video footage?"

"Of course I got the video footage," Nigel said. "You told me to. I always do what I'm told."

No, you don't. "Why didn't you lead with that?!"

"You didn't ask." He just stood there, staring up at me.

"I'm fucking asking now, Nigel. Who took Brooklyn?"

"Not Mr. Pruitt."

"Told you," Tanner said.

I glared at him. "Nigel, spit it out." Every second we spent talking about this was a second I didn't have to get Brooklyn back.

Nigel pulled out his phone. "Magnus King. He's been a member of Club Onyx for quite some time." He pointed to his phone where a video feed was playing. "There he is. See. The big, beefy man who's stealing your helicopter for your special surprise for Brooklyn."

I watched in horror as Magnus King carried Brooklyn into the helicopter.

"The escape is in poor taste in my humble opinion," Nigel said. "Men never steal other men's air carriages."

Yeah, that was a dick move. But that wasn't what I was worried about right now. "Is that video feed live? We can still stop them." I just needed to make it to the roof.

"No. It's from about five minutes ago."

I watched as the helicopter took off from the roof. They could be going anywhere. "Who the fuck is Magnus King?"

"He's a known enforcer for the Locatellis. I told you something sinister was afoot. They're probably seeking revenge for the death of their only heir. You know, since Poppy blew him up with that car bomb."

Fuck. This was bad. Really bad. I pulled out my phone and tried to call Mr. Pruitt again. But it still went straight to voicemail. "We need to go to Mr. Pruitt's apartment. He'll know where to find the Locatellis."

"No need," Nigel said. "I've already checked in with my spy network of houseboys. Or in this case, housegirls. The Locatelli's are very sexist and only hire housegirls. They forget that modern day boys can also do housework..."

"Nigel focus," Tanner said.

"Right. The helicopter landed at the Locatelli Hotel in New York City. They're keeping her there. Probably to murder her for revenge. Luckily, it's just down the street."

I took a deep breath. I was done panicking. I was done thinking about the worst case scenario. No one was murdering my girl. I turned to face my friends.

First things first. Brooklyn would want me to make sure Jacob was safe. I took another deep breath. "James. Penny. I need you to go home and make sure all the kids are safe."

Penny's eyes grew round. "They wouldn't...they..." her voice trailed off. "James." Tears started falling down her cheeks.

James nodded at me. "I'll call you as soon as we get back to the apartment. We'll make sure Jacob is okay." He grabbed Penny's hand and they ran off.

"I should go with them," Daphne said. She tried to hide the tremor in her voice, but failed. "And I'll go get Tyler and Hailey too. They'll want to make sure Axel is safe."

"Thanks, Daphne." I hadn't even thought about Tyler and Hailey. But of course their son was in danger too.

She gave Rob a swift kiss and then ran off to find Tyler and Hailey in the crowd.

I turned to my brother. "Mason, Bee. Make sure my house is safe." I was worried we were bugged. Or…worse. I couldn't get the car bomb image out of my head. I pulled out my key and handed it to Mason. "I know Brooklyn will want to go home as soon as I get her back. And I don't want any surprises. Double check the cars."

"We're on it." Mason squeezed my shoulder. "Go get her back."

"And you two are coming with me," I said to Rob and Tanner.

"What about me?" Nigel asked and cocked his gun.

"You go see Mr. Pruitt." I was a little worried that Nigel was going to accidentally shoot someone if he kept waving that around. And I'd prefer if it was Mr. Pruitt and not me.

"But he's not a part of this…"

"Yes he is. This is all happening because of him. Get whatever information you can out of him."

A smile slowly spread across his face. "I'll get it all! I haven't tortured anyone in ages!" He sprinted off with his gun in the air.

What the fuck? I shook my head.

"So what's the plan?" Tanner asked.

I'd let Brooklyn down a thousand times back in high school. And I wasn't going to let her down ever again. "Follow me."

CHAPTER 2

Friday

Brooklyn

I'd seen so many lives cut short. I'd lost so much. But I still closed my eyes tight and prayed to a God I didn't believe in. *Please let Jacob be okay. Please.* Tears streamed down my cheeks, wetting the mask on my face. *Just let my baby be okay.*

But I couldn't shake the feeling of what I already knew to be true. Everyone I loved died. *Everyone.* And I loved Jacob more than I'd ever loved anyone. He was everything to me. A piece of my soul. And if anything ever happened to him… I knew that would be it. My heart would finally stop beating too. I couldn't handle any more pain.

"Silent now, huh?" the man who'd kidnapped me said as he put me down on something soft and covered my shoulders with a towel. "One mention of your son and you're quiet as a mouse."

I wanted to scream again. Instead, I clenched my jaw. I'd never do something that would risk my son's life. But I also wasn't sure if anything I did would keep my son safe. Because I loved him. And I was bad fucking luck.

My thoughts slammed together as tears spilled down my cheeks. I could hear Miller's voice when I'd told him I was bad luck. *"If anything you're my good luck charm."*

And I heard Matt's voice too when I told him I was bad luck and that everyone I loved died. *"What about my parents? And what about Mrs. Alcaraz? And what about me? I'm still here loving you. I'll always be here loving you."*

I took a deep breath.

I'm not bad luck.

Miller believed that.

Matt believed that.

And I needed to start believing it myself.

Nothing else bad was going to happen to me or my family. Because I wasn't 16 and in high school and being bullied by my crazy half-sister. I wasn't the same girl anymore. I was Brooklyn Miller. Soon to be Brooklyn Caldwell. And I fucking believed in myself.

I clenched my jaw harder as I tried to think of a plan to get out of this mess. But all I could hear was the blood pounding in my ears.

I'd heard the ticking down in my head earlier. I'd heard it and ignored it. *Again.* And this was what I got for not trusting my instincts. I'd never make that mistake again. I knew when I was in danger and I just needed to believe when my body warned me.

Matt would know I was gone. There had to be cameras everywhere in that fancy club. But I didn't know how long he'd take. And a part of me hoped he'd just go to make sure Jacob was safe.

I took another deep breath. For some reason, my mind kept wanting to focus on homecoming with Isabella. No, I wasn't the same girl I'd been in high school. But I was the same in one way. Sixteen years ago, when Isabella had kidnapped me during the dance, I hadn't waited for someone to come rescue me. I'd rescued myself. And I knew I could figure out a way out of this too. I just needed to think.

I was definitely sitting on something soft. A couch maybe? And I knew he'd taken me to the roof of Club Onyx. We'd only been in the helicopter for a few minutes before we landed. So we were still in New York City.

But...I couldn't even picture any of the buildings nearby the Caldwell Hotel. That wasn't anything to go off of. *Think!*

I'd started hearing the clock ticking down when my father started texting me incessantly. Saying we needed to talk. Whatever was going on had to do with him. And as long as I wasn't screaming for help, there was no reason for my kidnapper to do anything to my son. "How do you know my father?" I asked as I started fidgeting with the restraints holding my wrists together.

"Everyone knows your father, Brooklyn."

I remembered my father saying something odd when we first met. Something about me not reading newspapers because I didn't recognize him. Was he really that notable in this city? I was pretty sure he was only notable in one circle. The worst one. The one that did this kind of shit. "Did he...did he do something to you?"

"No. This isn't about me."

Then why the hell did you kidnap me?! "Is there something you want? Money? You can have everything in my account." I still had that bank account filled with my father's money that Miller and I didn't touch. "Millions."

He laughed. "I don't need your money."

"Then what do you need?"

"I told you. This isn't about me."

"Then who is it about?"

"My boss. And your father."

His boss and my father? Yeah, that definitely screamed mafia to me. My dad had told Matt that he was retired. But of course that was a lie. Because the only thing my dad knew was lies.

I tried to focus on my kidnapper's words. He was doing this for his boss. So he was just doing his boss's dirty work. Which meant he was like Miller. A bodyguard of some sort? An enforcer? Maybe he wanted an out just like Miller had. Maybe there was a heart of gold hidden somewhere inside of him. Somewhere deep inside of him. Miller had never hidden his heart from me. He'd always been kind. "If this isn't about you, then maybe we can come to some sort of arrangement instead?"

"And what exactly did you have in mind?" His fingers lightly touched the bottom of my chin.

I shifted back and he laughed. *Don't touch me.*

"You're a little timid for my taste," he said.

"You don't know me." I wasn't timid. I knew how to defend myself thanks to Miller. If this man hadn't threatened my son, I probably wouldn't be sitting wherever I was still blindfolded and at his mercy. After the deer had scared me in the middle of the night at the lake house, Miller insisted that I learn to use a gun. But he taught me how to defend myself in other ways too. I kept playing with my restraints, trying to find a weak point. The ones around my wrists weren't as tight as the ones on my ankles.

"I know everything about you," he said. "Your mother died when you were 16 and you moved in with your uncle. But your uncle got sick too and then you moved in with your father. You were engaged very young, probably so that you could hide your true last name and not be in danger at all."

That definitely wasn't why, asshole. I loved Matt. And my father didn't want to hide me from guys like this. He was trying to keep me safe from Isabella. Hell, my father had been trying to get me to take over for him not too long ago. This man didn't know me at all.

"And then you mysteriously died. But my boss never believed that. It took us a while, but we eventually found you."

No. The blood in my veins turned to ice. *No.*

"Richard Pruitt has been off his game for years. Ever since his grandson was born. His heart just isn't in the business. And my boss is done taking orders from him. And we're definitely never going to take orders from *you.*"

I felt the tears falling down my cheeks again. "It was you." He'd killed Miller. He'd put the bomb in my car. "You killed my husband."

"No. Not me. Unlike your father, my boss likes getting his hands dirty. He did it himself. And the bomb was meant for you."

"I'm going to kill him," I said. I was surprised by the words that tumbled out of my mouth. I wasn't even sure I meant them.

But I hated that he laughed. "Sure you are."

"A life for a life," I said. I held back a sob as I twisted my wrist, trying to break free and failing. I'd wanted to kill my father for Miller's death. I hadn't been able to pull the trigger then. Maybe I'd be able to pull it on a stranger. A stranger who'd stolen everything from me.

"That's the whole problem. You already took a life out of retaliation. You killed Luigi Locatelli's only heir."

"I had nothing to do with that."

"And now he'll stop at nothing until your whole family is wiped from the map," he said, ignoring me.

My whole family? Jacob. My heart started racing faster as the restraints dug into my wrists. I needed to get back to my son. I needed to protect him.

"That's no use," he said and grabbed my wrist so I'd stop fidgeting. "You're not getting out of this. My boss will be here any minute to finish the job."

"You don't have to do this," I said. "You don't have to listen to your boss. You can be free. You can do whatever you want. I can help you."

He didn't respond. Which seemed like a good thing. It probably meant he was thinking about it. *Please be like Miller. Please want an out.*

"If you let me go, I'll help you," I said. "I promise. You don't need to work in this business. We'll figure a way out together."

"Not everyone's life is a fairy tale," he said.

Was he kidding? Did it look like I was in a fucking fairy tale right now?!

"And even if I did let you go…he'd still find you. He'd find you and kill you. And then he'd just kill me too."

Honestly he was probably right. Look at what happened to Miller. We'd just wanted to be free. I pictured our lake house. And him proposing under the lights hanging in the sky. The smile on his face. "*We're written in the stars.*"

Tears started streaming down my cheeks again. I'd gotten Miller out. But his life was still cut short.

There is no out.

Fuck. I leaned over. *I can't breathe.*

There's never an out. Miller knew.

I gasped for air and leaned over more. Miller knew his past would eventually catch up with him. That's why he'd written me that note. That's why he'd taught me how to defend myself. He knew he wouldn't be around forever.

There is no fucking out. There never had been. I'd been living in a fairy tale, just like my kidnapper had said. It was a dream. It was never going to last.

I can't breathe.

And who was I kidding? I hadn't saved myself 16 years ago when Isabella had left me naked and stranded in the middle of the city. I'd run to James for help. And my dad had shown up.

Whenever I was in danger, I always ran to someone for help. *Miller. Matt.*

God, Matt. I squeezed my eyes tight as my lungs refused to expand.

When I was a teenager, Matt had a bad habit of not showing up when I needed him. But ever since I came back to New York, he'd always shown up. And I needed him now. If my life was a fairy tale, I needed him to be my knight in shining armor.

And wasn't he? He'd been the reason I kept breathing when I first moved to the city. He held me when I cried about my mom. He'd been there for me after my uncle's funeral. And he'd loved me fiercely for 16 years.

Please, Matt. I need you.

CHAPTER 3

Friday

Matt

When Mr. Pruitt had taken Brooklyn from her uncle's funeral, I'd tried to come to her rescue. But I'd gone to the wrong apartment. I'd had no idea that Mr. Pruitt had a second hidden apartment where he'd taken her. I'd tried to show up. But I'd failed her.

The second time she was kidnapped, I'd thought she was dead. I'd had this hope in my chest that maybe...maybe she was still alive. I'd done everything in my power to find her. But I was just a kid. And I'd failed her again.

Now though? I knew exactly where she was thanks to Nigel's network of houseboy spies or whatever the fuck he'd said. And I wasn't a dumb kid anymore. I wouldn't fail this time.

I looked up at the Locatelli Hotel that was just down the street from Club Onyx.

"We shouldn't walk through the front doors," Tanner said. "They probably have cameras everywhere."

Rob nodded. "I hate it, but Tanner is probably right for the first time ever. Maybe we can sneak in the back door?"

"No, the back door will be tightly guarded," Tanner said. "Every man knows you must protect your back entrance from intruders."

"What exactly are we talking about right now?" Rob asked.

"Proper etiquette for locking doors."

"Are you sure that's what you're referring to? Because it kind of sounds like you think Magnus King has a very specific fear of being taken by behind from a stranger."

"Get off it, old chap. This isn't a time for jokes. My best friend's fiancée has been taken."

"Matt's *my* best friend. And you're the one procrastinating by talking about back doors…"

"The kitchen," I said. Brooklyn told me that when she had to sneak into the hotel at homecoming, she'd gone through the kitchen entrance.

"Magnus King takes it in the butt in the kitchen?" Rob asked.

"What? No. We can sneak in through the kitchen. What the hell are you two talking about?" I was trying not to pay attention to their bickering.

"I have no idea," Tanner said. "I actually have a list of all Club Onyx members sexual preferences and Magnus King has never once taken part in…"

"Stop it," I said.

"He started it," Tanner and Rob said at the same time and pointed at each other.

For fuck's sake. How did they not realize how similar they were? *I should have asked James and Mason to come with me instead.*

I walked past the first alley. There weren't any trash bins, so that must not have been where the kitchen was located. I hurried toward the alley on the other side of the hotel. *Bingo.* There were trash bins back here, but you could barely smell them over the aroma of freshly baked bread. The kitchen door was propped open with a brick. Brooklyn was a genius.

"Wait." Tanner grabbed my arm. "What's the plan now? Should we…"

"Dress like waiters?" Rob and Tanner said at the same time. They glared at each other.

It wasn't a bad idea. We were practically dressed the part already. I pulled off my tux jacket and tossed it to the side. Rob and Tanner did the same. Except Tanner folded his and gently put it on top of Rob and my discarded jackets.

"What are you doing?" I asked.

"It was expensive."

"You cheap ass, you're a billionaire."

"Because I'm fiscally responsible and never throw anything away like you millennials. Anyone who's lived through the depression understands."

"So my great grandparents understand you?" *And you're a millennial too.*

He shrugged. "I mean…probably. Not that I've ever met Bobby or Clara. Because that wouldn't make sense. Since I'm your age."

"Younger than me." And how did he know my great grandparents' names?

"Right. It's hard to keep track of time. Let's focus on the task at hand, shall we? Because if you're not careful, you'll blink and 50 years will go by." He walked through the open door.

Rob caught my arm before I could follow. "Why did you have to bring him too? He's so annoying."

"Can you please just get along for two seconds? All that matters right now is that we save Brooklyn."

Rob sighed. "Yeah. For Sanders."

Tanner walked back out wearing an apron and a chef's hat. "For my waiters." He chucked two aprons at us.

I didn't know how he'd gotten those so fast. But it didn't really matter. I put the apron on and tied it behind my back. We followed Tanner into the kitchen.

"Back to work!" Tanner yelled in a demanding voice.

"Yes, Chef Rhodes!" everyone in the kitchen shouted. There weren't many people working this late, but the handful of line cooks in here looked terrified as Tanner walked past them. Like they were worried he'd yell at them or stab them with a knife or something.

How in the hell did he convince them that he… Never mind. I didn't care. They were probably just tired from working all day and weren't paying attention to the fact that Chef Rhodes was not the executive chef here.

Tanner winked at me and turned back to his new staff. "And what are you going to say if someone asks you about where I am?"

"That no one has seen you or your friends, Chef Rhodes!" they all yelled in unison.

Okay then.

"This way." Tanner walked backwards through a door.

Rob and I hurried after him.

"Have you been here before?" Rob asked.

"No, never. Why would I come here when I frequent Club Onyx? And keep your head down, Robert, there's cameras everywhere."

"But they called you Chef Rhodes," Rob said as he trained his eyes on the ground.

Tanner shrugged. "Because they know how to show respect. Unlike some people I know."

"Where do you think they're keeping her?" I asked before the two of them could start fighting again. "Shit." I pulled them down a different hallway just as a security guard walked past in the other hall. "Do they seriously patrol the place?"

"Well, they have something invaluable, do they not?" Tanner said. "And Magnus King has a penthouse suite in all the Locatelli Hotels around the world. They'll be up there."

I found a stairwell and pushed open the door, doing my best to keep my head down. "Why do you know so much about Magnus King?"

"Because I've been trying to find him his perfect match for years. The more details I know the better. I feel like I'm close."

Rob laughed. "You own a sex club, man."

"The purpose of Club Onyx is to find true love…never mind. Neanderthals will never understand."

"Did you just call me a neanderthal?"

"If the hideous shoe fits."

"What's wrong with my shoes?" Rob looked down.

"They're not Odegaards."

"Of course they're not. That company sucks. The owner is a lying, crazy person with an insane complex that makes him label friendships inaccurately."

"I'm going to kill you by beating you to death with your basic ass shoes," Tanner said.

"Whoa." I stepped between them on the stairs. "Enough."

"He started it," they both said at the same time again and pointed to each other.

It was like hanging out with Scarlett and Sophie. "Do you two not understand the severity of what is going on right now? Brooklyn needs me. And for once in my fucking life, I'm not going to let her down. So get your shit together or leave."

Tanner cracked his knuckles. "We're ready. Right, Robert?"

I looked down at the step Rob was on.

Rob nodded. "Shit, someone is coming!" He gestured up the stairs where the sounds of footsteps were coming from. "Act normal."

Tanner started whistling and then ran up the stairs toward the noise.

"That's not normal!" Rob hissed. "And why are you running toward the person?" But he started running up too.

Fuck. I ran up the stairs after them.

"Top of the morning to you, good sir," Tanner said.

The security guard stared at him. "What did you just say to me?"

"Did I say something weird?" Tanner asked and turned to us. "I don't think I did."

You definitely did.

The security guard pulled out his radio. But before he clicked on the button, Tanner karate chopped him right in the throat.

He coughed and bent forward and then toppled to his knees.

What the fuck?!

He fell onto his side and didn't move at all.

"Did you just kill him?" Rob asked.

"No." Tanner cocked his head to the side. "I mean, I don't think so. I'm a little rusty. I hope I didn't hit his throat too low." He shook his head. "No, he's just asleep. I'm sure of it." He smiled. "Not rusty after all. High five."

I just stared at him. I was seriously worried he'd just killed that security guard, despite what he said.

"Fucking ninja," Rob said instead of high-fiving him.

"No, I'm not classically trained in that." Tanner leaned down and grabbed the guard's radio. "Come on, we better go before he wakes up." And then he started sprinting up the stairs again.

Rob and I glanced at each other. Yeah, I had no idea what that was either. I grabbed Rob's arm and we followed Tanner up the stairs.

We didn't run into anyone else. But Rob and I were completely out of breath by the time we reached the top floor. Tanner was just standing there breathing normally though.

"How are you not tired?" Rob said. "This hotel is fucking tall."

"Oh. I lift the weights. And…cycle? Yes. And…what's that other thing people do all the time to stay fit? Shot put."

"Who the hell shot puts?" Rob asked.

"Olympic athletes. Check yourself. And I feel like I'm really close." He looked a little dazed. "Like…really close."

"Well, you did say she was on the top floor," Rob said.

"No. I'm talking about Magnus King's match. I have the oddest sensation that it could happen tonight."

Rob laughed. "Why are you even thinking about this right now?"

"Because it's a full time job. You'd be terrible at it."

"Running Odegaard?"

"I have many jobs, Robert!"

Jesus. "Stop it. Seriously. We need to focus…" my voice trailed off as a guard walked out the door talking into his radio.

"There's no sign of any intruders yet…" his voice trailed off when he saw us. "What are you all doing out of the kitchen?"

Rob karate chopped him in the throat. And…nothing happened. "Fuck," Rob said. "Why did it work when Tanner did it?" He looked down at his hand in confusion.

The guard grunted and stepped toward him.

But Tanner spun around and kicked the back of the guard's knees, making his legs buckle. Tanner did a weird back flip over his head and then slammed the base of his palm into the center of the guard's chest. The guard gasped for air and then fell backward, his body sprawled out in the middle of the stairwell. Completely lifeless.

"What the fuck, Tanner?!" I yelled.

"Sorry." He winced. "Like I said…I'm a little rusty."

"Stop killing people!"

"I haven't killed anyone. He's asleep. Just like the last one."

"I don't think he's breathing," Rob said.

"He is. It's just shallow. You're acting like I'm an evil assassin."

"I have no idea what you are!" Rob yelled. "That's the whole problem. Oh my God, we're all going to jail." He groaned. "I'm not meant for prison. I like tits too much. Fuck my life. Now I need to talk to Magnus King about how to properly protect my back door."

"We're not going to prison," I said calmly, even though I wasn't entirely sure. "They kidnapped Brooklyn. And we were just…defending ourselves."

"Neither of them ever touched us," Rob said.

"It's fine," Tanner said. "He'll wake up." He kicked the guard's lifeless leg.

"Are you part of the mafia too?" Rob looked totally freaked out.

Tanner laughed. "They wish. They'd never be able to afford me. Plus I'm too busy running all my companies and hanging out with you guys. All your dramas are practically a full time gig, you know. And look." He snapped his fingers in front of the guy's face and whispered something to him.

The security guard groaned but didn't open his eyes.

At least he was conscious. I was relieved that Tanner hadn't killed him.

"See," Tanner said and put his hand on Rob's shoulder. "No need to take it in the butt after all. But seriously do you feel that in the air?"

"What, a dick?"

Tanner laughed. "No. Love, man. There's love in the air. Seriously, I'm so close I can taste it!"

I'd only seen Tanner look this excited when he'd told me that Kennedy fucked Felix.

"Are you implying that Brooklyn is going to fall in love with Magnus King?" Rob asked.

"Huh," Tanner said. "I didn't think of that. But it wouldn't be unprecedented. She's fallen in love with her captor before…"

"Quit it." I glared at him. "No one is falling in love with Brooklyn tonight."

"She was naked when he took her," Rob said. "And if your painting is accurate, he might fall in love with her…"

I hit him in the back of his head.

"Ow." He rubbed the spot. "I'm just saying we should be prepared for what we're about to walk into."

"I'd be so pissed if that's the love in the air I feel," Tanner said. "I didn't even introduce them. What a waste."

What the fuck were the two of them going on about? "Brooklyn isn't sleeping with Magnus King right now." I knew my girl. She was a fighter. She was the strongest person I knew, even if sometimes she didn't believe it. And I'd bet she was punching Magnus King square in the nuts right now.

CHAPTER 4

Friday

Brooklyn

My kidnapper untied my mask and put his hands on my shoulders.

I cringed at the bright light of the room.

"Are you alright?" he asked.

No, I'm not alright. You fucking kidnapped me. You told me Luigi Locatelli plans on killing my whole family. And I can't breathe!

I blinked as his face came into focus. He actually looked…kind. If a kidnapper really could look that way. He seemed genuinely concerned about me gasping for air though.

"It's just a panic attack," I gasped and bent forward.

"Do you get these a lot?" He kept his hands on my shoulders and it was oddly comforting.

I took a shaky breath. "Only when I think about my world falling apart."

He didn't respond. He just stayed there with his hands on my shoulders.

I took another deep breath. It didn't matter how kind my kidnapper was suddenly being. I still needed to get out of this room. My son needed me. Matt needed me. My friends needed me. I wasn't as forgettable as I once thought. And I wasn't going down without a fight.

I exhaled slowly as I looked around the office we were in. It was all white with modern furniture. Lots of sharp edges. I could use that to my advantage.

"Feeling better?" he asked.

I will be in a second. I lifted my knees as fast as possible so I could kick him in the groin.

But his hand fell from my shoulder and he grabbed my ankles before I made contact. "Nice try." He stayed on eye level with me.

I hated how kind he looked.

"Was that whole thing an act or…"

"I wish." Having panic attacks at the exact wrong moments weren't exactly helpful.

"Would some water help?"

"Only if you want it to be spit in your face."

He smiled. "I like the feisty side of you better." He let go of my ankles and stood up. He folded his arms as he stared down at me.

I tried to twist my wrists again but it was no use. I couldn't get out of these restraints. Even if I had incapacitated him for a few seconds, I only would have been able to hop around the room completely useless. The angles of the desk and other furniture were sharp, but not razor sharp. I needed him to feel comfortable enough to unclasp my wrists and ankles. I needed him to like me.

I stopped fidgeting and stared at him. "My husband worked for my father."

"I know."

"He was a bodyguard. Are you one too?"

"No." He didn't offer any more information.

"So do you just do the company's annual kidnappings?"

"Annual?" He smiled. "No." The way he said it made it seem like it was a lot more frequent than annually.

"Do you like your job?"

"It has its perks." His eyes fell to my chest.

I looked down. The towel he'd put around my shoulders had fallen. "Can you please untie me so I can put something on?"

"So you can try to kick me in the nuts again? I don't think so." But he lifted the towel back around me, this time tucking it beneath my arms to keep it in place. It was also probably so that I wouldn't be tempted to sucker punch him. If I did, my towel would fall.

"What's your name?" I asked.

"King. Magnus King."

Right. He'd mentioned something about being a king but not my prom king. I'd had no idea what he was talking about. "Magnus King. Huh."

"What?"

"It's just…that's the kind of name that belongs to a boss. Not a second-in-command."

"Trust me, I know."

I stared at him. "So you know you can do more than the semi-annual kidnappings?"

"Semi-annual?" he smiled. "Sure."

How many kidnappings a year did he do?! I tried to shake away the thought. "So maybe you should be in charge. Locatelli no longer has an heir. He's focused on revenge instead of running his business. You said my father lost focus. Locatelli has too. Maybe this is your chance to take over."

"So when Locatelli walks in this room to kill you, I should kill him instead? That's your plan?"

"Yes?"

"Hmm."

I lifted my shoulders to try to look more confident. "It's a good plan. You don't want to be working for someone else. You can run this whole town."

"There's only one problem. As soon as he steps down, I'm taking over anyway. There doesn't have to be any bloodshed."

"Except for mine? And my family?"

He pressed his lips together. "Did you want something to eat? Anything you want. It's on me."

"A last meal? Really?"

"Or maybe you want something stronger than water? Maybe some banana juice?"

I just stared at him.

"Or we could play a game? There's ping pong on the roof."

What kind of kidnappee wanted to get drunk and play ping pong? Seriously, who was this guy? "The only thing I want is for you to let me go."

"Brooklyn, I'm sorry, but there is no going forward from this. The Locatellis and Pruitts have been butting heads for years. It was always going to come to this."

That would have been nice to know. My father had mentioned unrest in the families before. I'd had no idea what that entailed. "But there doesn't have to be any animosity. If you let me go, I'll forget this ever happened. I'll tell my dad not to retaliate. And we're cool, right?"

"You're not in charge yet."

And I never will be. "But my father will listen..." *Shit. No.*

"What?"

"My father said he stepped down." *Maybe.*

"No he hasn't."

"He says he has. Which means my cousin Poppy is in charge." And we didn't exactly have a great relationship. I couldn't negotiate anything on her behalf. She was crazy.

Magnus lowered his eyebrows. "I would have heard if that was true. And you're the one taking over. Not your cousin."

"I want nothing to do with any of this. And I told my father that if he wanted to be part of my life and my son's life that he had to step down. And…he did." But did I really believe that? Did I believe anything that man ever said?

"Locatelli would have told me." He frowned and pulled his cell phone out of his pocket.

"Unless your boss was just using this feud between him and my father to get you to do what he wanted."

He didn't respond. He was busy texting someone.

Fuck this. I looked around the room again. There was seriously nothing helpful. "Actually, about that last meal. I could eat."

Magnus looked up from his phone. "Yeah? What would you like? Lobster? Or we have a great signature steak dish."

A steak *knife* would be perfect. "I'd love to try the steak."

He nodded and kept texting.

The door opened.

I half expected it to be the fastest room service order ever. But it was just a man with gray hair and a hardened face and no steak knife to help me escape. He gave me a quick glance and then sat down behind the white and black marble desk. He propped his feet up on top of it.

Magnus did not look particularly pleased. This seemed like it was his office.

"Brooklyn Pruitt," the old man said without looking at me. But he said my last name with such disdain. "Do you know who I am?"

I certainly had a guess. "Luigi Locatelli."

"Good. So you're all caught up. How long do you think it'll take for your father to come to your rescue? Half an hour? More?" He glanced at his watch. "I really want to get this over with as fast as possible."

Magnus stepped in front of me. "Poppy Cannavaro took over," he said. "Did you know?"

"Yes. And it doesn't matter."

"Of course it matters. Richard Pruitt has single-handedly kept the Cannavaros in line for decades. You know the Cannavaros are fucking nuts. Without him they'll…"

"He killed my son, King."

"Because you tried to kill his daughter."

Locatelli slammed his hands on the desk and stood up. "We're finishing this tonight. Understand?"

I started fidgeting with my restraints again as I looked around the room for anything helpful. I could pick up the lamp and hurl it at Locatelli's head…

"The Cannavaros will wipe us off the map next if you go through with this," Magnus said.

"No. They won't."

"Are you forgetting that Pruitt is married to one of them?"

"I have a deal set up with the Cannavaros," Locatelli said. "We're on the same page."

That couldn't be true. For all Poppy's faults, she loved my father. Her parents had died when she was young. She'd relied a lot on my father growing up. She never would have agreed to hurt him.

But…she'd also relied a lot on Mrs. Pruitt. *Oh, fuck.*

"We get rid of the Pruitt line and we're the head of the families," Locatelli said. "The Cannavaros have agreed. Simple. Clean. And no retaliation. The plan is flawless."

This wasn't just about my dad. It was about Mrs. Pruitt and her hatred of me. And my mother. She'd wanted me out of this town just as badly as Isabella had. But why now? I'd passed on taking over for my dad. I didn't want any part of her legacy. I just wanted to live my life. And my dad had stepped aside. Was his wife really that spiteful?

But I had a sinking feeling it went back farther than me reappearing in the city. Maybe Mrs. Pruitt had teamed up with the Locatellis a while ago. Maybe it was her that ordered the hit on me at the lake house. And she'd just gotten Locatelli to go along with it. She'd wanted me dead this whole time.

"So I'll ask again," Locatelli said and rounded the desk. He walked in front of me and pulled a gun out from his waistband. "How long do you think until your father arrives?"

My dad wasn't coming. I'd cut him out. I wasn't answering his texts or calls.

I stared at the gun and tried to keep my breath even. Tanner had told me to respond. He told me that if my dad was reaching out it was probably important. What if my father had been trying to warn me? I felt like I was going to be sick.

"Patricia was right about you," Locatelli said, a sinister smile splitting across his face. "You're much too weak to take over."

Patricia Pruitt could go to hell. "Mrs. Pruitt is insane." *And I'm a lot stronger than I look, asshole.*

"The divorce became final this morning," he said. "And I really think she'd prefer it if you called her Ms. Cannavaro now. The Pruitt name isn't going to be worth much in a few minutes. Really, where is your father? He truly is off his game." He glanced at his watch again.

Wait, what? They were divorced? My father had mentioned that they lived separately. He never said they were divorcing. Had he done that for me? I swallowed hard. Did it even matter? Tears bit at the corners of my eyes.

It did matter.

It mattered to me.

I'd told my father I wanted nothing to do with him unless he stepped down. Cutting ties with the Cannavaros could have been seen as a part of that. And he'd once told me that there was no out. Had he known they'd come for him? And had he done it anyway? For me? For Jacob?

My heart felt funny in my chest. My father was a liar. A thief. A mobster. But I knew somewhere deep down he did love me.

I'd tried so hard to remember the bad things about him over the years. But...he'd done everything from a place of love. Even if he'd done it all wrong.

Even this. There was no way he'd know the Locatellis would take me. He probably just expected them to take *him*. And he probably had tried to warn me.

I just wanted the truth. All of it. "Did Mrs. Pruitt order the hit on me? At the lake house? Was it you or her?"

"We made an arrangement."

"Was it your idea or hers?" *Just tell me.*

There was a knock on the door. "Room service!" called a deep voice from the other side.

Locatelli turned to Magnus. "Did you order something?"

"A last meal."

"Was that really necessary?"

"She deserves a final meal. I don't tell you how to do your job, so don't tell me how to do mine."

"Excuse me?"

Magnus ignored him and threw open the door. "Who the hell are you?"

Tanner was standing there in a chef's hat.

Wait…Tanner?!

CHAPTER 5

Friday – A few seconds earlier

Matt

"Should we just knock and say housekeeping?" Rob asked as we stared at the door with Magnus King's name on it.

"What kind of shoddy hotel has housekeeping coming around this late at night?" Tanner said. "Utterly ridiculous."

"Do you have a better idea?"

"Obviously." Tanner pointed to his chef's hat. "A late night snack." He knocked on the door and yelled: "Room service!"

"What the hell are you doing?" I said. "We didn't come up with a plan yet."

"I find it better to just act on impulse. I rarely plan anything. It always works out okay."

Of course everything worked out okay for him. Because he knew some kind of weird technique that put people to sleep almost instantly. Or killed them. I still wasn't entirely sure.

"You don't have any food trays," Rob said. "Magnus is obviously going to know you're lying. Besides, won't he know you're not the chef at this hotel?"

"Magnus King is rich. He barely pays attention to who's on staff." Tanner shrugged. "Look at me. I have no idea who cooks my meals on a daily basis."

"Isn't it Nigel?" I asked.

"Oh. Right. Yes, probably. But I don't know the particulars. He may hire it out for all I know."

I was pretty sure he made everything. Or else he wouldn't have asked me how much meat I wanted in my lunches. I shook away the thought. What the hell was I thinking about right now? "But won't he recognize you? You said you've been working on setting him up with someone."

Tanner shrugged. "He definitely won't recognize me. I just have one of those faces that blends into a crowd."

"Do you though?" I asked.

"Of course. Trust me, he has no idea who I am."

"But you just said you were helping him..."

"Forget about that. And don't mention it to him. I blend in. Trust me. It would be rather impractical to stand out everywhere I went."

"Then you should stop wearing neon green tuxes with zigzags all over them," Rob said.

"That's not me, Young Robert. How many times do I have to tell you? Look at the very normal tux I'm wearing right now. And definitely don't mention the colorful tuxedos or man bun to Magnus. It will confuse the poor lad."

"What the fuck are you talking about?" Rob asked.

Tanner just shook his head.

"Fine, maybe he won't recognize you," I said. "But what should we do? Should we just stand here?"

"To the side." Tanner pushed Rob away from the door.

Rob wasn't expecting to be pushed and almost fell over. "What the fuck, man?"

"I'll distract Magnus with my charm. And then you two rush him? Good? Good."

I ducked to the side right as the door opened.

Magnus King, the guy from Nigel's video feed, answered the door. "Who the hell are you?"

Yeah, this was a terrible plan.

"I'm Chef Rhodes," Tanner said. "Ask anyone from the kitchen."

Why the hell did he tell him his name?! Now he was definitely going to recognize him.

"Chef Rhodes? There is no…"

I didn't wait for him to finish his sentence. I rushed in and slammed my shoulder into his stomach.

The guy was built like a brick wall, but Rob jumped onto my back to add to my momentum and all three of us toppled to the floor.

"Matt!" Brooklyn screamed.

I turned my head to see her. She stood up, but immediately tripped and fell to her knees. She had a towel wrapped around her and her wrists and ankles were still bound. But she was alive. She was still breathing. The relief I felt was quickly erased when King slammed his fist into the side of my jaw.

Blood flew out of my mouth.

King grabbed me in a headlock, wrapping his arm around my throat.

Fuck. I clawed at his arm.

Rob scrambled to his feet and looked around for something to help. "Do something!" he yelled at Tanner.

"But Matt told me not to kill anyone!"

I gasped for air as King tightened his arm around my throat. I silently pleaded with my eyes to Tanner. *Help me.*

"I don't know what you want me to do!" Tanner yelled. "Is murder okay now?"

Rob pulled a lamp from the socket and slammed it down on King's shoulder. The glass shattered into a million pieces.

"What the fuck?" King groaned and released me from his grip.

I sat up and then slammed my elbow into his face.

"Son of a bitch," he said and grabbed his jaw.

I stood up and was about to kick him when I saw a glint of metal out of the corner of my eye.

"Enough," said a deep voice.

We all froze. There was an older man standing in the corner of the room with a gun pointed in our direction.

He smiled. "Matthew Caldwell. Your family has snubbed mine for years. Do you think you're better than me?"

I'm not a mobster, if that's what you mean. I wiped the blood off my mouth with the back of my hand. "I'm just here for my girl. Let her go and you'll never hear from me again."

"Ah yes. Brooklyn Pruitt." He walked over to Brooklyn on the floor, grabbed a fistful of her hair, and pulled her to her feet.

She didn't scream. But I saw the tears biting the corners of her eyes.

I swear to God. I took one step toward him, but he turned the gun to the side of Brooklyn's head.

No.

"Take care of Jacob," she mouthed silently at me. "Promise."

I couldn't lose her again.

"Please," she mouthed again. She didn't look scared.

But I was terrified. I couldn't live without her. Not again.

Tears started streaming down her cheeks now. "Matt. Promise me."

I nodded. Of course I'd take care of her son. But I couldn't lose her. I'd only just gotten her back. *Baby.*

Locatelli gripped her hair tighter, pulling her head back so I couldn't see her eyes anymore.

For years I couldn't remember the hue of her eyes. I didn't want to forget again.

King pushed himself off the ground. "I really think we should talk about this," he said.

"Well, this has been fun," Locatelli said. "But it's time to take care of the trash."

I grit my teeth. Isabella had said something like that to Brooklyn once. When she'd found out that Brooklyn's uncle was the janitor. And no one was allowed to talk to Brooklyn like that ever again.

"Let her go," I said as evenly as possible. "If you think it's been bad being snubbed by my family, just wait until we reign hell on you."

"Your family won't lift a finger unless they want to be next. The city is mine now. As soon as I end the Pruitt line."

What the fuck was he talking about?

"Luigi," Magnus said and lifted his hands to his sides in peace. "We really should talk about this. Teaming up with Patricia Cannavaro is a mistake. You can't trust her."

Patricia Cannavaro? Was he talking about Mrs. Pruitt? *Mother fucker.* I should have known she was behind this somehow.

"Did someone order room service?" said someone from behind us.

I turned around to see a very bewildered guy in an actual server's uniform holding a tray of food.

Tanner pulled off the cloche to reveal a steak dinner. "Ah. Perfect. Just what I was looking for." He lifted up the steak knife, spun it around, and threw the knife. It sunk into Locatelli's forearm.

He screamed and dropped his gun.

A shot fired off, the bullet landing in the drywall.

"Fuck!" Locatelli yelled and released his grip on Brooklyn's hair so he could pull out the knife.

Brooklyn fell to the ground. "Matt!" she yelled as she somehow managed to kick the gun toward me with her bound ankles.

I grabbed it off the ground and held it in front of me.

Locatelli dropped the knife from his hand and stared at me.

I'd never held a gun before. I'd never even imagined killing someone before. Well, that wasn't entirely true. I used to dream of offing Mr. Pruitt for what he did to Brooklyn.

But this guy in front of me? Practically a complete stranger? I clenched my jaw. He'd kidnapped Brooklyn. He'd been seconds away from killing her. He deserved to die.

The gun shook slightly in my hand.

I could feel everyone's eyes on me.

"Get over there," I said to Magnus King. "With him."

"I'm not with him. I don't agree with anything he's fucking doing."

"Over there. Now."

Magnus kept his hands in the air and walked over to Locatelli. I saw him eyeing something on the side of his desk. It looked like there was a button hidden at the top of one of the legs. A panic button probably. But he hadn't hit it.

"Matt, don't," Brooklyn said. She'd grabbed the knife off the ground and was working on cutting through her restraints.

"Rob, help her."

Rob hurried over and grabbed the knife. He quickly got her free and helped her to her feet.

"Get her out of here," I said and held the gun a little tighter. I didn't want her to see this.

Sixteen years ago, Mr. Pruitt took Brooklyn away from me because he thought I couldn't protect her. He thought Miller would do a better job taking care of her than me. But Mr. Pruitt was fucking wrong. I could protect her. I'd do anything to keep her safe. But the fucking gun kept shaking in my hand.

Rob tried to pull Brooklyn out of the room but she refused.

"Matt," she said.

I took a deep breath and stared at the man I was about to kill.

"Matt, it's okay. We can just call 9-1-1."

Nothing about this was okay. "Miller wouldn't have even hesitated." So why the fuck was I hesitating?

"You're not Miller." She gently put her hand on my arm.

I can protect you too. I clenched my jaw. I had to do this.

"This isn't you," she said again.

But it needed to be. For once in my life I fucking needed to show up. The gun started shaking more in my hand. I just needed to pull the trigger. I needed to show her I'd always be there to protect her.

"I don't want you to be anyone but you, Matt. Please."

I turned to look at her. Tears were streaming down her cheeks. Her beautiful blue irises were rimmed with red. I refused to ever forget the color again. I refused to let anyone ever take her away from me. The gun kept shaking in my hand.

Brooklyn wound her fingers around my arm. "I love you exactly the way you are."

I felt tears falling down my cheeks.

And a gunshot echoed in my ears.

No.

Blood splattered on the wall behind Luigi Locatelli's head and he fell to his knees. The shot had gone clean through his forehead.

I didn't.

I stared at the gun in my hand in horror. My stomach churned. I was a murderer. I was just as bad as her father.

Brooklyn let go of my arm. She looked…horrified. Disgusted. By me. She was staring at me like she didn't even know me.

I didn't mean to.

I dropped the gun. All I'd ever wanted was to protect her. I'd wanted to be enough. Because no matter how much I wanted to live in the present, I was haunted by the past.

She'd chosen Miller. And I knew a piece of her wished that he was the one standing beside her right now. I'd never fill that hole in her heart. I'd never be what she truly wanted or needed.

Especially now, based on the way she was staring at me.

CHAPTER 6

Friday – A few seconds earlier

Brooklyn

Matt wasn't a murderer. And neither was I.

Yes, I'd dreamed of killing my father. Yes, I'd dreamed of wanting revenge for Miller.

But if I had the gun, I wasn't sure I'd actually be able to pull the trigger.

It was one thing to want something. It was an entirely different thing to actually do it.

I knew Matt wanted to protect me. And I was so grateful. I was grateful that he'd shown up. I was grateful that he was even contemplating doing this. But Matt wasn't Miller. And I didn't need him to be. I just needed him to be...*him*. "I love you exactly the way you are," I said. And I meant it.

Tears ran down his cheeks. It looked like he was about to lower the gun.

But then a shot rang out. The bullet pierced Locatelli right in the middle of his forehead.

No. I was glad Locatelli was dead. He deserved it. But I hadn't needed Matt to pull the trigger for me. I didn't need him to be something that he wasn't.

Matt stared down at his gun in horror.

Oh, Matt. My heart shattered for him.

"What the fuck?!" Magnus King yelled and lifted his hands higher in the air.

Matt dropped the gun. He looked like he was going to throw up.

I knew he'd done it for me. But I hadn't wanted him to. I didn't want him to ever feel like he needed to be different. I didn't want him to feel like he wasn't good enough exactly the way he was.

I'm so sorry you thought I wanted that. I hugged him.

He put his arms around me. I pressed the side of my face against his chest. His heart was racing so fast.

There were so many times that he held me when I needed him. It had always felt like he was taking my pain away. And all I wanted to do was take away his.

Tanner put his hand on Matt's shoulder. "Your first kill is always the hardest. Taking another man's life is no easy feat. But you will get over it. Trust me."

"What the hell, Tanner?" Rob said. "How many people have you killed?"

"I just meant from shows I've seen. War shows. It's a history thing, Robert, you wouldn't understand. But you will get over this, Matt," he said.

I had a feeling that Matt wasn't going to get over this. Because this wasn't him. And this wasn't me. We didn't want to be part of this world. I didn't want danger to be lurking around every corner. *Danger. Shit.* I pulled back. "Jacob? Is he okay?! We need to go…"

"Just got the text from James," Rob said. He showed me the picture on his phone. James was sitting on the floor in his tux reading Jacob a bedtime story. "All the kids are safe. Although Penny crying woke them all up. Just so you know, the first thing Matt did was send James to check and make sure Jacob was okay."

Matt. I hugged him again. If I hadn't already said yes to his proposal, I would have now.

"Perfect shot, Uncle Richard."

I pulled back from Matt and turned toward the door to see Poppy standing there with Nigel and my father. The gun in my dad's hand was smoking.

"Dad?" my voice cracked. He'd come. Even though I told him I wanted nothing to do with him. And *he* was the one who'd pulled the trigger. *Oh thank God.*

"Angel," my father said calmly. "Are you alright?"

I nodded.

"Oh thank fuck," Matt said and looked up at the ceiling in relief. "I thought I killed him." He still looked like he was going to hurl. "Jesus."

I wanted to breathe a sigh of relief that Matt wasn't the one who had shot Locatelli. But Poppy was behind all of this. And it wasn't exactly soothing seeing my father so easily murder someone right in front of my face.

"Everyone stay where they are!" Nigel yelled. "I have a hand grenade and I'm not afraid to use it!" He lifted the grenade above his head and waved it around.

My dad turned to him. "Put that away before you hurt someone, son."

Nigel smiled up at him. "Do you think of me as a son?"

"I barely know who you are. Put the pin back in that now."

"I think I misplaced the pin," Nigel mumbled. "I expected to be using it." He looked around the floor and started checking his pockets.

"Why does no one ever offer you their jacket when you're in duress?" My father asked and walked over to me. "James let you run around that hotel half naked back in high school. And here you are again in nothing but a towel." He shrugged out of his suit jacket and put it around my shoulders.

I remembered him taking care of me after Isabella tried to murder me at homecoming. I remembered the smell of the cologne on his jacket making me feel safe. But I also remembered the smell of his cologne at the lake house making me feel anything but safe. I felt trapped. I knew there were a lot of sides to my father. I knew that he loved me in his own way. And I wanted to give him the benefit of the doubt. I at least wanted him to be alive long enough so we could talk about everything. All of it. I was just about to open my mouth when my dad turned to Magnus.

"As for you," my father said. "No one touches my daughter without my permission." He lifted his gun.

"Wait!" I stepped in front of him. "Magnus was just following Locatelli's orders. And he was actually kind of nice about the whole thing."

"He kidnapped you," my dad said.

So did you. But I knew my father didn't see it that way. He'd thought he was protecting me from Isabella. He thought he was doing the right thing. "Magnus isn't the bad guy here. And Locatelli was just a pawn, dad. Your wife is behind all of this. All the Cannavaros are. You should be threatening *her*." I pointed to Poppy. "Poppy betrayed you. She's working with your wife to..."

"No, Poppy was the one that warned me what Patricia was up to. I told you, Angel. Poppy is on our side. She found out what Patricia was doing. Well, not just what she was currently doing. What she *did*. I'm so sorry, sweetheart. But I was wrong. It wasn't just Luigi Locatelli who had a hand in Miller's death. It was Patricia's plan."

I swallowed hard.

"That's true," Poppy said. "Aunt Patricia completely lost her mind when you returned to the city. Well, actually before you returned. Since she was the one that planned to blow you up. Which for the record, I only just found out about recently. I told Uncle Richard as soon as I uncovered the truth. And I tried my best to talk to Aunt Patricia. But she wouldn't listen to reason. And why do you not believe that I'm on your side? I killed the Locatelli heir for you. Well, a little for Matt." She winked at him. "How are you doing, sugar tits?"

"Stop it, Poppy," Matt said and put his arm around my shoulders.

I melted into his side.

"And I've been trying to warn you all week that you might be in danger," my dad said. "Why haven't you answered any of my calls or texts, Angel?"

Because I thought you killed my husband! I hadn't believed that he was innocent. But now? Tanner had already told me that my father hadn't done it. But I'd kind of needed Locatelli to admit all of it to truly believe it. "Did you really step down, Dad?"

He nodded. "You told me I had to. So I did. Poppy has taken my place."

"I love being on top," she said and winked at Matt again.

"What the fuck?" Matt mumbled under his breath.

"Why now? Why not when my mom..." my voice trailed off. *Why not when my mom needed you?*

"Patricia's parents were still alive then. And Poppy's parents," he added a little quieter.

"Oh, it's okay, Uncle Richard. They definitely would have offed you for running out on Aunt Patricia. My parents were totally nuts. No need to hide it."

So are you, Poppy.

"I'd only just taken over," my dad said. "I didn't have the alliances I do now. I never would have survived. And I would have put your mother in danger. And you. But as I told you before…I didn't know you were born. I didn't know, Brooklyn. Or maybe I would have done things differently. I want to believe that I would."

Tears pooled in the corners of my eyes. He'd wanted my mother to get rid of me. He'd thought that she had. And it was hard not to wonder how everything would have turned out if he'd known the truth.

But you couldn't rewind time. I knew that better than anyone. All you could do was move forward. "But won't Mrs. Pruitt retaliate now?"

"You mean Ms. Cannavaro. She's no longer my wife. Distancing myself from the mafia was what you asked me to do in order to be a part of your life and my grandson's. So I took that very seriously. And…" He looked at his watch. "Oh, look at the time." He smiled. "A helicopter crashed into the Hudson River two minutes ago. My ex-wife was on board. There were no survivors."

I should have been horrified. My father wasn't looking at a news report. He was just checking the time. He'd clearly just had his ex-wife murdered. But having Mrs. Pruitt out of my life made me breathe a little easier.

My dad hadn't murdered Miller. And he'd gotten revenge for Miller's death. Twice over. Three times if you counted Locatelli's son.

And he really had retired. He was out. For real. For *me*.

"Did you seriously kill her?" Rob asked.

My dad turned to him. "It's better not to say these things out loud, Robert."

"Yeah, probably not," Rob said. "And um…speaking of killing people. We need to go check on a few security guards probably."

"They're fine," Tanner said. "Why do you never believe anything I say?"

"Because you're a crazy person."

"Ah, Poppy," my father said and turned to her.

I pressed my lips together. Was I the only one that caught the transition there?

"I think it's best if you team up with Magnus from here on out. The two of you can take over where I left off."

"But, Uncle Richard..." protested Poppy.

"No buts," he said, shaking his head. "It's cleaner this way. Two families can keep everyone else in line easier. And he has certain skills that you do not. And it expands your connections and power."

"I have to say I don't love this idea either," Magnus said.

"Would you rather be on the ground next to your boss?"

Magnus cleared his throat. "No, sir. But the Cannavaros...they're...they're..."

Crazy?

Poppy glared at him. She knew what he was inferring too.

"You'll keep each other in line, yes?" my dad said and turned back to me. "Now where were we? I see you're engaged again! For real this time. Because I'm done meddling." He lifted his hands to show that he was innocent.

Matt told me that my father never intended to let us get married back in high school. That he's always planned to take me away from the city. But I couldn't hold on to that anger anymore. Besides, his meddling let me live a beautiful life with Miller. It gave me sixteen years of happiness. It gave me Jacob. The only thing I regretted was hurting Matt. I'd loved my little bubble. And I loved my life right now too. I'd always love both.

"I think a celebration is in order. Magnus, order us a bottle of your best champagne, will you?"

"I really think we should discuss this a bit more," Magnus said. "Maybe privately?"

"Do you really think this is a negotiation? You were working with Locatelli to murder me and my entire family."

"I didn't know why…"

"And now you'll be in the know. Poppy, get closer to Magnus and discuss things, will you? I don't want to be a part of this anymore. I'm retired." He moved his hands together to show them that he actually wanted them to move closer together.

"Wait!" Tanner yelled and stepped in between Poppy and Magnus. "Magnus King, I want to formally introduce you to Poppy Cannavaro." He grabbed both their hands and made them shake. "That counts, I think," he said. "I introduced them. You all saw it, right?"

"That definitely counts," Nigel said. "Has anyone seen the pin to my grenade? My thumb is getting tired. And explosions aren't always good for coitus."

"Ew what?" Poppy said. She glanced at Magnus with her nose turned up.

Nigel kept pulling out his pockets. "Love is in the air. Don't you feel it? I just hope it's not explosive."

I had no idea what Nigel was talking about. I just wanted out of this room. And away from that grenade. I looked up at Matt. "Take me home."

CHAPTER 7

Friday

Matt

Mason and Bee were still working with a member of James' security to make sure my house hadn't been tampered with. I didn't want to take Brooklyn back there until we got the all-clear.

I stared at Brooklyn's back. She was just standing in the doorjamb of Scarlett's room where all the kids were asleep.

I wanted to comfort her. But I didn't know how when I was still a little shaky. I didn't know if I would have actually gone through with pulling the trigger. But when I'd thought I had? I'd never felt so much regret.

All I wanted was for Brooklyn to be safe. But I wasn't a killer. She told me that I was exactly what she wanted. That she didn't need me to be someone I wasn't. But there was a part of me that knew she'd always miss Miller. Not that she wished I was him. Just that she wished he was still here.

A sob escaped her throat.

I never could stay away when I knew she needed me. "Baby." I put my hand on her shoulder and she jumped.

She turned her head away from me to try and hide her tears.

"Come here." I pulled her against my chest.

"I don't know what I would have done if I had lost Jacob too."

I ran my fingers through her hair. God it killed me to see her cry. "It's over now." *For real this time.*

"It's hard to believe that when the pain never stops."

I held her tighter.

Someone cleared their throat.

I turned to see Penny standing there.

"I was just checking in," she said. "I don't know how much longer Mason and Bee will be. But you two should spend the night. Rob and Daphne are staying too. A slumber party of sorts." She smiled.

Honestly that sounded great. Being with our friends right now helped. "Count us in, Penny." I looked down at Brooklyn. She nodded in agreement.

"Brooklyn, would you like a hot shower? And you can borrow some of my clothes to sleep in."

Brooklyn was still in a towel with the Locatelli Hotel logo on it, with her father's jacket draped around her shoulders.

"Penny," Brooklyn said. "I'm so sorry about ruining your birthday. I don't even know what to say."

"Are you joking?" Penny grabbed her hand. "This is one of my most memorable birthdays ever. And you don't need to apologize for something you had no control over. Brooklyn, we're family. We're all in this together." She squeezed her hand.

Brooklyn smiled through her tears. "Actually, a hot shower sounds great."

"Come with me." Penny pulled her away from Scarlett's bedroom.

I exhaled slowly and grabbed my hand that kept shaking. I needed to calm down. Brooklyn needed me right now. And I was too in my head. I sat down on the stairs and closed my eyes for a second. I didn't know why I was still so shaken. I hadn't pulled the trigger.

"Rob told me what happened," James said.

I opened my eyes.

He sat down next to me with a sigh. "What a night, huh?"

I forced a laugh. "This was definitely not how I wanted prom to go."

"Honestly, it was about as bad as my original prom."

This time my laugh was real. "Mine too."

"At least Penny and Brooklyn got an authentic Empire High prom. Terrible."

I shook my head. "And it wasn't even Tanner who ruined it."

James laughed. "Promenade."

"Right." I took another deep breath.

James looked over his shoulder and then back at me. "I know Brooklyn came to my room that homecoming for help. But I definitely wasn't her first choice. She needed you 16 years ago. And she needs you now." He nodded toward his bedroom door.

I knew about how the two of them showered together after homecoming. "You want me to recreate *your* moment with her 16 years ago?"

"Unless you want me to join her in the shower again."

"Fuck off," I laughed.

He smiled. "Go on. Besides, I could use a minute alone with my wife. It is still her birthday for another few minutes."

I didn't need to be told twice. I wasn't a cock-blocker. I stood up and wandered into their bedroom. Penny was in their walk-in closet, probably searching for something for Brooklyn to change into. I quickly snuck into the bathroom and closed the door behind me.

The sound of Brooklyn crying could be heard over the water falling on the tile.

I opened the shower door.

She was sitting in the corner of the shower with her arms wrapped around her legs. Naked. Her hand was wrapped around her necklace. She was clutching the rings Miller had given her. But my ring on her finger shimmered in the light. The steam all around her made her look ethereal. She lifted her head and stared at me. She smiled, but it looked so sad.

I knew she'd been in her underwear when James joined her in the shower 16 years ago. And that James had been fully clothed. I was not trying to recreate whatever the hell that was. But I also wanted her to know that I was just here to make sure she was okay. So I kicked off my dress shoes and climbed into the shower still in my tux.

She laughed as I sat down next to her and let the water fall all over my pants.

It only took a few seconds for my clothes to cling uncomfortably to my skin.

"Why does every dance I attend end this way?" She let go of her necklace and stared up at me with her big blue eyes.

"It's a pretty great tradition. As long as *I'm* the one in the shower with you."

She slid her hand into mine and rested her head on my shoulder. For just a few seconds we sat there getting soaked.

It was oddly comforting. To just sit and let the water cascade down on us. It felt...safe. I took a deep breath, trying to erase the image of the gunshot from my head.

"I'm so tired of being scared, Matt. I'm tired of always feeling like I'm running out of time."

"Hey." I tugged her arm and pulled her onto my lap. "You're not running out of time."

She straddled my waist and I watched the beads of water drip down her tits.

No, James had definitely never seen her like this.

Her forehead fell to mine. For just a few minutes we breathed in each other's exhales.

My hand finally stopped shaking.

And her tears disappeared.

"I just want everything to stop hurting," she whispered against my lips.

I didn't know what exactly she was referring to. She'd been clinging to the rings dangling from her neck. Was she thinking about Miller? Was she thinking about her father? Her uncle? Her mom? She'd known so much pain that I couldn't possibly know what was plaguing her.

"Please make it stop," she whispered.

No, I didn't know what was hurting her in this moment. But I knew how to take away the pain. Because I knew she was the only one that could take away mine.

I slowly lowered my mouth to hers. Her lips were salty from her tears.

"Please," she whispered. "I just want the pain to stop." She shifted forward, grinding against me.

Fuck. I buried my fingers in her wet hair. Sometimes Brooklyn just wanted to be held when she cried. Other times she just wanted to forget for a moment. And I was really good at distracting her.

I kissed a path down her chest, tracing the water cascading down her skin.

When she'd first come back to town, fucking her was the only thing that made me feel better. And it would make us both feel better now. I knew exactly how to take away her pain.

My tongue swirled around her nipple.

She tilted her head back in the water.

I lightly bit down, tugging her nipple with my teeth.

Her moan disappeared into the steam as I kissed down her stomach.

"You're safe," I whispered. I kissed her hipbone. "We're safe here."

"In James' shower," she said, her laughter filling my ears.

"Don't talk about James right now."

She laughed again. "We really shouldn't be doing this in here." She put her hands on my shoulders and stood up.

James shouldn't have been with her the first time she'd needed help.

And I wanted to erase that memory from her mind. I caught her wrist before she could step out of the shower.

She stared down at me. "Matt."

I shifted forward onto my knees. She truly did look like an angel standing in the steam. And I was perfectly content worshiping her on my knees.

I placed a long slow stroke against her wetness.

"Matt," she moaned this time.

She'd asked me to take away her pain. I kept my eyes trained on her as I pushed her backward against the tile wall. I paused, my breath hot against her pussy and watched her chest rise and fall. Yeah, I knew exactly what my girl liked.

I grabbed her hips and thrust my tongue inside of her. She was so fucking wet for me. So soft. So sweet.

Her fingers tangled in my wet hair as my tongue swirled faster.

I lifted one of her thighs over my shoulder to get better access. I moved my lips to her clit and sucked. Hard.

"Matt." She grabbed the collar of my dress shirt to pull me up.

I raised my eyebrow at her and stayed on my knees. "Did you want something?"

"You."

"You know I like when you tell me exactly what you want." I circled her clit with my thumb as I looked up at her.

"I want your cock inside me."

"Hmm." I leaned forward and licked her pussy again. "Where exactly? Because I can think of a few places…" I gripped her ass cheek in my hand.

She groaned in frustration. "Matt if you don't fuck me right this second I'm going to lose my mind."

I'd definitely distracted her from her pain. And she didn't need to tell me twice. I stood up and grabbed her hands, putting them on the waistband of my tuxedo pants. She unbuttoned and unzipped my pants as I tried to get my dress shirt off. The fabric was too wet and clingy though and just stuck to my arms as more water fell on my shoulders.

She laughed as she tried to push my wet pants and boxers down my hips.

Fuck this.

I pulled my pants down just enough to free my cock and grabbed her thighs, lifting her legs around my waist. I slammed her back against the tile wall as I thrust inside of her.

She breathed a sigh of relief. Like my cock was the only thing that could soothe her.

Her sweet cunt was the only thing that could soothe me too. Especially when she gripped me like *that.*

I sucked on the side of her neck, marking her flesh.

Mine.

As she pulled me closer, I felt the ring on her finger on the back of my neck.

Mine.

I slammed into her harder.

She'd always be mine. And I'd never let anything happen to her.

I pictured the hole in Locatelli's forehead and closed my eyes tight. I'd always do anything to protect her. Even if it made me sick to my stomach. I thrust into her faster. The harder I fucked her, the better I felt. The easier it was to breathe. The less blood I saw in my mind.

And there was something really satisfying about taking her in James' shower. Brooklyn was mine. *All mine.* I moved one of my hands to her left breast and squeezed. And no one was allowed to touch her like this but me.

I was done feeling like I wasn't good enough for her. Like I wasn't what she wanted. She wanted me. For me.

Her fingers dug into the muscles of my back, trying to pull me even closer.

She wanted my cock.

My body against hers.

My love.

And she'd never run to anyone else again. Because I'd always be there for her. In any way she needed. I slammed into her harder, my fingers digging into her thigh.

I couldn't stop staring down at her. Sucking on her skin. Squeezing her tits. We were completely in the moment. Together. No fears. And definitely no pain. Unless I fucked her any harder.

"Feel better now, baby?" I said and bit down on her earlobe.

She shattered around me, gripping my cock.

Fuck. I emptied myself inside of her. Filling her pussy with my cum.

CHAPTER 8

Friday

Brooklyn

I felt surprisingly calm. Every time I moved, I was a little sore from my time in the shower with Matt. It pulled me back into this moment. Right here. With all the Untouchables and their spouses. Being here with them felt like home. And it made me feel young again. Like we were having a sleepover back in high school or something.

I blew on my mug of hot chocolate. It was like no time had passed at all. Yet…so much at the same time.

Matt pulled my feet onto his lap and smiled at me. He'd borrowed some clothes from James and the too small t-shirt clung to his muscles almost as much as his wet dress shirt had. Luckily Penny and I were about the same size. The leggings she'd let me borrow were more comfortable than anything I owned. And I couldn't help but think about the pair that Matt had ripped recently. I really needed to go shopping. I smiled. I definitely didn't think I'd be calm enough to be thinking about shopping right now.

"I can't believe you almost killed someone," Penny said to Matt. She was sitting on James' lap and he was absentmindedly tracing circles on her thigh.

They looked so at peace. I was so happy for him.

"I don't know if I would have done it," Matt said.

I wasn't so sure about that. It really seemed like he had been about to. But I was glad he hadn't.

"I thought you were gonna do it," Rob said. "You were all like, get Brooklyn out of here, I don't want her to see me kill this lunatic."

Tanner nodded. "He would have done anything to protect you, Brooklyn."

I knew. But he didn't need to. I lightly nudged Matt's thigh with my foot.

He caught my ankle and started to massage my sole.

I sighed and sunk farther into the pillows on the couch.

"Craziest birthday ever," Daphne said as she took a sip of wine. She seemed the most rattled still.

And I got it. She'd already lost someone close to her. I took a deep breath, trying to focus on Matt's fingers on my skin.

"The most memorable birthday ever," Rob added. "Only fitting for this lovely MILF."

"Stop," Penny groaned. But she was smiling so hard.

"A super memorable engagement too." He smiled at us.

I looked down at the ring on my finger. After all these years, it was still a perfect fit. And this time it meant more. Because this time it was permanent.

A comfortable silence settled around all of us. I looked over at Mason and Bee. I was so happy to see him so happy. His eyes met mine and he winked at me.

I rolled my eyes. He probably thought I was checking him out or something. I definitely was not. I took a sip of my hot chocolate.

"I have an idea," Rob said. "Let's play truth or dare."

"How do you play?" Tanner asked.

Rob groaned. "What is wrong with you? What full grown man doesn't know how to play truth or dare?"

"I grew up overseas."

Tanner used that excuse a lot for not understanding pretty common references. Did children really grow up so differently overseas? "It's when you choose to share a truth or perform a dare. And then the person asking gets to either ask a very inappropriate question or dare you to do something silly."

"Or dare you to do something inappropriate," Rob said and winked at me.

Daphne laughed and elbowed him in the side.

He bent over, pretending to be in pain. "Who's handing out the first dare? Birthday girl?"

"Sure," Penny said. She turned to Matt. "Truth or dare?" she asked.

He laughed. "Dare."

"I dare you to kiss your new fiancée."

"Technically she's my old fiancée."

"Hey." I lightly nudged him with my foot again.

"Careful with that." He grabbed my foot off his lap and pulled me closer. "And I will love you until you're old and gray, just so you know." He pressed his lips against mine.

Rob whistled.

I laughed and pulled back.

"Your turn, Matt," Rob said.

"Hmm. Truth or dare, Rob?"

"Dare of course."

"I dare you and Tanner to each say something nice about each other."

Rob groaned. "Seriously? Lame."

"You have to do it," Daphne said. "Be nice."

Rob shook his head. "Tanner, you look better without a man bun."

"Thanks," Tanner said.

Rob stood up. "He just admitted he sometimes has a man bun!" He pointed at Tanner. "Didn't you hear him?!"

Tanner just laughed. "And Young Robert…I think you have a wonderful imagination."

"That's not a compliment," Rob said. "You're calling me crazy. And I'm not crazy."

"Well, that didn't work," Matt said. "Rob, you're up."

He glared at Tanner. "I dare you to pull your hair into a bun and take off your glasses."

"I can't see anything without my glasses, but fine." He pulled them off. "And my hair is too short to put into that hairstyle." He ran his fingers through his hair.

I cocked my head to the side. Was it too short? I couldn't really tell.

Tanner cleared his throat and put his glasses back on. "Brooklyn." He smiled at me. "Truth or dare?"

"Um...dare?"

"I dare you to take your shirt off," he said.

I laughed.

"Whoa, what?" Matt said. "Not cool, man."

"Oh? Why?"

"We're engaged."

"Right, but..." Tanner looked down at his phone. "I looked up the rules and that was literally one of the examples." He held up his phone.

Sure enough it was on there. Wow, he'd seriously never played this before? I kind of thought he might be joking.

"Ask something else," Matt said.

"Okay. Brooklyn, I dare you to get a hickey from Rob like the one you already have on your neck."

I put my hand over where Matt had sucked on my neck in the shower.

"Okay," Rob said.

"What the fuck?" Matt said. He grabbed the phone from Tanner. "What the hell is this shit? You looked up adult slumber party games." He tossed the phone back at him.

"Right because we're adults."

"Choose something less *that*," Matt said.

I couldn't help but smile. I kind of loved how possessive Matt was being.

"Okay. Um…maybe just kiss Rob?" he said.

"What?!" Matt looked even more pissed about that.

I laughed. "It's fine," I said. "I'll just kiss him on the cheek." I set my hot chocolate down, climbed off the couch, and walked over to Rob.

He had a stupid cocky smirk on his face.

"Don't make this weird, Rob," I said.

"How am I making it weird, Sanders? Kiss me. I know you've been dying to."

"Definitely not."

"Pretty sure you have."

No. I leaned down to kiss his cheek.

But at the last second, he turned his head and pressed his lips against mine. I slapped his cheek and pulled back.

Luckily Daphne was just laughing. I was glad they were so secure in their relationship or else that would have been incredibly awkward. But I could feel Matt's heated gaze on my back.

"That reminds me of the good old days," Rob said and rubbed his cheek. "But finally! I didn't like being the only Untouchable that never kissed you."

"I never kissed Mason either, Rob." I felt my face turning red, realizing what I said. I turned to Penny. "Sorry," I said.

Penny smiled. "It's fine." She looked up at James. "Everything worked out."

James ran the tip of his nose down the length of hers.

I turned away and cleared my throat. "Okay, I dare Daphne to slap Rob."

"What?" Rob said. "Rude, Sanders. You didn't even give her a choice of truth or dare."

Daphne lightly patted the side of his face instead of slapping him. "If you're waiting for someone to dare you to have a threesome, it's not happening, babe."

He licked her palm and she screamed.

I laughed and sat back down next to Matt. "Sorry," I whispered.

His lips dropped to my ear. "I'm actually a little relieved to hear that you never kissed him back in high school."

"Of course I didn't. Why would you think I did?"

"Brooklyn, you kissed a lot of people back in high school."

I gaped at him. "Me? Really? What about you and the whole cheerleading squad?"

"Before I knew you."

I shook my head. But I couldn't stop smiling. Yeah, it really felt like we were teenagers again tonight.

"Okay, I dare Mason to kiss Brooklyn too," Daphne said.

"What?" Matt turned to her. "Traitor."

She just laughed and took another sip of wine. "Sorry, Matt." She giggled again.

"You really do not need to do that," I said to Mason. "Bee won't like it. So...don't."

Bee poured herself another glass of wine. "I'm actually really enjoying not having the heat on me," she said.

"Me too," Penny said.

"Agreed," Daphne added.

Yeah, hanging out with these guys could be *a lot* sometimes.

Mason took a swig of his beer, stood up, and stretched.

Why was he stretching?

"Bro," Matt said.

"Bro," Mason said back. "I'm the only one that hasn't kissed her. It's only fair."

"I hate all of you," Matt said.

I turned my head and tapped my cheek for Mason.

"I don't think so," he said. He grabbed my chin and turned me to face him.

It was strange. All these guys were hot. There was really no denying that. The Caldwells and Hunters were always too perfect for their own good. But I'd really only ever wanted to kiss Matt.

Mason shoved Matt's shoulder and then pressed his lips against mine.

"I hate this game," Matt mumbled.

I laughed against Mason's lips.

It was almost like he took that as a challenge, because his tongue darted across my lips.

"What the fuck?" Matt said.

I laughed again and pulled back.

Mason laughed too. "Yeah, that was like kissing my sister."

I pushed on his arm. Yeah that was definitely weird. And also in a strange way, it was kind of like kissing Matt. I shook the thought away. *Never again.*

"I'm going to kill all of them," Matt said as Mason collapsed back down next to Bee.

I snuggled into his side. "You're the best kisser," I whispered into his ear.

His body untensed.

I'd officially kissed every single Untouchable. And I'd already known it, but Matt was definitely the one for me.

"I feel like it's my turn," Tanner said.

"Don't you fucking dare, Tanner," Matt said.

Tanner laughed. "I was just kidding. After all, a *best friend* would never cross that line. I'm definitely going to be the best man now."

"You set me up," Rob said.

"I know your weaknesses."

Rob groaned. "That doesn't prove anything."

"You're both ridiculous," Mason said. "I'm definitely going to be the best man."

Tanner and Rob both turned to him. "No," they both said at the same time.

I laughed. I would be shocked if Matt didn't ask Mason to be his best man. But I kind of loved this rivalry Tanner and Rob had going on.

"I'm here, I'm here!" Nigel yelled and ran into the room. You could only see the top of his head. The rest of him was hidden behind a huge pile of pillows in his arms.

"Sorry," Tanner said. "I forgot to cancel this. It was part of the adult sleepover article I read."

What?

"Extra down in these ones," Nigel said and put them on the floor. "And I brought the lingerie too." He pulled a lacy bra out of a bag.

"What the hell is that for?" Matt asked.

"For the pillow fight. Like in the article Master Tanner sent me. And in my favorite movies about modern day sleepovers. If the lingerie doesn't fit, naked is fine too, based on my research. Actually naked is better." He dropped the bag and kicked it to the side.

What kind of movies was he referring to?

"Mademoiselle, you first," he said and smiled at me.

"No," Matt said firmly. "Truth or dare or whatever Nigel is referring to is over."

"But…" Nigel started.

"I didn't get a turn though," Bee said. "And it's only fair that I get to dare someone to do something."

I stared at her. She'd definitely had a few glasses of wine. And it seemed like the more she had, the more wild she got. I was so curious about her dare.

"Screw the lingerie," she said.

"Yes!" Nigel yelled.

She laughed. "No. We're flipping that shit on its head. I dare all of the guys to have a pillow fight in their boxers."

"Now that's a dare," Penny said.

"Here's to that." Daphne clinked her wine glass against Penny's.

"Take it off!" Bee yelled and hit Mason with a pillow.

Mason stood up and tore off his t-shirt. He winked at me again as he flexed his pecs.

I wasn't checking you out, weirdo. Although it was a little hard to look away. I watched as Rob jumped on the couch and ripped off his shirt as Daphne ducked out of the way laughing.

Penny climbed off James' lap. "You next."

"As you wish, birthday girl." He kissed her and then grabbed the collar of his t-shirt and pulled it off over his head.

All of these boys had definitely grown up.

"Oh my God, this feels like Daphne's bachelorette party all over again," Bee said.

Penny fanned her face.

"What happened at Daphne's bachelorette party?" I asked.

"All the guys put on a striptease for us," Bee said. "It was so hot. And James got soooo mad at Penny. Everyone really brought their A-game for her. And she was loving it."

"I didn't do anything wrong!" Penny said.

James lowered his mouth to Penny's ear and whispered something to her.

Her face turned bright red and she swatted him away. "It's pillow fight time. Unless you're backing down from a dare."

"Me? Never," he said and grabbed a pillow and tossed it at Matt.

Matt sighed and stood up.

My eyes raked down his body as he pulled off his too tight t-shirt. He tossed it at me and I laughed.

He lowered his sweatpants and kicked them off at me. Yes, everyone seeing him in his boxer briefs seemed inappropriate. But this show was all for me. Matt turned around and shimmied his butt in my face.

I laughed again and slapped his ass.

"We definitely have to do the same thing for your bachelorette party," Bee said.

"There's zero chance," Matt said. "I think tonight has been enough."

"Boo," Bee said and stuck out her tongue. But then she cheered as Mason tore off his sweatpants. And yes. He *tore* them off.

Tanner took his shirt off, folded it, and then turned to me. "Hold this for me." He handed me the shirt, grabbed one of the pillows Nigel had brought, and hit Rob with it.

Feathers burst out of it.

Rob grabbed a pillow too. More feathers burst into the air as he slammed a pillow against Tanner.

"Boys fight!" Nigel yelled and pulled off his shirt. He was surprisingly fit too. I'd seen him naked before, but I didn't remember his abs. I'd been rather distracted by his enormous monster dong. I stifled a laugh.

James jumped from one couch to the other, trying to get away from Mason.

Matt tried to break up Rob and Tanner hitting each other. They were being a little violent about it. And Matt was somehow taking most of the blows from the pillows.

"This is amazing," Penny said and plopped down next to me.

Daphne sat down on the other side of me. "It finally feels like we're all…whole."

Bee screamed and jumped on top of us.

"You're so drunk," Penny said.

Bee laughed. "Not even." She leaned across us and grabbed a pillow. "Are you guys thinking what I'm thinking?"

"Oh we're definitely joining in on this," Penny said.

We all got up and grabbed pillows.

"Attack!" Daphne yelled and we all charged into the fight. She jumped onto Rob's back and they somehow managed to both hit Tanner at the same time.

James and Penny started making out and Mason and Bee hit them with pillows.

There were so many feathers in the air now that I could barely see anything.

Matt caught me around the waist, holding me close so no one could hit me.

I looked up at the feathers floating all around us. It reminded me of the snow at the lake house. I closed my eyes for just a second and pictured Miller's smiling face. I felt him here with us. I felt him all around me. I opened my eyes and smiled.

Miller would always have my heart.

And so would Matt.

I could love them both at the same time. Daphne was right. I was whole again.

Matt leaned down and kissed me as the feathers fell all around us.

CHAPTER 9

Thursday

Matt

Brooklyn seemed okay the night after everything happened at prom. But each day that followed, she closed herself off a little more.

I poured us each a cup of coffee as I watched her sitting with her tomato plants on the floor. She was picking a few ripe tomatoes off the vines. But mostly she was just staring at them, lost in thought. I knew what the plants meant to her. I knew they tied her to her past.

I took a deep breath and handed her a steaming mug of coffee.

She shook her head. "Thanks, but I'm not thirsty."

Every time I tried to do something for her, she pushed me away a little more. I set the extra mug down on the counter. "Felix and Kennedy invited us out to dinner again tonight. Are you feeling up to it?" Felix had been texting me about going on a double date the past few days. They'd left prom early and had to find out second hand what had happened. I knew they were worried about Brooklyn. Just like I was.

"No, I want to make something with these tomatoes tonight. Before they go bad. Kennedy and Felix will understand."

They didn't understand. Neither did I. And I was starting to worry that Brooklyn was never going to leave the house again. "Have you thought anymore about costumes for the Halloween party next weekend?"

She shrugged. "I'm sure whatever you choose will be fine."

I didn't want to choose. I wanted us to look together. For a long time, there was no annual Halloween party. No one had been up to it after she'd died. But my parents restarted it a few years ago. And this was the first Halloween Brooklyn was back. I wanted to go all out. But she didn't seem interested at all.

"How about we go for a run?" I said and sat down next to her on the floor.

"That's okay."

"But you love to run."

She didn't look at me.

"I think the fresh air might do you some good."

"I'm not comfortable leaving Jacob here alone."

"He won't be alone. We can get Mrs. Alcaraz to watch him. Or Tanner. Or Nigel. Or whoever you feel most comfortable with."

"That's okay," she said again and picked off more tomatoes.

"Brooklyn," I grabbed her hand.

At least she didn't pull away from my touch.

"Maybe we should have your father over? You can ask him any other questions you have. To put your mind at ease."

"I don't want to see him."

"I'll skip work and stay here so you're not alone with him."

"You can't skip work again," she said. "You haven't been to work a day this week. And you told me you had meetings today." It almost seemed like she was excited to get rid of me.

"I'll figure it out."

She shook her head. "Really, you should go. And I don't want any visitors. If there's one thing I learned in the past few weeks it's that I should trust my instincts. And my instincts are screaming at me to stay here. Where it's safe. With you and Jacob. No one else."

I loved that she trusted me. But she was slowly breaking my heart. Life had given her an unfair hand. And she was starting to turn her back on it. I didn't want her to stop living because she was scared. "I just don't want you to waste any days," I said. I knew how important that was to her.

"Don't." She pulled her hand out of mine. "Don't use my mother's words against me."

"I wasn't, Brooklyn. I'm just worried about you."

"I need to be here. I don't know how to explain it. I need to be *here* where it's safe."

"What if we go to my parents' house for the day instead? We can jump in leaves again and..."

"You're not listening to me."

"I'm trying, but you're scaring me. Baby." I cradled her face in my hands. "You haven't even stepped outside in days."

"I'm protecting my family."

I was trying to understand. I really was. But...I didn't. "We're safe now."

"I know. Because we're *here*. And I'm not leaving." She stood up, making my hands fall from her face. "I don't know what else you want me to say."

"Baby, I just want you to talk to me..."

"Hiya, Coach!" Jacob said as he slid across the floor in his socks.

I laughed as he fell into my arms. The panic in my chest always subsided when Jacob was in the room. "Good morning, kiddo."

"Can we come to practice today? Pleeeeease?"

He'd been asking me every day. And every day, I looked at Brooklyn. Waiting for her to change her mind. Waiting for her to start moving forward again.

She shook her head.

I cleared my throat. "Not today, Jacob. Maybe next week."

"Noooooo. I want to come today. Mommy, please?" He turned to her.

"You heard, Matt," she said.

I pressed my lips together. I didn't love the way she was making it seem like I was saying no. I wanted nothing more than for Jacob and her to come to practice with me. But what could I say?

I ruffled Jacob's hair. "We can play outside when I get home, okay?"

"When will that be? And can Scarlett come?"

I looked up at Brooklyn.

She shook her head.

"I'll be home before dinner. We're going to have a quiet night in just the three of us. Your mom is making homemade tomato sauce. Doesn't that sound good?"

"Yessie. Sí. Oui."

I smiled. I looked up at Brooklyn to see if she was smiling too, but she wasn't paying attention.

I stood up, lifting Jacob upside down by his ankles.

He laughed as he tried to wiggle free. "Put me down!" he said through his laughter.

"What? I can't hear you!"

Jacob laughed harder. "I said put me down, Coach!"

"What?" I lifted him higher in the air.

"Coach!"

I plopped him down on the kitchen counter and stole another glance at Brooklyn. No smile. No laughter. I swallowed hard. I just wanted to help. I desperately wanted to help her smile again. But everything I did just seemed to make it worse. "I'll see the two of you later, okay?"

"Mhm," Brooklyn said, but she didn't look up or say goodbye.

"Call me if you need me, yeah?"

"Okay, Coach," Jacob said.

But still Brooklyn didn't say anything.

I gave Jacob one last smile and headed to the door. I needed to do something to fix this. But I didn't know how.

***

There was only one person that knew Brooklyn as well as I did. *Kennedy*. But Brooklyn refused to see her. I didn't understand why. Maybe Brooklyn was right. Maybe I wasn't listening. But I was trying my best. I just wanted to see her smile again.

I eyed my cell phone.

There was one other person that knew Brooklyn pretty damn well. *James*. But I didn't want to call him about this.

I kept staring at my phone. What if he was the only one that could help? He was the only person I knew that had dealt closely with the Pruitts. He knew them. He…he could definitely help.

I sighed. *Fuck it*. I hit James' number and pulled my phone to my ear.

He answered after a few rings. "Hey, Matt. How is Brooklyn doing?"

Penny had called trying to set up a play date for Scarlett and Jacob earlier this week. I'd let her know that Brooklyn wasn't up to it. I'd figured she'd told James too.

"Not great actually," I said. "I need your help. Do you think maybe you could talk to her?"

"Me?"

"She's scared to leave the house. She just…I don't know. She's closed herself off. I don't know what to do. And you know what it's like to be part of that world. Isabella tried to kill you."

James didn't say anything.

"And you made up with your dad. I know it's not the same as Brooklyn and her dad. But you were able to put the past in the past and move forward. I think maybe talking to you could help her. I don't know what else to do, James. I'm really worried about her."

"My next class doesn't start for another hour. I could swing by now."

I breathed a sigh of relief. "Thanks, man."

"Of course, Matt. I'll let you know how it goes."

Hopefully Brooklyn would let him in the house. I knew she didn't want any visitors. I was trying my best to listen. But…it was James. She'd talk to James. *Please let this help.*

CHAPTER 10

Thursday

Brooklyn

The thought of leaving the house made my chest hurt. I just knew in my gut that I was supposed to be home. That I was safe here. And I didn't know any other way to explain it to Matt.

I knew he was just trying to help, but if he asked me to leave the house one more time I was going to scream. I was exactly where I needed to be.

"Can we go to the zoo?" Jacob asked.

Not you too. I felt bad enough denying him football practice. "Not today, sweet boy."

"Can we go see Scarlett?"

This kid and his crush on Scarlett. "Maybe next week." That's what Matt had said. It was possible that I'd feel differently next week. *Maybe.*

"But I miss her."

I pressed my lips together. "Not today," I said. "But soon."

He sighed. "Can Abuelo Tanner come?"

I shook my head.

"What about Mr. Nigel?"

Jacob, please. I pulled him off the kitchen counter. "How about you go play with your trucks?"

"But they're not as fun without Mr. Nigel. He makes the engines roar."

"You can make the engines roar."

"Not the way he can."

I had no idea what that meant. "Use your imagination."

His shoulders slumped. He went into the living room and fell face down onto the couch in despair.

Jacob. Where had he learned that move? I had a feeling he'd picked it up from Nigel. I wasn't trying to torture him. I was just keeping him safe. "We can have cupcakes for dessert after lunch," I said. "How does that sound?"

"Cuppycakes!" He pushed himself up and then jumped off the couch. He fell to his knees on the carpet and started crawling around making his own engine revving noises. He was fine. We were all fine.

I turned to the stove to start the tomato sauce when there was a knock on the door.

"Abuelo Tanner!" Jacob yelled and ran to the door.

I dropped my spoon and ran toward him. "Jacob, no!"

But he flung the door open before I had a chance to stop him.

"Oh, hi, Uncle James." He said with a big smile. "Will you play trucks with me?"

So now he knew the word uncle? I'd have to teach him that for Tanner too. Although I did find it cute that he called him abuelo.

James crouched down to get on eye level with him. "That sounds like fun. But I need to talk to your mom first, okay, buddy?"

"Okay." Jacob ran back to his toys.

James smiled and stood back up.

"Is everything okay?" I asked.

"You tell me."

I sighed. "Matt sent you, didn't he?"

James stepped inside and closed the door behind him. "We're worried about you."

I shook my head and walked back over to the stove. "I'm fine," I said and turned off the burner before I accidentally burned the whole house down.

"I don't know if that's true, Brooklyn." He leaned against the kitchen island. "Matt says you haven't been leaving the house. You're pushing him away."

"I'm not pushing him away. I just want to be here. With him. I've told him that a thousand times."

"But you don't want to leave the house?"

"What do you want me to say? That I'm scared to leave?"

He nodded. "We can start with that. Why are you scared to leave?"

I folded my arms across my chest. "You know why."

"No, I don't. Your father took care of everything. You're safe."

Hardly. I just stared at him. "It's never ending."

"Penny took Scarlett and Liam to the park this morning. And came back home safely."

"You have security guards following their every move."

"Would that make you feel better? Having security? Because I can…"

"No," I said. "It wouldn't." It would remind me of Miller. It would remind me of everything I'd lost. Tears started welling in my eyes. "James, I've already talked about all this with Matt. He's just not listening. I have this innate sense that I need to be here. To be still. For just a while. And I need to trust that feeling."

"Okay. Well, let's be still then." He slid onto one of the stools.

I stared at him. I didn't know what he wanted from me.

"You spent a lot of your life on the run," he said. "I bet it's an adjustment staying still."

I put my hands on the counter. "I was at the lake house for 15 years, James. I'm used to being still." I frowned. I remembered right after Jacob was born. I'd had this innate sense that we needed to run. There'd been this doom in my chest. The feeling I had then wasn't like the feeling I had now though. It was almost the opposite. I just wanted to be calm. And comfortable. And…safe. I shook my head. Why couldn't I explain it right?

"Maybe that's the problem then. Living in the city isn't exactly still."

"That's not it. I like it here. I like being close to all of you guys. And Jacob loves it here." I looked over at him. *He'd like it a lot more if I let him out of the house though.*

James put his elbows on the counter and leaned a little closer. "After Isabella's death, I felt so much relief. For years, I'd felt on edge. But once she was really gone, I felt at peace." His eyes searched mine.

I did feel more at peace now. But still on edge. I couldn't explain it. And I was so tired of trying to.

"It was hard though," he said. "Because that feeling of looking over your shoulder doesn't just go away. I do understand, Brooklyn. Probably better than anyone."

I knew he understood. He'd been part of the Pruitt family for a short time. He got it. "What did you do? To get over that fear?"

"I leaned on Penny and…"

"I *am* leaning on Matt. He just doesn't like the way I'm leaning, I guess."

"You didn't let me finish. Yes, I leaned on Penny. But I leaned on all my friends. Would you have let me in today if Jacob hadn't answered the door?"

"Of course I would have."

"Really?" He raised his eyebrow at me. And for just a second, he looked 18 again.

I smiled and then sighed. "Honestly, James, I don't know."

"We're all here for you. You know that."

I blinked fast so my tears wouldn't start up. "I do know that. But I also know that I don't know how to talk about this. And Matt thinks I'm crazy. I don't want him to think that. But I just…I…"

"Want to be still."

"Yeah." I smiled. "That."

He looked over his shoulder at Jacob playing. "It's hard to stay still with kids though."

I laughed. "I know."

James turned back to me. "Sometimes being still is the same as being stuck."

I pressed my lips together.

"Did you know that my parents are divorced?"

"Matt mentioned that, yeah."

"It wasn't until Scarlett was born that I was able to have a real conversation with my father. About the way I grew up. About the way I felt about his absence. My dad was…awful. But I know it doesn't even begin to compare to how your father has been."

"Probably not."

"I forgave my dad. For all of it. I didn't realize how unhappy he was. How stuck he felt staying with my mother."

Where was he going with this? "I'm happy with Matt. I don't feel stuck. In the slightest."

James laughed. "I'm not talking about you and Matt. I'm talking about Mr. Pruitt. He's taken steps to make up for his wrongs."

"He *killed* his wife. That is not the same as just getting a divorce and owning up to his mistakes."

"Yeah, not exactly the same. But I think you'll feel a lot less stuck if you try to forgive him. It might put you at ease. You don't want to stay still forever, Brooklyn."

For some reason I wrapped my arm in front of my stomach. I looked down. I wasn't sure why I'd done that. It was something I did when I was pregnant with Jacob. Because I wanted to keep him safe. I dropped my arm.

"I can stay still for a bit though."

He nodded. "I wish I could stay still for a bit longer, but I have a class I have to get to." He stood up, rounded the counter and pulled me into a hug. "For the record, I don't think Matt cares whether you ever step foot out of the house again. He just wants you to be happy."

"I know." I pressed the side of my face against his chest.

"And I'm not trying to pressure you either. I was just here to talk. To let you know that we're all here whenever you're ready."

"Thanks, James."

***

Talking to James made me feel calmer. He did understand. I think he understood better than I even understood myself.

"Mr. Nigel!" Jacob yelled.

I turned around from the stove to see Nigel walking in through the door he'd installed in the middle of my living room. He had a huge basket in his arms.

I tried to give him a stern look, but I was pretty sure I failed. "Nigel, we talked about this."

"I did knock," he said.

Oh, did he? I'd been so lost in thought.

"Besides, I talked to Master Matthew about it. Not you. And I know you don't mind me coming and going as I please."

I mind a little. But I didn't mind how happy Jacob was to see him. The two of them walked into the kitchen.

Nigel put his basket on the counter, and then grabbed Jacob and put him beside it. "Your sous chefs are at your service, mademoiselle."

"What is all this?" I asked and looked into the basket. It was full of spice bottles.

"Matthew likes his food spicy."

"I didn't realize."

"That's okay. I've got you covered." He started pulling the spices out of the basket. "All the spices."

"But I want to play trucks!" Jacob said.

"What was that, Mr. Jacob? I didn't understand you."

"Camions!" Jacob said and pointed to his toys.

"Much better. You play. Your mother only needs one professional sous chef on this lovely afternoon." He put Jacob back down on the floor.

Jacob hurried back into the living room.

"What did Jacob just say?" I asked. "What does camions mean?"

"Trucks. He's a very fast learner."

Yeah, I know. With his mix of Spanish from Mrs. Alcaraz and French from Nigel, soon I wasn't going to understand him at all. "What is this?" I asked and lifted up a small shirt from the bottom of the basket.

"Oh, yes, I almost forgot." Nigel grabbed the shirt and a pair of athletic shorts from the bottom of the basket and walked over to Jacob.

I couldn't hear what they were saying, but in under a minute, Nigel had Jacob getting dressed.

What the…

Nigel walked over smiling. "Problem fixed."

"How... How did you do that?" Jacob always refused to put on clothes for me. *Seriously...how?*

"Mr. Jacob likes the finer things in life. He just needed a softer fabric. I know all the best fabrics from my time helping with Odegaard."

"Those are Odegaard children's clothes?"

"Yes, it was my idea. But Master Tanner started a new line just for Jacob."

"That wasn't necessary..."

"Of course it is. Anything for our grandson."

I laughed. "Jacob isn't your grandson, Nigel."

Nigel frowned. "Stop reminding me. I haven't found one of my own yet."

I rarely knew what he was talking about. "How much do I owe you for the clothes?"

"Nothing. And more will be arriving soon. I just needed to make sure he liked them first."

I pulled out my phone. "I need to thank Tanner."

"It was my idea though," Nigel said. "I like comfortable clothes too." He gestured to his lederhosen.

It didn't look very comfortable to me.

"And you can thank him later. We need to have an important discussion."

"About what?"

Nigel hoisted himself up onto the counter and I laughed.

He smiled at me. "Like James, I understand you too. I understand you best."

"Nigel, were you listening to our conversation?"

"Yes, of course. And I know you don't need a security detail because I'm keeping you safe. Thank you for trusting me."

That wasn't why. But it was nice knowing he was looking out for us. It did make me feel better. If I was being honest, I actually really liked it. Even though it infuriated Matt.

"I do appreciate it, Nigel."

"I know. And I like when you stare into the cameras."

Well, I definitely didn't do that. Unless there were cameras somewhere I didn't know about…

"But I also have had bouts of not wanting to leave the house. For a while, I was scared of the plague. I didn't leave my house for a year."

"The plague?"

"Yes. I lost my younger brother. And then I was terrified…" he stopped talking when he looked up at me. He cleared his throat. "I mean I saw a documentary about it. My brother coincidentally died soon after the documentary. And I was terrified. So I stayed home."

"Nigel, I'm so sorry. I didn't know you had a brother."

"It was a long time ago." But you could hear the sadness in his voice.

It wasn't *that* long ago. Nigel was young. Definitely younger than I was. "I'm really sorry." I grabbed his hand and squeezed it.

"It's actually nice having a little guy around again," Nigel said and looked over at Jacob. "My brother was about that age when the sickness got him."

What sickness? I wanted to ask more questions, but I didn't want to push him. "You're really good with Jacob. I'm sure you were good with your brother too."

Nigel nodded. "I'm a natural caregiver. I always have been. It's a blessing and a curse."

Okay.

"But I digress. What I mean to say is that I understand you. Once the plague ended…or…people forgot about the scary documentary…I still didn't leave the house for quite some time. People made fun of me around town. They used to throw rocks and sticks at me."

Oh my God. What town had he grown up in? And where on earth were his parents during all of this? Someone should have stopped him from watching that documentary. "I'm so sorry, Nigel. That's awful."

"Actually people still make fun of me for a lot of things." He sounded so dejected. "I think no one realizes that I can hear when they call me weird. Or maybe they do. Someone shouted it in my face one time. It was very hurtful. I don't think people realize how much words can hurt." He looked down at his lap.

I pressed my lips together. "You know what?"

He looked back up at me.

"People thought I was weird when I first moved to the city."

"Yeah?"

Maybe not weird exactly. But they definitely thought I was different. I nodded. "I didn't fit in at all. I didn't have lots of money like the other students at Empire High, and I was a complete outcast. Barely anyone spoke to me."

"I can't imagine you being an outcast, mademoiselle."

"Trust me, I was. And people used to say mean things to me too." I pictured Isabella calling me trash and laughing. And Mrs. Pruitt saying those awful things about my mother.

"People can be so cruel."

They really can be. "I think when someone is different, it scares people. But different isn't bad."

"It isn't?"

"Not at all. There is only one *you.* So why should you try to be anything other than you? I actually think being weird is a compliment. Who wants to be normal, anyway?"

"I train regularly on being a normal modern day boy, and I hate it."

I laughed. I had no idea what he was talking about. "Don't ever change, Nigel. Don't let the haters win. Screw them."

He smiled. "Yes. Screw them. Next time someone says something mean about me I'm going to throw my hand grenade at them. I finally found the pin, but I'm ready to take it out again."

"Well, maybe not that. It's better to just ignore them." I pictured Isabella's cruel smile. "Sometimes people that lash out are actually very unhappy in their own life. They're just trying to find something else to focus on so they don't have to look inside themselves and face their own demons. So just smile and keep being you. Ignore them."

Nigel smiled. "People hate being ignored. I love it!"

I laughed. "And maybe we can call them Wizzys behind their backs."

"Wizzys?"

"It was a nickname for Isabella. Not many people know it."

He beamed at me. "Deal. And you can stay home as long as you want," he said. "I'll keep you and Mr. Jacob safe, I promise."

I believed him. I felt tears welling in my eyes. I hated that people were cruel to him. He was one of the kindest people I'd ever met.

"Now, let's spice up this sauce!" He poured an entire bottle of chili flakes into his hand and hopped off the counter.

He was as bad as Jacob was with sprinkles. And I didn't know if Matt would like it *that* spicy...

CHAPTER 11

Friday – One Week Later

Matt

I didn't understand why Brooklyn wouldn't leave the house. But it didn't matter whether I understood it or not. All that mattered was that I gave her what she needed.

Pushing her certainly hadn't helped. Ever since I talked to James, I understood what I'd done wrong. I hadn't mentioned leaving the house once for over a week. I'd been trying to think of things that would make me feel better. Instead of what she needed. But I could give her this. I *loved* this.

"Matt, those pieces are huge," Brooklyn said and grabbed the knife out of my hand. "They need to be half the size. At least." She cut one of the pieces of bell pepper in half that I'd already cut. "Like that."

"I don't know if I should trust your cooking skills after you tried to poison me last week."

She laughed and handed me the knife back. "I told you that was all Nigel. He said you liked it spicy."

He would. I started cutting again. "I still don't understand why you let Nigel anywhere near our food. He can't be trusted around anything like that. Especially beverages."

She laughed. "He's a really great cook usually. I'm sorry about that sauce though." She leaned a little closer to me. "It really was too spicy," she whispered.

"Why are we whispering?" I whispered back.

"Because he's probably listening."

"I'm taking down the security system." I put the knife down.

"No." She grabbed my hand. "I like it."

I sighed. "Okay. At least we moved your painting into our bedroom so he can't zoom in on it all day."

Brooklyn laughed.

God I loved that sound. She was doing better. I could tell.

Jacob slid into the kitchen in his socks.

"Doesn't that remind you a bit of our first Halloween?" I asked Brooklyn.

"If he takes off his pants and starts singing we're in trouble."

I laughed.

"Let me finish this up real quick," she said and grabbed the knife back.

I pressed my lips together as I watched her expertly cut all my pieces in half. I was happy to be here with her and Jacob. But there was a small piece of me that was sad we were missing out on my parents' Halloween party tonight. I was really hoping she'd come around. They'd been so looking forward to it. *I'd* been looking forward to it.

But staying home would be fun too.

"When is cena ready?" Jacob asked.

"Cena?"

"Dinner, Coach."

"I don't know as much Spanish as you," I said and ruffled his hair.

"It'll be ready in just a minute," Brooklyn said.

"Do you want to pick out the movie tonight while your mom finishes up?" We'd been doing movie marathons almost every night the past week. Yes, I felt bad about missing out on Halloween. But I loved snuggling up to Brooklyn on the couch.

Jacob nodded and ran out of the room.

Brooklyn pushed around something in a pan with a spatula.

"You know..." I wrapped my arms around her from behind. "It's nice having homecooked meals every night."

She leaned her head back and looked up at me. "Well good, because I like cooking for you every night. But are you sure you want to watch movies tonight?"

"Of course."

"Hmm." She turned off the stove and turned toward me. "There's nothing else you want to do?"

"Nope."

She raised her eyebrow at me.

"I'm happy right here with you and Jacob."

"I know. But your mom texted me about the Halloween party. To see if we'd changed our minds."

"I'm sorry. I already told her we weren't coming. You don't have to text her back. I'll call her."

"I already texted her."

"Oh. Well, good." I wasn't sure what she wanted me to say. That I wanted to go? That I was sad we were missing out on a fun night with our friends? I cleared my throat. "Dinner smells amazing. Let me get the plates." I stepped around her but she grabbed my hand.

"I told her we were coming," she said.

"Wait, what?"

"I don't want to miss out. I'm not going to waste any more days." A smile spread across her face.

I picked her up and twirled her around.

Her laughter filled the room.

"Oh, shit," I said and put her down on her feet. "We don't have costumes." Well, that wasn't entirely true. "Actually, I do have your old Sandy costume."

"Why on earth do you have that?"

I shrugged. "Mr. Pruitt let me keep a few of your things. I think it's at my parents' house." A lot of her things were there.

"I'm very curious about what other old things of mine you kept. But Sandy doesn't exactly fit the theme of this year's party."

"Right." It was comedies and romcoms this year. "I'm sure we have something..."

"I actually already have it covered."

"You do?" How long had she been planning on going?

"Mhm." She was trying to hide her smile, but failing.

"What did you do?"

"You're going to love it, I promise. It almost tops your Risky Business costume. *Almost.*"

I had a feeling I was going to be half naked in a few minutes.

"Everyone's dropping the kids off at James and Penny's again. They're doing this trick-or-treat thing in their apartment complex. Ellen says she has it covered. And all their security will be there. And Jacob is so excited to see Scarlett. Serve up dinner real quick. I already ate because I need some time to get ready. So eat up. We don't want to be late." She hurried upstairs.

I couldn't stop smiling. "So you already knew about this?" I asked Jacob.

"Yessie. I'm going to be a football player. My abuelo made me an Empire High uniform."

I'd have to thank Tanner for that. "Good choice, kiddo. Do you know what Scarlett is dressing up as?"

"A princess, I think."

Yeah, that sounded about right. I served up dinner and the two of us started eating. "Do you know what your mother is dressing up as?"

"No. Do you?"

"Nope." But I couldn't wait to see it.

I was just finishing up the dishes when I heard Brooklyn's feet on the stairs. I turned around to see her walking down the stairs in a silky red dress. She looked amazing. But I had no idea what her costume was. She was balancing a huge gold frame from my painting room in her arms, and a very tiny bag was dangling from her wrist.

"Take a guess," she said and lifted the frame over my head. She let it fall around my shoulders.

"I have no idea. But you look like Cameron Diaz from The Mask."

She smiled. "I'll take that as a compliment. But no. That's not it." She tapped on the frame.

"I've got no clue."

"This will probably help." She opened the bag and held it out for me.

I pulled out a pair of my tan boxer briefs. I turned them over and there was a huge fig leaf sewed to the front. "Adam and Eve? I don't think Eve dressed like that, baby."

"No. The fig leaf. The frame."

I just stared at her.

She put her hand on her hip. "I'm a stage five clinger."

"Oh my God." I started laughing. "Wedding Crashers?"

"Yes!"

I laughed. I remembered watching that with her and her uncle. "So I'm the painting that the weird brother painted? This is the most ridiculous costume ever."

"It's perfect."

It really was. "I can't believe you planned all this."

"Did you really think I was going to make you miss out on the Halloween party? Now go change." She slapped my butt.

I hurried upstairs and changed. I was correct. This was the most ridiculous costume ever. But so fucking hilarious. I stared at the fig leaf that really didn't cover anything. It was good she'd sewn it to boxers or you'd be able to see everything it was trying to hide. My friends were going to get a good laugh out of this. Brooklyn had nailed it.

I pulled a pair of jeans over the fig leaf boxers. I didn't need to give Jacob any ideas about running around naked anymore. He'd been so good the last week thanks to Nigel and Tanner. I pulled on a shirt too. I'd just take everything off when we got to the party.

"Ready!" I called as I grabbed the frame. I hurried down the stairs. I was so excited to go to the party. It actually felt like Halloween as a kid, when I was so pumped to go get candy. And I couldn't stop smiling. Smiles definitely came easier when my girl was smiling too.

Brooklyn grabbed Jacob's helmet. She'd put black paint under his eyes and he looked like the cutest little running back. Especially with the regulation sized football tucked under his arm. He was going to have so much fun tonight.

We were just about to head out the front door when the stupid living room door opened.

"Wait for me!" Nigel yelled and ran into the living room through his private door. He was wearing all black except for the stripped scarf around his neck. His hair was askew like he'd just woken up. And he was holding a paint palette in one hand. He smiled at me.

Brooklyn laughed. "Nigel, that's perfect. I figured you'd be listening. You totally nailed it." She held up her hand for a high five.

He awkwardly shook her hand instead. "It seemed like an invitation to me. You can't be Gloria and Jeremy without me."

"I'm sorry, who are you supposed to be?" I asked.

"Todd Cleary," Nigel said and adjusted his scarf.

"Who?"

"The brother from the movie. The homo painter."

I laughed. "Nigel, you can't say that." But he'd totally nailed the look.

"Why not? That's what he was. And you and I?" He stepped closer to me. "We had a moment at the table earlier, didn't we?"

"When you were watching me eat?"

"No, before. So I painted you. Since you refused to paint me." He tapped the frame. "I call this painting…Celebration!" He waved his free hand through the air. "But you're not doing it right. Take off your pants." He reached for the button on my jeans.

I stepped back from him. I remembered his character from the movie perfectly now. He'd painted the painting I was supposed to be. And tied the character up in the bed and tried to do things to him. Nigel was very much like Todd Cleary. "Cut it out, Nigel. This was supposed to be a couples costume."

"A throuples costume, yes."

Brooklyn couldn't stop laughing.

"Let's play tummy sticks!" he said.

"Nope. No. Absolutely not. Go change."

Nigel turned to Brooklyn. "Someone is being a Wizzy."

Brooklyn laughed. "Such a Wizzy."

"What does that mean?" I said.

"It's a savage insult," Nigel said.

Well, yeah, I got that.

"I bet you're devasted right now."

"Go change," I said more firmly.

"The only other costume I have is Hitch. It's a nod to Master Tanner's expert matchmaking skills. But I'm out of shoe polish for my face so I won't quite fit the part…wait! Can I borrow some of that paint that you put under Mr. Jacob's eyes?"

"What for?" Jacob asked.

"No," I said firmly. "You're not allowed to put shoe polish or paint on your face. Come on, man."

"Why? It was fine a few years ago I think. Has that changed? I haven't checked my Halloween costume notes in a decade or two…"

"Just keep being the homo painter. It's fine." What the fuck was I even saying?

"Okay." He smiled. "Let's do homo things."

Brooklyn bent over laughing.

I was glad she was finally laughing again. But I did not love anything about this.

"What does homo mean?" Jacob asked. "And what's tummy sticks? Is that like when we fight with swords?"

"It's very much like sword fighting…" Nigel started.

"Nope," Brooklyn said and lifted Jacob into her arms. "Time to go!" She laughed all the way down the front steps.

"Let's go," Nigel said and slapped my butt like Brooklyn had earlier.

Yeah, I hated this. But I loved seeing Brooklyn so happy.

CHAPTER 12

Friday

Brooklyn

I took a deep breath as I walked into the foyer of the Caldwell mansion. It was decorated very similarly to how it had been the last time I'd been to one of their Halloween parties. Fake blood oozed down the banister and cobwebs wrapped around the chandelier. And down the hall to the left, screams could be heard.

I'd been so in love with Matt that Halloween. But for some reason, all I could think about was the first time I'd ever stepped foot inside here. That party I attended with Felix and Kennedy. I'd had no idea the party would be here or I probably wouldn't have agreed to come. I'd hated Matt. Loved, hated. It was definitely a fine line when it came to him.

But what I remembered best about that night was that I felt…hopeful. Hopeful for my future. And definitely a little scared. Especially when Rob pushed me into Matt's dark room. My eyes wandered up the stairs.

And God, who was I kidding? I hadn't hated Matt. I'd been so desperately in love with him. Yeah, stepping into his childhood home made me feel so freaking hopeful. Especially if I didn't think about how that night ended.

"What are you thinking?" Matt asked.

"That I feel 16 again." I smiled up at him.

And he smiled down at me.

"Well, there's one thing I can promise about tonight. It won't end the same as the last Halloween party we attended together."

"I should hope not. I also hope it doesn't end like that other party. The first time I was here."

He winced. "I owe you a thousand apologies, Brooklyn."

"For making me hide in the closet while you flirted with Wizzy? Mhm," I said with a laugh.

"I'm sorry." He kissed my forehead. "I'm sorry." He kissed the tip of my nose and I laughed again. "I'm so sorry about all of it." He placed a kiss on my lips.

"You are officially forgiven. Besides, before she showed up, it was one of the best moments of my life. Remember how I punched you because I thought you were a vampire?" That night really was crazy.

He tucked a loose strand of hair behind my ear. "I remember every second."

I was smiling so hard it hurt.

"Thanks for coming tonight. It means a lot to me."

Standing here with him, it was easy to not be scared. I was doing my best to try and keep the thoughts in the back of my head where they belonged. We were safe. Jacob was safe. I put my arm in front of my stomach and then immediately dropped it. I had no idea why I kept doing that. "Thanks for being patient with me. I know the past couple weeks have been hard. I just…"

"Wanted to be home, I get it. I love that I'm a part of that. And like I said, nothing is going to happen tonight, because you're not leaving my sight."

"Oh, I know, I'm not leaving your side for a second. There's a reason why I chose this couple." I gestured to our costumes, trying not to get distracted by what his fig leaf was hiding. "I'm going to be such a stage five clinger tonight."

He laughed. "Should we get in there?"

"Yeah, Nigel's costume doesn't make much sense without us." Matt insisted that Nigel go in while he took off his clothes in the car. But I was pretty sure he just didn't want to be seen in the party next to Nigel.

Matt groaned. "I hate his costume."

"It's hilarious."

"It's really not."

It so is. I tried to hide my laugh as Matt tucked me into his side. We made our way down the hall with the eerie music. Each step grew a little darker. I was gripping his hand so tightly, looking left and right, waiting for something to pop out. But…nothing happened.

The hallway was decorated with tons of tombstones. But there were no coffins for zombies or skeletons to pop out of. It was just tombstone after tombstone. The music had grown more sinister, but nothing else had.

I took a long, slow breath. "This isn't nearly as scary as last time…"

A ghost fell from the ceiling right in front of us, cutting me off. I screamed at the top of my lungs and pressed my back against the wall. Okay, yeah, this definitely felt like the Halloween party, not the other party. My heart was racing so fast.

Matt laughed.

"Not funny!" I said. "I nearly had a heart attack."

Matt caged me in against the wall. "I love making your heart race."

"You probably shouldn't make my heart race too much. Because it'll just get you excited too and you might tent your fig leaf."

He laughed and pulled back. "Fair. You really should have sewn on a bigger leaf."

"That's the biggest one I could find."

He smiled. He seemed very content with that explanation.

I grabbed his hand. "Come on. Let's get out of this hallway as fast as possible." I started running, pulling him with me.

He laughed when another ghost fell from the ceiling and I screamed. This shit seriously wasn't funny. This party probably wasn't the best choice after being too scared to leave the house in weeks. I stepped to the side to avoid another ghost. I knew it was all fake, but I couldn't seem to calm my racing heart.

There was a big wrought iron gate near the end of the hallway, several feet in front of the closed door at the end of the hall. We pushed it, but it didn't budge.

"What the hell?" Matt said and tried again to no avail.

There was a low groaning noise behind us and the floorboard in front of one of the tombstones shifted to the side. A zombie started slowly sitting up.

"Open the gate!" I yelled.

"I can't. It's locked."

Someone screamed behind us.

I turned around to see Penny clinging to James. She was waving around a flute like she was going to hit a ghost or zombie with it. And from her band camp t-shirt, I knew immediately that she was the girl from American Pie. But James' costume completed the couples' costume perfectly. His hair was really curly and he was dressed almost exactly like Matt. But instead of a fig leaf on his boxers, he had a pie tin over his junk.

I would have laughed, but the zombie was starting to climb out of the floor.

"Open it!" Penny yelled.

"It's locked," I said.

"Oh my God, how do we get out of here?!" She grabbed my arm.

Matt rattled the gate again. "Seriously, what the fuck?"

"I think we need a key," James said.

"The key!" Penny said. "The one in the invitation! Of course!"

I'd never seen the invitation. Matt had just told me about it. But I liked the idea of the extra security layer.

James put the key into the lock and turned it. The gate squeaked on its hinges, sending a chill down my spine.

The four of us ran toward the door at the end of the hall.

"Matt, your parents are sick," Penny said with a laugh. "Every year gets scarier. Where do they come up with this stuff?"

"They watch a lot of movies," Matt said. "Too many probably." He was just about to push the door open when it opened on its own. The hinges squeaked worse than the metal gate.

"Come in if you dare," boomed a voice from a hidden speaker.

I agreed with Penny. Matt's parents were twisted.

But when the doors finally opened all the way, the ballroom was significantly less scary. Creepy? Yes. But the zombies and ghosts were serving hors d'oeuvres instead of trying to attack us. Which I much preferred.

Cobwebs cascaded down the walls with huge spiders that were somehow moving about on them. Blood was splattered all over the cobwebs and the sound of chain saws could be heard beneath the music the band was playing. The side of the stage was decorated to make it look like the band was standing on top of an old VHS tape. But the music was upbeat and fun. And everyone dancing and drinking and chatting over in a pumpkin patch definitely calmed my nerves.

"I'm going to go get us drinks," Penny said. "I'll be right back."

Rob walked over to us. "Hey pie fucker," he said to James.

James laughed. "I'm obviously Jim from American Pie."

"Or you're just a pervert." He turned to me. "This party is great and all, but wanna come to the party in my pants, Sanders?"

"Um…what?"

He gestured to his costume. He had glasses on, a brown suit that looked like it was from the 80s, and he was holding a hand grenade. "I love dress." He poked my stomach. "I love breast." He poked the side of my boob. "I love nipp…"

"Dude, stop saying random stuff you love and poking Brooklyn." Matt swatted his hand away. "We know who you are. You're the weatherman from Anchorman."

Rob smiled. "Nailed it. Yup, I'm Brick." His smile grew. "I stabbed someone with a trident earlier."

I started laughing. "Ah, I remember that!"

"It's better with Daphne. Where is she? Oh, there she is." He pointed to the man walking up to us.

Wait, no. *Oh my God.*

Daphne was dressed like Ron Burgundy from the movie. She was wearing a fitted burgundy suit and had a fake mustache on.

"Hey, toots," Daphne said and slapped Rob's butt.

I wrinkled my nose. "What's that smell?"

"Do you like it?" She adjusted her tie. "I call it sex panther. It's illegal in eight countries."

I couldn't stop laughing. "You two are ridiculous," I said.

Daphne kissed his cheek.

"Stop that, it tickles," he swatted her hand away. "What are you supposed to be?" he asked us.

"You motorboatin' son of a bitch," Matt said. "You old sailor you!"

Rob just stared at him. "You want me to motorboat, Sanders? I mean…if you really want me to."

"I gotta get out of here, man," Matt added. "I got a stage five clinger. Virgin clinger." He pointed to me.

"If Sanders is a virgin she won't be for long in that dress." Rob winked at me.

How was he not getting who we were? "If you ever leave me I will find you," I said and booped Matt on the tip of his nose.

Daphne, Rob, and James were all staring at us like we were crazy.

"It makes more sense with Nigel," I said. "But I don't know where he…"

"You called, mademoiselle?" Nigel said and appeared next to Matt.

Matt jumped.

"We're trying to get them to guess our couples costume," I said.

Nigel nodded. "Our throuples costume, yes." He stared at Rob for a second. "Wait, why are you being me?" he asked.

"What?" Rob looked truly offended.

"The hand grenade. That's me from when I saved Brooklyn."

Rob laughed. "No, I'm Brick."

"Did he just call himself a brick?" Nigel turned to me.

"Forget about Rob's costume," I said. "Help us explain ours."

"Right. Let me get into character. I'm a homo painter, you see." He tossed his scarf over his shoulder and turned toward Matt. "I made this painting for you. Because of the moment we shared at the table."

"Nigel…" Matt started.

"Shush." Nigel said and put his finger to his lips. "Don't you love it? It's so sexual and violent."

Matt looked disgusted and moved his face away.

"Stop touching me," Matt said.

"But they need to know about us!"

It was actually a perfect rendition of him being tied to the bed in the movie. And I wasn't sure Matt even intended it to be. I could barely breathe I was laughing so hard. Rob, James, and Daphne were all laughing too. They had to know who we were now.

"Quit it, Nigel!" Matt yelled and slapped his hand away.

"Do you want me to hide in the closet?"

"Um…sure?" Matt said.

"Great! I'll pop out at just the right moment." Nigel sprinted off.

James laughed. "Wow, okay. That was a lot. But you guys are from Wedding Crashers."

"Bingo!"

"We actually have a third to our costume too. My dad is around here somewhere being super awkward and giving out sexual advice like the dad from American Pie."

I couldn't wait to see that.

"Wait, didn't the girl from Wedding Crashers have red hair?" Rob asked.

"Yeah." I shrugged. "It was last minute."

"Or was it because you didn't want to accidentally seduce my brother?"

I felt my cheeks turning red. "Definitely not."

"Or maybe it was because you were worried Matt would like you more with red hair? Because of his crush on Penny and all?"

I actually had thought about that...

"Shut it, Rob," Matt said. "I don't think Brick is supposed to think that much about anything."

Rob shrugged. "Fair. I was just curious. I feel like it was a little of both though, right?" He turned back to me.

"What did I miss?" Penny asked. She was somehow balancing a ton of shots in her hands.

Daphne turned to her. "I'm in a glass case of emotion!" she yelled and knocked the glasses out of Penny's hands.

"Jesus, Daphne," James said.

Penny just laughed. "You're getting the next ones, Ron Burgundy." She turned to me. "It took me a minute, but you're from Wedding Crashers, right? The stage five clinger and the Celebration portrait? Epic."

She didn't seem to remember that the girl had red hair. Or didn't care. Because it didn't matter.

"I love boob," Rob said and poked the side of Penny's boob.

"Stop it," she said and swatted his hand away.

"I love redhead." He poked her hair and winked at me.

Rob loved stirring the pot.

Matt pulled me in close. "I don't have a crush on Penny," he whispered into my ear.

"I know." I did know. He'd been in a bad place. Because of me. I looked up at him, but I caught sight of Mason and Bee out of the corner of my eye. "The Caldwells seem to prefer blondes. Speaking of which…why the hell are Mason and Bee dressed like *that*?"

CHAPTER 13

Friday

Matt

"THIS. IS. SPARTA!" Mason yelled and raised his sword in the air.

He was dressed like King Leonidas from 300 and Bee was dressed like the queen, in a very revealing draped white dress.

"Um...why are you dressed like that?" Rob asked. "Did you not read the invitation?"

"What?" Mason looked around at all of us. Then looked over his shoulder at literally everyone else dressed as characters from comedies and romcoms. "Fuck, what did the invitation say?"

"Mason, you told me the theme was movie characters," Bee said. "Is that not right?"

"Yeah," Mason said. "I definitely said that. But...I also may have skimmed the invitation."

"What?" Bee started looking around at all the costumes too.

"I was too busy to read the whole thing."

"It literally would have taken two seconds," Rob said. And then he poked the side of Bee's breast that was exposed. "I love boob."

She swatted his hand away. "What are you supposed to be? A pervert?"

"No," Rob said. "Well...kind of."

"He's dressed like Nigel," I said. "When he showed up with a hand grenade the other night."

Bee laughed.

"I'm not dressed like Nigel." Rob chucked his grenade into the center of the room where people were dancing.

Someone screamed.

"It's not real!" Rob yelled over his shoulder. He shook his head.

Apparently Rob did not want to be mistaken for Nigel. And I was a little worried that now that I'd said his name, he'd pop out like he'd promised. I looked around. He was nowhere in sight.

"We're not the only ones that didn't read the whole invitation," Mason said. "That guy is dressed like the guy from Scream." He pointed to someone who'd just walked in.

"Or he's dressed like the murderer from Scary Movie, which does fit the theme."

"Son of a bitch," Mason said.

But I was much more distracted by the two people next to him. They were both dressed like Dr. Evil from Austin Powers and they kept glaring at each other. Or maybe the shorter one was supposed to be Mini Me? She was dressed in a low cut grey shirt dress and had a bald cat in her arms. The skin-cap on her head and drawn in raised eyebrows just made her look insane though.

"Is that Poppy dressed like Dr. Evil?" Brooklyn asked.

I squinted to get a better look. "Oh shit, I think you might be right." No wonder I thought she looked insane.

"Bold move with the bald cap," Daphne said. "And I thought my mustache was good."

Brooklyn laughed. "I much prefer your mustache."

Kennedy rushed over to us in what I could only describe as a filled burlap sack. "There you guys are!"

"What are you supposed to be?" Brooklyn asked.

"I'm a sandbag of course." She put her hand on her hip, like she needed to sell it. But we all saw it.

Felix put his arm around her. He was wearing a pair of khakis and had no shirt on. And half of his chest was waxed. "Nope, she's a boob," Felix said and poked her.

But unlike when Rob did it, this made complete sense. I laughed, remembering when Steve Carrel's character said breasts felt like sandbags in The 40-Year-Old Virgin. Because he'd never touched one before.

"Dude, that's epic." I high fived him. They totally deserved to win best costume.

Kennedy flicked Felix where he was partially waxed.

"AH! KELLY CLARKSON!" Felix yelled at the top of his lungs.

Brooklyn laughed. "You two totally deserved to win best costume," she said, reading my mind.

"What about me?" Rob said. "I've been in character almost the whole time. Look." He screamed at the top of his lungs and knocked a tray out of a passing waiter's hands.

"You and Daphne need to stop making a mess," James said. "Someone is going to trip over all this stuff."

Rob screamed again.

Honestly, it was exactly what Brick would do.

"I see your parents," Brooklyn said and grabbed my hand. "Let's go say hello." She pulled me through the crowd to my parents.

They were dressed like the couple from How to Lose a Guy in 10 Days. Well, kind of. My mom was in a satin yellow dress and my dad was in a tux. But they were both covered in fake blood.

"You just couldn't resist making it gory," I said.

"Ah I'm so glad you could both come!" My mom went to hug me, but the frame was kind of in the way. "At least I'm clothed."

I laughed.

My dad snapped his fingers. "Wedding Crashers, right?"

Brooklyn nodded.

"Ah, there you are," James and Rob's dad said as he pushed himself in between my parents. He had glasses on and had left his hair curly like James. "I saw you across the room, Matt. And I noticed that although you're naked and your date looks gorgeous, you're not tenting your fig leaf. There's an easy fix for that. I brought some magazines." He lifted the paper bag in his hand. "Plenty of nudies. They'll help."

My dad burst out laughing and slapped Mr. Hunter on the back.

Wow, James wasn't kidding when he said his dad was going around giving awkward sexual advice. He was just like the dad in American Pie. And so much more fun as their third than Nigel was as ours.

"You must be Mr. Hunter," Brooklyn said and offered him her hand. "James looks so much like you."

I'd forgotten that the two of them had never really met before.

Mr. Hunter smiled and took her hand. "Well I should hope he looks like me. I made sure to put it in the right hole. Unlike when I caught him with that pie."

Brooklyn laughed.

"Who is that?" Mr. Caldwell asked.

I turned to see an old man walking into the party. I laughed. No, not an old man. Even though the wrinkles and crazy white hair looked very real, you could tell the guy wasn't actually old because he was ripped. He was in swim trunks and wearing a wrestling helmet, and he had his arms slung around two topless girls in cutoff jean shorts. They were wearing gold pasties, but it didn't make it any more tasteful. Tanner and I had watched Old School together recently. But I never would have guessed he'd come as *that* character.

"Is that Tanner?" Brooklyn asked. "He makes an incredibly realistic old man."

I laughed. *He really does.* "Yup, that's Tanner."

"Who is he supposed to be? And why does he have two topless girls with him?"

"It's from Old School," I said.

"Oh. Right. Are either of those girls the one he brought to prom?"

"Doubtful."

"Huh."

"My boy, Blue!" I yelled over to him.

Tanner smiled and walked over to us.

"You old sailor, you," I said. "Are they built for speed or comfort?"

"I actually am a navy man. World War 2. Thanks for noticing," Tanner said.

Was that in character? Or was he saying that for real? But then I got distracted because he leaned down and motorboated the brunette.

She giggled.

It had been a while since I'd been out with Tanner. I'd forgotten how quickly he went through women. And how sexual literally everything he did was. I wasn't sure Brooklyn had ever seen this side of him though. Despite the fact that they'd hung out quite a bit before I knew she was back in town.

"Definitely speed," Tanner said and then repeated the action with the blonde. "And I'd say comfort for these." He slapped both their asses.

I glanced at Brooklyn. Her eyes were completely round.

"Well I see you don't need any of my advice," Mr. Hunter said.

Tanner laughed.

"Except to stay safe and wrap it up."

"Don't worry, I won't set anything on fire here."

Mr. Hunter frowned. "What does that have to do with anything? If it burns when you pee, it might be syphilis, son. One time when I was your age…"

"Definitely clean, man," Tanner said.

"Well then. Have fun with your harem." Mr. Hunter turned to my parents. "Who should I mess with next?"

"Let's do Mason," my mom said and the three of them hurried off to torment my brother.

"Give me just a minute," Tanner said to his girls and tapped them on their asses again.

The two of them wandered off into the crowd.

"Wow." Brooklyn cleared her throat. "Are you dating both of them at once?"

"I don't really date," Tanner said with a shrug. "And actually, I'll probably try to set them up with someone here if I can."

"Swinger!" Rob yelled.

I jumped. I hadn't seen him walk up to us.

"That's it! You're a swinger. That's what you've been hiding!"

Tanner laughed. "I wouldn't classify myself that way. If I *was* a swinger, I wouldn't hide it. There's nothing wrong with group sex, Rob. I do dabble in it occasionally. There is something about having chicks in twos that I love."

Brooklyn's jaw actually dropped.

Yeah, Brooklyn did not know about this side of Tanner.

Rob glared at him.

"You're very unenlightened, Young Robert."

"And you're…you're…you're great at being old."

Tanner laughed. "Nice comeback. And I am old, so it's not really an insult."

"You're younger than me," Rob said.

"Time is a funny thing. It's not as linear as one might assume."

"I need to go find my trident," Rob said and stormed off.

I laughed. Had he actually brought a trident? When he said he killed someone with a trident earlier, I thought he was just quoting the movie.

"You look lovely," Tanner said and gave Brooklyn a hug.

"Tanner, I have so many questions," she said and pulled back. "But also somehow so much is clear at the same time. Like the two of you hanging out in this city together like a bunch of whores."

Tanner smiled. "I'd hardly classify myself that way either."

"You and Matt were terrible influences on each other. You were both hurting and instead of dealing with your feelings you just slept your way through half of New York."

Well, she wasn't wrong.

Tanner pressed his lips together. But he didn't say anything.

I didn't really know the extent of their friendship. But I knew they'd talked a lot. I knew he'd helped Brooklyn open her heart up to love again. So they must have shared some intimate details. And I could also tell that her words hurt him.

I cleared my throat. "Brooklyn…"

"I'm sorry," she quickly said. "I wasn't trying to judge you, Tanner. Things just started clicking into place in my head. I hadn't really pictured you as Matt's wingman. But of course you were. All his other friends are married."

I didn't think this was helping. She was making it sound like Tanner was some kind of replacement for my other friends. "Brooklyn, I don't think…"

"But it's like you said," she continued. "Everyone handles grief differently. And I'm really glad you were there for Matt. Truly. But when Matt told me you usually hang out with models I didn't really believe him. It doesn't really seem like…*you*."

Tanner still didn't say anything.

"If that is you, that's fine. I just couldn't picture it until literally a second ago because when we talk you just seem so down to earth. I definitely see it now though. It'll be a little hard to unsee, actually." She laughed. "But for some reason I just feel like maybe you'd love a sweet girl to settle down with."

Tanner grabbed a glass off a passing tray and downed the whole thing. "Maybe in a hundred years, Brooklyn." He sighed and put the glass back down on the tray.

"I don't get it," Brooklyn said. "You like setting matches for everyone else. Why not yourself?"

He opened his mouth and then closed it again. "If you'll excuse me, I think I need another drink." He walked off.

"Brooklyn, what was that?" I said. "You basically just said you used to think he was a nice guy, but now you think he's a womanizing asshole."

She put her face in her hands. "I'm so sorry. I'm mortified. It was like I couldn't stop talking."

"Hey." I pulled her hands down.

"Tanner is such a sweet guy. I just never in a million years expected him to show up with two topless women."

"It's Halloween. I mean, look at me." I gestured to my fig leaf.

She groaned. "I know, I'm such a jerk. I should go apologize."

I caught her hand before she could follow him. "Maybe give him a second, okay?" *Or maybe several minutes.* Because he'd just tossed one of the girls he'd come with over his shoulder and was walking out the door.

Tanner and I probably were bad influences on each other. But he was also one of my best friends. I wasn't sure what I would have done if I hadn't met him a few years ago. All my other friends had moved on with their lives. And I was just…stuck. Tanner understood that. He was there for me when no one else was.

Just because I was ready to settle down now, it didn't mean he had to be too. I knew what it was like when all my single friends got into serious relationships. I hated feeling like the odd man out. I knew exactly how Tanner was feeling right now. And having one of my friends' girls tell me to settle down hadn't helped me either. Despite Penny's best intentions.

"He's a good guy," I said to Brooklyn.

"I know he's a good guy. He's a *great* guy. He's honestly one of my best friends. And I feel like such an ass."

I laughed. "Well if you feel like an ass, maybe I need to make an ass out of myself too." I shimmied my shoulders to the music.

She laughed. "I really should go apologize."

I grabbed her hand and pulled her onto the dance floor where the rest of our friends were already dancing. Tanner definitely needed some time. And I wanted to dance until sweat dripped down Brooklyn's chest and I could trace the path with my tongue.

CHAPTER 14

Friday

Brooklyn

I laughed as the song finally changed to a slow one and Matt pulled me in close. I was glad he'd ditched the frame around his shoulders so that I could put my arms there instead. "I forgot how good of a dancer you were."

"We dance almost every night when you're cooking."

I smiled. "Yeah, with Jacob. That's different."

"You mean because at home you don't grind all up on me like a horny teenager?"

"Hey." I swatted his arm. But he wasn't wrong. I couldn't get enough of him. And they were playing music from the early 2000s. It felt like high school all over again. But also…different. I felt closer to him now than I had before. I think because I felt more sure of myself. I felt like I belonged in his world. Like I fit. I didn't have a single doubt in my head this Halloween. It helped that Isabella wasn't dressed in the same costume as me running around killing puppies.

I pushed the thought away.

"Ah! I see Tanner finally. I'm going to go apologize."

Matt kept his hands firmly on my hips. "And what exactly are you going to say?"

"That I'm sorry."

"That's all you're going to say?"

I laughed. "I mean, I'd like to talk about why he hooks up with two girls at once. It's a little hurtful."

"For who?"

"The girls."

"Did they look like they weren't having fun? They looked perfectly happy to me."

"I mean…yeah. But…" my voice trailed off as I stared up into his eyes. Wait, how did he know it wasn't hurtful to the girls? "Matt, have you ever been with more than one woman at once?"

"Do you really want me to answer that?"

I sighed. "No, probably not." I searched his eyes. "We're okay, right? Like…you don't want stuff like that anymore?"

"Eh. I've had enough nights like that."

I lightly shoved his chest.

He caught my hand. "No, I don't want that. I just want you. I think I've shared you enough for 16 years, Brooklyn. I'm never sharing you again for another second."

I couldn't help but smile. The less specifics I knew about our time apart, the better. Because I had a feeling he really did have a lot of nights like that. "Well you have to share me for one more second, because I'm going to go talk to Tanner."

Matt laughed as I hurried off.

"Tanner!" I yelled over the music. "Can we talk for a second?"

He smiled. "How about we dance instead?" He grabbed my hand and pulled me back onto the dance floor.

He looked a lot happier than he had an hour ago. And I wondered how much he'd had to drink as he smiled down at me.

"I'm so sorry about earlier. I was out of line…"

"It's fine," he said. "It's already forgotten."

"It's not fine. I was just surprised to see you with two girls at the same time."

"Too scandalous?"

"I mean, a little. Matt kind of explained it to me."

"How threesomes work?"

I felt my face blush. "I know how threesomes work." The logistics were a little blurry in my head, but I got the general idea.

"Do you really? Because I think if you'd experienced a good one, you wouldn't be staring at me in horror, but with lust in your eyes."

"Tanner, I'm trying to apologize."

"I'm not stopping you," he said with a smile.

"You kind of are. Stop distracting me."

"If you and Matt want to borrow Tatiana for the night…"

"Tanner, I just want to know why you do this when it's obvious you'd rather be in a relationship. I know you. I know you love love."

He shook his head. "I can't have what you have."

"Why?"

"Because I can't."

"Why?" I said again. "I mean, look at Matt. You probably thought he'd be a bachelor forever but he's in love."

"Because you came back, Brooklyn." His Adam's apple rose and then fell. "You came back."

God, my heart ached for him. "And your girlfriend didn't."

He smiled, but it looked so sad. "Are you trying to rub it in?"

"No. Definitely not. I'm so sorry, Tanner." I pressed the side of my face against his chest. "Sleep with a hundred women. Sleep with a thousand. I don't care. It doesn't change my opinion of you at all."

He sighed and rested his chin on the top of my head.

"But you told me that some people are lucky. That they get two great loves. Maybe you're lucky like me."

"Maybe," he said. "Ask me again in a thousand years."

"A thousand?" I laughed and pulled back. "I thought you said a hundred earlier."

"These things take time."

I shook my head. "You're ridiculous."

"And you're ridiculous for never having a threesome. Imagine another woman swirling her tongue around your nipple as you stare at Matt, wishing it was his mouth on you. Or her finger slipping inside your wetness, fucking your pussy, while you desperately beg for Matt's cock."

My heart started racing.

"You grinding against her hand as she bites down on your hard nipple. Your back arching as you push her head lower. All you need is a release. And her soft lips on your skin are turning you on more than you realized they could. Your fingers tangling in her hair as she pushes your thighs wider. You watch Matt start to stroke his length as she thrusts her tongue into your dripping pussy."

I swallowed hard.

He smiled. "See. You'd like it."

I rolled my eyes. "So you just sit there watching your two dates?"

"Until my control snaps."

Fuck. I pressed my thighs together.

"Like I said, you can borrow Tatiana for the night…"

"I'm good," I said.

"If you say so."

But suddenly my dress felt too warm. The heat coming off the other dancers was stifling. And I'm sure my cheeks were flushed.

"Have a good night, Brooklyn," Tanner said and dropped his hands from my waist. "Let me know how it goes."

I wasn't having a threesome. But Tanner was right. I was suddenly desperate for Matt's cock.

I weaved my way through the crowd and wrapped my hand around Matt's forearm. "Come with me," I whispered into his ear.

He didn't protest. He just grabbed my hand and let me guide him toward the creepy hallway we'd come in through.

This time, I knew where the ghosts were falling from, so it was easy to dodge them. But my heart was still racing as I pulled Matt into the foyer.

I let go of his hand and started walking up the stairs, letting my hips swap.

He groaned from behind me. "Your ass in that dress."

I smiled and kept walking. I went past Mason's old bedroom and opened the door to Matt's room. Unlike Halloween 16 years ago, there was no blood on the wall or on his bed. Isabella was gone. And we were safe. I turned around and pressed my palm on the center of Matt's chest, until his back hit the wall.

His eyes trailed down my body. "What exactly did Tanner say to you?"

"Nothing important." My fingers trailed down his abs, stopping just above his boxers.

"No?" He raised his eyebrow at me.

I shook my head. This wasn't about what Tanner had said. Well, maybe a little about what Tanner had said. But I was also thinking about all the times that Matt had pleased me in this room. And that I definitely owed him a few blowjobs. Or according to him, hundreds from our time apart. This room held a lot of memories. And most of them were like this.

I dropped to my knees and locked eyes with him.

He ran his thumb along my lower lip, smudging my red lipstick. "I can't wait to see this color smeared on my cock."

Jesus. I grabbed the sides of his boxers and slowly pulled down. His erection sprung free, almost hitting my cheek.

If he wanted my lipstick on his cock, I'd give it to him. I shifted forward on my knees.

His chest rose and fell as he stared down at me.

I loved when he stared at me like that. Like I was the only one that could please him. I slowly licked him from his base to his tip. And then I wrapped my lips around him.

He groaned and buried his fingers in my hair.

I moved up and down his length a few times before he started guiding my mouth. Faster and faster. He thrust deeper, hitting the back of my throat.

My eyes watered, but I didn't gag.

"Good girl," he said.

I loved when he called me that. I tightened my lips around him.

There was a knock on the door.

"Fuck," Matt groaned, his fingers gripping my hair harder. He kept guiding my mouth, ignoring the knock.

But then the door started to open.

He let go of my hair and I sat back as he shoved his hard cock back into his boxers. But we weren't hiding anything. My hair was a tangled mess, I was still on my knees, and the fig leaf did absolutely nothing to hide Matt's erection.

The girl smiled as her eyes trailed down Matt's body. "Tanner said you requested me?"

What?!

Matt looked down at me. "Sorry, what exactly did the two of you talk about?"

"I told Tanner no." I pushed myself up off my knees. But he'd probably seen how turned on I was.

"Are you sure?" She bit her lip and stared at Matt.

"I mean…" Matt said and shrugged at me.

I slapped his arm and he laughed.

And Nigel popped out of the closet.

Oh my God. Had he been in there the whole time?

"Get out of here!" Nigel yelled at the girl. "You can't just walk in on a couple during coitus, it's completely inappropriate."

"Nigel, what the fuck?" Matt said.

Nigel smiled. "I popped out at just the right time. Like I promised." He walked over and grabbed the girl's arm and pulled her out of the room. And then he slammed the door and turned around to face us. "I got rid of her. You're welcome. I'll just go back to the closet now and pop out again soon."

"No, Nigel," Matt said. "You need to leave too. We've talked about this."

"But I'm supposed to be in the closet."

I laughed. I couldn't help it. Nigel was hilarious. He was playing my brother in the movie so perfectly.

"See?" Nigel said. "Mistress Brooklyn understands me. Don't be a Wizzy, Master Matthew."

I put my hand over my mouth to hide my laughter.

Matt glared at him. "I don't know what this inside joke is, but stop it."

"Never." Nigel smiled.

"You know what?" Matt said. "Tanner mentioned that he's going to wrestle that girl in a tub filled with KY Jelly. Just like in Old School. But I'm afraid they're doing it all wrong."

Nigel's eyes grew round. "Of course that's wrong! You can't but KY Jelly in a tub! It'll clog the pipes! I need to go to him. Will the two of you be okay without me?"

"Yes, Nigel. We'll be good."

"I'm sorry I have to run so quickly. Enjoy your coitus!" He ran out of the room so fast.

Matt turned to me. He opened his mouth and then closed it again. "I'm so confused."

"I didn't know Nigel was in there either, but it *does* fit the movie."

"Yes that. But I was actually talking about the girl that came in. Seriously, baby, what did you and Tanner talk about?"

I pressed my lips together. "Nothing, really."

"Nothing? He just sent one of his dates up here to join us."

I cleared my throat. "Well, he was describing a threesome to me."

Matt lowered his eyebrows, waiting for me to continue.

"And the…benefits of doing that."

He just stared at me for a moment. "And what are the benefits?"

"How badly I'd want you the whole time."

"Hmm. And how badly is that?"

I swallowed hard and my throat made a weird squeaking noise. "Desperately."

His mouth fell to my ear. "Let's make one thing perfectly clear. No one touches you but me." He grabbed my thighs and lifted my legs around his waist.

I laughed as he tossed me onto his bed. But he silenced my laughter with a searing kiss. His hand slid up the inside of my thigh and his fingers gently brushed against my thong. I was so turned on that in a few seconds I forgot what we'd even been talking about.

"I took you so many times right here," he said as his index finger slid beneath my thong. "Just like this." He traced my wetness with his finger.

God.

"But you told me I don't need to be gentle with you anymore." His fingers fell from my skin. And then he grabbed my hips and flipped me over.

I caught myself so my face didn't hit the mattress.

"And you really shouldn't have worn a dress like this..." He pushed the fabric up over my ass. "...unless you wanted to be fucked." He pushed my thong to the side and thrust into me hard.

CHAPTER 15

Friday

Matt

Brooklyn had been worried that I wouldn't love her as much now as I did when she was 16. But she couldn't be more wrong.

I slammed into her harder. And she pushed back on the bed, trying to match my pace.

Yeah, I loved Brooklyn now more than ever. Especially the way her ass jiggled each time I thrust into her. I ran my hand over her ass cheek and squeezed it. The heels she was wearing just made her ass look even more perfect.

She'd been teasing me in this red dress all night. Grinding against me on the dance floor. And she was so fucking wet, coating my dick in her juices. I pulled out and stared down at my slick cock and then slammed it back into her.

Brooklyn arched her back, making the dimples above her ass more apparent. She was so fucking perfect. Every inch of her.

My hand slid to her hip. I knew she was close. My fingers dug into her skin as her pussy started pulsing around me.

"Matt," she moaned.

The way she said my name pulled me over the edge. I thrust forward, all the way to the hilt, and exploded inside of her. My name on her lips. And my cum deep inside her pussy where it belonged.

"Mmm," she sighed and relaxed on the bed.

I slowly pulled out of her, watching my cum leak down the inside of her thigh. I'd never get tired of the sight of that.

I collapsed on the bed beside her.

She turned her head and smiled at me.

Some days, when I looked at her, it still felt like she was just an image in my head. I reached out and traced the engagement ring on her finger. It sure felt real to me.

"What are you thinking?" I asked.

"That I like grown up Matt."

I smiled. "I love you."

"I love you too. But there is one other thing that I'm thinking about." She rolled over on her side and propped her head up on her hand.

"And what is that? If Tanner is right about chicks in twos?"

"No," she said with a groan. "Definitely not. I was wondering what other stuff you kept of mine." She was staring over my shoulder.

I turned to see a framed picture of us on my nightstand. She'd already seen my paintings of her. She knew how much I'd missed her. How desperately I wanted to hold on to her memory forever. This didn't have to be weird.

"Let me show you," I said. I grabbed a tissue and placed it against her leg.

She finished cleaning up as I pulled my boxers back on. I grabbed a key from my nightstand and slid my hand into hers.

Her eyebrows pinched together as she stared at the key. But she didn't say a word as I led her down the hall.

We stopped at the door of her old bedroom here. She spent every night in my bed. But all her things had been in this room. Mostly things she'd gotten after she moved in during high school. I put the key into the lock and turned it.

I coughed and waved my hand through the dust in the air. I hadn't been in here in ages. And no one else had a key. I switched on the lights and turned to Brooklyn.

She didn't look back at me. Instead, she walked into the room.

There was a dusty picture of us on her nightstand. She stared at it for a moment and then went to the closet.

I swallowed hard as she opened the double doors.

All her things were packed away inside. There were garments covered in plastic hanging up. And clear plastic bins lined the floor. Everything was packed away, neat and tidy. Almost like it was waiting for her to come back.

"Did you do all this?" she asked and touched the plastic outside one of her dresses.

I shook my head. "No. My mom. I couldn't do it." I'd been such a fucking mess.

Brooklyn let her hand fall to her side. "But you kept everything? Why?"

I swallowed hard. "Because getting rid of it would make everything that happened feel…real."

She didn't reply. She just folded her arms across her chest and kept staring.

And I didn't know what to do. It was like she was hugging herself. Piecing herself back together. And I wasn't sure if she wanted a minute to herself or not. I cleared my throat. "I guess it makes sense now. Why your father didn't let me keep more of your things. You needed them."

She shook her head, but still didn't say anything.

I'd always wondered about her Keds. And her mother's dress. Some of her framed pictures. Even my varsity jacket that I'd given her. It was like her father had locked away all her favorite things from me just out of spite. Because it certainly hadn't seemed like he'd cared about her death. But it all made sense now. She really had needed them. Some of those same pictures now lined our mantel back home.

"Sixteen years." She wrapped her arms tighter around herself. "Sixteen years, Matt." Her voice cracked.

She didn't need to hold herself together. Not when I was here to hold her. I walked up behind her, wrapping my arms around her.

Her head melted back against my chest.

For a few minutes, we just stood there, staring at our past.

Brooklyn sniffed. "I guess you should have dressed like the stage five clinger tonight instead of me."

I laughed. "I've always been obsessed with you." I rested my chin on top of her head. "I'm not ashamed to admit that."

"I never stopped loving you either," she said. "I guess I should have dressed like a monster tonight."

"You're not a monster, Brooklyn."

"Aren't I? My heart has always belonged to you *and* Miller."

I tried not to let her words affect me.

"I'm a monster for holding on to you for the fifteen years I was with him. And I'm a monster for repeatedly talking about him to you. Because I just keep hurting you. But my heart will always be torn. I'll always love you both."

I held her tighter. "I know. I understand." I did. It hurt, but I did. "We're going to be okay."

She sniffed again. "I'm not okay, Matt. I don't know if I'll ever be okay again." She let one of her arms fall, wrapping it in front of her stomach.

And I wondered if she was thinking about the child she'd lost. "You will be, Brooklyn." I'd make sure of it.

We stood in silence for a few more minutes.

"Oh my God." She pulled away from me and pushed some of the plastic covered garments aside. "You kept it."

"Kept what?"

"My wedding dress."

I actually didn't know that was in there. I had stayed away from this room after my mom packed away all Brooklyn's things. Painting her had been my therapy. Going through her old things would have hurt more than it helped. I tried to step around her to see the dress.

But she immediately spun around to block me. "You're not allowed to see it. That would be bad luck."

I smiled. "Seriously?"

"Seriously."

My eyes searched hers. "Does that mean you're planning on wearing it soon?" We had barely spoken about being engaged. With everything that happened. But I wanted to move forward. I was done with living in the past.

"I..." Her voice trailed off. She pressed her lips together and looked down at the ring on her finger. Or maybe she was peering down the front of her dress at where the rings Miller gave her were hanging against her chest.

"I...I...can't..." Tears started falling down her cheeks.

Baby. I reached out and wiped her tears away with my thumbs. She didn't need to say it. I had my answer. She wasn't ready. "I'll wait another lifetime if I have to."

She laughed through her tears. "I don't want to wait a lifetime. But...I'm not ready. Yet. Soon though. I promise."

I knew she was still grieving. But I was worried that she'd always be.

I was glad my ring was back on her finger where it belonged. But she should have had a wedding band too. She'd said it herself. She'd always been mine, even when we were apart.

And we were already acting like a married couple. Maybe it was the officiality of marriage that unsettled her. A piece of paper that said she was mine. Instead of his. "I'm not asking you to forget him," I said.

She stared up at me with her big blue eyes. "I know."

Then what was the problem? "You said yes to my proposal."

"I did."

She really wasn't giving me much to work with here. "A marriage proposal."

Brooklyn exhaled slowly. "And what's so wrong with being engaged?"

"Nothing. But we haven't really spoken about it since the night I proposed. Or our plans. We haven't even told Jacob." I knew she'd been excited to tell him. Before she'd been kidnapped. We had been on the same page. We'd both been excited. And now it felt like we kept taking steps backward.

She pressed her lips together. "I want to tell him."

"Okay."

"Let's do it tomorrow."

"Yeah?" This felt like a good step.

She nodded. "Yeah." She looked over her shoulder at all her old clothes and then back at me. "But before you get any ideas in your head, I need to say one thing. I can't marry you in December, Matt."

That had been our original plan. A wedding right before Christmas. Instead she'd married Miller on Christmas day. Did she think that marrying me in December would be a betrayal to Miller? Because her getting married to him on Christmas certainly felt like a fucking betrayal to me. But I swallowed down the words on the tip of my tongue. "How about November then?"

"Next November?"

I shook my head. "This November."

"November is in just a few days, Matt."

"You already have a dress."

She laughed. "I doubt that dress still fits me."

"Then you can get it altered."

"When I said soon, I didn't mean next month."

"Then what did you mean?"

She shrugged. "I don't know."

I was pretty sure if I let her have her way, she'd just stay engaged to me forever. And that wasn't okay with me. She was always meant to be Brooklyn Caldwell.

"Let's talk to Jacob about everything. And then go from there."

I nodded. One step at a time. As long as we weren't going backward, I could be patient. Well, patient-ish. I'd been tiptoeing around her the past few weeks, terrified that I was losing her. But she was talking to me now. We were going to be okay.

"Thank you," I said. "For coming tonight. For talking to me."

"Thank you for being patient with me."

Patient-ish, I thought again.

"I really don't know what's been going on with me. I tried to talk to you about it. But I can't really put it into words. I just want to be..."

"Home," I said, finishing her sentence for her.

"Yeah." She smiled. "Home."

"Did you want to get going?" I was grateful that she'd come tonight. But snuggling up to her on the couch actually sounded pretty good right now.

"I think I still owe you a few more Halloween dances," she said.

"A few? Years worth, Brooklyn."

"Then we should definitely get back downstairs." She grabbed my hand and pulled me toward the door. But she looked over her shoulder one more time at the open closet.

I wondered if she was picturing that dress. And walking down the aisle to me. I hoped so. I hadn't been joking when I said we should get married next month. Any time, any place. I'd been ready to marry her since I was 16 years old.

Her fingers tightened in mine as we made our way through the spooky hallway.

"Shit," I said when we reached the gate near the end.

The zombie started rising from the floor behind us.

"What?" Brooklyn asked.

"I don't have the key."

"What do you mean you don't have the key?" She held my hand even tighter.

"The invitation really should have said to bring it…"

The lights flickered and went out in the hall.

"Finally. I've been waiting to talk to the two of you all night," said a deep voice from behind us.

CHAPTER 16

Friday

Brooklyn

I didn't even have time to scream. Matt pushed me behind him. I couldn't see anything in the darkness. But I still heard the zombie groaning.

"Who's there?" Matt said.

"It's just me," said the deep voice.

A voice I was pretty sure I'd never forget now. *Magnus King.*

"I've been waiting to talk to you," he said.

We had nothing to talk about. What was he doing caging us in against this gate? I grabbed Matt's arm.

"Why is it so dark?!" yelled a high-pitched voice. And then she screamed bloody murder.

The zombie groaned again. But this time it sounded like it was because he was in pain.

The gates creaked open behind us.

"Step away from my friends or you won't be able to walk ever again," Tanner said.

I'd recognize his voice anywhere.

The lights turned on and Tanner was standing next to Matt. Tanner didn't look intimidating in his old man costume. But his authoritative voice made up for it. And after seeing him throw a knife at Luigi Locatelli, I had no doubt that he could hurt anyone he wanted.

"What the fuck is going on?" Magnus said. "Everyone calm down." He reached into the hole in the floor to help Poppy up.

The zombie actor did not look happy that Poppy had fallen on him.

Magnus and Poppy were both dressed like Dr. Evil. It was an off-putting sight for several reasons. But mostly because the taller one had kidnapped me a couple weeks ago. And the shorter one was Poppy, which was off-putting all by itself.

"Magnus," I said. "Poppy."

"I was just trying to apologize," Magnus said. "For the other night."

Poppy rolled her eyes. "I don't know why Uncle Richard is making us do this. Brooklyn knows we're on her side."

I didn't. Not really. I just wanted nothing to do with any of them. "I like the Mini Me costume," I said to her.

"I'm not Mini Me. He is." She pointed to Magnus.

Magnus laughed. "Definitely not, sweetheart."

"Don't call me that. I'm not your sweetheart. And you're Mini Me because I'm the one in charge."

"You can think whatever you want to think," Magnus said.

Someone else cleared their throat behind us.

I spun around to see someone standing there in the ghost mask from Scary Movie. There was a bloody knife in his hand.

The lights cut off again.

And this time I did scream.

Matt stepped in front of me again.

But honestly, I didn't know which was worse. A masked stranger with a bloody knife? Or Magnus and Poppy?

When the lights turned back on, Tanner had the masked man in a headlock.

"What are you doing?!" Magnus yelled. "It's just Richard."

Tanner looked at Magnus and then back down at the guy in a headlock. "Richard Reginald Pruitt?" Tanner asked. "Is that you?"

"Yes," my dad grunted.

Of course my father was dressed like a murderer.

Tanner let go of him and my dad coughed and fell to his knees.

"Sorry, old chap," Tanner said. He grabbed him by the back of his black robes and pulled him to his feet. "You're all good."

He coughed again.

Realizing who it was didn't make my heartrate go back to normal.

"What's with the bloody knife?" Matt asked.

My dad pulled off his mask. "It's part of the costume. It's fake." He tossed it on the ground and it bounced. It must have been made from plastic.

"Speaking of costumes," Poppy said. "I love what you have going on, Matthew. I have no idea what you're supposed to be, but it's very form fitting."

Matt turned around so she couldn't keep staring at his butt in his tan boxers.

I just ignored her. "What are you doing here, Dad? You're not even friends with the Caldwells."

"I was invited."

"That doesn't really answer my question."

"You've been avoiding me ever since I neutralized Luigi and Patricia had her…accident."

Accident? Yeah right. I wasn't sure why he seemed so confused about my not speaking to him. He'd killed two people. And I knew in my gut that he'd had a lot more people killed than that.

"I thought we were on the same page," he said. "I stepped down from my position. I want to be a part of your life. That's why I'm here."

I didn't want him here. And despite him trying, my opinion of him that I'd formed 16 years ago hadn't changed. I didn't want him to be part of my life. Miller wouldn't want him to be part of our son's life. I'd had a couple weeks to think more about this. And I wasn't going to cave. I couldn't. I'd never put my son at risk. "I can't do this, Dad."

"I just want to be part of your life."

That wasn't what I wanted.

"I didn't hurt Miller. And I'm sorry if I ever hurt you."

If he'd ever hurt me? He'd stolen my fucking kidney! I took a deep breath. I'd come to terms with all that shit years ago. It had led me to Miller. It had led me to having Jacob. I couldn't regret or be spiteful about any of that. And I knew he hadn't been involved with Miller's death. I understood what happened. But it didn't mean my father wasn't dangerous.

"I'm sorry," he said again. "Angel, I'm so sorry."

Tears started welling in my eyes. "I forgive you." It felt like a weight had been lifted off my shoulders as soon as I said it. James told me he'd felt similarly once he'd forgiven his father. He was right. Holding on to that pain was only hurting myself. I did forgive my dad. I had to, or else the pain would eventually swallow me whole.

"So, maybe I can come over tomorrow? And spend the afternoon with you and my grandson."

I shook my head. "I forgive you, Dad. But I don't trust you. I don't know if I'll ever trust you."

He pressed his lips together. "Just tell me what you want me to do. I already stepped down. I…"

"I need time," I said. I wasn't sure if time would help. But I knew I needed it.

"Brooklyn, you're the most important part of my life…"

"She said we needed time," Matt said and put his arm around my shoulders.

My father was great at manipulating me. If I was the most important person in his life, he would have done things differently 16 years ago. He would have listened to me and sent Isabella away instead of me. He would have put me first. I wasn't the most important person in his life. I was just all he had left.

When he'd shown up to save me from Locatelli, I'd been ready to put everything aside. To move forward. I couldn't explain why my mind had shifted over the past couple weeks. But I felt different. I needed to be home. And safe. I needed to protect my family.

"Okay," my father said. "Take all the time you need. I'll be waiting." He leaned down and hugged me.

It caught me off guard and I almost stepped back.

But then I closed my eyes and breathed in his familiar scent. It twisted around in my head. All the good and bad. I hugged him back. Because despite everything, he was my dad. And maybe one day we'd be able to repair everything. But that day wasn't today.

He sniffed and pulled back. "Magnus, Poppy, thank you for making your apologies. But we should be going."

Poppy definitely had not apologized for anything. She'd just hit on my fiancé. But I expected nothing less from her.

"Take care of my girl," my dad said and patted Matt's back before departing down the hall with the two Mini Mes.

"Well he has that wrong," Tanner said when he disappeared. "You're our girl," he said and winked at me.

I smiled.

"And speaking of girls…how did the two of you enjoy Tatiana?"

"We did not," I said.

"Oh?" Tanner stared at Matt. "What did you do wrong? I swore you said you could handle at least three…"

"Stop it," Matt said.

"Were you about to say three girls at once?" I sighed. "My future husband is a total slut."

"No, apparently he's not a harlot at all," Tanner said. "If he couldn't please both you and Tatiana."

I shook my head. "We didn't have a threesome, Tanner."

"Oh, no," Tanner said, completely horrified. "Matt, were you not able to perform?"

"Jesus," Matt said. "No. Stop talking about threesomes." He turned to me. "You said you wanted to dance?"

I laughed. "Actually, can we just get out of here? I want to go have that conversation with Jacob."

He smiled. "Absolutely. Later, Tanner."

"Comfort *and* speed, my boy." Tanner slapped Matt on the back and then walked back toward the party.

"Ignore him," Matt said.

"It's a little hard to ignore Tanner. In a good way."

Matt laughed.

I smiled. "Matt?"

"Yeah?" We started walking down the hallway.

"Thank you for having my back."

"Always." He kissed the side of my forehead.

***

If I was being completely honest with myself, I had been delaying this conversation with my son. Because this was hard to explain. And I had this horrible feeling that I wouldn't be able to make him understand.

"Let's go get ready for bed," I said when we walked into our house.

"Never!" Jacob yelled and ran into the living room. He sat down and started zooming his trucks across the floor.

"Someone has had way too much candy tonight," Matt said.

I laughed. "Apparently so." I stared at Jacob playing.

"I'm really not trying to pressure you into anything you don't want to do. I was just trying to talk." He gave me a sad smile.

I knew he wasn't pressuring me. But I was done standing still. I was done wasting time. I'd already wasted so much of his. Hurting him was the only thing I regretted. I wasn't going to hurt him anymore. "Come with me." I grabbed his hand and led him over to the couch. We sat down. "Jacob?"

"Yessie?" He didn't look up from his trucks.

"Matt and I need to talk to you. Can you come sit with us for a minute?"

He ran over to the couch and jumped on top of me.

Ooph. He was definitely hyper. This conversation would have been better outside under the stars. Or in his bed with the fake stars on his ceiling. I looked up at one of the pictures of Miller up on the mantel. It was okay. He was here. And he'd always be here.

I blinked fast so I wouldn't start crying. "Jacob, you know how much I love your dad."

He nodded.

"And I will always love your dad."

He frowned and looked at Matt.

That wasn't a good start.

I stared at Jacob. He looked so much like Miller. And I knew how much Miller would have loved Jacob's football costume. Down to the cute little black lines under his eyes. I would always keep the memory of Miller alive for us. "Your father isn't replaceable."

"I know," Jacob said. "My daddy is my daddy."

Yeah. None of this was coming out right. "But I also love Matt."

Jacob looked at Matt again.

"And I know you love Matt too," I said. "So I really want him to be part of our family."

"Like an abuelo? Or…like a brother? Scarlett has a little brother."

"No, not like either of those things." I pressed my lips together. "Matt proposed to me. And I said yes."

Jacob just stared at me.

I knew he didn't know what any of that meant. What was I doing? But I couldn't think of what to say.

Matt reached out and grabbed my hand.

Jacob stared at our intertwined hands and frowned again.

"I'm hoping to marry your mother," Matt said. "One day. When we're all ready."

I slowly exhaled. He'd worded it much better. I squeezed his hand.

Jacob shook his head and looked up at me. "But you're already married to my daddy."

His present tense killed me. "I will always love your father. And he's always with us. Right here." I put my hand on the center of his chest.

Jacob looked down at his lap. "I don't need another daddy. I just want mine back."

God. "Sweet boy, Matt isn't replacing your father. Okay? He could never do that. And if I could bring your father back, I would. I'd give anything to have him back." I wasn't sure if my words were hurting Matt. But we'd talked about this. He knew I'd always love Miller too. And I didn't know how else to explain this. It felt like my heart was breaking all over again.

"I'm sorry about your father," Matt said. "I know how wonderful he was to you guys."

I squeezed his hand again as I tried to hold back my tears.

"I'm just hoping to be part of your family. And I'm hoping you want that too. I love you and your mom so much."

I blinked faster. Matt was much better at this than me.

"I don't want to call you dad," Jacob said.

"I'm not asking you to, kiddo. You can call me whatever you want. Just like before."

"Okay, Coach."

Matt smiled.

"Can you play trucks with me?" asked Jacob.

"I can definitely do that." Matt picked Jacob up off my lap and set him back down on the floor. "You okay?" he said to me.

I quickly nodded. "I just need a minute." I hurried out the back door before either of them could see me cry.

I wrapped my arms around myself and stared up at the sky. "I don't want to hurt anymore, Miller."

I swear the brightest star in the sky twinkled.

I finally let the tears stream down my cheeks. "It's okay, right? This was what you wanted?"

It twinkled again.

Miller had always been so understanding. So caring. He'd want all my scars to heal. He'd want me to be happy. I took a deep breath.

I don't think my heart would ever heal from losing him. But I knew he wanted me to keep living. I pressed the tips of my fingers against the rings hanging against my chest.

It was always easier to take deep breaths when I touched those rings.

When Miller had proposed to me, I'd hesitated. But I'd said yes because it didn't feel like a betrayal. I hadn't broken any promises to Matt when I'd said yes. I'd promised Matt all my firsts. And Matt had technically still been my first fiancé.

But when I'd gotten pregnant with Jacob? That's when I'd known it was time to make it official. And breaking one promise cascaded into breaking a whole lot more. Like a dam breaking. I'd married Miller right away. It was like Jacob had given us permission to embrace life. I felt guilty and hopeful at the same time. So freaking hopeful.

I let my hand slowly fall to my stomach.

The star twinkled again.

In inhaled sharply and looked down at my stomach.

I had felt this way before.

Protective.

Wanting to stay home.

Emotional.

Hopeful. Exactly what I was just recalling. *Really freaking hopeful.*

I spread my fingers out on my stomach. When was my last period?

CHAPTER 17

Saturday

Matt

I looked back up at Brooklyn in the stands. She was on her feet cheering like everyone around her. There were just a few seconds left on the clock and we'd demolished the other team. Normally, that would be enough to make me happy. But I was a hell of a lot happier now that I could look up in the stands and see the real Brooklyn instead of a ghost of the past.

Tanner had Jacob on his shoulders and they both looked almost as happy as Brooklyn did. *Almost.* It felt like a lifetime since I'd seen Brooklyn so...present in the moment.

"Nice game, Coach," Kennedy said. And then she waved up to the stands at Felix. He was standing up there with Brooklyn too, and I was relieved that I didn't feel jealous at all. The four of us really could be just friends. Finally.

"You too," I said.

She laughed. "I don't really do much now that Jefferson can kick. And I'm especially not helpful when I have a hangover." She rubbed her forehead.

I hadn't had much to drink at all at the party last night. And I wasn't sure Brooklyn had anything to drink. Maybe that's why she looked the happiest in the crowd.

"I'm glad you were able to get Brooklyn out of the house again," said Kennedy. "I've been so worried."

I thought about what she'd said to her father last night. "She just needed some time."

"But everything's okay now?"

I stared at her smiling. "Yeah, everything's okay now." Telling Jacob the news last night hadn't exactly been smooth. I knew Brooklyn was still grieving. She'd gone outside for a bit after we'd told Jacob, but when she came back in, she was all smiles. We were ready to move forward. And I was okay with waiting to get married. As long as she was wearing my ring, we were good. And my old varsity jacket. I smiled up at her again. The jacket was way too big for her. But I'd never seen her look sexier.

The ref blew the whistle, signaling the end of the game.

"Victory is ours!" Nigel yelled. "We slayed the beasts!" He sprinted out onto the field.

Kennedy laughed. "He does know that team we're playing is the tigers, not the beasts, right?"

"I have no idea what goes through Nigel's head." I high fived all the players and smiled as they enjoyed some of the cookies Brooklyn had made for them.

The stadium slowly emptied out.

"I'm going to cut out early from cleanup," Kennedy said. "I need some Tylenol and a nap. I'm pretty sure Nigel has it covered anyway."

Nigel was currently removing fingerprints from his water glasses with a towel.

I wasn't sure why he kept bringing fancy glasses instead of paper cups.

"See you later," I said.

"Coach! Coach!" Jacob yelled as he sprinted toward me. "We won!"

"Yeah we did." I lifted him into my arms and balanced him on my hip. "Where'd you get this?" I tapped the Eagle in the middle of his long-sleeved shirt. He hadn't been wearing this when we left the house. And I didn't even realize that Empire High made clothes in children's sizes.

"My abuelo gave it to me."

"Thanks, Tanner," I said as he joined us on the field.

"Young Jacob and I have the same taste in fashion. Don't we, my boy?" He put his fist out.

Jacob fist-bumped him.

"How about we go help out Nigel with...whatever he's doing," Tanner said and lifted Jacob out of my arms. The second Jacob's feet hit the ground he ran over to Nigel.

"Brooklyn wants a word," Tanner whispered to me.

I looked up at the stands. She was still sitting there. But instead of smiling down at us she was staring off in the distance. "Is everything okay?"

"Oh, I think everything is more than okay," Tanner said.

"What's going on?"

"She didn't tell me."

"Then how do you know it's fine?"

"Because I can read people like the back of my hand."

"So...what does she want to talk about?"

"I'm going to let her fill you in. Congrats, Matt. I'm really happy for you." His smile faltered. "Truly. You're living the dream." His smile was gone now. He patted my back and then joined Jacob and Nigel.

What the hell was going on? Tanner looking serious was never a good thing. He'd been congratulating me but looked sad as fuck. I walked up the steps.

Brooklyn turned toward me at the sound of my steps. And her smile was back now.

I sat down next to her. "I like seeing you this happy." I gently nudged her with my shoulder.

Her smile just grew. "I am so happy."

"I can see that."

She laughed.

"I didn't realize how invested you were in the Eagles winning."

"So invested."

I laughed. "Tanner said you wanted to talk?"

"I do want to do that."

I just stared at her.

She took a deep breath, her chest rising and falling slowly. "You know, I always pictured a big family." She stared out at the field.

I swallowed hard. We hadn't spoken about this since she told me about her miscarriage. She hadn't liked the way I'd responded. I'd wanted her to see a specialist. But she just wanted to know if that was okay. If we could move forward just the three of us. Of course we could.

"We do have a big family." I placed my hand on her knee and stared out at Tanner, Nigel, and Jacob tossing the ball around. "All our friends. All our nieces and nephews."

She didn't respond.

"And there's more than one way to have children."

She still didn't respond.

When Brooklyn's mother died, she'd been an orphan. She was lucky that she'd had such a kind, caring uncle to take her in. But if she hadn't? There were lots of kids out there that didn't. "I'm happy just the three of us," I said. I tried to think about my words before I said them out loud. "I know you're scared of trying again. And I just want you to know that I'm open to talking about adoption."

"Hmm."

"Is that a good hmm or a bad hmm?"

She laughed. "I didn't realize how much you'd been thinking about this. I've been thinking about it a lot too."

"Yeah?"

She nodded. "I actually can't stop thinking about it." Her smile was back now. "And I have something for you." She reached into her purse and pulled out a jewelry box. The kind you'd find a fancy necklace in. It wasn't wrapped, but there was a white bow tied around it to keep it closed.

I wasn't a big jewelry person. And I had no idea what this had to do with our discussion.

"I have so much respect for people who adopt," she said.

I smiled. "Me too."

"But I…I want a little you."

Yeah. I wanted a little her too. "Have you thought more about maybe going to see a specialist?"

"I think maybe you should open this." She placed the jewelry box in my hands.

I had no idea what this had to do with our conversation. But she nodded at the box. I was about to pull on the bow, but she grabbed my hand to stop me.

"I love you." It suddenly looked like she was going to burst into tears. "So much."

"I love you too." All I wanted to do was pull her into my arms. "We don't need to talk about this right now if you don't…"

She shook her head. "No. I can't think of a better time to talk about this. Here, you know?" She gestured toward the field. "I wanted to give this to you here."

I had no idea what she was talking about.

"But just don't get too excited." She shook her head. "No, be excited. Positive vibes, you know?"

What the hell was going on?

She let go of my hand. "Open it."

I pulled on the bow and then lifted the lid. It was not jewelry. I'd never actually seen one of these up close. But the big positive sign in the middle definitely gave it away.

"You're…you're pregnant?" I lifted my eyes from the pregnancy test.

Tears were streaming down her cheeks now. "Yes. I took like five different tests this morning."

"We're going to have a baby?"

She nodded.

Holy shit. I pulled her onto my lap. I buried my face in the side of her neck, holding her tight. I didn't even know what to say. So I just said the same thing again. But this time it wasn't a question. "We're going to have a baby." I couldn't believe it.

She kept crying. "I'm so hopeful. But I'm so scared, Matt. What if…" her voice trailed off.

"Don't go there," I said. She didn't need to voice her fears. I knew what she was worried about. "Positive vibes, right?"

"Positive vibes."

I held her tighter. And then realized I probably shouldn't be holding her so tight. Or maybe it was okay? I had no fucking clue. But I pulled back so I could stare at her. "We've got this," I said firmly. I'd take her to whatever doctors we needed. I'd travel across the world to make sure this baby was okay. Brooklyn had experienced enough pain in her life. She'd earned this win. And I hated that she was worried. This moment was perfect. She was perfect. "We've got this," I said again. "I promise."

She wiped the tears from her cheeks and nodded. "We've got this."

I moved one of my hands to her stomach.

She laughed. "You can't feel anything yet, Matt."

"Oh, I know he's in there."

"A boy, huh?" She smiled up at me.

I dropped my forehead to hers. "Nah, I take it back. It's a girl. I can't wait to have a little you running around."

I kept my hand on her stomach. "You're pregnant." It came out as a whisper. I couldn't believe it.

"I'm pregnant," she said and laughed.

God, I wanted to freeze time.

"I think maybe we should go ahead and plan that wedding for next month," she said.

I lifted my head. *Fuck freezing time.* I wanted that wedding. "Really?"

"Really. Before I get huge."

"You're going to look beautiful with my baby inside of you."

She shook her head. "No, I definitely will not."

"You definitely will." I cradled her face in my hands. "I should have known we'd have a shotgun wedding."

She laughed. "We have a lot to plan in a very short amount of time. But we know just the person to help."

"Justin."

"Justin," she agreed with a nod.

I smiled. "We're getting married. And we're having a baby. I don't think I could possibly be any happier."

"Me either."

I dropped my forehead back against hers. This was what I'd pictured back in high school. Our wedding. Children. I'd waited half of my life for my dreams to come true. I felt the tears falling down my cheeks. "Us against the world. The four of us."

She leaned back, wiping away my tears with her fingers. "The four of us. I really like the sound of that."

I pressed my lips against hers. I really liked the sound of that too.

CHAPTER 18

Sunday

Brooklyn

I couldn't stop smiling. We'd agreed not to tell anyone the news yet. But I was so freaking hopeful. I was worried I might feel…numb. Trying to somehow push away the pain from the past. But Matt seemed so sure everything was going to be okay. And I think because of his excitement, all I could feel was excitement too.

Matt walked up behind me, wrapping his arms around me. He put his hands on my stomach and kissed the side of my neck. "Justin will be here any minute," he said.

"I can't believe you didn't tell Justin why we needed to see him. He's going to freak out."

"It seemed like a better thing to do in person."

I turned around so I could look up at him. "We don't even have a date."

Matt shrugged. "Sometime in November."

"November starts in two days. What if Justin is already fully booked?" I pressed my lips together. "What am I saying? He's the best. Of course he's already fully booked."

"Justin *is* the best," Matt said. "Which means he'll figure it out."

"I really don't want to do it without him."

Matt smiled. "And we won't."

I believed him again. His positive attitude was hard not to accept as truth. After all, Matthew Caldwell had always gotten everything he'd wanted. Including me. I stood on my tiptoes and kissed him.

There was a knock on the door.

"Let me get it." I hurried over to the door and opened it.

Justin was wearing a red velvet vest and matching top hat and bowtie. His bare chest was covered in glitter. He looked like a very sparkly ringleader. He slammed his walking stick on the ground. "Why are you not in costume?" He looked over my shoulder at Matt. "Why are neither of you in costume? Although I do love the outfit, Matt. 'Tis my favorite season."

Matt looked down at his gray sweatpants.

"Are we supposed to be dressed up?" I asked.

"It's Halloween weekend! I thought you were inviting me to a big bash."

Oh. I can see why he probably assumed that. And now I felt awful that we hadn't invited him to the Caldwell Halloween party on Friday. This was why Matt should have told him why we were calling.

"Sorry," I said. "No party. At least…not until you help us."

Justin's eyes grew round. "I can't help you throw a Halloween party at 8 o'clock on Mischief Night. Have you lost your minds?" He walked past us and into the kitchen. "I didn't eat any carbs today because I was saving the calories for tequila. You better at least have tequila."

"I can definitely make you a drink," Matt said.

"No. We're doing shots! You both owe me shots." He sat down at the kitchen island.

Matt grabbed two shot glasses and poured them both a shot.

"You too, babe," Justin said and handed his glass to me.

Shit. "I'm good." I tried to hand the glass back, but he refused.

"No, you need to be on our level."

"Do you want a chaser or anything?" Matt asked, trying to distract Justin.

"You don't need a chaser with that label. We just need a third glass."

Matt cleared his throat and looked at me.

"I..." my voice trailed off. "I'm not very thirsty."

"Girl, it's Halloween Eve! I did not put glitter on every inch of my body if we're not getting wasted together tonight."

Every inch? Why? I shook the thought away. "I'm sorry, Justin. I just...I..." I didn't know what else to say.

"Shut the front door!" he yelled.

"I didn't say anything..."

Justin squealed. "You're pregnant?!"

Okay, yeah. I guess I'd made that kind of obvious. Matt and I hadn't told anyone yet. But Justin's reaction made me smile. I looked up at Matt.

He smiled at me.

I nodded. I wanted Justin to know.

"We are," Matt said.

"I'm going to be an uncle!" Justin said. "Brooklyn, you're glowing. I'm glowing. We're all glowing! And don't you dare drink that!" He snatched the glass out of my hand and pulled me into a hug.

I definitely wasn't going to drink that.

Justin squealed again and tapped his glass against Matt's. "To the new daddy in town." He winked at him.

Matt laughed and they both downed their shots.

"Oh my God, I know why you invited me over tonight," Justin said. "You want me to plan your baby shower, is that it? You're not very far along because you're not showing. So..." he tapped his index finger against his lower lip. "...We need like an April shower or something?

Yaasssss! I love spring showers. And a summer baby! Is that right? A summer baby?"

I couldn't stop smiling. Matt rounded the counter and put his arm around my shoulders. "We were just playing with a due date calculator online. We think it'll be a June baby."

"This is perfect. I can already see it. I've got you. Let's do a Saturday brunch! Gah a Caldwell baby. This is front page news."

Is it really?

"Who's on the guest list? I should call your mom," he said to Matt. "The two of us need to talk."

"Actually, no one else knows yet," Matt said.

"No one else knows?" Justin's eyes grew round. "You're telling me first?" He looked like he was about to cry. "I love you guys." He grabbed the bottle of tequila. "I feel very overwhelmed right now." He took a swig right from the bottle. "But I'm amazing at keeping secrets. I won't tell a soul. We'll start the planning in secret. Until you're both ready to shout it from the rooftops."

I'm glad he was so happy to know first. But we hadn't exactly planned to tell him tonight. And I loved Justin, but I had no idea if he was actually good at keeping a secret or not. I was nervous to tell people because… I shook the thought away. That wasn't going to happen again. Maybe telling people early was a good thing. Maybe it would just multiply Matt's positive vibes tenfold.

"I can't believe my girl is having another baby!" Justin said. "And speaking of girls…we can't really figure out the flower arrangements until we know if it's a boy or girl. But we can choose a theme. Do you know what you want the nursery to look like yet? We can play off that."

"We haven't had time to think about it," Matt said. "And actually, we have something else we need your help with."

"The announcement! Of course!"

Justin was about to freak out. "No, not an announcement about the baby," I said. I didn't even know what that was. "Matt and I need your help planning our wedding."

"I'm literally going to die! When? When?!"

"November," Matt said.

"The fall! Matt, you divine beast, you have exquisite taste. The fall is still so hot for weddings." He pulled out his phone. "Let me check my calendar for next November. We'll figure something out."

I pressed my lips together. Not *next* November.

"Are you at all open for a Friday wedding?" He kept staring at his phone.

"Yes," I said. "But we didn't mean next November."

"Phew," he said. "Because I didn't have a single opening. I almost had a heart attack. So the following November? Fantastic. We definitely need two years to plan it. This is going to be the wedding of the century. And I have Saturdays open. Does one of these work?" He put his phone in front of my face.

"We actually don't want to wait two years," Matt said. "We're thinking *this* November."

"This November?" Justin sounded eerily calm.

"Mhm," Matt said.

"*This* November?" he said again in a hushed voice.

I nodded.

"This November?!" he screamed at the top of his lungs.

He was going to wake Jacob.

"You can't get married *this* November! November starts in two days, you maniacs! I'm a wedding magician, not an all-powerful genie!" He downed more tequila directly from the bottle. "This is like the sexy little Hunter brother wedding all over again."

What? I turned to Matt.

"Another shotgun wedding," Matt clarified.

Right. I think Daphne had mentioned something about that.

"And technically the older Hunter brother too. My heart with that man!" Justin sighed at the thought of James.

So apparently Bee and Mason were the only ones not pregnant when they got hitched.

"But no," Justin said. "Not happening. I can't do this November. Look at my calendar!" He turned it back to next month and showed me.

Each day was filled with several different things. All in different colors. He was very organized. And very busy.

"We really need you," Matt said.

"We really want you," I added.

It looked like Justin's head was about to explode. "No."

"Justin," I said.

"Brooklyn!" he screamed.

"Please." I grabbed his hand. "I made a promise to you 16 years ago. And I feel like you made me a promise too."

He exhaled slowly. "You're lucky you disappeared for so long because I have a huge team now," he said. And then he slapped his hand over his mouth. "I didn't mean that. I mean, I do have a huge team now that can help me. But I wish you hadn't disappeared for so long, Brooklyn."

I smiled. "I knew what you meant."

"Of course I'll plan your shotgun wedding," he said. "You're my favorite human." He started blinking fast like he was going to cry.

"Thank you."

He waved his hand through the air. "Don't make me cry. I'll ruin my glitter."

I laughed. "So what do we need to do first?"

He groaned. "I thought I was going to be partying tonight, not planning the quickest wedding turnaround in the history of my business. God, just pick a date." He tossed Matt his phone. "You know I'll always put you first. Whatever actress or singer you're stealing me away from can deal with my assistant. You're my A-team."

Matt and I stared at Justin's crazy calendar.

When I thought of November, I thought of playing football in the backyard with Miller and Jacob, our feet crunching in the grass. I closed my eyes. And I also thought about Matt. I thought about Thanksgiving. And the Friday after that I lost everything.

"I have an idea," Matt said. "And there isn't even a famous couple we'll be stealing you away from. At least, I don't recognize those names."

I peered at the date Matt was pointing at. Friday the 25th. The day after Thanksgiving. I stared up at him.

"The worst day of my life," he said. "I think we need a new memory for that day."

I smiled. "I love that idea." The 25th also reminded me of Christmas. And we'd originally planned a Christmas wedding.

"Yeah?" Matt asked.

"Yassssss!" Justin screamed. "Fuck the Livingstons! I hate that bridezilla bitch anyway."

Wow. Okay.

"I was hoping you'd choose the Livingstons wedding day! This is amazing! She wanted to dress in all black for Black Friday and her dress was hideous. I never thought I'd hate someone who loved shopping so much."

I laughed. "So we can make it work?"

"All hands on deck, honey. But yes, we can make it work."

"And I can help," Nigel said.

Justin screamed at the top of his lungs when Nigel walked up to us.

"Who are you and where did you come from?" Justin said as he caught himself from falling off his stool.

I would have wondered where he'd come from too. But Nigel was always very quiet when he came through his door.

"I'm Nigel," Nigel said.

Justin just kept staring at him.

"And I'm their houseboy."

"Oh." Justin turned toward Matt. "You have a houseboy? Interesting."

"He is not our houseboy," Matt said firmly.

"I am," Nigel said. "They just don't know it. And I am at your service, Mr. Belle. It sounds like you're going to need me."

"I have a whole team," Justin said. "But I will let you know if we need anything."

"Well, where is the venue?" Nigel asked.

Justin opened his mouth and closed it again.

"I think it's probably where they wanted their first wedding to be," Nigel said. "And I booked it ten minutes ago. What's next?"

"You…you already booked it? How?"

"I told you. I'm a houseboy." Nigel stood up a little straighter. "You got a problem with that?"

Justin shook his head and turned to me. "Is that still where you want to get married? Right there on that bridge?"

I looked up at Matt. "I can't think of a better place."

"Me either," Matt said with a smile.

"Well, I have a million things to do," Justin said. "As soon as I get all this glitter off."

"I can help with that," Nigel said.

"With the glitter? Or the wedding planning?"

Nigel shrugged. "Technically all of that is in my wheelhouse. A quick bath will help with the glitter. But the wedding planning is more pressing, Mr. Belle. I have a million *and one* things to do."

Justin glared at him for a moment.

And Nigel glared back.

It reminded me of when Nigel and Jacob were feuding. "Justin, if you do need extra help, Nigel is really good at stuff like this too."

Justin sighed. "If you insist. Well, come on then, Nigel. Because I have a million *and two* things to do."

"I have a million *and three* things now," Nigel said as they both walked toward the front door. "Wait! I almost forgot!" He turned around, ran back over to me, and gave me a huge hug. "Congratulations on the baby, mademoiselle."

I should have known he'd be listening. This baby was definitely not staying a secret.

"Master Tanner was right. I told him that he was wrong, because I hadn't heard anything yet. But of course he was right. He's always right about these things."

Tanner had kept weirdly staring at my stomach yesterday at the game. I had no idea how he'd known I was pregnant. But he'd certainly seemed to.

"And just so you know, I think you're the best mom. For loving everyone exactly how they are." He squeezed me tight.

Oh, Nigel. I hugged him a little tighter.

"But I must get going! Best man duties! And don't worry, I have the camera feed of all the angles of your house on my phone, so I'll keep my new grandson or granddaughter safe. And Mr. Jacob of course. Au revoir!" He ran out the door after Justin.

There was a lot to unpack there.

"Best man duties?" Matt groaned. "Why on earth does he think he's going to be my best man? First Rob, then Tanner, and now Nigel?"

We'd talked a lot about our wedding parties 16 years ago. At the time, Matt wasn't speaking to James or Rob. He'd really only wanted Mason beside him. But I kept adding more and more people to my wedding party, trying to make him add James and Rob. So he'd kept adding random guys from his football team.

He was no longer feuding with the Hunters though. And Nigel and Tanner had become a huge part of our lives. "Well, who is your best man going to be?"

CHAPTER 19

Monday

Matt

"This is ridiculous, Matt," Brooklyn said as she pulled out a tin of muffins from the oven.

"Muffins are never ridiculous." I tried to grab one but she swatted my hand away.

"You know I'm not talking about the muffins. If you already know who you're going to ask to be your best man, shouldn't you just tell everyone?"

"Where's the fun in that?"

She laughed and shook her head.

"Besides, we wanted everyone to come over anyway for the game tonight." The Giants were on. It seemed like the perfect time to finally have all my friends over at the same time. I'd never hosted one of the game nights before. I'd always been worried someone would find my art studio.

"Muffykins!" Jacob yelled and ran into the kitchen.

"Not until you put a shirt on…" Brooklyn's voice trailed off because Jacob was already fully clothed. "Oh. Well. You can have one then. Are you excited to see Scarlett?"

"Oui."

She lifted him onto the counter and handed him a muffin.

I never knew when Jacob was going to be speaking Spanish or French. But I should have known when Nigel had been over here all afternoon. I turned to Brooklyn. We'd wanted to wait to tell everyone she was pregnant, but with Nigel, Justin, and apparently Tanner loose with the information…we didn't think we had that long before the news came out with or without us. We were visiting my parents tomorrow night to tell them the good news. And tonight we were telling all our friends.

But we'd agreed to talk to Jacob before everyone came over tonight. Jacob needed to know first. We'd gone to the doctor this afternoon. Brooklyn was definitely pregnant. And if I was being completely honest, I wasn't sure I could have kept it a secret either. She was lucky I wasn't screaming it from the rooftops already.

"We need to talk to you about something, kiddo," I said.

He swallowed a mouthful of muffin. "What's up, Coach?"

This was a lot of information within the span of a few days.

I thought Brooklyn might jump in, but she was just staring at me. I cleared my throat. "You know how the other day when your mom told you that I was joining your family?"

"Oui."

"And you were wondering if I was going to be your brother? Is that something you want? A little brother?"

He shrugged. "Not really."

Oh. Okay. I wasn't expecting that answer. I didn't really know what to say. I hadn't expected him to say no.

"But you like Scarlett's little brother, right?" Brooklyn asked.

Jacob shrugged again. "Liam's okay. But he cries a lot. I like Mr. Nigel better."

What did Nigel have to do with any of this? I turned to Brooklyn.

"Nigel?" Brooklyn asked.

"Yeah, can he be my brother? He's as good at playing as my abuelo. But he does the car noises better."

All I could think about was Jacob calling Nigel "brother Nigel" now. I laughed.

Brooklyn put her elbows on the counter to get on eye-level with Jacob. "I love that you think of Nigel as a brother. But I think there's still room in our family for one more sibling. A little brother *or* a little sister. It's always good to have more playmates. Wouldn't that be fun?"

"I guess," Jacob said. "As long as I don't have to share a room. I like that Mr. Nigel has his own house. Can my new brother have his own house too?"

Jacob really did not like the idea of sharing his room. He'd said something similar to Brooklyn when she asked if I could move in. That it was fine as long as I had to share a room with her instead of sharing one with him. But I valued my privacy too. I understood that.

"You won't have to share a room," I said. I didn't need my painting studio anymore. Because I had the real Brooklyn back.

"Okay," Jacob said. "Did you already order the baby? It seems like you already ordered one."

Order? What? "We didn't order a baby. But we made one."

Jacob stared at me for a moment. "How?"

Oh fuck. I really hadn't thought this conversation through. "We made one because we love each other."

"But how?"

Brooklyn laughed but did not offer any help.

So I said the first thing that popped into my head: "Magic."

Jacob's eyes grew round. "With a wand?"

I mean…that was one way to put it. "Yes. With a wand."

"Wow. I can't wait to tell Mr. Nigel!"

At least he hadn't called him brother Nigel.

"Tell me what, Mr. Jacob?" Nigel asked.

I jumped. *Jesus*. He needed to start knocking.

"I'm going to have another brother."

"Or sister," Brooklyn said.

"Another?" Nigel asked and hoisted himself up onto the counter.

"Yeah, he'll be one of us," Jacob said.

Nigel smiled.

I knew he'd been listening to that whole conversation. And he looked very pleased. And for some reason, for the first time ever, I realized just how young Nigel looked. I wasn't sure if Tanner had told me Nigel was in his twenties, or I had just assumed. But he could easily pass as a teenager. And Brooklyn kind of treated him like a kid.

There was a knock on the door.

"You boys behave," Brooklyn said and hurried over to answer it.

"Shhh," Penny said as she walked in trying to calm a crying Liam. She started bouncing him on her hip.

I'd been so happy just being an uncle and soon-to-be-step-father. But if I was being honest with myself, I'd always wanted more. I walked over to Penny and lifted Liam out of her arms. I'd always been good at calming him down. I didn't know whether I was going to have a son or daughter. But either way, they wouldn't be that far off from Liam's age. Or R.J.'s. Rob had just walked in carrying little R.J. in his arms.

I'd given up on that hope that one day all our kids could play together. Those longs summer days spent out by my parents' pool. Or throwing around a football. Or playing videogames. I'd given all that up when Brooklyn died.

I rubbed my hand up and down Liam's back as he quieted down. And for some reason, tears started welling in the corners of my eyes. I just felt so damn lucky. I watched my friends come into the house. It was the first time we were all together here. Brooklyn, Tanner, James, Penny, Mason, Bee, Rob, Daphne, Kennedy, Felix, and all the kids. This really felt like a home. And for 16 years, I hadn't had that feeling.

"You okay?" James asked and lifted Liam out of my arms.

"Yeah, man." I sniffed.

"Are you sure?"

"Honestly, I've never been better." I patted Liam's back.

"If you say so." He looked concerned.

And I got it. I usually only cried when I was missing Brooklyn. Usually when I was wasted and missing her. But I wasn't pissed off at the world anymore. I was just so fucking happy. And it had been a really long time since I was actually happy.

I cleared my throat, trying to get the emotion out of my voice. "We have some good news. Come on into the kitchen."

James walked into the family room first to put Liam down into a play pen for the babies.

Jacob, Scarlett, and Sophie had already started playing in the family room. And all my friends gathered around the kitchen island. I wasn't sure why I'd gotten a bottle of champagne, since Brooklyn couldn't drink it. But we were celebrating and it was the first thing that came to mind. I popped the cork and started pouring glasses.

"What exactly are we toasting to?" Mason asked and lifted up his glass.

"Yes, what in the galaxy could we possibly be toasting to?" Tanner asked and winked at me. "Because I sure have no idea."

But he did already know. Somehow.

"Well, Brooklyn and I have chosen a date for our wedding." I smiled down at her.

"Friday November 25th," Brooklyn said. "*This* November."

Kennedy squealed. "I'm so happy for you guys!"

Brooklyn smiled.

Mason raised his eyebrows. "Congrats, sis." He pulled her into a hug.

She laughed. "Thanks, Mason."

"Moving fast, Sanders," Rob said. "What, are you pregnant or something?"

Daphne elbowed him in the side.

"Ow, woman." He tickled her side back in retaliation.

She almost spilled her champagne as she burst into a fit of giggles.

I smiled as I stared at all our friends. "Actually…yeah," I said. "Brooklyn's pregnant."

Everyone was quiet for a moment.

"Oh my God, Matt!" Penny said. She ran around the kitchen island and threw her arms around me as Kennedy almost knocked Brooklyn over with a big hug.

I'd been a little worried to tell Penny. I knew she couldn't have more kids and I knew how badly she wanted more. But I should have known she'd be happy for me. She was one of the kindest people I knew. And I felt those damn tears in my eyes again.

"And Brooklyn." She turned around and hugged Brooklyn too. "I'm so happy for both of you."

Rob was just about to take a sip of his champagne, but then stopped. "It is yours, right?" he asked.

"What the fuck, Rob?" Mason said.

"It's a valid question. Sanders only just came back."

I knew it was mine. When Brooklyn first told me she wasn't sure she could have any kids, I'd been worried she was pregnant with Miller's child. But she'd assured me that wasn't possible. I hadn't even let the possibility cross my mind.

Brooklyn cleared her throat. "It's definitely Matt's."

"But like…are you 100% sure?" Rob asked.

James hit Rob in the back of the head.

"Why does everyone keep hitting me?" Rob shoved him away.

"I'm so happy for you guys," Bee said.

"And I'm glad everyone finally knows now," Nigel said.

Everyone turned to Nigel.

"Wait, you told Nigel before you told us?" Rob asked.

"Yes," Nigel said. "As the best man I know everything first."

Rob stared at him. "What the hell did you just say to me?"

"As Matt's best man, I learned all the news first. I'm helping with the wedding. And I'll be in charge of the little one once he or she is born. Probably a she. That's what Tanner thinks."

I don't think we'd talked about him watching our new baby…

"Tanner already knew too?" Rob asked. "Seriously, what the fuck?"

Tanner held up his hands. "I just guessed."

"Good." Rob turned his attention back to me and glared. "Dude, is Nigel your best man?"

Definitely not.

"Yes," Nigel said.

I ignored him. "That's actually the other reason I invited you all over here. The game doesn't start for another half hour. So I figured we could start the night with a different game. A little best man competition."

"A best man competition?" Nigel asked. "Whatever for? I'm the best man in the room."

"Maybe," I said. "We'll know soon. After a series of challenges."

"Not a chance in hell, Nigel," Rob said. "*I'm* the best man."

Tanner laughed. "You young silly boy, Robert. I'm the best man. Right, Matt?"

"I'm not a silly boy!" Rob yelled.

"I told you this was ridiculous," Brooklyn whispered to me. "Super ridiculous."

"But fun," I said.

She laughed and shook her head.

"Okay, to start," I said and rubbed my hands together. "Tell me why each of you should be my best man."

"I'll go first," Tanner said. "I got the two of you back together. I did that." He tapped his chest. "And who's the one that's been hanging out with you the most these past few years while all these guys have been married?"

James laughed. "He has a point."

"And Brooklyn and I are very close too. Right, Brooklyn?"

Brooklyn smiled. "Yes. But I'm staying out of this competition." She held up her hands.

"We're all close with Brooklyn," Rob said.

"You call her by a last name that she hasn't had in years," Tanner said. "You know the old her. Not the new her."

"Sanders is a term of endearment. And I'll keep calling her that even after she's a Caldwell. Because that's our thing. Right, hot stuff?" Rob turned back to her.

Brooklyn held up her hands again.

"Okay," Tanner said. "One final point. I'm Matt's best friend."

"Son of a bitch," Rob said under his breath. "False. My turn. I'm Matt's best friend. I know literally everything about him. And I've known him much longer than that creep over there."

"I'm also a kind person," Tanner said.

"False," Rob said again. "You're a liar who prances around town in weird suits and elf shoes!"

"It's not nice to call people weird, Young Robert. Stop being a fascist."

"Yes, don't be a Wizzy," Nigel said.

"I'm nothing like Isabella and I'm definitely not a fascist," Rob said. He shook his head like that insult truly offended him. And then he shuddered. "Back to my point. It's always been us, Matt. The *four* of us really." Rob smiled. "And it'll always be us." He shrugged. "I love you man. You know that. And nothing will ever change that."

Brooklyn put her arm around my back.

Yeah, I'd felt that straight to the heart too.

Mason cleared his throat. "What Rob said. Minus being a fascist."

Rob groaned.

"Also, I'm your brother," Mason said.

"We're all brothers," Rob said. "We always have been."

Mason ignored him. "And you already asked me to be your best man the first time the two of you were engaged."

"Because we were feuding," Rob said. "That hardly counts. You were his last resort."

Tanner laughed. "Ah, see? Just because you've known Matt longer doesn't mean you were a good friend to him that whole time."

"Matt kissed my brother's girlfriend. What was I supposed to do? High five him?"

"See," Mason said. "Rob's just admitted that he doesn't think of you as a brother."

"I didn't..." Rob's voice trailed off. "You tricked me."

"I think you should pick whoever you want to pick," James said. "And we'll all be happy with that decision."

"Unless it's not me," Rob said. "And stop sucking up to him."

James shook his head. "I'm not sucking up to him. We both know that I'm not Matt's best man." He pressed his lips together. "I wasn't always there when you needed me. And I'm sorry for that."

I shook my head. "You tried. Actually, you tried more than anyone else. I knew you'd be there if I needed you."

James lowered his eyebrows. He never took a compliment well.

Brooklyn held on to me a little tighter.

I cleared my throat and turned to Felix. "What about you?" I said, knowing he'd say something funny.

"I don't think I'm a part of this," Felix said with a laugh.

I shrugged.

"Um...well...we're friends. But I've kissed Brooklyn so I'm pretty sure that means I'm out of the running."

"A million years ago," I said. "Besides, the past is in the past."

"Exactly," Rob said. "The past is in the past. Not that you stand a chance here, Felix. No offense. I doubt you're even in the wedding party. But back to the past thing. Tanner and Nigel don't even have a past with you."

Mason set his glass down. "I would also like to add the point that neither James nor Rob asked you to be the best man at their weddings. But you were mine at my wedding."

That was definitely the best point that had been made.

"I only asked James out of obligation," Rob said. "Because he asked me to be his."

James laughed. "Really, man?"

"No," Rob whispered. "But I'm trying to win here. Be cool."

Nigel cleared his throat. "My turn. I should be the best man because I love you the most. I'm your manny and your security detail. I'm always at your beck and call. I'm your bath butler. I'm your wardrobe stylist. I pack your meaty lunches. I'm your waterboy. We go on top secret missions together. I got you out of that mess with Poppy. I saved the day with a hand grenade. I'm your muse. I'm your office assistant. Brooklyn loves me like one of her own children. I'm Jacob's best friend. And I will do *anything* for you. *Anything*." He smiled up at me.

A lot of that was true. Well, at least some of it. *Huh*.

Rob sighed. "Dude, I'm your best friend. Just tell Tanner and everyone else and let's get this thing going. The wedding is in less than a month. We have things to plan."

"Exactly. That's the next part of the best man competition. If you were the best man, what would you plan for my bachelor party?"

Brooklyn laughed. "And with that, do you ladies want to go in the family room with me? I don't think we need to hear about what horrible things they're planning to do."

"As fun as whatever this is, yes," Bee said with a laugh. "It's a little weird watching all these grown men kissing Matt's ass."

Daphne laughed and linked her arm through Brooklyn's. "Well, if they plan anything like what they did for my bachelorette party, you're in for a real treat."

CHAPTER 20

Monday

Brooklyn

"I'm so happy for you guys," Daphne said as we all sat down on the couch.

"Thank you." I didn't know the Untouchables' wives that well. But they already felt like family.

"If there's one thing I know about the two of you, it's that you do everything fast," Kennedy said with a smile.

"We definitely weren't planning this," I said. When we were playing around with the pregnancy due date calculator, we figured out that I probably got pregnant when we'd had sex in the auditorium. None of that had been planned. But it had all happened for a reason. I was about to be swallowed whole by my pain. Matt had saved me. This baby saved me.

"So we have less than 4 weeks to plan this thing," Penny said. "We're all hands on deck. What do you need from us?"

"Well, Justin is already working on it. And Nigel is helping. I think the actual wedding will come together pretty quickly with those two."

Penny nodded. "Definitely. Justin is the best."

"He really is," Bee said.

Daphne nodded in agreement.

I couldn't believe that they'd all used Justin for their weddings. I was so proud of him for chasing his dreams. He'd wanted me to launch his career. But he'd never needed me. He just needed to believe in himself.

Justin definitely had the wedding handled. But that didn't mean I didn't need something from my friends. I couldn't remember the last time I was so nervous. I cleared my throat. "I know we don't know each other that well. But Matt was telling me about who he wanted for groomsmen…"

"Wait, do you know who he's choosing as his best man?" Daphne asked. "Because please just rip the Band-Aid off. Rob is going to be going on and on about this until he knows."

I laughed. I was sure he would be. "My lips are sealed."

"Traitor," Daphne said with a smile.

"I don't know what they're even doing over there," Bee said.

We all turned to see the guys in the kitchen.

Nigel was lying in the middle of the kitchen island. At least he had all his clothes on this time.

"Why is he full spread on your kitchen counter?" Penny asked.

Bee laughed. "I feel like full spread would imply that he was nude with his legs spread."

Penny wrinkled her nose. "That is not what I meant. Nigel would obviously never do that."

Actually…he had kind of done that. At least he'd covered his junk with a pan. I had no idea what him being on the counter had to do with the best man competition. It seemed like Matt was freeballing it. I shook my head. That was a weird thing to think when I'd just been thinking about Nigel full spread on the kitchen counter.

I cleared my throat. "Anyway. What I was getting at was that Matt and I were hoping to have an even amount of bridesmaids and groomsmen. I know that I don't know all of you very well. But at the same time it feels like I've known you forever. Penny, Bee, and Daphne, will you be my bridesmaids?"

"I was hoping you'd ask," Penny said with a smile. "Of course!"

"Absolutely," Bee said. "You're going to be my new sister. I honestly would have been sad if you didn't ask."

"I can't wait," Daphne added. "This is going to be so much fun."

I breathed a sigh of relief. This really was the best group of friends I could ask for.

I turned to Kennedy.

And she looked so…sad.

But she quickly hid the expression from her face and smiled. "It's going to be a beautiful wedding, Brooklyn." She reached out and squeezed my hand. "And you probably already have a photographer, but there's no way I'm not sneaking in a few of all you guys together. More memories for your mantel."

What was she talking about?

"I think the game is probably on now." She grabbed the remote and turned on the TV.

I stared up at the mantel. There was one person noticeably missing from the pictures. My best friend. For so long I'd tried to forget about my past. I regretted shutting her out. Just thinking about all our time apart made my chest hurt. Did she seriously not think I was going to ask her to be part of my wedding party? After everything we'd been through? She was my best friend. She always had been. "Kennedy?"

She forced another smile to her face. "I really am so happy for you. There is no one else in the world that deserves all of this happiness more than you. And I can't wait to meet your new baby."

Even though she was hurting, I knew she meant every word. She took a big sip of her champagne.

I just stared at her. "Kennedy," I said again. "I was hoping you'd be my maid of honor."

She almost spit out her champagne. "What?" she coughed.

"Did you seriously think I wasn't going to ask you to be one of my bridesmaids?"

"I…I don't know. You just asked everyone else but me, what was I supposed to think?" She laughed.

"That I wanted you to be my maid of honor." I leaned forward and hugged her. "Just like how I asked you before. Nothing has changed." In 16 years, not much had changed at all. I still loved Matt. And Kennedy was still my best friend.

She squeezed me tight. "I would love to be your maid of honor." She pulled back. "Puta mierda, Brooklyn. I was really sad for a minute there, but that was going to turn to anger real quick. I was getting ready to give a whole speech about my maid of honor credentials like those idiots in the other room."

I laughed and turned to see what they were up to. And Rob, Tanner, and Nigel were all sprinting into the room.

I screamed as Rob lifted me up into his arms. "I win!"

"What are you doing?" I slapped his arm.

"Capture the Princess."

"What the heck is Capture the Princess? Put me down." The best man competition was out of control.

"I honestly have no idea. It's something Tanner suggested." Rob set me back down on the couch. "But I won. Even though it was his stupid idea."

"You have to be able to save the bride in case of an emergency," Tanner said and wiped something out of his eyes. It looked like he'd been splashed with water. "Which

I've already proved when I helped save her from Locatelli."

"I also helped," Rob said.

"I threw the knife."

"I brought the hand grenade," Nigel said.

Tanner kept wiping his face.

"Tanner are you okay?" I asked. "Do you need a towel?"

"Young Robert threw his champagne in my face so he could get to you first."

"Okay. That's enough," I said. "Matt just tell them."

"I'm actually kind of enjoying this," he said.

I shook my head. "Everyone just sit down and watch the game." I grabbed Matt's hand and pulled him into the kitchen. I got some paper towels and turned to face him. "Someone is going to get hurt."

"They're big boys. Their feelings won't be hurt."

"No, I mean actually hurt. Champagne in the eyes must sting. What if Rob had...I don't know...thrown boiling water at Tanner?"

"Rob wouldn't have done that."

"How sure are you? Just tell them who the best man is."

"We've only done a few of the things on the best man competition list though."

I shook my head. "Why was Nigel on the counter again?"

Matt laughed. "I don't know. Something about the best spread? He was showing us how much room all his food would take up that night. They keep coming up with their own ideas on how to prove that they're the best man. I only got to one of my things. The bachelor party."

"Well, who had the best idea for that?"

Matt shrugged. "They were all fine. But I already know what I'm doing for my bachelor party."

"Which is?"

"You."

I laughed. "Seriously, what are you planning on doing?"

"You," he said again.

I rolled my eyes. "You're really not going to tell me?"

He put his arms around me, his hands settling on my lower back. "It's sexy when you roll your eyes at me."

"Just tell me what you're planning." The fact that he wouldn't tell me had me dying to know.

"I am telling you. Unless you want me to go to the Blue Parrot Resort like we did for James' bachelor party. That was Rob's suggestion."

"I have no idea what the Blue Parrot Resort is."

Matt smiled. "Well, maybe the two of us could go sometime." His hands slid to my ass.

I sighed. "Matthew Caldwell, you're trouble."

"Am I?" He smiled down at me.

"So much trouble." I couldn't help but smile too. "Now go tell your friends that you love all of them. But that you already know who your best man is."

"Or...I can at least make them do the ring test."

"I thought you were joking about the ring test."

Matt shook his head. "Definitely not. It's what I was looking forward to most."

"Where are you even planning on getting five monkeys?"

"Tanner has an animal guy."

I stared at him. Claude, yeah. Tanner had mentioned him to me once too. I shook my head. "This is going to be a disaster."

"Or it's going to be really fun."

"Well, in this made-up competition, who's winning so far?" I asked.

"Actually? Probably Nigel. He knows me really well. Like...too well."

I laughed. "Maybe you should add him as a groomsman. I think he'd really appreciate it. And his speech was really nice. He does help us out so much. I want him to know we care about him."

"But we already have that all figured out. We want to have an even amount of groomsmen and bridesmaids."

I bit the inside of my lip. "Actually, I have one more person I want to ask."

"Is this like when you kept adding random people trying to make me add James and Rob back in high school? Because I'm sure Nigel would be fine just helping Justin out with the planning."

I shook my head. "No. I really do have someone else I want to ask."

"Okay. Who is it?"

"I know he's going to be so busy that day. But I really want to ask Justin."

Matt smiled. "I think that's a great idea." And then he sighed. "Shit, am I really about to ask Nigel to be in my wedding party? What is my life?"

CHAPTER 21

Tuesday

Matt

"Rob, you're late," I said as he strolled onto the field a half hour after practice ended.

Nigel shook his head. "A proper best man must be on time if not early."

Nigel had a great point.

Rob pulled up his sleeve to look at his empty wrist. "How 'bout that? I forgot my watch."

I was pretty sure I'd only ever seen him wear a watch once. "Do you even own a watch?"

"Of course I do," Rob said. "I have a whole collection. I blame James for this. He should have texted me."

James lifted his hands. "How is you being late my fault? We both knew the time."

"Was that the last part of the best man competition?" Mason asked. "Because Rob definitely failed. And I was here first."

"Whoa, whoa, whoa," Rob said. "You're acting like I'd be late on the day of the wedding. I would never do that. Daphne wouldn't allow it."

That was true. Daphne would make sure Rob showed up on time. But this technically was part of the best man competition. And Rob had definitely failed. "You're a half hour late, man."

"But I won Capture the Princess last night. And you know my bachelor party idea is the best. Oh and…I'm your fucking best friend."

Tanner laughed.

"Don't you laugh at me, you secret Christmas elf!"

"Young Robert." Tanner shook his head. "It's very hard to take you seriously when you're saying such silly things. An elf? Really? Green isn't my color. And I'm taller than you. I could hardly be categorized as one of the big man's *little* helpers."

"Well, maybe your dick is little."

Tanner laughed. "No. But yours probably is."

"Speaking of our private members, I have an idea!" Nigel yelled.

We all turned to him.

A smile slowly spread across his face. "Let's have a dick measuring contest to determine who wins the best man competition."

"What does that have to do with being a good best man?" I asked. This wasn't a dick measuring contest. It was a best man competition. Why did everyone keep suggesting such weird things for this? I had a whole plan.

"It has everything to do with it," Nigel said.

That was not an answer. He just wanted a reason to whip out his giant monster dong. "Keep it in your pants, man. Okay, where was I? I invited the five of you here today because..."

"Wait," Rob said. "Nigel is right. The best man has to have big dick energy. Let's do it." He grabbed the front of his belt.

"Rob, stop it. We're in the middle of a high school football stadium." And he did not want to have this contest with Nigel. Because Rob would 100% lose. I'd seen what Nigel was packing on my kitchen counter. And I never wanted to see it again.

"But this will settle everything. Right guys?" Rob looked over at Mason and James.

"If you want to finally realize you have the smallest dick, fine by me," Mason said.

What did my friends not understand about being at a *high school* right now? We were going to get arrested. And no one was going to beat Nigel. We were all perfectly well-endowed. But Nigel's dick was made for a freaking elephant.

"So we're doing it?" Nigel asked. "Good. Biggest dick wins. Agreed?" He turned to Tanner. "You're in, right?"

"What the hell, Nigel," Tanner said. "You know it's too dangerous for me to participate in this."

What on earth does that mean?

"I'm sure your dick isn't so big that it's dangerous," Rob said with a laugh.

Tanner ignored him, folded his arms across his chest, and glared at Nigel.

"I have to ensure that I'll win," Nigel said. "I'm sorry, Master Tanner, but I have to fight dirty. It's the only way I know how to fight." He started to lower his pants.

"Don't you dare drop your pants on this field, Nigel," I said.

He inched them a little lower as he stared at me dead in the eyes.

"Anyone who whips out their dick is kicked out of the best man competition."

"But..." Nigel started.

"No buts. Zip it up."

He sighed and zipped his pants back up.

I cleared my throat. "Now, where was I?" This afternoon wasn't going according to plan at all. I blew my whistle and Tanner's animal guy wheeled out a covered cage.

"Hi, Claude," Tanner said. "Matt, I didn't know Claude was your animal guy too. Good choice. He is the best. But what does being a best man have to do with animals?"

I'd gotten Claude's information from Nigel. But I'd actually had Nigel organize all of this. Which also made his random dick measuring contest idea not make any sense. He knew what I was going to ask everyone to do already.

"It's what the animal symbolizes," I said. "The most important part of being a best man is holding on to a valuable item." I stared at all of them.

James raised his eyebrows. "Are you talking about the ring right now?" He glanced warily at the covered cage.

"Yes. You have to protect the ring at all costs." Brooklyn was probably right. I was having way too much fun with this. Especially since I already knew who I was going to ask.

Something clanged against the inside of the cage and Rob jumped.

"What are you about to make us do?" Rob asked.

"Take care of something valuable," I said. "And what's more valuable than a living thing?" I nodded at Claude.

He pulled the cover off the cage.

There were five monkeys jumping around inside. One of them threw a banana peel out of the cage and it almost hit Mason in the face.

"Sorry," Rob said. "What exactly are you about to make us do?" he asked again.

"You have to take care of your monkey for the rest of the day. Whoever takes care of it best will win this last part of the best man competition."

"You're serious?" Rob asked. "You know I've never had a pet, man."

"You'll be fine."

Rob shuddered.

"Sounds good," Tanner said. He walked over to the cage, took out a monkey, and placed it on his shoulder.

The monkey reached out to touch Tanner's hair, but Tanner snapped his fingers, and the monkey put his hand back down.

Huh. Weird. I didn't know Tanner was so good with animals.

"This is nothing like a ring," Rob said and picked up one of the monkeys. "But if I can handle two kids, I can surely handle a monkey."

The monkey immediately put its hands on Rob's right pec.

"Why is it so handsy?"

I shrugged. "Maybe it's a skin-on-skin thing?"

"I'm not getting naked with my monkey."

Nigel grabbed a monkey too. "Who's a good little simian?" He rubbed him under the chin.

Like always, I didn't know what Nigel was talking about.

James walked over to me and put his hand on my shoulder. "You do already know who you're choosing, right?" he asked, so no one near the cage could hear.

I laughed. "Yup."

He smiled. "Then I'm going to sit this one out. I'm not risking giving anyone in my family some kind of weird monkey disease. Even if Scarlett would love having a monkey in the house."

"Fair."

"I'm also not handling a monkey for the next…" Mason looked down at his watch "…eight hours. But I would like to point out that I have a watch. Not that it matters. Because I already know I'm your best man."

I clapped him on the back, but didn't reply.

Mason gave me a hard stare.

"I mean…you're not even doing the ring test."

"I'll gladly hold your rings on the day of your wedding. I'm not fondling a monkey though. But I'll be at your house later so you can beg me on your knees."

I laughed. "Never."

"We'll see."

"It tried to bite my nipple!" Rob yelled.

He'd taken his shirt off. Apparently he was taking the skin-on-skin thing seriously.

"None of my kids ever tried to bite me. How long do we have to care for these things?"

"Everyone come by my house at midnight. Whoever's monkey is the happiest wins. You two come too," I said to James and Mason.

"Right. So you can beg me," Mason said.

"Never," I whispered.

"See you lads at midnight." Tanner saluted me. And his monkey almost pulled off a salute too before Tanner turned and walked away.

Wow. Okay. Tanner was definitely winning this thing. Especially because Rob's monkey was still trying to bite him. And Nigel's monkey didn't look like he liked being held like a baby. He kept trying to slap Nigel's face.

***

"Is it even legal to have a monkey as a pet in New York City?" Brooklyn asked.

I shrugged. "No idea."

"Your friends could be arrested."

"Trust me, it's better than what they wanted to do."

"Which was?"

I laughed. "Nigel wanted to have a dick measuring contest."

Brooklyn laughed too. "Well, that would have ended poorly for everyone else."

"He also tried to do it in the middle of the Empire High football stadium."

"Yeah, your friends are definitely going to get arrested."

"Trust me, it'll be fine. No one will get in trouble."

"Matthew Caldwell." She sighed and leaned against the counter. "I almost forgot that you never get in trouble. Even though you are trouble."

I laughed. "Me? Trouble?"

"You gave your friends monkeys to take care of. And none of them have experience with monkeys. And they're in the middle of a crowded city. You're trouble. Especially since the best man competition is rigged."

"They all know that already." I wrapped my arms around her. "It's just a bit of fun."

"As long as no one gets hurt."

I placed a slow kiss against her lips. "No one is getting hurt."

"I'm holding you to that."

"Besides, Mason and James refused to participate."

"Smart men."

I smiled down at her. "Have you asked Justin yet?"

"No, I'll ask him whenever he calls or shows up next. He has a lot on his plate. I don't want to add anything else."

"He's going to be excited."

"I know." She stood on her tiptoes and kissed me again. "I really want to stay up to see which monkey is the happiest. Whatever that means. But I'm not going to make it."

I laughed and looked at the clock. It was only 9. "I have an idea." I grabbed her hand and pulled her into the family room. I turned on a movie, sat down, and gestured for her to lie down.

She smiled and rested her head on my lap.

I looked down at her stomach. Brooklyn had been worried that I didn't love this version of her. And she was about to change again.

But she had it all wrong. I loved every version of her more and more. I was pretty sure the pregnant version of her was going to be my new favorite.

I ran my fingers through her hair. And two minutes into the movie she started lightly snoring. I barely paid attention to the movie. I just kept running my fingers through her hair and staring down at her. *How did I get so fucking lucky?*

A knock on the door made Brooklyn open her eyes. "Did I fall asleep?" she said with a yawn.

"And almost woke up the whole house with your snoring."

"I did not." She lightly slapped my thigh and pushed herself up.

The knock sounded on the door again.

"I can't wait to see this," Brooklyn said.

I opened the door. Rob was standing there. Without a monkey.

He smiled and walked in. "Would you look at that? I'm first. Early even. I think that makes up for earlier, don't you think? You should just crown me best man now."

"Rob, where is your monkey?"

"What monkey?" Rob asked.

"The monkey I gave you to take care of."

"Oh." He laughed. "That monkey." But he didn't offer any more information.

There was another knock on the door. Tanner and Nigel walked in with their monkeys in tow. And Mason and James showed up right after.

I turned back to Rob. "Where is your monkey?" I asked again.

"What monkey?" Rob asked, like we hadn't just been over this.

"Where is it?" I said again.

"It's fine," Rob said with a laugh.

"But where is it?"

"Well. Funny story…" his voice trailed off as he stared at the TV.

The movie had ended and the news had turned on. A red banner was scrolling along the bottom of the screen that said: "Monkey terrorizing downtown Manhattan." And there was footage of a monkey running down a sidewalk throwing trash at people and grabbing their butts.

What the fuck?

A reporter on the sidewalk started talking. "As you can see, the monkey is groping…"

"Nothing to see there," Rob said as he grabbed the remote and switched off the TV.

"Was that your monkey?" I asked.

"I mean…I don't know if there's any way to tell. That could be anyone's monkey."

"Well, did you lose your monkey?"

"Did I lose my monkey?" Rob laughed. "Um. Yes. Yes, I did do that."

Brooklyn burst out laughing. "You guys are ridiculous. Shouldn't you go catch that monkey or something?"

"We should let the professionals handle that," Rob said. "That monkey is way too handsy. Or…my monkey was way too handsy. I don't know if that was my monkey on the TV."

"It was groping people," James said with a laugh. "That's definitely your handsy little monkey."

"Well don't look at me. It's not like I taught him to grab ass. He was born that way."

Tanner cleared his throat. "As you can see, I took the best care of my monkey. Look at this. Blow a kiss."

The monkey blew me a kiss.

How the hell did he teach him to do that?

"Well, my monkey is asleep," Nigel said. "He's very docile. Look." He held up his sleeping monkey. "I'm clearly the best at caring for the animals. Like I'm the best at caring for peoples."

His monkey was definitely knocked out. And I was a little suspicious that he'd drugged it. Like he'd drugged me that one time when I was "hysterical."

"Tanner wins," I said.

"Yes!" Tanner put his fist in the air and his monkey did the same. "I believe that means I'm the best man. I won the most tasks. Matt, I will not let you down." He rubbed his hands together. "I've got everything covered. This is going to be the best day of your life."

"You absolutely did not win," Rob said. "And Matt definitely doesn't want you beside him in all those wedding pictures. He wants his *best* friend. Me."

"Wait, there's…pictures?" Tanner asked.

"Yeah, man," I said. I was confused about why he seemed surprised about this. He'd been to weddings before.

"Oh." He laughed. "Like pictures you're keeping very private? And not on display? And that you'll burn upon your death?"

"Um…no," I said. "We'll get some printed out for the house. We'll print out some for you too. And everyone in the wedding party. And my parents of course…"

"No," Tanner said.

"No you don't want pictures?"

"No, I don't want you to take pictures."

"We're taking pictures at our wedding, Tanner," Brooklyn said. "Everyone takes pictures at their wedding."

"Well I...I didn't know that," he said.

"How could you not know that?" I asked.

He cleared his throat. "Because I grew up overseas."

He used that excuse all the time. But it made zero sense.

He cleared his throat again. "So the privacy settings and burning of pictures isn't up for negotiation?"

Brooklyn and I looked at each other. "No," I said.

He sighed. "Well, I have to respectfully step down from the best man competition." He looked devastated. "I need to be on the edge of every picture."

"Why?"

"So I'm easily removable."

Rob laughed. "See. Barely a friend. He wants to be removed. Perfect. Put him on the end. And I'll be right next to my best friend." He clapped me on the back.

I was so confused. Tanner had been dead set on being my best man. What was going on?

"I also need to regretfully decline being the best man," Nigel said.

"Why?" I asked.

"I do not like being photographed. I will also be on the edge of the photo so I can easily cut both Master Tanner and myself out of the picture upon your d..."

"Shh," Tanner said.

"Right," Nigel said. "But I never wanted to be the best man anyway. Because I already have my title." He smiled. "I'm the best boy!"

Brooklyn laughed. And for some reason I laughed too. *Okay, Nigel.*

"Great," Rob said. "Mason and James weren't participating, so it's me, right? I'm the best man? Fuck yes!"

"Actually…" my voice trailed off and I looked over at Mason.

Mason smiled.

"Mason, I asked you 16 years ago, and I'm asking you again. Will you be my best man?"

"What?!" Rob yelled.

"Yes," Mason said. "I won't even make you beg."

I laughed.

"No," Rob said. "I'm your best friend. Even Tanner admitted…"

"I didn't admit to anything," Tanner said. "I just don't want there to be photographic evidence…"

Nigel elbowed him in the side.

"Right." Tanner nodded. He shoved his hands into his pockets. "I have nothing else to say."

I had no idea what was going on. "And James, Rob, Tanner, and Nigel, I'd love for you guys to be my groomsmen," I said.

James nodded. "Of course, man."

"No," Rob said. "I'm the *best* man."

"Rob, you can stand right next to Mason," I said.

Rob smiled. "Deal. That still makes me the best friend. Since Mason is your brother. And you were always going to ask me to be your number two, right? Even without whatever the hell is going on with Tanner being scared of cameras?"

I actually didn't know. And I was happy I didn't have to make that choice. Tanner and Nigel had made it easy on me. And I wondered if that's what they were doing. Because they really were good friends. I smiled at Tanner.

He shrugged like it was no big deal.

But it was. And I appreciated it. I'd appreciate it even more if he didn't cut up all my wedding photos though.

CHAPTER 22

Thursday

Brooklyn

I laughed and lifted my plate off the table. "Justin, you're getting glitter in the food."

"You're getting glitter in the food," he said back sarcastically as he slammed a book full of color swatches closed and glitter went everywhere. "Well, maybe if we didn't have to do literally all the planning in one night, you wouldn't have glitter in your hors d'oeuvres."

This probably wasn't the best time to ask him to be a bridesmaid. Or a bridesman? I wasn't exactly sure what it was called. But it definitely wasn't a good time to ask. *Maybe at the end of the night.* I blew some of the glitter off my plate and ate another one of the little pastry puffs that tasted like cheesesteaks. "Well this cheesesteak pastry thing has my vote."

"Agreed," Mason said as he grabbed another from the tray.

I smiled at him. It was really sweet of Mason and Kennedy to come with us. And Mrs. Alcaraz and Mrs. Caldwell. The two of them were talking to one of the seamstresses. They seemed to think my old dress would still work. I hoped that was true.

I couldn't believe that in just a few weeks *I'd* be Mrs. Caldwell. Everything was happening so fast, it felt surreal. Like I was in some kind of dream instead of reality. Because my reality was being curled up on a couch at the lake house in Miller's arms. I felt tears pulling in my eyes. No, my reality was that Miller was gone. There was no safe haven lake house. I needed my mind to stop playing tricks on me.

I took a deep breath and put my hand on my stomach. It was easier to hold on to the present when I knew I was needed here. Right now. In this moment. I looked around Justin's studio. It was really easy to be present in here. There were seamstresses altering dresses, people in suits running around with clipboards for some reason, place settings on display, and other couples discussing cake options. It was colorful and chaotic and just so very Justin.

I turned to Matt. "Which is your favorite appetizer?" I asked.

"Whatever you choose sounds good to me."

He kept saying that to any suggestion I had. But at this rate I was going to choose everything. "But which appetizer is your favorite?"

He leaned closer to me so no one could hear him. "Baby, there's only one thing I'm interested in eating on our wedding day."

"Right. The cake." But I was going to have a lot of opinions about that too…

His lips fell to my ear. "Not the cake, Brooklyn. *You.*"

Jesus. I crossed my legs under the table.

"Good, you chose one. I'll choose the rest," Justin said and snapped his fingers. The waiter started clearing away the appetizers. I quickly grabbed one more cheesesteak pastry before the plate was snatched off the table.

Justin was definitely in his frantic mode. Whenever we weren't quick enough, he just said he'd figure it out. But actually…I was okay with that. I trusted him. And he still had all our original wedding plans. I wasn't sure what had made him keep them all those years ago. But I was so glad he did.

"When are you going to ask him about being in the wedding party?" Matt whispered.

"It doesn't really seem like a good time right now."

"I don't think he's going to calm down until after the wedding."

I bit the inside of my lip. Matt was probably right. I just needed to ask. "Hey, Justin?" I said as the waiters started to bring out dozens of different cakes.

"If you're about to ask me why you don't get to try any entrees, save your breath. There's no time. You'll have steak and crabcakes."

"That sounds great…"

"Don't you dare *but* me right now. There's no time for buts!"

"I wasn't going to. That truly sounds great. I just wanted to ask…"

"No, you can't choose the wine list, Brooklyn. You're pregnant."

I wouldn't know how to choose a wine list even if I wasn't pregnant. "Justin…"

"Save your breath, you're choosing cake #7." He pointed to a beautiful cake with yellow icing. I smiled. My mother would have loved it. I felt an ache in my chest. I'd do anything for her to be here with me right now.

"Justin, she's trying to ask you an important question," Matt said. He put his arm around my shoulders.

"She doesn't get to ask any questions until she answers all of mine." He held up a stack of papers. "Like, who's walking you down the aisle?"

I swallowed hard. I really didn't want to talk about that.

Matt cleared his throat. "Justin. Just hear her out. It's one question."

"I don't have time for questions!" Justin downed the rest of his cup of coffee. "I need more caffeine!" He snapped his fingers and a waiter with coffee appeared.

I really didn't think he needed more caffeine right now.

"You're going to want to make time for this question," Matt said calmly. He nodded at me when Justin had finally quieted down with his new coffee mug in hand.

At least if he was drinking he wouldn't be able to interrupt me. "Justin, I know you're going to be busy the day of the wedding, so I'm not sure how it'll work exactly, but I'd love for you to be in the bridal party."

Justin spat his coffee out all over the table. "Excuse me?"

"Jesus, Justin," Mason said and wiped some coffee spittle off his tie.

Kennedy laughed.

I couldn't help but laugh too. "Justin, I was hoping you could be a bridesmaid. Or bridesperson?"

"Shut the hell up!" Justin yelled.

Was he upset? Or excited? I felt like I was wording it wrong. "Or…bridesman?"

"Brooklyn." He put his hand to his chest. "You beautiful last-minute goddess. I would love nothing more. And I will look amazing in a yellow tux."

"You really will."

He screamed at the top of his lungs and threw his arms out, accidentally knocking over the yellow cake. "Oops. But this one really is divine, just trust me." He licked a little icing off his fingers.

"I do," I said.

"Save that for your gorgeous hunk of a husband," Justin said and winked at Matt. He sighed "To think, the two of us almost kissed."

Kennedy laughed. "Wait, the two of you almost kissed on your date?"

"No," Matt said.

At the same time, Justin said, "yes."

Matt laughed. "Definitely not."

Justin shrugged. "I remember it differently in my dreams." He clapped his hands together. "Now that all the food is situated, it's time we try on that dress. So you boys need to get out of my studio and leave the rest of the work to the ladies."

"We barely ate anything," Mason said. He turned to Matt. "I came here straight from work and I was promised lots of food."

"Want to go get some takeout or something?" Matt asked.

"No need." Justin snapped his fingers and waiters balancing tons of takeout containers walked over to the table. "You can have all the leftovers. You can take forever eating on your own time. Now leave."

Matt leaned down and kissed my cheek. "Are you sure you don't want me to stay?"

"You can't see me in my dress. It's bad luck." I swallowed hard. I hated thinking of anything else bad happening.

"Nothing bad is going to happen. But if you insist."

I put my hand on Matt's cheek. I wanted to believe him. But there was this little voice in the back of my head. Bouncing around, trying to make me listen. *Everyone I love dies.* I immediately pushed it away. Matt had taught me that wasn't true. That's why we had friends and family with us here. That's why he was here. "Have fun with Mason." I let my hand fall from his cheek.

I thought he'd stand up and leave, but instead he leaned in closer. "Tell me what you're thinking."

I pressed my lips together. I was missing Miller. I was missing my mom. I was worried I'd never get to meet this baby. And I was worried that one day soon, if we walked down the aisle, I'd be missing Matt. Because I *was* bad luck. My heart was just aching. With pain from my past and worry for my future. And I didn't know what to say. Because we'd talked about all this. I just didn't know how to let go of that fear that my whole world would be ripped apart again.

"It's okay," he whispered. "Just tell me. I know you're missing him. I know this is all fast. If it's too fast..."

I quickly shook my head. "That's not it." *Not exactly*. I wasn't sure my heart would ever stop aching for Miller. But it felt like my heart beat better around Matt. Like if I was ever going to heal, I needed him by my side. Tanner had told me that it was hard to grieve alone. He was right about that.

"This is what I want," I said. I grabbed Matt's hand. "You're what I want." I lowered my voice even more. "I'm just...scared." I didn't need to say anything else. He knew all my fears.

"There is nothing to be scared of." He dropped his forehead to mine.

I slowly breathed in his exhales. Matt wanted me to be honest with him. That was our deal. That I could tell him everything on my mind. "And yes, I do miss him."

He didn't respond. But he squeezed my hand.

"And I wish my mom were here. I've been thinking about her a lot ever since I found out I was pregnant."

"I wish I could have met her," he said.

"Me too." She would have loved Matt. And she would have loved Miller. She would have understood my heart belonging to both of them. Because her heart had belonged to two people too. Me and my father. She'd chosen me. But she'd still only ever loved my father.

"Matthew and Mason, you need to leave now," Justin said. "Or I will have someone remove you from the premises."

I couldn't help but laugh.

Matt cradled my face in his hand. "You are so loved, Brooklyn. And I know it's not the same, but my mom and Mrs. Alcaraz are so excited to be here."

"I know."

"But…I have an idea about your mom."

I stared at him. "What's your idea?"

"I'll tell you when you get home." He gave me one last kiss and then helped Mason with all the takeout containers.

Justin turned toward me. "Now get your sexy ass into that dress so we can assess the damage."

I hated how he'd put that. But it made me smile. I turned to watch Matt walk out the door. He somehow managed to balance the containers in one hand as he ran his index finger across the tip of his nose.

Our secret signal.

I had no idea what Matt was planning, but whenever he had a surprise, I knew it would be a good one. I took a deep breath and turned to Justin. "Okay, let's assess the damage."

It didn't take long to realize that the dress no longer fit.

Justin sighed and stopped attempting to button the buttons that trailed down the back of the dress. "Curse you and your fantastic curves."

It was a compliment. Kind of. My hips were a little wider. And I was definitely a little wider around the rib-cage. Unfortunately the dress was very unforgiving. It had been designed to be skintight, giving the sheath dress a more fitted form. I stared at the lace trailing down my arms. I still absolutely loved the dress. It was flowy and bohemian and as timeless as I hoped it would be. But it didn't fit at all.

If I was 16, maybe I'd just try to lose a few pounds. But I was 32. And pregnant. And that wasn't an option. "It's not going to work."

"Well, come let the ladies see. We're all going to figure it out together. But it is a shame that it was already fitted."

Yeah. I held my hand to my chest as I walked out of the changing room. Not because I was worried the dress would fall. The sleeves made sure of that. But my chest still ached. I really wished my mom was here.

Mrs. Caldwell smiled. "You look more beautiful now that you did when you were a teenager."

I felt my cheeks flush. "Thank you."

"But your ass and boobs are way bigger," Kennedy said.

"Por favor, mi amor," Mrs. Alcaraz said.

I laughed. "It's fine. She's right. It doesn't fit at all."

Mrs. Caldwell stood up and walked around me, inspecting the dress. "Well, we need a little extra fabric from somewhere. What if we lower the neckline?"

Justin gasped. "Yes. I love it. Show off the girls." He started writing something in his notebook.

"Oh." I kept my hand on my chest.

"And we can use the extra fabric to expand the waist a pinch," he said.

"How much fabric exactly?" I asked.

Kennedy stood up, grabbed my hand, and lowered it from my chest. "I know back then you were worried about the dress being too sexy. But girl…you're not a teenager anymore. I say if you got it, flaunt it."

I smiled. "But seriously…how low cut are we talking?"

Justin tuned his notebook to me. He hadn't been writing anything down. He'd been sketching. The neckline originally cut right beneath my neck. But the new neckline plunged in a deep V. A very deep V.

"We can find a matching tulle," Justin said. "Put a little right here?" He drew a line where the neckline originally was. "So it'll be sheer. Classy and sexy AF." He looked up from his notebook at me.

I didn't bother to ask why we couldn't put a matching tulle along the waist to make it fit. Because the drawing Justin had done was perfect. Kennedy was right. Back then, I'd been worried about my dress being appropriate. I wanted Mrs. Caldwell to like me. And I'd been so nervous picking out the dress with her.

But she was standing here nodding her head. I didn't think it mattered if I showed up in a burlap sack. She loved me, because her son loved me. I made him happy. And that's all she wanted.

I turned back to Justin. "I love it."

"Yeah?"

I nodded. "What do you guys think?"

"I think you're going to look amazing," Kennedy said.

"It's perfect," Mrs. Caldwell said. "Matthew is going to love it, Brooklyn."

I smiled and turned to Mrs. Alcaraz.

There were tears in her eyes. "I wish Jim could have seen you. He'd be so proud of you, Brooklyn. So proud."

I wish he could be here too. If he was, it would have made the who is going to walk you down the aisle question easier. I would have asked him in a heartbeat.

"Mama," Kennedy said and wiped beneath her eyes. "Stop, you're making everyone cry."

Mrs. Alcaraz sniffed. "Sí sí. But he'd be so proud of both mis niñas. How strong you both are." She grabbed one of Kennedy's hands and mine. "And I am proud too."

She really was trying to make us cry.

"I think we could all use a group hug," Mrs. Caldwell said and put her arms around the three of us.

Justin put his arms around us too. "I love my girls."

I smiled through my tears. Matt was right. My mom wasn't here, but Mrs. Caldwell and Mrs. Alcaraz were pretty great stand-ins.

CHAPTER 23

Thursday

Matt

"And the duck goes..."

"Quack," Jacob said with a yawn and put his head on my shoulder.

I smiled down at him. We had a new routine. He loved reading his favorite books in the dark with a flashlight. While the stars glowed above his bed.

Usually Brooklyn was with us though. I was a little worried he'd be hard to put to sleep without her tonight. But he hadn't made a fuss. He just seemed excited to read his story.

"And the lion goes..."

"Roar." He yawned again.

"And the monster goes..."

Jacob started snoring lightly. Usually he was jumping around to this part of the book. But Tanner had been playing football in the backyard with him when I'd gotten home from Justin's studio. Mason and I had joined them, and the four of us had kept playing for at least another hour. Jacob was tuckered out.

I smiled as Jacob snored again. He actually sounded just like Brooklyn when she was really tired. For a second I just stared at him sleeping. His little head on my shoulder.

For years, I'd tried to pretend I didn't want a family. That I didn't want to be a father. But I couldn't be more wrong. This little guy made my heart feel so full. I knew he wasn't my kid. But it was hard to believe he wasn't when we were playing football. Or reading like this. Or dancing around the kitchen. This kid was a piece of me. I guess because Brooklyn was a piece of me.

I'd meant what I said to Brooklyn. That I would have been happy just the three of us. I kissed the top of Jacob's head and gently moved him so he was lying down. I tried my best not to move the bed too much as I climbed off. I put the book down on his nightstand, switched off the flashlight, and tiptoed to the door.

"Goodnight, Daddy," Jacob said.

I froze. I thought my heart was already full. But hearing him call me that? I turned around to say goodnight too.

But Jacob was staring up at the ceiling.

I swallowed hard. I don't know why I thought he was calling me that. Jacob had told me he didn't want me to be his dad. That he wanted to keep calling me Coach. And I was fine with that. I understood that. I just...I had a slip up. But my chest felt all funny now. Of course he wasn't talking to me.

Jacob turned back to me and smiled. "Goodnight, Coach. I love you."

I blinked and for a second and didn't say anything at all. That hit differently. Because it was definitely for me. Jacob loved so freely. He trusted me to keep him safe. To keep his mom safe. To make sure they were both happy. No, I wasn't his dad. But I could definitely be his coach. "I love you too, kiddo."

He closed his eyes, rolled over on his side, and held one of his stuffed animals tight.

I stared at him for another moment until I heard him snoring again. And then I closed the door.

The house was eerily quiet now that Tanner and Mason had left and Brooklyn still wasn't home. I picked up some of the toys that were strewn on the floor. As I put the last truck in the basket, I paused at one of the photos on the mantel. Of Miller and Brooklyn smiling at the camera. I exhaled slowly and walked toward the back door. There was something I needed to do. I closed the door quietly behind me.

"Hey," I said and stared up at the sky. "I know you don't like me, man." How could he possibly?

The wind blew and the city felt so still.

"But I do promise to keep Brooklyn safe. And I promise to take care of Jacob. And to love them both. I promise you that."

The wind blew again and I closed my eyes.

"I'll pick up where you left off. Loving them." I exhaled slowly and opened my eyes again.

The stars looked a little brighter in the sky.

And I could tell why this helped Brooklyn and Jacob so much. Because the stars felt alive. Like they were listening. Hell, maybe they were.

I cleared my throat and stared at the stars. "Thank you, Miller. Thank you for taking care of Brooklyn when I couldn't. Thank you for being what she needed. And thank you for trusting me to be what she needs now." I nodded. I hoped he understood. I hoped he knew that Brooklyn wasn't just moving on. That her heart was still broken. And that she was letting me help heal her. That she was giving me a second chance that I probably didn't deserve. But I wasn't going to fuck it up this time. This time it was forever.

I nodded at the stars once more and then went back inside. It felt like a weight had been lifted off my shoulders. Like I'd somehow gotten Miller's permission.

I didn't move any of the pictures on the mantel, but I grabbed the couple I had framed and added them. One was of me and Brooklyn back in high school. I'd pulled it from the photo album Kennedy had made for us as a wedding present. It had been taken after one of my football games. In it Brooklyn was kissing me even though I was still in my uniform and all sweaty. I loved that photo. And I added one from prom too.

Tanner had brought over a huge stack of photos from prom that he'd gotten the photographer to print out. And he and Nigel were only in a few. And always on the end. He specifically asked me not to frame any of them.

I asked him why he really didn't like being photographed. He'd just shrugged and said it was a billionaire thing. And that I wouldn't understand until I was a billionaire.

So I put one of all the Untouchables on the mantel instead. One with Rob jumping on my back and kind of ruining the photo in the best way. Then I added one of all of us with our wives and girlfriends. It was definitely missing Tanner. But I respected his billionaire wishes. Hell, maybe I would understand one day. It was probably just a privacy thing.

I grabbed the big picture I had framed and walked into the entranceway. I'd moved the naked portrait of Brooklyn to our bathroom. I lifted up the new frame and hung it in the portrait's place. It was another picture from prom, of me dipping Brooklyn backwards as she laughed. God I loved the sound of her laughter.

I stepped back and stared at the photo. *There.* I took a deep breath. Now it felt like my home too. *Our* home. Together. For our family.

I heard the key in the lock.

Shit. She was back early. I ran into the kitchen and turned on the music, low enough to not wake Jacob.

"What is this?" she said with a laugh.

I hurried back into the entranceway and dipped her like in the picture.

She turned toward it and smiled. "Seriously, what is going on?"

I leaned down and kissed her and then pulled her back upright. "Oh, this is how I'm always going to welcome you home," I shimmied my shoulders.

"Hmm, I'm reconsidering everything now," she said with a smile.

I pretended to look shocked. "Baby, I know you love my dance moves." I broke out the robot and she laughed again.

"I truly will expect this every time I come home now," she said.

"Done." I twirled her around and pulled her in close.

The music was upbeat, but we started swaying in the entranceway.

"I like the new picture."

"I like you," I said. I'd been worried about her when I left her at Justin's studio. But she looked do damn happy right now. I'd planned a whole night around making her smile again. But I was sure I could make her smile even bigger.

"I should go say goodnight to Jacob," she said.

"He's sound asleep."

"Yeah? He was okay tonight? I was worried…"

"He was good. He had fun with Tanner while we were out. And Mason came over for a bit and the four of us played football outside."

"I'm sure he loved that."

"He did. He was so tuckered out that we barely made it through half a book before he fell asleep. Come here, I want to show you something else." I pulled her into the family room.

She dropped my hand and looked at the new pictures on the mantel. She smiled when she reached the one of us from high school. "I remember that day."

"I remember that night," I said.

She laughed. "Yeah. I remember that too."

"I was thinking we could reenact it."

"You want to reenact your parents being out of town? And your brother being at a party?"

"Yes."

"We're not 16 anymore, Matt."

"No. But we were rarely all alone back then. And we're rarely alone right now."

She squealed as I lifted her into my arms. I carried her into the kitchen and put her down on the island. I needed a new memory of someone naked on this kitchen counter.

Sixteen years ago, we'd skipped a party after my team won so that we could be alone. Brooklyn insisted she'd wanted to bake something. But I'd only had one thing on my mind then. And I only had one thing on my mind now.

I stepped between her legs, pushing her thighs apart.

"This is not what I was expecting when I walked in the door tonight," she said.

"I want you to love surprises again. So I'll keep surprising you until you do."

She smiled. "I've always loved *your* surprises. Just not my dad's."

I really didn't want to talk about Mr. Pruitt right now. For just a few minutes, I wanted Brooklyn to forget about all the pain she was carrying around. I slid my hands up her thighs, forcing her skirt to rise up higher. I ran one of my thumbs up the side of her thong and circled her hip bone. "I love this part of you." Where her soft flesh met a hard line.

A soft moan escaped her lips.

"So you remember that night?" I asked, lowering my mouth to her skin. I kissed the inside of her thigh.

She didn't reply, but she grabbed the back of my head.

"Greedy girl," I whispered and nipped at the skin on the inside of her thigh.

She tightened her grip in my hair.

My fingers dug into her hipbone as I pushed her thong aside with my free hand. She was already glistening, begging for my tongue. "I remember making a mess. Kind of like what you're doing now." A drop of her wetness had landed on the granite countertop. *So fucking sexy.*

"I think we made a bigger mess than that," she said.

She was right. We'd made such a mess. I locked eyes with her as I licked her wetness off the counter. *God.* I'd meant what I said during the tasting tonight. I could fucking live off her sweetness. I lifted my head from between her thighs.

"Matt..."

"Do you know what else I remember?" I asked as I walked around the island toward the fridge. "That you were still bad at asking me for what you wanted. That you had no problem spreading your thighs for me in the middle of my parents' kitchen. But were too shy to ask me to make you come with my tongue."

Her jaw dropped.

I opened the fridge and grabbed a bottle of whipped cream. Which I'd picked up exactly for this occasion. Because I'd wanted to make a mess with her too.

I rounded the counter again and spread a line of whipped cream up the inside of her thigh. "Baby, we both know you're not shy." I licked the whipped cream up halfway. "You're feisty." I licked the rest of the way up.

But she didn't say a word. So I squirted whipped cream up her other thigh and moved my head away from her pussy. "You're bold." I licked halfway up and she moaned. "And it turns you on to ask for exactly what you want." I licked the rest of the way up. "So tell me." I put a dollop of whipped cream on her pussy. "Tell me exactly what you want baby. So I can feast on you. And don't you dare ask me to poke you in the pants."

An exasperated laugh escaped her throat. "Matt, we're going to wake…"

"Don't worry, I won't let you make too much noise." I had an idea for that.

A smile spread across her face. "Okay." She slowly spread her thighs wider like the little vixen I knew she was. "In that case…I want you to lick my pussy until I can't even remember what day it is."

Oh, I could guarantee she was going to remember today forever. But she had asked nicely. I shook the cannister of whipped cream and put a line on my thumb. I pressed the pad of my thumb against her lips. "Suck."

She opened her lips and wrapped them around my thumb. She'd be quiet enough, moaning around my finger, wishing it was my cock buried in her throat.

And in the meantime, I could focus on what I'd been dying to do all night. I lowered my mouth to her aching pussy. I placed one, long stroke along her wetness.

Her lips tightened around my thumb.

Just thinking about it being her lips around my cock turned me on even more. I buried my face in her pussy, her sweetness mixing with the taste of whipped cream.

I grabbed her thigh and hoisted it over my shoulder for better access.

Her moaning my name around my thumb and the taste of her were enough to drive me insane. I swirled my tongue around her wetness and her lips wrapped around my knuckle.

I'd had every intention to just please her. But the way she was gripping my thumb? If she wanted the real thing…

I pulled back. She reached out to grab me, but I was holding her in place with my hand around her chin.

"Don't worry, baby." I undid my pants with one hand. "I know you'd rather gag on the real thing."

Her eyes fell to my hard cock.

"Lie back." I slid my thumb out of her mouth and smiled when she immediately complied.

I kicked off my boxers and pants and rounded the counter. I put a line of whipped cream on my length as I stared down at her.

I liked when she rode my face. But tonight I was setting the pace. I climbed onto the counter and she tilted her head back to see me from upside down. The angle made her neck look even longer. And I knew she could handle every inch of me. I pressed my tip against her lips and she immediately opened her mouth for me.

Good girl.

I thrust into her mouth as I leaned forward. I breathed in the scent of her pussy. *Time for my favorite dessert.*

CHAPTER 24

Friday

Brooklyn

"I don't know if he still owns it," I said as Matt cut the engine.

"I think he does," Matt said.

"Well, even if he does, I don't know if the code will be the same anymore."

"I think it will be."

"Really?" I asked. "My father is cold, and cruel, and heartless." I stared out at the apartment building that my father had bought for my mom when they'd dated. And I knew my words weren't the entire truth. My father could be warm…to me. He could be kind…to me. And he did love me in his own way.

"He kept the apartment for 16 years," Matt said. "Who's to say he hasn't kept it for another 16?"

I shrugged.

"We don't know until we try. You said you were missing your mom. We can bring some of her stuff home. We can keep her memory alive too."

Too. He meant like we were keeping Miller's memory alive. In a lot of ways, Matt was the same as he was 16 years ago. But he was way more patient now. Way more understanding. He was exactly what I'd needed back in high school. And he was exactly what I needed now. We'd both changed. And somehow we fit together better than ever.

"And it just so happens that we need something old, something new, something borrowed, and something blue.

We can probably find something in there that checks a few of those boxes. What do you say?"

I took a deep breath. I knew what I was really worried about. "What if he got rid of all of it, Matt?" What if all I had left of my mom were some old pictures, my beat up Keds, and my mom's dress?

"We won't know until we look."

I hadn't spoken to my dad at all since the Halloween party. I'd told him I forgave him, but that I needed time. And for once he was actually respecting my wishes. There was a small piece of me that hoped he'd changed too over the years. But I wasn't sure he was capable of change.

This wasn't really about my dad though. Matt had come up with the idea that we should visit here. He'd told me after we washed all the sticky whipped cream off ourselves last night. He knew I was missing my mom. And I hadn't even thought about this place.

I smiled over at him. "Okay," I said. "Let's try." I unbuckled my seatbelt and stepped out of the car. The cool autumn breeze made me shiver.

Matt wrapped his arm around me as we walked into the building. Not much had changed about the entrance. There was still a friendly doorman, although he wasn't the same person. And no one asked us any questions as we walked over to the elevator.

"So far so good," Matt said as he hit the button for the right floor.

Sixteen years ago, my father had locked me in this apartment. And I wondered if that was how my mother had felt when they dated. Locked away. A secret. I couldn't imagine how scared she'd been when she found out she was pregnant. I put my hand on my stomach as the elevator slid to a stop. Matt put in the code.

And...the panel turned red and started blinking.

I felt my shoulders slump. I'd wanted to believe that my father had kept the apartment. I hadn't meant for this to turn into some kind of strange test. But my father had somehow failed.

Matt looked back down at the paper. "Wait, I think I forgot a number. One sec." He put the code back in. And this time the panel turned green and the elevator doors slid open.

I swallowed hard. Not a single thing had changed since I'd last been here. I stepped inside and turned in a circle. Everything was pristine and white, minus the couch that we'd pulled into the family room. The couch my mom had picked out. And the door at the end of the hall with all her things was still open instead of locked. I could just make out a hint of her perfume.

"He kept it," I said.

"Of course he did."

I looked up at Matt. "How were you so sure?"

Matt shrugged. "I don't like your father. I don't think I ever will. And I'll never understand why he did the things he did. But…" his voice trailed off as he stared at the couch. "…I do believe he did everything because he loves you. And he loves you because you're a piece of your mom. Just like I love Jacob because he's a piece of you."

For so long, I thought my father just wanted me for spare parts. But I knew there was truth in what Matt said. Or else my father would have sold this apartment 32 years ago. "I meant what I said at the Halloween party. I do forgive him. But I just don't know how to move forward from everything. Justin keeps asking me who's walking me down the aisle. And I don't know what to tell him."

"You don't need anyone to give you away," Matt said. "Because you know exactly who you are and what you want. So you can walk down the aisle yourself and right into my arms. Where you belong."

I smiled. "Right where I belong." I pressed the side of my face against his chest. Maybe he was right. I didn't need my father to walk me down the aisle. He didn't need to give me away. Because he didn't own me. He never had.

I just didn't want to regret not asking him. Hell, I wasn't even sure I wanted to ask him to the wedding. But I'd give anything for my mom to be at my wedding. And my uncle. It just seemed like it would be a mistake if I didn't invite my one living relative.

But I wasn't here to think about my dad. I was here to keep the memory of my mom alive. I pulled back. "Let's go find something old and borrowed. And blue if I'm lucky."

Matt slid his hand into mine and we wandered down the hall and into the room filled with my mom's things.

The smell of her perfume was stronger in here. And I didn't know whether to laugh or cry. God I missed her.

"Is there anything in particular you're looking for?" Matt dropped my hand and opened a cardboard box.

"This is all stuff she owned before she had me. I kinda just want to look at everything."

Matt laughed. "We could just bring all of it home with us. I can call a moving company."

"I don't know if it'll all fit." We needed less stuff, not more. "We don't even have a room for the baby right now." I opened a box too and rummaged around through it. There were some clothes, but nothing small enough that I could incorporate into my wedding.

Matt didn't respond.

"I still want you to be able to paint." I appreciated that he wanted to transform his studio into the nursery. But painting relieved his stress.

He still didn't respond.

I rummaged around in the box some more. There was a small velvety jewelry box. I lifted the lid and stared down at the bracelet inside. It was beautiful. It would definitely work as something borrowed. But if it was here…it meant my father had probably given it to her. She'd left it behind for a reason. Did it really count as borrowing something if my mom hadn't even wanted it anymore? I snapped the lid closed. "Matt, I think I might just wear my Keds on our wedding day." They'd make me feel close to her. And they were old.

He still didn't respond.

I turned around. He had a stack of envelopes in his hand. He was frowning as he stared at them. He reached into the box and pushed some things around, the frown on his face deepening.

"What is it?" I asked.

"Isn't this the address to your uncle's apartment?"

I closed the distance between us and looked at the envelope on top. "Yeah." The envelope was addressed to my mom though. And the return address was this apartment, but there was no name.

Matt fanned out the envelopes. They were all addressed to my mom. "None of them are opened."

I looked down at the box. There were more unopened letters in there. Dozens of them. I picked one up. They'd all been mailed, but "return to sender" was stamped on all of them. "What are all these?" Had my mom mailed herself a bunch of letters for some reason? I squinted at the date on the one in my hand. It was from several months before I was born.

Matt started to open one of them.

"Wait." I grabbed his hand. This felt like an invasion of privacy. Which I knew was silly, since we were here to go through her things.

"Don't you want to know what these are?" he asked.

I thought about the letter Miller had left me. It had helped. Maybe these letters would help, even though they didn't seem like there were for me. But…what if they were for me? Somehow? Someway? Like she knew one day I'd find these when I needed them most. I nodded.

He pulled out the paper and unfolded it. We both read it silently.

My love,

I didn't mean what I said. Of course I didn't mean it. Just come home. We'll figure something out. Us against the world, remember?

-R.P.

"R.P.," Matt said. "That must stand for Richard Pruitt. Are these all letters your dad sent your mom?" He stared back down at the letters filling the box to the brim.

My heart started racing. I grabbed another envelope and tore it open.

My love,

Please forgive me. Can we just talk? I miss you. I need you.

Yours always,

-R.P.

"Brooklyn…" Matt said. But I grabbed another envelope and tore it open.

My love,

Your brother made it very clear that if I come to the apartment again he'll call the cops. But I just need to talk to you. I know what I asked you to do was wrong. I know that. And I'm asking you to forgive me. I didn't mean it. We can leave the city. We'll start a new life. I just need you to write me back, baby. Tell me yes. Tell me we can start over.

Love always,

-R.P.

"She never opened these," I said. "They were all returned here. But she was living with my uncle after she broke up with my dad." I pictured being sick back in high school. My uncle had told me my mother had terrible morning sickness right there in that bathroom. She'd moved in with him after my dad told her to have an abortion. But my dad kept saying he was sorry in these letters. Was he sorry for asking my mom to get rid of me? Is that what he was saying?

"And the thing he's asking forgiveness for?" Matt asked.

My heart felt funny in my chest. "I think he's saying sorry for asking her to get rid of me."

Matt lowered his eyebrows and stared back at the letter in my hand. "He said he was willing to leave the city. He wanted the three of you to be a family, Brooklyn."

Us against the world. That's what he's said in one of the letters. My mom used to say that to me. How many of her other phrases came from her time with him too?

She'd always loved him. Why had she refused to read the letters? Why had she sent them back?

I pressed my lips together. I knew why. Because she chose me. She was strong and brave and she knew what she wanted. *Me.* I ignored the tears welling in the corners of my eyes and grabbed another letter. And another. And another. So many letters, confessing his love. Begging for a fresh start. Talking about when they first met. The love they shared. Tears started streaming down my cheeks as I grabbed another letter.

My love,
Us against the world. The three of us.
Please let me see you. I'm begging you.
-R.P.

The *three* of us. I wiped my tears away so none would fall on the words. The letter was dated from a few months before I was born. He was definitely talking about me. There was no doubt in my mind. He'd regretted what he asked my mom to do. He really had wanted to be a family. He had hope that she hadn't gotten rid of me. He'd been willing to risk everything and run away with her. And she'd never known.

"Matt," my voice cracked. "My father was trying to apologize. He was trying to take back what he said. He *did* want me."

I wasn't a mistake.

I wasn't an inconvenience.

He'd wanted to be a part of my life.

"Why didn't he tell me that?" I asked. "He let me believe him asking her for an abortion was the end of the story. But it wasn't the end. He tried to fight for her. He tried to fight for me."

Matt pulled me into a hug. "I don't know," he said.

I rested the side of my face against his chest as I stared down at the box. Matt rubbed his hand up and down my back as I tried to make sense of what these letters meant. But there was only one conclusion I could come to: My father wanted me to think he was a monster. Because he felt like one. He'd asked my mom to do something and he regretted it. And for 16 years, he thought my mom had gone through with it. He'd regretted all of it.

I'd already forgiven my father. But these letters? They changed everything. They gave me hope for a future with him in it. He'd wanted me. He'd actually wanted me.

And it wasn't some manipulative gesture. There was no way my father knew I'd come here. This wasn't some game where he was using me as a pawn. And that's what made this real. My father had never meant for me to see these letters. He kept them because he loved my mom. And he regretted not having a life with me in it.

I pulled back and looked up at Matt. "I need to talk to him."

Matt nodded.

"I can't believe he tried to win her back." I hit my father's name on my phone and pulled it to my ear. I didn't know what I was going to say. But it didn't matter, because my call went straight to voicemail.

"How about we just go see him?" Matt asked.

"Is that really okay? He's put us through so much. I..." my voice trailed off.

Matt shrugged. "He's your dad, Brooklyn. I get it. If you want to talk to him, I understand. If you want him in our lives, I understand. This is your choice."

"Thank you." I heard the sound of a clock ticking down in my head. *No.* There was actually an old clock sitting in the corner of the room. I wasn't out of time. I tried to push the sound out of my head as I looked back up at Matt. "Can you grab that box?" I wanted to read the rest of those letters.

***

I knocked on the door again. I knew my dad had sent most of his staff to the Hamptons with Mrs. Pruitt. But wouldn't they be back now? Since she was gone?

I knocked again.

And again there was no answer.

"Maybe he's at work," I said, but then I shook my head. My father had quit the business. Another thing he'd done for me. Seriously, where was he?

Matt glanced at his watch. "Maybe he's at lunch?"

Yeah. Maybe. I just really needed to talk to him. I had one of the letters folded in my hand. The one that said "the three of us." I wanted to know why he'd lied about changing his mind about wanting me. He'd tried to fight for me. Just like he'd tried to fight for me when he found out I was alive when I was 16. Just like he gave up his business to fight to be in my life now. What if I'd completely misjudged him?

I lifted my hand to knock again, but the door finally opened.

Donnelley was standing there. "Hey, Brooklyn," he said. "How are you?"

How was I? *Conflicted. Hopeful. Torn. Sorry. Confused.* But that wasn't really what Donnelley was asking. "I'm good. Is my dad here?"

He shook his head. "No."

I swore I heard a bit of sadness in his voice. And then I started to hear the clock in my head again. I looked behind him, expecting to see the old grandfather clock. But it was missing. The apartment looked…empty. Minus the people walking around carrying boxes. What was going on? I turned back to Donnelley. "Where is my dad?"

"He's gone, Brooklyn."

Gone? What did he mean *gone*? I walked past him and into the foyer. There were more people packing up things in the dining room. But I was focused on the empty wall where the portrait of him, Mrs. Pruitt, and Isabella had once hung.

Gone.

The word echoed around in my head.

Gone.

Gone.

Gone.

The word collided with the sound of the clock ticking down in my head. He couldn't be gone.

"Brooklyn," Donnelley said. "He'd hoped you'd come by."

Hoped. Past tense. I shook my head. *No.* One of the movers almost bumped into me.

It felt like a fist was gripping my heart. My dad couldn't be gone. We hadn't gotten a chance to move forward. I had so many questions. I… *No.*

This wasn't happening. I turned away from Donnelley and looked up the stairs. Donnelley was wrong. My father had to still be here. He had to.

"Dad!" I called up the stairs. "Dad?!"

"Brooklyn…" Donnelley put his hand on my shoulder, but I shook him off. He was supposed to protect him. How had this happened?

"Dad!" I yelled and took a step toward the stairs. He had to be up there.

"Baby," Matt said and grabbed my wrist to stop me from running up the stairs.

I turned toward him. And he looked…haunted. He was staring up the staircase instead of at me. And I wondered if he was reliving something. Reliving the moment he found out that I had "died." Right here. Sixteen years ago.

Matt had said things to me the day before I disappeared that he regretted.

And here I was 16 years later, regretting what I *hadn't* gotten to say to my father.

"He can't be dead." My voice cracked. "He…he can't.

Matt pulled me into a hug.

A sob escaped my throat. I knew Matt said I was loved. That I had family. But my father was my only living relative other than Jacob. He was my family. My only family. And I hadn't gotten a chance to tell him that I loved him.

"What's wrong?" Donnelley asked calmly.

Of course he wasn't upset. He was finally free from my father. Miller had said there was no out. But there was…once my dad was dead.

I pulled back from Matt and wiped the tears off my cheeks. "I know you didn't like him," I said to Donnelley. "Over the years, I hated him enough for both of us, trust me. But I…I needed to talk to him." One more time at least.

I gripped the letter in my hand. I'd wasted time with him. Why did I never learn my lesson? Why did I always waste so much fucking time?

"Well, do you want me to call him?" Donnelley asked.

"What?" Matt said.

"I mean, I don't know if he has service, but we can see if he picks up."

I shook my head. "Wait. He's not dead?"

Donnelley laughed. "No. Why would you think that?"

"Because you said that!"

"No I didn't. I said he was gone. He left a couple days ago." He laughed again.

"That's not funny," I said. "All his stuff is being packed up and you told me he was gone! What was I supposed to think?"

"It's a little funny," he said. "We both know Mr. Pruitt is invincible."

Yeah, now that he had my kidney. "Where did he go?"

"He didn't really say. He just said he needed a break from the city. I think he wants a fresh start." Donnelley shrugged. "He's selling the apartment. That's why everything is being packed up. Let me give him a call." He pulled out his phone.

I turned back to Matt. "I thought…"

"Me too," he said. "This was where I found out about you. On that Friday after Thanksgiving."

Yeah, I could see it in his eyes. The pain. We were both moving forward, trying out best to leave the past in the past. But the scars would never truly go away. It was a good thing we were going to give Black Friday a new memory in a few weeks. "I'm sorry, Matt." I wanted to tell him I wish we could rewind time. That the past 16 years hadn't happened. But he knew I couldn't say that.

He pulled me back into a hug. "I'm so glad you're alive. And that your father is too."

"He didn't answer," Donnelley said. "His connection is spotty. It might be a while before we can get ahold of him."

I kept my arms around Matt. "You have no idea where he is?"

"Oh no, I know where he is. I just don't know where he's going yet. I don't think he even knows. He's on his yacht."

I didn't realize my father had a yacht. "And you don't know how long he'll be gone?"

"No idea," Donnelley said. "He just…I don't know. I think he's having a mid-life crisis or something."

Or he was leaving the city because he'd given up his career for me. And then I told him I still didn't want him in Jacob's life. Or mine. He didn't have anything left in New York.

"I need to reach him before our wedding. I want him to come. Actually, I'd love for you to come too, Donnelley."

Donnelley looked back and forth between us. And for the first time his eyes settled on the ring on my finger.

I swallowed hard. Because I already knew what he was thinking. That this was a betrayal to Miller.

Donnelley pressed his lips together. "I don't know, Brooklyn. Miller…"

I pulled back from Matt. "Yeah. No." I shook my head. I didn't need him to say the words out loud. But he didn't understand. Miller wanted me to be happy. He'd want me to keep living. And hadn't I just reinforced the idea in my mind that time was limited? I wasn't wasting another second. I cleared my throat. "Of course. I understand."

Donnelley nodded.

"Actually, Donnelley, if you'd reconsider, I'd really like you to come," Matt said. "You were friends with Miller. You knew him even before Brooklyn did. It would mean a lot to both of us if you got to know Jacob. He's going to want to know all your stories about his dad. And we want that too. It would mean a lot to all three of us. The four of us, actually." He put his hand on my stomach.

All four of us. Every time I thought I couldn't love Matt more, he surprised me.

Donnelley looked down at my stomach. "You're pregnant?"

I nodded.

"Is it…is it Miller's too?"

"No." It was the same question Rob had asked. I'd wished that I was pregnant after Miller's death. I'd cried when I'd gotten my period. I understood that hope. And I could tell Donnelley that this wasn't planned. That we'd never meant for it to happen. But I wasn't going to justify this to him. I wanted this baby. I needed this baby.

Donnelley turned back to Matt. "Yeah, man. I'll come. It's what Miller would have wanted."

Matt put his hand out for him.

Donnelley hesitated for a moment, but then shook it. "Congrats," he said. "To both of you." He turned back to me and smiled.

Donnelley always had been sweet. And for some reason, his approval made me feel better. Almost like talking to the north star always made me feel better.

"And I'll keep trying to reach Mr. Pruitt for you, Brooklyn," he said.

"Thank you." I felt tears welling in the corners of my eyes again. God, every day I felt like I got more emotional.

CHAPTER 25

Thursday

Matt

Brooklyn looked down at her phone and then pushed it away from her on the coffee table.

It had been almost a week since we'd found the letters. And there was still no word from her dad. We'd read every single one of the letters.

I didn't like Mr. Pruitt. I didn't forgive him for what he'd done to us as teenagers. But my heart had never been as big as Brooklyn's. I knew these letters changed things for her. It was pretty clear that Mr. Pruitt regretted asking her mom to have an abortion. And it was pretty clear how much he'd loved her mom.

Brooklyn wanted to make things right because of that big heart of hers. I didn't know what that looked like for our future. Mr. Pruitt coming to Sunday football games? I kind of hoped not. But if she wanted him in our lives, I'd make do. Brooklyn had already forgiven him for everything. And I knew that was hard for her. The least I could do was not be an asshole to him.

"Brooklyn, I'm asking a vital question here," Justin said and put his hand on his hip.

I hadn't realized he'd spoken either. I was more focused on Brooklyn's frowns. I wanted to turn them back into smiles. But I didn't know how to fix this. What if we couldn't get a hold of Mr. Pruitt before the wedding? What if he missed it?

"Sorry, what did you say?" Brooklyn asked.

Justin squinted his eyes at her. "The rehearsal dinner. On Thanksgiving. In two freaking weeks! Where? Where the hell could we possibly have it? It's Thanksgiving, Brooklyn! Thanksgiving!"

"Maybe we can all just calm down…" I started.

"Matthew Caldwell, do not tell a boy to calm down!"

I didn't. Justin was a grown ass man. But I kept my mouth shut because he seemed extra hyper tonight.

"We're having it at Master Tanner's house," Nigel said.

Brooklyn jumped.

I hadn't seen him come into the family room either. I needed to add a bell to his door. Or put a collar with a bell on him. I shook my head. *No, he'd probably like that too much.* "You need to knock, Nigel," I said. "You keep startling Brooklyn."

"Ah yes. Mademoiselle, my apologies. I know you're in a fragile state. I will try to remember to possibly start knocking. For you and you only." He lifted her hand and kissed the back of it.

Brooklyn laughed.

She was always quick to smile when Nigel was here. And I guess if anyone was a good distraction for her father being AWOL, it was a strange little man in lederhosen.

"Master Tanner?" Justin asked. "Say." He clapped along with the word. "More." He clapped again.

"He's my master," Nigel said. "I told you I was a houseboy. What else do I need to say?"

Justin raised his eyebrow. "More." He clapped.

"It's just Tanner," I said. "Tanner Rhodes. The two of you have met before."

"Oh. Yes. I know the fine specimen you're referring to. Tell me, Nigel, does he like being called master in the bedroom?"

"He is a fan of master bedrooms, yes. He has several."

"Interesting. But that is not what I asked," Justin said. "I'm asking…"

"Can we get back to the rehearsal dinner thing?" I asked. "Nigel, what did you say about Tanner's place?"

"We're having Thanksgiving there. You already told me yes. And you can't go back once you've accepted a formal invitation. It was very formal. I think you may have signed something. Remember?"

"Um…" I definitely hadn't signed anything. Had Nigel started forging my signature?

"It was earlier this fall. When you were single. You specifically requested an American Thanksgiving." He put air quotes around American. "We talked about how many people would be attending. I put you down for one because you didn't need a plus one. But I can add an extra seat for Brooklyn." He smiled at her.

Oh. I did remember him saying something weird about an American Thanksgiving. And being rude when I asked if Kennedy could come.

"We'd need a lot more seats than just one more though," Brooklyn said. "Matt's parents. And the whole bridal party. Jacob of course. All the kids too probably to make it easier for everyone. And maybe my dad?" She glanced at her phone again.

"It definitely won't be appropriate for children," Nigel said.

"I always need him to say more," Justin said. "Why does he never say more?"

I'd never had the problem of Nigel not saying enough. If anything, he always said too much. In way too much detail.

"I'm going to text Tanner," I said and grabbed my phone.

"But I already have permission," Nigel said. "I'll make it good, I promise."

I shot Tanner a text anyway. "He's weird about his privacy though," I said. "He has all those sheets over everything."

"I'll remove all the sheets then," Nigel said. "And the statues and portraits underneath. Since they're not for you."

"Who are they for?" Justin asked. "And what are they of? Tanner?"

"Not many by that name, no," Nigel said.

"That's a very confusing answer," Justin said. "Who are they of?"

"I'm not supposed to say the names. It's against the rules." He turned back to me. "If you don't want it at Tanner's we can have it in my new house!" He pointed to the door into his home.

I did kind of want to see it... *But no.* It was probably very weird. And I didn't want our rehearsal dinner to be at Nigel's. It was strange enough that he was a groomsman.

There was a knock on the door.

"Company?" Justin asked. "We've barely gone over anything. Whoever it is better be ready to make some decisions for this rehearsal dinner."

I walked over to the door. *What the hell?* Tanner was standing there in a suit and a bushy mustache.

"What's with the stache dude?" And how had he grown it so quickly? I'd just seen him a few days ago. Or had it been more like a week? *Huh.* I definitely hadn't seen him as much as I used to before Brooklyn was back. I think the last time I saw him was when we'd played football in the back yard with Jacob and Mason.

"What?" He touched his upper lip. "Oh." He ripped it off and concealed his scream with a cough. "Ow. Sorry about that. It was for a sex thing."

"What sex thing?"

He gave me a funny look. "Mustache rides. What else would it be for?" He patted my chest and walked in. "I'm glad you texted. It's been forever since we had a proper boys night. I…" his voice trailed off when he saw everyone in the room. "Oh. Yeah, this works too." But he sounded kind of sad. He cleared his throat and walked past me. "Hey, Brooklyn." He sounded cheery again as he sat down next to her on the couch where I'd been sitting.

"I'm so glad you're here," Brooklyn said. "We have a huge favor to ask you."

Tanner nodded. "If this is about your third, we can…"

"No," I said firmly.

"You are a fascinating creature, Tanner," Justin said. "Or…should I call you *Master* Tanner? If you're ever needing a third, you can write my name down."

Tanner laughed. "I appreciate the offer, good lad. But I only partake in dalliances with women. I bet I can find you someone though. Are you only interested in a throuple? Or…"

"Oh my God," Brooklyn said. "Justin, do you remember Donnelley?"

"Donnelley." Justin tapped his index finger against his lips. "Donnelley, Donnelley, Donnelley."

"He's one of my dad's bodyguards."

Justin smiled. "Oh. Yes. That big bear of a man! Yum. Ah, it's been years. Well, I guess about 16, huh? To be young again..."

"He's coming to the wedding," Brooklyn said with a smile.

"Shut the front door! He's not on the guest list! You can't just add random hotties without consulting me! Especially bears! You know what they do to me!"

Um…

"I'd really like him to come," Brooklyn said.

"Me too!" Justin yelled. "Damn it. This changes everything."

"Does it though?" I asked.

"It definitely changes what I'm doing with my hair."

Okay, this seemed unimportant to the rehearsal dinner discussion. "Tanner, we were hoping we could have the rehearsal dinner at your place. Since we were planning on having Thanksgiving there anyway. But we'd need a few more place settings."

"Yeah. Sure. That's fine. Um…" he looked at Nigel. "We'll have to move a few things around. But we can make that work. How many people exactly? I'll have to figure out how many bathrooms to open."

What was he talking about?

Justin tore off a sheet of paper and handed it to him. "Here is the guest list. And my number just in case. You're a billionaire, right?"

"I am," Tanner said as he scanned the list. "Why is Robert on this list?"

I sighed. "Tanner, he's one of the groomsmen. You know this."

"I figured you'd change your mind about that decision."

Did he though? "You can sit at opposite ends of the table."

"But it's Thanksgiving and I'm not thankful for him. And it's my house. And he certainly can't sit at the head of the table."

Brooklyn laughed. "Tanner. Please." She squeezed his arm.

He smiled at her. "Yeah, okay, fine. But he better not go poking around and trying to get in any locked rooms."

Rob most definitely was going to try to do that.

"How many locked rooms?" Justin asked. "And what's inside of them?"

"Dozens including the wine cellar," Nigel said.

"Are any of them sex dungeons?" Justin asked.

"Well if you count…"

"Nigel," Tanner hissed.

"I can neither confirm nor deny any such rooms exist," Nigel clarified.

"I think I'm in love with the two of you," Justin said.

Nigel shook his head. "I will let you down easy, Mr. Justin. I love the boobies."

Brooklyn laughed.

"Big ones. But only real ones. I need them to jiggle around my face when I do the…" he motorboated the air. "My favorite thing in the world. And I've been all over. Every country in lots of decades. I have a rating system…"

Tanner cleared his throat.

"But I do have a rating system," Nigel said.

"The other thing," Tanner hissed. "The lots of decades thing."

"Right. *This* decade," Nigel said. "Because I'm a young boy. I went to high school in the 60s."

That can't be right.

Justin shook his head. "Math is not my forte, and even I know that's not right." He turned back to Brooklyn. "Any word about your father walking you down the aisle?"

Brooklyn shook her head. "No service yet. I just checked with Donnelley again too. No word. I'm worried we won't be able to reach him in time."

"Where did Richard go?" Tanner asked.

"No one knows where he's going," I said. "He's on his yacht somewhere."

"Oh, a fellow yacht man."

"Wait, you have a yacht?" Why didn't I know that?

"Of course I have a yacht." Tanner laughed. "I'm a billionaire. You wouldn't understand."

I was pretty sure I could afford a yacht. I just had no need for one. And the upkeep was probably a lot...

"So you're having trouble getting a hold of him?" Tanner asked.

"Yeah, he doesn't have service," Brooklyn said. "I've called him a dozen times and left voicemails and texts."

"Why the change of heart?"

"I found all these old letters he wrote my mom. She never saw them, they were all returned unopened to him. But he loved her so much. And he wanted me. I..." her voice trailed off. "I never knew."

"I can get a hold of him for you," Tanner said.

"You can?"

"Of course."

"How?" I asked.

"It's a boat thing, you wouldn't understand."

"I know stuff about boats."

"Not as much as us," Nigel said. "Port and starboard. Stern. Dinghy. Windward and leeward. It's a billionaire thing."

Why was Nigel being so savage right now? He wasn't a billionaire either. *Wait. Is he?*

"Can you really help?" Brooklyn asked.

Tanner nodded. "He'll be at the wedding. I promise. As the best man in theory but not in title, I've got it covered. And I'll be hosting the rehearsal dinner. I'm definitely the best man. Definitely at least better than Young Robert."

I mean, if he could really get Mr. Pruitt to the wedding, that would be better than anything Young Robert was doing. I laughed. *Young Robert.* All Rob wanted to do was plan the bachelor party. And I didn't even want one. "We'd really appreciate it," I said.

"Anything for my best friends," Tanner said with a smile. But his smile looked a little sad. He cleared his throat and stood up. "I guess I should be going if that's all. I don't want to impose. And I have some things to do and such." He pulled his mustache out of his pocket. "So I guess I'll be going then."

Tanner and I used to hang out most nights. Hell, I'd been living with him not that long ago. And I realized that maybe since Brooklyn got back, I'd kind of neglected him. He was an important part of my life. And I wanted him to know that.

"Unless you want to stay for a movie or something?" I said. As soon as everyone left, Brooklyn and I were just going to snuggle up on the couch. We'd gotten in the routine when she decided not to leave the house. I loved our nights just us. But I'd love this too.

"I mean…if you're sure it wouldn't be a bother," Tanner said with a shrug, like he didn't care. But I could tell he wanted to stay.

"That sounds great to me," Brooklyn said.

Tanner smiled and put his mustache back in his pocket. "Yeah? I do love a good motion picture."

Brooklyn grabbed his forearm to pull him back down on the couch.

Well, I didn't love that he'd be sitting between us. But yeah, I was happy he was here.

"Movie night!" Justin yelled and sat down too.

"The whole gang together," Nigel said and plopped down, taking up the last seat on the couch.

I needed a bigger couch.

I sat down on the carpet in front of Brooklyn. She lifted her legs and put them over my shoulders like I was her stool.

"Ah much more comfortable," she said.

I nipped at the inside of her knee and she laughed.

She leaned forward and ran her fingers through my hair.

I tilted my head back and looked up at her from upside down.

"I love you," she whispered silently as the guys fought over which movie to watch.

"I love you," I whispered back.

In two weeks, we'd be getting married. I'd be getting everything I'd ever wanted since I was a teenager. *Her.*

CHAPTER 26

Friday

Brooklyn

Another week went by, and there was still no word from my dad. My wedding was in one week. And I really didn't think he was going to make it.

I put my hand on my stomach. "It's okay," I said out loud. "That's what pictures are for." But I knew it wasn't the same.

Focusing on the baby, the wedding, and worrying about my father just so happened to be the perfect mix of distraction. I was…happy. I couldn't help but laugh and smile every day. But that was mostly because Matt was always by my side. And I was worried about tonight. I didn't want to fall asleep without him. I was worried I'd reach out to empty covers and panic.

Some nights I still rolled over, expecting Miller to be sleeping beside me. It was always worse in the quiet. And Matt always chased away the shadows on my soul. He always hugged me as I cried.

And as much as I liked my friends, I didn't think they'd understand me waking in the middle of the night sobbing over Miller when I was about to marry Matt. What would they say to him if that happened? What would they think of me?

I put my hand on my stomach again.

"Is he kicking yet?" Matt asked as he walked into the kitchen.

"You know the baby is too small for all that."

"I know no such thing." He leaned down and put the side of his face against my stomach. "I think I hear him."

"Or her," I said.

"Or her." He listened for another second and then kissed my belly before standing up. He must have seen the worry on my face because he lowered his eyebrows. "What's wrong?"

"Nothing, Mr. Best-Coach-in-the-City. I'm so proud of you." I looped my arms behind his neck. Empire High had won their last game of the regular season last weekend. And they'd be playing in the championship game the weekend after our wedding. They already knew they'd made it to the championship game, but it was still fun watching them all celebrate their final regular season win.

"Thank you. But…what's wrong?" he asked again.

I sighed. He could read me so well. "I don't need a bachelorette party," I said. "I don't even want one. I just want to hang out with you. And you refuse to tell me where you're going. You won't even tell me what you're doing."

"I did tell you. *You.*"

I groaned. He kept saying that. "You're impossible. I'm going to be worried all night."

"How much trouble can we get into? We'll be with Jacob."

It was really sweet that he was bringing Jacob along. But also…what the hell were they doing? "That's part of why I'm worried. All my favorite men will be out of the house."

Matt smiled. "I think you'll be plenty distracted."

"I don't think so." I pressed my lips together.

"Tell me what's going on in that beautiful head of yours."

"You know I have nightmares some nights. I…" my voice trailed off. "I don't want the Untouchables' wives to see that."

"Can I tell you a secret?"

I nodded.

"You were the first woman in the Untouchables' lives. It's not about them liking you. It's about you liking them."

I laughed. "That's not how anything works. I don't just get to come back after 16 years and pretend I'm the queen of all the Untouchables' wives."

"That's exactly how that works. And they're good people, Brooklyn. If you wake up in the middle of the night, Penny will hold you while you cry. Daphne will know just the thing to say to make you feel understood. And Bee will make you laugh."

I smiled. He was probably right about that.

"And Kennedy knows you almost as well as I do. You're going to be okay. Besides, you'll see me sooner than you think."

"Gah, what does that mean? What are you doing?!"

"You," Matt said.

I shook my head. "I texted Mason about this. And he said we were doing this a week early because you're going to get so shit-faced."

"He said that? Huh." Matt shrugged.

"Well, is that what's happening? Or…"

Matt shrugged again.

"You can't take Jacob to a bar."

"He'd be a really good little wingman though, don't you think?"

I narrowed my eyes at him.

Matt laughed. "I promise I'm not taking the kid to a bar. That would be very inappropriate."

"So where are you guys going?"

"Mommy, Mommy!" Jacob slid into the family room. "I'm going to boys night!"

I lifted him into my arms. He'd tell me the truth. "And what are you doing at boys night?"

"Boy things," he said.

"Like what?"

"Boy things. Right, Coach?" He looked up at Matt.

"Right," Matt said.

Wait, had they practiced that? *Matt!*

"Like what?" I said again.

Nigel walked into the family room wearing black leather lederhosen. "Strippers and hos!"

Oh God. That's what I was afraid of. And I didn't realize they made lederhosen that looked like that.

Nigel cleared his throat when he saw Jacob. "I mean…bidders and grows!"

"What's growing?" Jacob asked.

"The…bidders?" Nigel said and shrugged. "I don't know. Pretend I didn't say anything." He turned to Matt. "Are you ready, big boy?"

"Don't call me that," Matt said.

"Ready *little man*?" Nigel asked. "I feel like that's more suited for the child. But if you insist. I understand wanting to be the cutest boy in the room."

Matt shook his head and turned to me. "We should be going."

I put Jacob down and he ran to the door and put on his sneakers.

"Going…where?" I asked.

Matt smiled. "Wouldn't you like to know."

"Yes. I desperately want to know."

He placed a quick kiss against my lips and turned around.

"Matthew Caldwell, tell me what you're doing tonight."

"You," he said with a wink. And with that, the three of them walked out the front door.

I sighed. Luckily I didn't have too long alone to think about what the hell was happening. Because there was a knock on my door almost immediately.

Kennedy walked in holding a bunch of balloons. "For the record, it is really hard figuring out what to do for a bachelorette party when the bride can't drink."

"So you landed on balloons?" I smiled.

"I did my best," she said with a laugh and tied them to a chair. "How are you feeling?"

"Good. Excited. Nervous. No, just excited."

Kennedy smiled. "Has Tanner been able to get ahold of your dad yet?"

I shook my head. "Not that I know of." But I knew Tanner was capable of amazing things. He'd gotten me to give Matt another chance. He'd been a big part of the reason why I was here right now. I had hope that he'd pull through on this too.

"If anyone can pull off a miracle, it's him. He's like, really lucky."

I wasn't so sure about Tanner being lucky. He'd had a really hard life, from the little he'd told me. It was one of the reasons why we got along so well. It felt like he understood me. He gave me hope that you could go through all the pain and make it out on the other side okay. Mostly at least. Sometimes when he thought no one was looking, he still looked sad. Tanner threw himself into his business to deal with the pain. Like I was throwing myself into wedding planning. Maybe his billions involved a little luck. But I think they were the result of a lot of pain. And needing an escape from it.

"Speaking of lucky..." Kennedy said. "You're sure you don't want to hit a casino or something?"

"A casino?"

"I've never planned one of these things before!"

There was another knock on the door. Penny, Bee, and Daphne had arrived.

And their smiles and hugs made me realize I had no reason to be nervous. Not because I was the OG girl that had joined the Untouchables. But because they were all so nice.

"I know you can't drink," Daphne said, but I've pumped enough milk for a few days and I'm going wild."

"Same," Penny said. "Also, Daphne says the funniest things when she's drunk."

"Count me in too," Kennedy said.

The three of them walked into the kitchen. And Bee just stood there by the door, fidgeting with her coat she was hanging up.

"You okay?" I asked.

"What? Oh, yeah." She smiled and looked over at the three of them. And then leaned in a little closer to me. "Mason and I are actually trying to get pregnant. I didn't really want to tell everyone. But they're going to be suspicious if I'm not drinking, right?"

I smiled. She'd told *me* though. "Just take a glass and pretend," I whispered. "They won't notice a thing after they've downed theirs."

"You're probably right." She exhaled slowly. "Thanks, Brooklyn. Wouldn't it be amazing timing if I got pregnant soon too?"

I smiled. "The best timing." That would be wonderful. That was my dream back in high school. For all the Untouchables to have kids that grew up together, just the way they did. Except no one's parents would be like Mr. and Mrs. Hunter.

"I always felt a little behind since Penny and Daphne each have two kids. But maybe I was just meant to have kids at the same time as my new sister."

I started blinking fast. "Bee."

"I'm sorry. I didn't mean to make you cry."

"You're fine," I said. "Pregnancy hormones, I swear."

"For a second, I thought you were horrified by the thought." She laughed.

"Not at all. I would love that. I'm so excited for the two of you. Fingers crossed."

Bee nodded. "Fingers crossed."

Kennedy handed Bee a glass.

"Thanks," she said and didn't take a sip.

"I feel like we should be drinking out of penis glasses or something," Daphne said.

"Ah," Kennedy said. "Penis glasses probably would have been better than balloons."

"Did someone say penis glasses?" Justin asked as he walked into the house without knocking.

He must have picked that up from Nigel.

"Because I have all the penis things, honeys." He lifted the box in his arms. "It's not a party without that D."

I laughed as Kennedy pulled out a giant foam penis.

"Pin the splooge on the tip," Justin said.

"Oh, of course." Kennedy nodded and picked up a foam picture of what looked like the squirt emoji. "We need to hang this up."

"Is there a clock somewhere?" Penny asked while Kennedy and Justin looked around for a perfect place to hang the foam penis. Did she want to hang it over a clock for some reason?

"Um...yeah." I pointed to the display on the oven. "Why?"

She stared at it for a moment. "No reason." But she was smiling ear to ear.

"What's going on with you?" I asked.

"Nothing, what's going on with you?" she said way too defensively and took a huge sip of champagne.

I shook my head. "You know something, don't you?"

"Me? No. Never."

I laughed. "You totally do. Tell me what the guys are doing tonight. I'm dying here."

"Drinking too much, probably," she said. "Actually, maybe I should call James. Just to check in." But she didn't look nervous at all. It seemed like she was acting. She made a big show of pulling out her phone and calling him.

It probably would have worked, but I knew how happy James was with her. He wasn't drowning like he had been in high school. He wouldn't be drinking too much tonight. He would never risk his life with Penny and his family.

Penny shook her head and laughed. "Mhm," she said into the phone. "Sure you are." She pointed at her phone and rolled her eyes. "Men," she mouthed silently.

Yeah, that was acting. Bad acting. I grabbed her phone from her.

"No, don't..." she started, but I already pulled the phone to my ear.

"Yeah, we're just setting everything up," James said. "I'll see you soon, baby."

"Setting what up?" I asked.

There was a long pause.

James cleared his throat. "Brooklyn?"

"Yes. Now tell me what you guys are doing."

"Um..." he coughed. "Nothing."

"You just said you were setting something up."

"I didn't say that," James said.

"Yes you did."

He laughed. "No. I don't think so."

I heard muffled voices on the other end.

"Is that Matt? Can you put him on?"

"Matt's a little busy," James said.

"Doing what?"

There was another long pause.

"Hey, *baby*," Rob said. He must have stolen the phone. "I knew you and James still had something going on. But you're choosing the wrong Hunter brother."

"Rob, can you please put Matt on the phone?"

"No can do, baby."

"Stop calling me that."

"You only like when my brother calls you that? Interesting. Noted though."

"No, I don't..." my voice trailed off. There was no use arguing with him.

"I prefer Sanders anyway. Although it's not super sexy when you're riding me. I'll figure it out. But in the meantime, now that I have you, we do need to talk."

"We do?" I asked.

"Yes. About that favor you owe me..."

"I don't owe you a favor."

"We've already been over this," Rob said. "We don't need to debate this again. You owe me a favor. And I know what I want."

"Which is?"

"Well, I was saving it just in case you were on the fence about marrying Matt. I was going to use it to make you walk down the aisle. But you love him for real or whatever, so I don't need to waste it on that."

Part of what he'd just said was really sweet. Would he have actually used it for that? I smiled. "Okay, what do you want?"

"I'm circling back to the prank idea. On Thanksgiving."

"You don't need to remind me."

"I'm not talking about the prank 16 years ago. I'm talking about this Thanksgiving. Your rehearsal dinner. I want you to help me pull a prank on Tanner."

Was he serious? Tanner was being so sweet to let us have the rehearsal dinner at his apartment. "Rob, no."

"No means yes."

"No, no means no."

"You have to do what I ask. That's how deals and favors work, Sanders."

"Absolutely not. It's my rehearsal dinner." All my friends were staring at me. "No pranks."

Penny laughed and shook her head. "Rob."

"You don't really get a say here…" Rob started.

"I thought we were friends," I said.

"Friends, lovers, potatoes, potahtoes."

"We were never lovers, Rob."

Daphne shook her head. "He's being extra Rob-y tonight, huh?"

I nodded.

"Only in your dreams, Sanders," Rob said.

"I'm not pulling a prank with you on Thanksgiving. That's not even funny. You know what happened last time."

"That's why it'll be so epic. No one will see it coming. I'm glad you're in. Because I'm gonna need the blueprints to Tanner's place."

I shook my head. "How would I even get them?"

"I don't know. But I'll make the pudding."

"No pudding." I groaned.

"So much pudding. It's a classic Hunter-Sanders mess around."

"Robert Hunter, no."

"Brooklyn Sanders, yes. You owe me. And you waited 16 years to give me my favor. So it has to be very extra. And it has to be this. No negotiation. I'm taking Tanner down on his own turf. He won't even see it coming."

I thought about the hole in the ceiling 16 years ago. He was going to ruin Tanner's apartment. And probably blame it on me. The night before our wedding. "No," I said more firmly.

"I feel like you should be spanking me right now," Rob said. "Or at least calling me daddy."

"Grow up."

"Never."

"This is ridiculous." But for some reason I was smiling.

"No, it's perfect. And so are you, *baby*. Love you. Gotta go. Let me know if you change your mind about that threesome. In the meantime, Matt needs help with the poles."

"Poles? Like stripper poles?"

Rob made a fake static noise with his mouth. "Sorry, you're breaking up." He made the noise again and then the line went dead.

What. The. Fuck. I looked up at my friends. "He's going to ruin the rehearsal dinner."

"I won't let him," Daphne said.

I wanted to believe her. But no one could control Rob when he was planning a prank. I knew that first hand. Luckily I had several days to figure out how to stop him.

Penny glanced at the clock again.

Seriously, what the fuck is happening?

CHAPTER 27

Friday

Matt

"We're going to get arrested," Mason said as he finished his bottle of beer and tossed it on the ten-yard-line.

I shook my head. "I got permission from the principal."

"You got permission to drink on the field, run around like maniacs, and have sex on school grounds?"

I laughed. "No, not exactly." But the season was over anyway. At least until the championship game in December. That would leave plenty of time for the field to be fixed up.

"Then we're going to get arrested." Mason made a one-handed catch on a pass from Rob. "So we better get this touchdown before the cops show up." He turned to Jacob. "You ready, little man? This one's coming to you." He pointed the ball at him.

"Ready!" Jacob yelled and crouched down with his hand on the ten-yard-line.

He was the perfect little wide receiver. I smiled. *Kind of like me.*

"Hut, hut!" Nigel yelled.

I wasn't sure why he was yelling that. He was on the other team. It was me, Mason, Tanner, and Jacob against Rob, James, and Nigel. Team Caldwell versus Team Hunter. And somehow they were up by a touchdown. Nigel was their secret weapon. For someone who seemed to know very little about football and sports in general, he was kind of a beast. But I also didn't want to admit that the Hunters were whooping us.

Mason stepped back from the line. I sprinted behind Jacob, trying to create a clear path for him to the endzone. Jacob caught the ball perfectly. He turned to start running, but James lifted him into his arms and started sprinting in the opposite direction with him.

Jacob laughed as James carried him toward the wrong endzone.

Fuck. I ran after them. I was almost there when James handed Jacob off to Rob.

"Lateral!" James yelled.

"Jacob, squirm free!" I yelled as Rob crossed the twenty-yard-line.

And a second later Rob bent over, releasing him. "Little dude kneed me in the junk," he groaned, gipping the front of his sweatpants as he fell to the ground.

I laughed as Jacob sprinted toward the correct endzone now.

Nigel tagged him out on the five-yard-line.

Jacob had almost dodged him. Maybe he'd be even better as a running back.

"Who taught him to do that?" Rob grimaced.

"Shake it off." I put my hand out for him.

"Easy for you to say. Your balls didn't just get violently attacked."

I laughed and helped him back up to his feet. And then I ran over to Jacob. I put my fist down and he fist bumped me.

"Good job, grandson," Tanner said. "You did that perfectly."

"Thank you, Abuelo." Jacob fist bumped him too.

Wait. Did Tanner tell Jacob to hit Rob where it hurt? Rob was still limping a little. I stifled a laugh. Okay, yeah.

Tanner definitely told Jacob to knee Rob in the nuts. I probably should have said something about that not being okay, but we were still losing right now.

"Hut, hut!" Nigel yelled even though no one was lined up.

I sprinted to the endzone and so did Tanner.

Mason tossed the ball to the right to Tanner.

James jumped up. He almost caught the ball, but he ended up tipping it.

It landed perfectly in Tanner's arms.

And then Rob completely decked Tanner.

Jesus. I ran over to them. "It's tag football, not tackle, man." I'd made that explicitly clear. The last thing I needed was for someone to break a leg before the wedding. I grabbed the back of Rob's shirt and pulled him off of Tanner.

"He started it," Rob said.

Tanner laughed and sat up, but didn't stand. "How did I start it exactly?"

"By being super Tannery."

Tanner brushed a leaf off his shoulder. "That's the only way I know how to be, Young Robert."

"Stop calling me that! I'm not young. We're all adults here. Well, except Jacob. And...maybe Nigel?" He turned to Nigel. "How old are you, man?"

"It's very rude to ask a boy his age," Nigel said.

Rob shook his head.

"You really should have played in high school," Mason said and slapped James' back. "That was almost an interception."

"Yeah." James shrugged.

I knew he'd wanted to play back in high school. But his parents wouldn't let him. And for some reason Rob played soccer instead of joining the football team. It would have been way more fun doing this together. But that's what nights like tonight were for.

"Enough of this lame tag team stuff," Rob said. "It's tackle football now. Unless you guys are scared of us." He lifted his chin like he was ready to start a fight right now.

"Scared of Team Hunter?" Mason chuckled. "Never."

Rob turned to me and raised his eyebrows.

This was a bad idea. A very bad idea. But I wasn't backing down from the challenge. Besides, it had been a long time since I'd played a real game of football. "Bring it."

"Hut, hut!" Nigel yelled and grabbed the ball. He tossed it at James to throw.

James threw it back at Nigel almost immediately. Nigel ducked under my arms and side-stepped Mason. Tanner and Jacob ran after him, but it was too late.

Son of a bitch, Nigel was so fast and sneaky. Nigel slammed the ball down in the endzone and did a backflip.

I blinked. Where did he learn to do that?

"My nimble little man!" Rob yelled and high fived him.

I shook my head. "Huddle," I said to my team. "What's the plan here, we can't let them win."

"Should I do what Abuelo told me again?" Jacob asked.

"Probably don't do that again," I said. "But it was great."

Jacob nodded.

Tanner patted his shoulder. "Maybe do that again."

"Let's do *the* play from high school," Mason said and nodded at me.

The play. He didn't have to say anything else. This one always scored. "And break!" I yelled and ran into position.

As soon as Mason stepped back with the ball, I sprinted forward straight at James. But then I broke hard left and ran toward the endzone.

Mason faked the ball toward Tanner. And even though Mason didn't throw it, Rob tackled him.

I turned to look over my shoulder again just as the ball sailed through the sky and landed perfectly in my arms.

And then James slammed into my side. Luckily I had more weight on me. There was no way I was going down. Not this close to scoring.

I heard yelling to my right but ignored it. I elbowed James off of me and sprinted into the endzone. "Suck it!" I yelled and slammed the ball down. I turned around and all I saw was carnage. *Oh shit.*

"Fuck," James said. He was holding his hand over his face and blood was seeping out between his fingers.

And Rob and Tanner were in a fist fight nowhere near the endzone.

And Jacob and Nigel were circling each other like they were about to lunge.

"Everybody stop!" I yelled.

Rob paused with his fist in the air, like he'd been caught red-handed. Which he had. Tanner shoved him off as I ran over to Jacob. I scooped him up before he could tackle Nigel. And then I turned to James.

"I'm so sorry," I said. "I didn't mean to hit your face."

James laughed, but then winced. He lowered his hand. "It's fine."

But it wasn't fine, his nose was gushing blood.

"Tilt your head back." I put my hand on his forehead so he'd look up.

"This is why we should have stuck to tag football," Rob said. He tore off his shirt and tossed it at James. "You Caldwells and your crazy ideas."

"It was your idea," I said as I helped place the shirt under James' nose.

Rob lifted his hands. "This is your bachelor party, man. I didn't plan this. Sounds like the best man's fault."

"I agreed to tag football, not this," Mason said. "This was all you, Rob."

"Psh. I don't remember suggesting this," Rob said.

"I remember it," Jacob said. "You said 'It's tackle football now. Unless you guys are scared of us.' And we weren't scared of you."

Damn right, Jacob.

Rob laughed. "Okay yeah, fair. That sounds like me. In my defense, I drank a lot before we started playing."

I stared at him and sighed. "You have a black eye, Rob."

"I do not."

"Yes you do. Brooklyn is going to kill me. She was so excited about the wedding photos."

"You should see the other guy," Rob said.

I turned to Tanner. Who looked perfectly fine. Not a hair out of place.

Tanner laughed. "You barely touched me." He lightly kicked the back of Rob's legs and Rob fell to his knees.

"Stop it with that kung fu stuff, man," Rob said. "I was trying to have a good old-fashioned brawl. Not whatever you're doing."

"So you want me to crack a bottle of vodka against your head?"

"What?" Rob shook his head. "No." He stood back up. "But I'm not against putting your head in a toilet."

Tanner shuddered. "What in the world? Where do you even come up with this stuff?"

"It's a swirly," Rob said.

"A what-y?"

"You've never heard of a swirly? What planet are you even from?"

Nigel cleared his throat. "This planet. Can we finish the game real quick?" he asked.

"No." I gestured to the bloody shirt covering most of James' face. "The game's done. It's a tie."

"But ties are for simps and paupers," Nigel said.

What the hell did he just say? "No, we're done."

"But..."

"Nigel, the game is over."

"I really am fine," James said. He lowered the shirt. The blood had stopped but the lower half of his face was covered in blood. And Rob's black eye was looking worse by the second.

"It's a tie," I said firmly. "The Hunters and Caldwells are even."

Rob made a farting noise with his mouth.

"So does that mean it's time for the strippers I ordered?" Nigel asked.

"What? No."

"But it's a bachelor party..."

"I specifically said no strippers." I turned to Mason.

"I told them all that," Mason said.

"But every bachelor party must involve strippers," Nigel protested.

I just stared at him. "Why do you think that?"

"It's a rule I think."

I shook my head. "Definitely not."

"But I looked up bachelor parties extensively," Nigel said. "Lots of videos. Every single one has strippers. So I hired enough for us each to have two. Because we're rich boys. And we earned twice the reward."

"We have a child here, man," I whispered and nodded down to Jacob.

"It'll be good for him. I wish I had started my rating system when I was a young lad. He'll get in early and really learn what kind of boobies he likes. Unless you want me to give him my rating system…"

"Stop talking," I said.

"But I even ordered two strippers for Francois." Nigel smiled. "So I actually get four. Because I'm Francois," he whispered.

As if I could ever forget him pretending to be Francois the handsy waiter.

Tanner elbowed Nigel in the side and Nigel was finally silent.

"What's a stripper?" Jacob asked.

"That's um…" my voice trailed off.

"A person doing an honest day's work," Nigel said.

I mean sure. That was actually a good way to put it. But also I didn't want Jacob to start saying he wanted to grow up and be a stripper. "It's something that you shouldn't repeat though," I said.

"Why? Does Mommy not like strippers?"

Probably not. "It's like a touchy gray area for some people."

Jacob just stared at me. "So just talk about them with the boys at boys night?"

"Exactly," Tanner said. "Wow, he learns fast." He ruffled Jacob's hair.

Jacob smiled up at him.

And that seemed to be the end of that. *Thank God.*

"My head hurts," James said. "I think I'm gonna lie down." He lay backward on the field and closed his eyes.

He looked really pale. *Shit.* "We should probably call a doctor." I set Jacob down and pulled out my phone.

"No need," Nigel said. "I have an elixir for that. One second." He hurried over to the table of waters he'd set up. He sprinted back over with two glasses of green juice. "This will help heal the nose and stop the bleeding. And put some color back in your cheeks." He handed one of the glasses to James.

"And this one will help the swelling stay down," he said and handed Rob the other glass. "Actually, let your brother have a sip of that too. So his nose calms down."

Rob looked down at the glass. "What's in here?"

"My secret green juice recipe," Nigel said with a smile.

Rob made a face and stared down into his glass.

Jacob tugged on Mason's sweatpants. "Uncle Mason, can you get me some juice?" he asked and looked up at him. "I'm thirsty too."

Mason smiled. "Of course, let's go get some…"

"Dude, did you skeet in this glass?" Rob asked.

Nigel looked shocked. "Do you want me to?" And then he smiled again.

"What? No." Rob shook his head and looked even more grossed out as he stared down at the contents of the glass. Why did Nigel always respond to that question that way? He definitely skeeted in his secret green juice.

"Maybe let's wait on the juice," Mason said and patted Jacob's shoulder.

Jacob shrugged.

"I thought your green juice was for hangovers?" I asked.

"I have a variety of recipes. Drink up boys and I'll call the strippers. Wait." His shoulders slumped. "No strippers. But I did already pay for them. So I guess I just get them all after the party ends. All 14 of them." He smiled. "That's 28 boobies to rate. So many strippers for me."

"Don't worry, I won't tell my mommy," Jacob said.

"Good lad." Nigel nodded at him.

I pressed my lips together. I wasn't sure we were teaching Jacob the best things here.

Mason must have seen my face because he grabbed Jacob's hand. "How about some water instead, kid?"

"Yessie."

They walked off to the water table.

"Speaking of water, we should probably hit the baths," Nigel said. It's almost time for the kidnapping."

I looked down at my watch. He was right. "Are you sure this is a good idea?" I asked. "After everything?"

"That's what makes it more thrilling," Rob said. "And you know girls give the best head when their hearts are racing."

"Yeah, but…"

"It's the *one* thing you let me plan. Let me have this," Rob said.

I laughed. He was right. About the kidnapping thing. Not the overall plan. I'd been planning this for weeks. And it was time to kidnap my girl.

CHAPTER 28

Friday

Brooklyn

"They were all basically the same as they are now," I said.

"You have to give us more than that." Daphne took another sip of her champagne. "Seriously, what were the four of them like back then? I need all the details."

"Honestly? Kinda mean until they let us into their circle," Kennedy said.

Penny shook her head. "I feel like I'm picturing them as little gangsters. Probably because of the name the Untouchables."

I laughed. "In a lot of ways they were. Except the mobsters were in my family, not theirs."

Daphne nodded. "But like…what were they *like*?"

I laughed again. "I don't know. They were…" I let my voice trail off. Kennedy was right. They had been kind of mean. But there was a lot more to it than that. I'd gotten to know them better than she had. I could so easily picture them back in high school. James trying to forget his pain by drinking and smoking too much. Mason having the weight of the world on his shoulders. Rob masking his issues with jokes. And Matt. I remembered thinking he was the only one who truly knew how to smile. But I was wrong. He was hiding pain too. "They were all a little…sad," I said. And I'd made Matt so much sadder. I pressed my lips together.

Penny put her hand to her chest. "I'm just picturing baby James all sad now."

"*Teenage* James," I said with a laugh.

"But baby James is such a better name for little James."

Teenage James wasn't as innocent as a baby. Especially when he was spending his free time blackmailing me. But the name baby James was definitely better than wasted teenage blackmailer. I hated what I'd done to Matt. But I hated what I'd done to James too. I'd added so much more pain to all their lives. And none of them deserved any more pain.

"And all I've ever known is sad Matt," Penny said. "Until now I mean," she clarified.

Hearing about the time we were apart killed me. I still couldn't believe he hadn't moved on. I couldn't believe I was sitting here right now about to marry him. I couldn't believe any of it. Someone needed to pinch me every day leading up to the wedding.

"The idea of sad baby Matt makes me want to cry," Penny said.

"I guess they were all just sad, waiting to meet the loves of their lives. All girls from Delaware that had significantly less money than them. So random. And none of you knew each other? Like you didn't introduce each other to them?"

Penny smiled. "No, it was fate."

"Lucky bitches," Justin said.

Bee smiled. "So weird though, right? Like what are the odds that four rich guys from New York City married four normal girls from little old Delaware?"

"Because they all had crushes on Brooklyn," Daphne said with a shrug.

"Definitely not true," I said.

Penny laughed. "James proposed to you. If that's not a crush, I don't know what is." She didn't sound upset about it. And I really appreciated how chill she was about this.

"It was a cry for help," I said. "He knew he had to marry a Pruitt and anyone would choose someone other than Isabella."

Penny's eyebrows pulled together. "What do you mean he *had* to?"

"Oh, I..." I'd never gotten a chance to tell James what Isabella had told me. That their parents made a deal or something. I didn't even really remember exactly what she'd said. And everything she said was crazy. I needed to leave the past in the past.

"It was just a crazy rumor," Kennedy said.

"Oh." Penny shook her head. "Good. James and his dad are finally in a good place and I'd hate for anything to cause another rift. It's been nice having Mr. Hunter around. And the kids love him. It's been really nice seeing James and his dad actually acting like father and son. I think James really needed that to move forward from everything."

I nodded. Yeah, the past could stay in the past. Buried with Isabella and whatever other lies and rumors she'd tried to spread. My father had told me there wasn't an arrangement between him and Mr. Hunter. And I needed to believe him. We were turning a new leaf. But thinking about my father made me press my lips together. I wanted to believe that Tanner could figure out how to get a hold of him. But we were running out of time.

I glanced at my phone again. Still no word from my dad. James forgiving his father helped them move forward from everything. I needed to have a real conversation with my dad. And I wanted to do it before my wedding. I wanted to get married without a cloud hanging over my head.

"Brooklyn, what was it like living with a gangster daddy?" Justin asked. "God, just saying it out loud is so hot."

Bee laughed. "Such a *daddy*."

"Right?" Justin said. "I'd call him daddy any day."

"He's more scary than hot," Kennedy said.

I smiled. Kennedy nailed that description, just like she had when describing the Untouchables. But just like with the Untouchables…there was more to the story. So much more now. I thought about the stack of letters in my bedroom. "He was really protective. But it was confusing. I know now that he wanted me healthy for my kidney. But I do think he cared about me." I remembered him worrying about me. It felt real. It felt like how a father would worry because it felt like how my mother worried about me. "And he wanted to protect me from Isabella. I know that was real. Because she was terrifying."

"Ugh." Penny took a sip of her champagne. "Whenever I hear that name I still shiver a bit." She shimmied her shoulders to get the ick out of her system.

"Yeah, me too," Kennedy said.

I nodded. "Me three."

"Me four," Justin said. "I still can't believe she cut up all those beautiful clothes. That alone was a crime. She should have been in jail for life."

"We're just lucky we didn't have to really know her," Bee said and put her arm around Daphne.

"Except for the fact that she shot Rob when we first started dating," Daphne said. "I wish I could have karate kicked her out that window. Not that I know karate. But I would have learned it for her."

Justin laughed. "Here's to a common enemy." He lifted his glass. Everyone but me clinked theirs together.

And no one said anything when Bee didn't take a sip. I really hoped she got pregnant soon too.

It was so strange. These women knew the Untouchables now. And Kennedy and I knew them better from high school. I loved hearing stories about the four of them.

Except about the time they drifted apart. I hated that. But they were all back together now. *Happily off doing God knows what at a bachelor party.*

"I don't know how you did it," Daphne said. "Being uprooted from your life and being forced to live with a father that your mother didn't want you to know. You're incredibly brave, Brooklyn."

I hadn't felt brave then. "I wasn't. The only thing that kept me going while I was living with my father was Miller. He made me feel safe. He wasn't cruel like my father." I'd given Miller a piece of my heart as soon as he'd shared his ice cream with me. I felt tears welling in my eyes.

The wave of grief hit me hard. Sitting here with my friends that were celebrating my new relationship felt...heavy. I was still mourning Miller. And I was bad at hiding it. This was why I didn't want Matt to leave me tonight. Because I knew this would happen.

Daphne grabbed my hand. "It hits at strange moments, I know." She squeezed my hand. "You don't have to hide how you're feeling around us. Ever. Okay?"

I nodded.

And then she pulled me into a hug.

How had I ever lived without a friend as understanding as Daphne?

"I'm sorry, we shouldn't have brought up your hot daddy and all that," Justin said and hugged my other side.

I laughed through my tears.

"Let it all out, gorgeous." He kissed my cheek.

"Group hug!" Kennedy yelled and slammed into my side. Penny and Bee joined in too.

I couldn't help but smile through my tears. Miller had held me together after everything. But now I had so many people to lean on. It was like Miller had known that if I came back here, it wouldn't just be because I needed Matt.

It was like he wanted me to have all these people in my life. To hold me when I cried. Since he couldn't.

It was strange to feel so unlucky but so lucky at the same time.

"I love you guys," I said.

"We love you too," Penny said.

"Well, I love you most, since I knew you first," Justin said.

"Justin, I knew Brooklyn first," Kennedy said.

Justin pulled back from the hug. "Semantics. If I was straight, Brooklyn and I would already be married and we all know it. That's true love. Which is more powerfully than best friend love."

I laughed and wiped away the rest of my tears.

"What do you find funny about that?" Justin asked. "Don't make me mouth kiss you again."

The power cut out and Justin screamed at the top of his lungs.

"Justin, let go, I can barely breathe," Penny said with a laugh.

"Sorry, gorgeous, but I'm not moving until the power is back on."

I would have been freaking out, but everyone was laughing. It was hard to be scared when I was smiling.

"Do you know where the circuit breaker is?" Daphne asked.

"I honestly have no idea. Should we go look for it?" I reached out for her in the darkness and found her hand.

"Yeah, we can definitely fix this," she said.

"Maybe you can. I have no idea how to. Let me get my phone so we can see." I rummaged around for my phone on the coffee table. I hit the flashlight feature. The room lit up. And standing behind the couch were six men with black ski masks over their faces.

I screamed at the top of my lungs and dropped my phone, bathing the room in darkness again.

And then all hell broke loose.

The sound of glass shattering rung in my ears.

Penny screamed. "Get off me!"

Someone groaned.

One of the guys had definitely been hit based on that groan. Probably by Penny.

"Flip the couch!" Bee yelled.

That was a good idea.

Before I could move, someone put their hand on my shoulder. Men I didn't know really needed to stop touching me. I threw out my elbow. But whoever my elbow collided with didn't even flinch. He put his hand over my mouth. He was messing with the wrong person. I bit down on one of his fingers.

He cursed under his breath and released me from his grip. I crouched down feeling along the ground for a piece of glass. I'd heard something else shatter. I wrapped my hand around the stem of a wine glass. *This will do.* Whoever these guys were, they'd walked into the wrong house. I'd been kidnapped for the last fucking time! I stood up and spun in a circle, waiting for my eyes to adjust in the darkness.

"Get my mommy!" Jacob yelled.

"Jacob?" Panic wrapped around my throat. "Jacob, where are you?!" I reached out my empty hand in the darkness, searching for him.

"I'm a kidnapper!" he said happily.

Wait. What?

The lights turned back on. Broken glass and wine covered the floor. And pillows had been thrown everywhere. A glass lamp was shattered. I recognized Matt, Rob, James, Mason, Tanner, and Nigel even though only Rob had his mask off. They were scattered around the room. I was pretty sure it was Mason who'd knocked over the lamp because he was trying and failing to put it back on the end table. There was also a very little kidnapper I hadn't seen before because you could only just see the top of his head over the couch. *Jacob.* I breathed a sigh of relief.

"Jesus, Brooklyn," said Mason and he dropped the lamp again.

I looked down at the wine glass in my hand. The top was broken, the glass shards sticking out precariously. It was the perfect weapon. But not against my friend. I let it fall to the ground.

"Oh, sorry," Rob said who had his arms wrapped around Penny. "Thought you were my wife." He let go of Penny's waist.

"I didn't mean to give you a black eye!" Penny threw her hand over her mouth. "I'm so sorry, Rob."

Rob laughed. "You definitely didn't give me a black eye. You lightly swatted my thigh. I thought you were just groping me." He winked at her and then grimaced from his black eye.

Penny made a grossed out face and Rob laughed.

"How did you get a black eye?!" Daphne said and hurried over to him.

"I don't remember," he said. But then he quickly added: "But you should see the other guy."

Tanner chuckled beside him. "Yeah, right." He pulled off his mask.

"You guys," James said and pulled off his mask too. "I thought we weren't taking our masks off?"

Penny gasped. "James, what happened to your face?!" She rushed over to him, cradling his face in her hands.

Why were they all beat up? God, they were going to look like a street fight gang in the wedding photos.

"Did you kidnap a bunch of big strong men with mean right hooks before this segment of kidnapping or something?" Justin asked. He was looking back and forth between James and Rob. "Tell me more."

"Kidnap, kidnap!" Jacob said and started jumping up and down on the couch.

"Is that a yes?" Justin asked with a smile.

"Kidnap, kidnap!" Jacob kept hopping.

He went to leap off the couch but I grabbed him before he could jump down onto the glass on the floor. I turned around and saw Matt. He'd been standing behind me. I should have felt bad about elbowing him so hard. And biting his hand. But I did not.

"Enough of the chitter chatter," Nigel said. "We need to kidnap our prey."

"Dude, read the room," Rob said. "The ladies are pissed."

That was an understatement. "Matt, what the…" my voice trailed off because I was seconds away from cursing and I didn't want to curse in front of Jacob. I stared at Matt's masked face. "What is wrong with you?! Kidnapping? Really? You thought *that* of all things was a good idea after everything?"

He cleared his throat. "Baby…"

"Yeah we did," Rob said and lifted his hand for a high five. But Matt didn't high five him.

I had a feeling this had been Rob's master plan…

"Kidnapping commence!" Rob yelled. He threw a bag over Daphne's head and then flipped the light switch.

Fuck.

Bee screamed.

"Coach, over here!" Jacob yelled.

I felt Matt's arms around me again. And this time I breathed in his familiar scent. "Kidnapping, Matt? Really?"

"If you'll excuse me, little dude," Matt said and pulled Jacob out of my arms. And then Matt put a bag over my head and lifted me over his shoulder. The bag was silky soft. And it felt more like something from a sex club than a hardware store. Maybe Tanner had planned this instead of Rob…

The whole thing was ridiculous. But for some reason as I was hanging upside down, I was smiling.

"Who's touching my butt?!" Kennedy yelled.

"Sorry," Tanner said. "My hand slipped. It's hard to make purchase in the dark with gloves."

"And who's touching my butt?" Justin asked in a much more excited tone.

"I'm not touching your butt," Nigel said. "My hand is definitely on your thigh."

"Then raise it," Justin said.

"No thank you, sir," Nigel said.

"Call me sir again."

"No."

Was Nigel carrying Justin right now? Justin had a whole foot on him. How was he doing that?

Matt carried me out of the apartment.

"Why does everyone look like they got into a brawl?" I asked. No wonder Matt hadn't told me what his plans were. Because I would have said no to all of this.

"We were playing football," Matt said.

Of course they were.

"Don't worry, Mistress Brooklyn," Nigel said. "I will have them looking right as rain before the wedding. Fresh faced and dapper. Because they get to be in pictures."

He was throwing too many sayings at me to believe him. There was no way Rob wouldn't be sporting a black eye at the wedding.

"You're so strong, Nigel," Justin said. "What's your workout routine?"

"Thank you," Nigel replied. "I'm a natural athlete. I don't need to waste time with modern boy jazzercise."

What is he talking about? I shook my head. "And you have an eye on Jacob?" I asked Matt.

"I'm right here, Mommy," Jacob said.

"I haven't let him out of my sight," Matt said.

That wasn't entirely true. Because no one had been able to see anything back there.

It was like he knew I didn't believe him, because he added: "I'm holding his hand. He's right here. He's safe."

I smiled. This must be the strangest sight ever. A bunch of men with women thrown over their shoulders. And one man over Nigel. And Matt holding a miniature kidnapper's hand.

"Where are we going?" I asked.

"It wouldn't be a proper kidnapping if I told you that."

"You should probably tell your fiancée who's been legitimately kidnapped a few times where we're going."

"It was Rob's idea," Matt said as he pulled me off his shoulder and set me down on a leather seat.

I had a feeling we were in a fancy car.

"He was sad about not being the best man. I thought he could have this win. Besides, this isn't the real surprise."

"And what's the real surprise?" The car started moving and I grabbed onto Matt.

"You'll see."

I kept a hold of Matt's arm. I could make out a few other voices. Penny and James were definitely here. And I heard Rob laughing. We must have been in a limo.

I couldn't believe Rob had come up with this plan. Right after telling me he was going to pull a prank during my rehearsal dinner. He was out of control. It was like my coming back to town had turned him into a high schooler all over again. Or maybe he was just always this poorly behaved?

We pulled to a stop and Matt grabbed my hand, helping me out of the limo.

"Ready?" he asked.

"As long as this is where the kidnapping bit ends."

He laughed. "No more kidnapping, I promise." He pulled the bag off my head.

I blinked. We were standing on the Empire High football field. But there were several tents erected on the field and a fire pit on the 50-yard-line.

Oh my God, we're going to get arrested.

CHAPTER 29

Friday

Matt

"Matt," Brooklyn said and looked up at me. "I don't want to spend our wedding behind bars."

I laughed. "I have the principal's permission."

"To set his field on fire and put a bunch of holes in it from tent poles?"

"Mhm," I said. *Not exactly.* But no one was watching. "I wanted to bring you here after the prom. That's what the helicopter was for. But we got…interrupted."

"That is the understatement of the century," Brooklyn said.

Rob stepped in front of us. "I tried to convince Matt to kidnap you for the proposal. But he said no. And then all *that* happened. So this time, he trusted my judgement." He slapped me on the back. "Besides, it's like a redo of prom. Which was already a redo of the prom you missed. And now this is a redo of the proposal. But you're already engaged… My reasoning got lost somewhere in there, but you got it. Surprise! Do you want a s'more?" He held up a bag of marshmallows.

"Yessie!" Jacob grabbed the marshmallows out of Rob's hand and ran toward the fire.

Brooklyn laughed as Rob ran after him.

I pulled Brooklyn in close. "On prom night I planned it just being us here," I said. "But I thought you might like this. All of us together." I ran my fingers through her hair, untangling it from her time with a bag over her head.

"I love it," she said.

I smiled down at her. "Yeah? The whole thing or…"

She lightly shoved my arm. "Fine. I guess even the kidnapping thing was a little funny."

"You bit me," I said. "You're definitely going to pay for that."

"And how exactly am I going to pay for that?" She smiled up at me.

"You'll find out in the tent later," I winked at her.

"Aren't we sharing a tent with Jacob?"

"Tanner offered to look after Jacob tonight." I looked over toward the fire pit. Everyone was already sitting around laughing and toasting marshmallows. Jacob was sitting on Tanner's knee.

"That's very nice of him," Brooklyn said. "I really wish Tanner was more open to finding someone. He'd be a really good dad."

Tanner was patiently trying to show Jacob how to roast one of the marshmallows. Jacob seemed to be listening. But then he whacked him with the stick instead of putting the marshmallow over the flame.

Brooklyn sighed. "I told Jacob to stop doing that. He's going to hurt someone."

I laughed. I wasn't sure why Tanner was letting Jacob do it. But he didn't seem to care at all. "I'm sure Tanner would tell him to stop if it hurt."

"Jacob likes to play swords with sticks…" her voice trailed off when Jacob walloped Tanner with a sticky marshmallow. "Oh no."

But Tanner just laughed and pulled the marshmallow off his cheek.

"See, Tanner's fine," I said.

"It's like Jacob can do nothing bad in your eyes. I'm always the one that has to reprimand him." She immediately pressed her lips together.

I saw the flash of pain cross her face. And I wondered if she used to say that to Miller. I cleared my throat. "We have hot chocolate too. Your favorite."

She smiled up at me. "Thank you. We're all going to be high on sugar. There's no way anyone is going to get any sleep tonight."

"No one has any plans of sleeping." I leaned down and lightly bit her earlobe in retaliation for earlier.

She laughed. "Lead me to the hot chocolate, fiancé."

"As you wish, fiancée." I wrapped my arm around her and led her over to our friends.

I grabbed us each a cup of hot chocolate before sitting down beside her.

She smiled at me as she blew the steam from her cup.

I couldn't wait to have those lips wrapped around my cock later.

"So about the tent situation," Rob said. "Is it a spouse thing? Or a who we're escorting down the aisle thing?"

Daphne lightly shoved his arm.

"I was just asking," Rob said. "Because Bee is going to be next to Kennedy. And I'm next to Mason. So I think that means Bee and I are supposed to shack up together tonight."

"Don't make me kill you," Mason said.

"James and Penny are actually paired up," Rob said. "Which is incredibly lame if you ask me. Then Tanner with Daphne..." Robs voice trailed off. "Never mind. Let's do the spouse thing for the tents. And maybe I can just escort Daphne down the aisle too? I think that makes more sense."

"Afraid I'll steal your beautiful wife away?" Tanner asked.

Daphne blushed.

"Over my dead body," Rob said.

Tanner shrugged. "That can be arranged."

"Don't make me whoop your ass again."

"Language," Brooklyn said.

"Earmuffs, grandson," Tanner said.

Jacob dropped his stick and threw his hands over his ears.

Tanner cleared his throat. "If you want to joust, I'll go right now, Young Robert."

"Joust? What century are you living in?"

"Fine, a gentlemen's duel," Tanner said. "Unless you don't know your way around a pistol?"

"Shall I fetch your dueling pistols, Master Tanner?" Nigel asked. "Hair trigger? Or normal?"

"Stop it, guys," I said.

"I will not…" Rob said, but Justin cut him off.

"Back to what you were saying earlier," Justin said. "Does that leave me with Nigel? Because count me in."

Nigel sighed like Justin was exhausting him. "I don't even sleep." He put a marshmallow on his stick and put it over the fire.

Tanner cleared his throat.

"I mean…I sleep," Nigel said. "Just not often. Because of all the errands Master Tanner sends me on. I'm a boy with no breaks. The life of a dedicated house boy."

No breaks? I knew that wasn't true. Nigel rarely ever worked. He had more time off than I did. Maybe he was just trying to turn Justin down nicely.

"Why are all the hot ones so insane and so straight," Justin said with a sigh.

Nigel smiled at the compliment. Even though only half of it was a compliment. And I still wasn't sure that Nigel was completely straight. Because he still looked at me very provocatively. And still tried to dress me most mornings.

As if Nigel knew I was thinking about him, he smiled over at me. "Do you want me to roast your marshmallow for you?" he asked, his smile growing.

Was that some kind of weird sexual innuendo? I didn't want him to roast my junk. "No thank you."

Nigel pulled his marshmallow off the flame, quickly made a s'more and handed it to Jacob.

"Thank you, Mr. Nigel," Jacob said.

"What was that, Mr. Jacob? I didn't understand you."

"I meant merci," Jacob said and bit into his s'more. His eyes lit up. "This is the best s'more I've ever had!"

"And for you, mademoiselle," Nigel said and handed Brooklyn a s'more.

"Thanks, Nigel." She took a bite. "Wow, this really is the best s'more ever. What's your secret?"

"A boy never tells his secretses." He pointed finger guns at me.

Oh God. I grimaced as Brooklyn took another bite. He better not have somehow snuck some jizz in there. But I knew he hadn't. Because he'd been in front of us the whole time. There was no way he could have skeeted anywhere. And now I was a little jealous that I said I didn't want one. Because he kept handing them out and everyone was raving about them.

"Don't be jealous, Master Matthew. I made you one without your consent anyway," Nigel said and handed me one too. "I know that's how you like it."

Without consent? Or just like...he'd made it the way I liked? I shrugged. *Fuck it.* I took a bite. Damn, it really was good.

"Rob, your eye is looking a lot better," Brooklyn said.

"Are you checking me out, Sanders?"

Brooklyn rolled her eyes. "No. But...really your eye looks better."

Daphne put her fingers under Rob's chin to turn his face toward hers. "Brooklyn's right. The swelling's really gone down. It even looks a little less purple."

"All in a day's work," Nigel said. "Now what should we do first? Strippers?"

"Stop it," I said.

"But they're on their way."

"Here, man? Seriously?" I glanced at Jacob. He was having trouble keeping his eyes open. He'd probably be out in a couple minutes.

"I told you I was going to spend the night with all of them. So don't pretend to be gobsmacked. And I already erected my tent. It'll be fine. I'll be as quiet as possible." He waved his hand through the air. "My tent is going to be very full though. Stretched to the seams, if you know what I mean."

Rob laughed.

"Now if you will excuse me. But here are more s'mores." He grabbed a try and handed it to me before sprinting toward his tent.

When had he made all these?

"He's almost as weird as you, Tanner," Rob said. "But in a good way."

Tanner laughed. "The only reason you don't like me is because you're threatened by me."

"Psh," Rob said. "I have way more muscle than you."

"Do you though?" Tanner asked. "And I'm taller than you. I feel a very threatened aura coming off of you right now."

"You're just asking for it," Rob said.

"And yet you're the one with a black eye."

"Come on," I said. "Let's just get along. Let's play a game or something."

"We could do truth or dare again," Mason suggested. "That went real well last time."

Yeah because they all got to lay one on my fiancée. "Definitely not that," I said. I'd been a little annoyed about how that had gone down last time. But I'd let it slide because I'd wanted to keep Brooklyn's mind preoccupied after her kidnapping. My girl didn't need to be distracted right now though. And no one else was kissing her ever again but me.

"How about spin the bottle?" Rob smiled. "That's always a good time."

"And definitely not that either." Why did my friends keep trying to hook up with Brooklyn?

"I'm not opposed to either of those," Justin said. "I feel like I missed out on something scandalous. But I have a game along those lines. How about seven minutes in heaven?"

Actually, I could get down with that one. I glanced over at Jacob again. He'd fallen asleep in Tanner's arms. "Perfect, Justin. We're up first," I said.

"We are?" Justin stood up.

"Dude, I meant with Brooklyn."

"You really should have been more specific. Come with me, Brooklyn." He stood up and put his hand out for her.

"What? No. *I'm* going with Brooklyn."

"What did I just say about being specific?" Justin sat down and crossed his arms over his chest.

Brooklyn squealed when I pulled her over my shoulder again.

"What is seven minutes in heaven?" Tanner asked. "Where are they going?"

Rob groaned. "Seriously? Where did you say you grew up again?"

"Abroad. All over. You wouldn't have heard of it."

"Seven minutes in heaven is when you hook up in a closet for seven minutes."

"But there aren't any closets here," Tanner said. "And why would you hook up in a closet when there's perfectly good tents?"

"You are the most ridiculous human I've ever met," Rob said.

Brooklyn laughed as their argument drifted away into the night. "Back to the kidnapping thing?" she asked. She lightly slapped my butt.

"We got a little interrupted earlier." I ducked under the flap of the tent and zipped it up behind us. And then I sat down, pulling her onto my lap.

She straddled my waist. "Just seven minutes, huh?" She placed her hands on my shoulders.

The air was hushed in here. It was just the two of us. I couldn't even hear Rob and Tanner bickering. "Just seven minutes," I said and tucked a loose strand of hair behind her ear. She was so fucking beautiful.

"Well, you better hurry up and fuck me, big boy." Her eyes grew round as soon as the words tumbled out of her mouth.

I laughed. "Did you just call me big boy?"

Her face flushed. "You know what I meant. We probably only have like six minutes left. And my hormones are going crazy right now." She reached for the hem of my shirt. "Arms up."

"I love how demanding you're being."

"But you're not listening." She had my shirt pushed up over my abs, but got distracted and trailed her hand down them.

"I really didn't think kidnapping you was going to turn you on this much," I said.

"It didn't. I told you, it's the hormones."

"Hmm." I put my hand on the side of her face.

"Matthew freaking Caldwell, why aren't you taking your pants off?"

I couldn't stop smiling. "Because I'm not giving you a quickie in…" I glanced at my watch. "…five minutes. I brought you in here to make out with you. Which is what seven minutes in heaven is."

"For like…tweens. We're adults. Seven minutes in heaven is getting railed."

Brooklyn was usually a little shy about telling me what she wanted. Maybe it was the hormones. But this was very fun. "We're kind of reenacting being teenagers here," I said. My hand slid back into her hair and she moaned. "So I'm going to kiss you. But that's it, baby."

She groaned in frustration. "We had sex when we were teenagers."

"I remember just kissing you an awful lot before that though."

She shook her head. "Seriously? You just want to make out?"

"In the middle of the Empire High football field." I smiled. "Yes, yes I do." I grabbed the back of her head and pulled her face toward mine.

Brooklyn immediately wrapped her arms behind my neck, pulling me closer.

It reminded me of when she used to jump into my arms after a win back in high school. Her running down the stands toward me had always been one of my favorite sights. And her thighs wrapped around my waist was one of my favorite feelings. I wanted to grab her hips and pull her closer. But that would just lead to me giving her what she wanted. And I was trying to keep this PG until everyone went to sleep for the night.

She was kissing me in *that* way though. The kisses where her tongue swirled around mine impossibly slowly. This was how she kissed when she wanted more. And I knew there weren't PG thoughts running through that gorgeous head of hers. She probably still wished she was bagged. Maybe she wanted to be tied up again, completely at my mercy. I felt myself growing hard. She started grinding against me as I buried my fingers in her hair. I had a whole thing planned for later. Some candles and romance.

A soft moan escaped her lips.

Fuck it. My dirty girl didn't want romance right now. She wanted to be moaning my name.

I flipped us over, slamming her back against the ground. "You want to know what I really wished I could have done to you in the middle of this field 16 years ago?" I didn't wait for her response. I just pushed her leggings and thong down her thighs, leaned forward, and thrust my tongue into her greedy pussy.

Her thighs tightened around my head.

Baby, I'm not going anywhere. This was the reward I'd wanted after every touchdown I'd made in high school. And her lips around my cock. I really loved my girl on her knees.

She bucked her hips up. I still had the taste of s'mores on my lips. The sweetness on my tongue mixed with the taste of her.

"Matt." She moaned and buried her fingers in my hair, pulling me closer.

She seemed perturbed about her fluctuating hormones. But I was really fucking enjoying this. I loved taking care of her. Pleasing her. Teasing her. I lightly rubbed my nose against her clit.

"I swear if you don't fuck me right now I'm going to scream."

I laughed against her pussy.

Her fingers tightened in my hair.

I lightly bit down on her clit in response. She'd earned that from biting my finger. I knew she was seconds away from coming. And we were probably way over our seven minutes. But I wasn't going to deny her request for my cock.

I placed one last slow stroke against her wetness. Then I shoved my pants down and leaned over her.

She wrapped her hand around my cock. I let her guide me into her soaked pussy.

So fucking tight. I pulled back and slammed into her. Again and again.

"Harder," she moaned.

Yeah, I really liked her crazy hormones. If she wanted it harder, I'd give it to her harder. "You like fucking the star wide receiver, baby?"

She moaned.

"You wish you could touch yourself while you watch me on the field?"

Her fingers dug into my back.

"Because I pictured you spreading your thighs right in the stands. Even though everyone was watching." I slammed into her again. "But you're so greedy for me you can't even wait until after the game."

"Matt," she moaned.

I grabbed one of her thighs, wrapping it around my waist, the angle letting me go even deeper. "That's what I liked to picture. Your fingers deep inside your greedy pussy, imaging my cock buried inside of you. Everyone staring, but knowing you're all mine."

Her nails scratched down my back.

"I imagined running up into the stands and fucking you in front of everyone. Claiming you. You're no one's dirty little secret, Brooklyn."

Her pussy clenched around me. I dropped my forehead to hers as I exploded inside of her. My chest rose and fell as her fingers fell from my back.

"Mmm," Brooklyn sighed and smiled up at me. "I have to say…I never thought about doing this on the Empire High football field."

"No? This has always been a fantasy of mine. Right in the stadium."

"It's *always* been a fantasy? So that means you've never done it before, right?"

"I mean…not in the middle of the field."

She lightly shoved my chest. "I forgot that you used to be a whore in high school. And…after."

"That's not a very nice thing to call your baby daddy."

She laughed, making her pussy clench around me again.

Fuck. I slowly pulled out of her. I watched some of my cum leak down her inner thigh. *So fucking hot.*

The sound of the zipper on our tent made me jump. I quickly pulled up my pants and moved in front of Brooklyn before the flap opened.

"It's been like 20 minutes," Mason said. He smiled as he looked back and forth between us.

Mason never knocked. Not that you could knock on a tent. But it was a bad habit he had.

"No one came to tell us the time," Brooklyn said. She cleared her throat. "We were just making out."

"Sure you were," Mason said. "But we need your help. It's us, Bee, Tanner, and Kennedy against the Hunters and Justin. And Tanner is terrible at charades."

"Charades?" Brooklyn asked. "I love charades."

I looked over my shoulder. She was completely composed. I grabbed her hand and helped her to her feet.

Rob was standing in front of the fire pretending to drive a car around.

"This is the second word of a two-word movie," Bee said to us as we sat back down.

"Driving a Lamborghini!" Tanner yelled. Jacob was asleep in his arms. He didn't seem at all phased by the yelling.

Rob shook his head. He pretended to drive around some more and then stopped, playing with some gears in the car.

"Driving a Bugatti!" Tanner yelled next.

Rob shook his head again. "What the fuck is wrong with him," he said under his breath.

"Driving a Tesla!" Tanner nodded like he'd definitely gotten it that time.

"Why so specific?" I asked. "And why are you guessing three words for the second word? Are you trying to guess the whole thing in one go?"

"The more specific the better in charahhhdes." He said charades really weird. With a long, drawn out "ah" in the middle.

"Charades," I said, correcting him.

"Charahhhdes," Tanner said. "Yes."

"And it's a movie, Tanner," Bee said. "What movie has the word Tesla in it?"

He shrugged. "I don't know. I'm not very up to date with the movies. I just watched all those new early 2000s movies for the Halloween party though."

"*New* early 2000s?" Mason shook his head. "They're old, man."

"Hardly."

"Park!" Daphne yelled.

"Damn it, Daphne!" Rob stopped driving. "Quit guessing for the other team."

"Sorry," she said and drank another sip of hot chocolate.

I was pretty sure hers was spiked.

Especially since she then hiccupped. "But was I right?"

"Yes." Rob shook his head and started motioning with his hands.

"First word," Bee said. "Three syllables. Third syllable. We're guessing the last syllable!" she yelled at all of us.

I forgot how competitive she was.

Rob pretended to throw up into the fire.

"Vomiting into a fire!" Tanner yelled.

"Dude, way too specific."

"It's charahhhdes, Matthew," Tanner said. "Oh! Burmiting!"

"Burmiting?" Mason asked.

"When you burp and a little vom comes up," Tanner said. He shook his head. "I'm just going to guess the movie. Mansfield Park! Wait, is that a movie? I know it's a book. But all of Jane Austen's books are movies, right?"

"I think it's a movie too," Brooklyn said. "Is that right, Rob? Is it Mansfield Park?"

"No that's not right. Why the fuck would I be doing Mansfield Park? I said it was a classic."

"That book is a classic," Tanner said.

"Not a classic movie. You didn't even know if it was one. And Mansfield only has two syllables. I said three, damn it."

"Ah!" Tanner yelled. "A classic you say? Central Park!"

"I literally just said it's a movie," Rob said.

"You're really not supposed to be talking, Rob," Bee said. "Isn't that a disqualification?"

Rob threw up his hands.

"Central Park is a movie," Tanner said. "A modern day classic."

"I've never heard of it," I said.

"Of course you have! It was from the 30s, good lad. It came out just a few years ago when the newfangled moving pictures were all the rage."

We all stared at him.

Tanner froze for a second. And then started laughing. "Just kidding. Not about the movie. Central Park *is* a movie and it's a classic. I meant about everything else. Like timeframe wise. But you'd like the movie, Brooklyn. It's about some kids getting mixed up with New York City gangsters. Never mind," he quickly said. "Let's forget I said anything."

Rob shook his head. "I don't know what all that was. But regardless… Central is two syllables too you maniac."

Tanner shrugged. "I was just joking around."

Rob started pretending to throw up in the fire again.

"Sick!" Bee yelled and pointed to Rob. "You're getting sick!"

He nodded.

"It's Jurassic Park!"

"Yes that's it! Thank fuck," Rob said and sat back down. "You're all so terrible at this game. One of you is up."

"I'll go," I said.

"No, not you," Rob said. "I already know you're just going to squat and pretend to poop for Winnie the *Pooh*. Next."

How did he know that? I shrugged. Okay, maybe I did like to do that one for charades. But it had been forever since we'd played this game together.

Brooklyn laughed as I sat back down and put my arm around her shoulders.

I smiled down at her. This was not at all a normal bachelor or bachelorette party. But all that mattered was that she was smiling.

"One week," she whispered.

"One week." I'd waited a lifetime for her to be Mrs. Brooklyn Caldwell. And this time next week she finally would be.

CHAPTER 30

Thursday – Thanksgiving Day

Brooklyn

I always felt a little sick to my stomach on Thanksgiving. Remembering what happened that day 16 years ago was always hard. Matt's words had haunted me for half my life. And my father's betrayal the following day haunted me too. So yeah, this time of year my stomach tended to churn. But today I was *actually* sick. Not from memories of the past. I leaned over and threw up in the toilet.

Matt pounded on the door. "Brooklyn?!"

"I'm fine," I groaned as I leaned over the toilet bowl again. God, I hated throwing up.

He jiggled the handle, but I'd locked the door. "Brooklyn, what's going on?!" he yelled.

"I'm fine," I said again and coughed.

But instead of listening to me, he kicked the door in. The wood splintered and the door hit the wall and almost fell off its hinges.

I stared over at Matt standing in the doorway with a bewildered expression on his face. And I couldn't help but laugh. And then I leaned over the toilet and threw up again.

"Jesus." He knelt down beside me on the floor and pulled my hair back for me. "What's going on? Is it the baby? Do you feel okay? Should I call the doctor?" He put his hand on my stomach.

"It's just morning sickness, Matt." I laughed again, but again it made my stomach turn over. My cheeks puffed up, but I didn't throw up anymore. I was pretty sure there was nothing left in my stomach. I took a deep breath and stared at him. "I can't believe you just broke down the door because of a very normal pregnancy symptom."

"I didn't know what was going on." He moved his hand from my stomach to my back and slowly ran his hand up and down my spine.

"I'm okay, I promise. I just need some paper towels."

He grabbed some paper towels off the vanity for me. "Are you sure that's what it is? Morning sickness?"

I tore off a paper towel and wiped my face. "Positive." I took another deep breath and my stomach didn't roll over this time. I sat back on my heels and Matt kept rubbing my back. "I'm okay. And so is the baby. It's actually a good sign."

"Throwing up is a good sign?" He shook his head. "Tell that to our door."

I laughed. "You're a barbarian."

He kissed my cheek.

I slid away from him on the floor. "Don't get anywhere near me. I need to brush my teeth and wash my face."

He caught my wrist so I couldn't hide from him. "I'm not going anywhere."

If I wasn't already on the floor, I probably would have melted onto it. This was probably the grossest thing I'd ever done in front of him. But he was still staring at me with stars in his eyes. And he'd broken down a freaking door to get to me.

He pushed some hair off my face. "You scared me. No more locking the bathroom door."

"Is that a house rule?" I raised my eyebrows at him.

"Yes." He smiled.

"I didn't think we had any rules in this house. We're kind of lawless."

His smile grew. "As much as I like the sound of being lawless with you…no locking the door."

I looked at the broken door. "I don't think that's going to be a problem."

"I'll fix it."

I glanced over his shoulder.

"What are you looking at?" He turned around, but there was nothing there to see.

I shook my head and laughed. "I just kind of thought Nigel would pop up and say 'No, I'll fix it,' before you got a chance to do it yourself."

Matt laughed. "He probably would have, but he's busy getting everything ready." The smile on Matt's face grew. "Our rehearsal dinner is tonight."

I couldn't wipe the smile off my face either. "It is. And I can't wait to go to town on some turkey. I'm pretty sure Thanksgiving was made for pregnant women."

He chuckled. "I'm sure it was."

"And hopefully I don't throw up again tonight."

"I thought it was *morning* sickness?"

"I got sick more than just in the mornings with Jacob."

"Interesting." Matt helped me to my feet. "Is there anything I can get you that will help with that?"

"Actually a cup of tea might be nice."

He nodded. "A cup of tea. Got it. I need to order some books about all this baby stuff. So I don't break any more doors."

"You do that. While I freshen up." I pushed him out of the bathroom. I would have closed the door, but it was hanging off its hinges.

He chuckled and walked away.

I pressed my hands against the vanity and stared in the mirror. My days fluctuated between thinking about the baby constantly to trying not to think about the baby at all. Just in case. But this really was a good sign. A great sign. I smiled. The baby was healthy. I removed one of my hands from the vanity and ran it over my stomach.

This Thanksgiving was going to be perfect. It was going to erase the Thanksgiving 16 years ago from my head.

I was glad we'd decided to do our rehearsal dinner tonight and our wedding tomorrow. It felt like we were fixing a wrong from out past. I didn't regret what I'd done in my time apart from Matt. But I wanted to fix this wrong for him. I wanted to erase the last words he spoke to me back then. I wanted to erase all the hurt. I wanted to move forward. *All four of us*. I couldn't stop smiling.

And Rob hadn't even texted me once about the silly prank he said he was going to pull. So hopefully that meant he was ready to move forward too. There was no way I still owed him a favor from back when we were teenagers. There were time limits to that kind of thing. And this favor was expired.

I quickly washed my face and brushed my teeth. Matt had a cup of tea waiting for me downstairs on the kitchen counter. Jacob was sitting on the counter next to the cup.

"Mommy, Mommy!" he said. "We get to go to Abuelo's castle!"

"Yes we do." I tickled his side. I was very curious about Tanner's apartment. He must have had very medieval decorations or something.

"We can still play football today, right?" he asked and looked up at me.

It was a family tradition. And I wanted to keep those traditions alive. But this Thanksgiving was a little different from most. "Tanner doesn't have a yard to play in," I said.

"Yes he does."

I shook my head. "He lives in an apartment."

"No, he lives in a castle."

I smiled. "Okay, but..."

"We are going to play," Matt said. "It's tradition, after all. And we're not leaving for a few hours. We'll play right now." He smiled over at me.

I'd told him about our tradition of playing football all morning, eating way too much turkey, and watching the football games.

"Just you and me though, kiddo. Your mommy needs to drink her tea."

I laughed. "Oh, I'm playing too." I took a quick sip of my tea and helped Jacob off the counter. "Race you to the back yard!"

Jacob started running, but Matt stopped me, pulling me into his arms.

"Shouldn't you be resting?" he asked.

I shook my head. "And miss out on one of my favorite traditions? Never."

"You sure?"

"I promise that I'm fine." I stood on my tiptoes and kissed him. "Now you better bring you're A-game. Because we take our Thanksgiving football very seriously."

"Oh, game on."

I patted his chest and spun around, making sure to sway my hips.

He groaned behind me.

I laughed and sprinted the rest of the way to the door.

***

"You look beautiful," Matt said when I walked into the living room. He stood up from the couch. He was wearing a fitted black suit. We were dressed way too fancy for Thanksgiving dinner. But we'd agreed to go all out for the rehearsal dinner. And Matt looked so yummy.

"You said the same thing a few hours ago when I had leaves in my hair," I said.

"Well you were beautiful then too. But this dress." His eyes scanned down my body in that way that heated my skin.

Justin had convinced me to buy a white dress for tonight too. This one was short and made of a satiny material that made me feel all fancy. It flared out at my hips and when Matt grabbed my hand and twirled me around, the skirt lifted and fluttered.

I stopped when I saw all the books on the couch. "What are all of these?" I let go of his hand and lifted one of the books up that already had a bookmark.

"I told you I needed to buy some pregnancy books. They were delivered when you were in the shower."

"I thought you meant like…next week. And I didn't think you'd buy the whole bookstore." I laughed.

He shrugged and looked a little embarrassed. "Well, you've done all this before. And I want to make sure I know what I can do to help out."

He was the sweetest. I opened to the page he'd bookmarked. It was all about morning sickness. He'd highlighted a few things. I scanned down the highlights. "Wait, they make anti-nausea candy drops? I don't remember them having anything like that when I was pregnant with Jacob."

Matt smiled. "We should give those a try."

I liked when he said *we* like that. "We definitely should."

"Do you want me to order some now?" He pulled out his phone.

I laughed and grabbed his hand. "Stop torturing the delivery people on Thanksgiving. We'll go shopping after the wedding."

"After the wedding." He smiled. "God I love the sound of that."

Jacob came running into the room. He skidded across the floor in his socks.

"You all ready?" Matt ruffled his hair.

"Yessie. Just let me get my sword." He picked up a stick off the floor. "Ready."

"We can leave the sword here I think, kiddo."

"But you need a sword in a castle, Coach. How else will we play knights? I'll get one for you too." He went over to his basket full of toys and pulled out a second stick. "And one for my abuelo!" He selected a third stick.

I shrugged. That made sense to me. "You definitely need swords to play knights," I said.

Matt laughed. "Okay, you guys. Let's get going." He helped Jacob into his coat and shoes. I pulled on my coat too as I smiled at Matt lacing Jacob's shoes. Matt was always meant to be a dad. I felt tears welling in the corners of my eyes. God, it was like I had no control over my emotions. I blinked fast, getting rid of the tears. Tonight was not for tears. We were celebrating.

Someone must have been burning leaves nearby because the smell of fall was everywhere when we walked outside. Matt opened the car door for me before getting Jacob situated in the back seat. The heat was turned up full blast, but it was still chilly. I would have been lying to myself if this smell and this temperature hadn't reminded me of Matt over the years. I smiled as Matt pulled away from the curb. Soon the city would be decorated for Christmas. I'd never seen the city in winter before. And I couldn't wait to see everything lit up even more. I couldn't wait to spend every season with this man.

"I love seeing you this happy," Matt said.

How could I not be happy? My 16-year-old self dreamed of this day just as much as my 32-year-old self. "I love you."

Matt smiled as he paid attention to the traffic.

It didn't take us long to get to Tanner's apartment. I looked out the window. "This looks very fancy."

"Because it's a castle!" Jacob said.

I smiled. "I can't wait to see it. Grab the swords!"

"Got 'em, Mommy."

I held Matt's hand and Jacob's hand as we walked toward the apartment. A doorman opened the door for us, welcoming us in from the cold.

Matt dropped my hand and pulled an envelope out of his inside suit pocket. He handed it to the doorman. "Happy Thanksgiving," he said.

"Happy Thanksgiving," the doorman said with a big smile.

"What did you give him?" I asked as we stepped in front of the elevator.

"Oh." Matt shrugged like it was nothing. "Just a little present."

"What kind of present?"

He scratched the back of his neck. "When I visited your um…grave," he whispered so Jacob didn't hear. "I used to see your uncle's grave too. And it always reminded me of how I never really knew him until you. His job was important. And I just treated him like he was invisible. So I don't want anyone who I come in contact with to ever feel that way. I was living here for a while. I know the doorman. And I wanted to make sure to thank him."

Tears were welling in my eyes again. "Uncle Jim would have really loved you doing that for people." I couldn't think of a better way to honor him.

Matt smiled down at me.

The elevator doors dinged open and Jacob jumped back. "Nunca," he said.

"Sweet boy, Tanner lives at the very top of this building." I couldn't walk up all these steps in heels. "Let's just give the elevator a try."

"Nooooo," Jacob said and took another step back.

"I have an idea," Matt said. "How about you close your eyes and count to 100?"

"I don't know how to count to 100."

Matt and I looked at each other. "You go on up," he said. "I'll take the stairs with Jacob."

"It's so many stairs," I said. "Jacob, maybe…"

"I want my abuelo," he said. "He never makes me get in those." He pointed one of his sticks at the elevator.

"Tanner is busy getting ready…"

"But I neeeeed him," Jacob said. "Pleeeeeease."

I could never say no to that. I looked at Matt and nodded.

"Okay, I'm going to go get Tanner then," Matt said. "Unless you want to go up?" he asked me.

"You go ahead. We'll wait here."

Matt stepped onto the elevator and the doors closed behind him.

"Jacob, there's nothing scary about elevators. They help you get from one place to another quicker."

"I'm not in a hurry," he said.

I smiled. "And they're kind of fun. It's like…a ride."

Jacob shrugged. "Like at the carnival?"

Miller and I had taken him to a carnival once about a year ago. But we'd left pretty quickly because I was paranoid that I'd felt someone watching us. Well…not paranoid. Someone probably had been. Jacob hadn't gotten a chance to get on a ride.

"Yes, like the carnival," I said.

Jacob shook his head. "I didn't want to ride those rides. And I don't want to go in the elevator."

"Okay, sweet boy. But it's always good to try something at least once."

"Not if you know you don't like it."

"Hmm." He did kind of have a point. But I really needed him to start riding elevators.

The doors dinged open and Tanner walked out. He was wearing a dark suit with stitches that glimmered slightly in the bright light down here.

"Stop checking me out, woman," he said. "We've been over this. I can't date my best friend's girl."

I laughed. "I wasn't. But I do like your suit."

"Thank you. And you look beautiful, as always." He turned to Jacob. "Hey, little man." He held up his hand.

Jacob high fived him. "I want you to do the magic thing! So I don't have to go on that." He pointed his stick at the elevators again.

"Right," Tanner said. "The stairs. Yup, we can do that."

"Nooooo," Jacob said. "The magic portal to your castle."

Tanner laughed and looked at me. "Kids and their imaginations," he said.

"But, Abuelo…"

"You go on ahead, Brooklyn," Tanner said. "We'll see you in a few minutes after taking the stairs."

Jacob scrunched his mouth to the side as he stared up at Tanner.

Tanner really was good at playing make-believe with Jacob. I stepped toward the elevator.

"Oh and Brooklyn?" Tanner said and caught my wrist. "If you need to talk at all tonight, I'm here."

I nodded. I knew. Tanner was the easiest person to talk to about loss. Because he'd lost someone too.

"And about your dad," he said and let his hand fall from my wrist. "I tried everything. I know his boat is getting the transmissions. I don't know why he hasn't responded."

My father was getting Tanner's messages? And just...didn't care? I knew my face fell.

Tanner cleared his throat. "Or maybe he's not. Maybe he..." Tanner shrugged. "I don't know, Brooklyn."

"It's okay." I forced a smile onto my face. "I really appreciate you trying. And we already have a pretty great abuelo here, don't we, Jacob?"

"The best abuelo," Jacob said.

Tanner smiled. "Thanks, little man."

I oddly wanted to burst into tears. So I quickly got onto the elevator. "I'll see you two up there. Have fun taking the stairs."

"We're not taking the stairs, Mommy," Jacob said.

Tanner laughed. "Kids," he said again.

Jacob sighed. "Abuelo's being silly."

"Abuelo is being silly," I said.

Tanner laughed again. "See you up there." He picked Jacob up as the doors slid closed.

I took a deep breath. My father wasn't coming to my wedding. I probably should have realized that as the wedding got closer and closer. But I'd still been holding out hope. I took another deep breath as the doors slid open.

"What's wrong?" Matt asked as soon as he saw me.

"Am I that easy to read?"

"I know when you're upset." He pulled me off the elevator and into his arms.

"My dad isn't coming. Tanner said he got messages through but that my dad didn't respond. And I know you're not upset about him not coming…"

"I'm upset if you're upset."

I pressed the side of my face against Matt's chest. The letters I'd found made me think my father truly loved me. But him ignoring an invitation to my wedding didn't feel great. It was possible he hadn't seen the messages though.

It felt like the letters all over again. My mom had never seen any of them. Maybe that's what was happening here. "Just because Tanner got messages to my dad's boat doesn't mean my father saw them though."

"Yeah, maybe," Matt said. "I know you dad would be here if he knew he was wanted."

I nodded. My dad wanted to be part of our lives. That I knew for sure. I took another deep breath. "Let's just be happy."

Matt smiled down at me. "Oh, I'm very happy. I'm marrying you tomorrow."

I laughed. "Come on, let's get inside."

He put his arm around my shoulders and guided me toward the bridge.

Wait, what? "Why is there a moat here?" I shook my head. *Wrong question.* "*How* is there a moat here?" No wonder Jacob thought this was a castle.

CHAPTER 31

Thursday

Brooklyn

"I think Tanner owns the apartment beneath his or something too," Matt said.

"That doesn't really answer my question." I paused on the footbridge and leaned on the railing to look at the water. A few fish swam by. "Is this even like…to code?"

Matt laughed. "Probably not. At least he took the tarp off. Usually it's covered. I thought there were sharks under there for the longest time."

"Hm." I watched another colorful fish swim by. "No sharks. But it's very cool."

"A little flashy if you ask me," Matt said.

I laughed. "Come on. I can't wait to see the rest." I pulled him across the bridge and knocked on the apartment door.

Nigel threw the door open. "Happy Thanksgiving!" He was wearing an apron that said "Kiss the Chef" with a little turkey stitched to the side. He was also wearing an Indian headdress, which was a pretty bold move. The feathers trailing down his back almost hit the floor. None of it made any sense over top of his lederhosen.

Matt shook his head. "What are you wearing?"

Nigel adjusted his headdress. "I couldn't remember if you wanted a traditional Thanksgiving or a modern day one. I forgot to write it down. So I did a mix. This is my war bonnet."

Matt shook his head again. "You maybe shouldn't be wearing that, man."

"Why? It's a celebration! And this is a sacred headdress."

"Not for you though."

"It's very sacred to me," Nigel said. "I keep it with all my bonnets in locked boxes. I treat all my relics with respect."

A strange smell suddenly hit me. My nose scrunched up and my stomach churned. *Oh no.* "Nigel, what are you cooking?" I took a deep breath through my mouth to try and calm my stomach.

"Like I said…it's a mix between a traditional Thanksgiving and a modern day feast. So we have your classic turkey with all the fixings, including my world-famous biscuits. I even made a Jello mold which was all the rage in the 60s. One of my favorites. The dish. Not the era." He shuddered. "And I also have the classics. Fresh hand-caught and butchered venison of course. A variety of fish. Cod and bass have been highlighted *heavily.* And eel. Those slippery devils were hard to catch. We also have an assortment of other wildfowl besides the turkey, fully plucked by yours truly. And so much corn. Corn bread, corn on the cob, corn off the cob, and corn porridge of course. There is no feast without a porridge if you ask me."

Well, that explained the warring smells in the air. Especially the *heavily* highlighted fish courses. "Wow that sounds…yummy."

Nigel smiled. "There's a little something for everyone." He straightened the straps of his apron, seeming to emphasis the "Kiss the Chef" written there. "I wanted it to be special for you, mademoiselle."

"Thank you, Nigel." I gave him a hug and kissed his cheek.

He was smiling ear to ear when I released him from the hug.

An alarm started going off.

"That's the porridge! Hors d'oeuvres are circulating. Help yourself to a beverage. But don't go into the wine cellar, it's off limits. And Mr. Jacob is already in the other room waiting for you with the other guests." He sprinted off.

Wait. Jacob? How did he get up here so fast? I must have heard him wrong. I shook my head. "There are a lot of smells in the air."

"Are you okay?" Matt asked.

I nodded. The smells were making me super nauseous, but there was nothing left in my stomach to come up. "I think so." I stared at one of the paintings on the wall that was covered with a sheet. "Why are all the pictures covered?"

"No idea," Matt said. He grabbed my hand and started leading me down the hallway. "But usually there's a lot more of them. And statues too."

"Statues of what?"

He shrugged. "I don't know. They were all covered too. Tanner's always doing renovations."

We walked by the kitchen where Nigel was pulling something out of the oven. I held my breath. I'm sure the food was great. But it was way too many things going on at once. And he was lucky he wasn't catching his headdress on fire.

We walked into the huge great room, with floor to ceiling windows that looked out at Central Park and the city. The sun was just setting, casting a beautiful glow over the city scape. But the decorations inside were just as breathtaking. There were white pumpkins and white candles in gold holders all over the room. And there was a huge white flocked Christmas tree that almost reached the ceiling. A white fur rug was wrapped around its base. It looked like it had just snowed in that corner of the room. There were little gold leaves hanging from the branches instead of Christmas ornaments. It was elegant and beautiful.

The open floor plan flowed into the dining room that had the biggest table I'd ever seen. It looked like one of those ones you'd see a king eating at, surrounded by all his loyal subjects. And there were several cornucopias on it. Actual cornucopias. I'd learned about them in school, but I'd never actual seen one before. Fresh fruit and vegetables poured out of them. The white candles and gold accents continued into this room too. But the real thing that brought everything together were the string lights stretching the length of the huge open floor plan. Strings of gold leaves and twinkle lights dipped from one side of the ceiling to the other. It somehow screamed Thanksgiving and Christmas all at once.

I swallowed hard. Maybe that was the point. Matt and I were originally supposed to get married around Christmas time. This tied everything together. But my eyes started watering at the twinkle lights. "It's beautiful."

"I know they were busy setting it up all day," Matt said. "It's perfect, huh?"

I smiled up at him. "So perfect."

"Touchdown!" Jacob yelled. Jacob and Tanner were sitting on the couch watching football.

What the... We'd literally been standing in the entranceway. There was no way they'd passed us. And there were a million stairs they'd needed to climb.

"How are you two already up here?" Matt asked as he escorted me over to the huge white couch.

Jacob stood up on the couch and turned around. "The magic portal!"

Tanner laughed. "The stairs."

"But Abuelo…"

"The stairs," Tanner said again.

Jacob sighed like Tanner was exhausting him.

"We were standing in the hallway," Matt said. "You didn't pass us."

Tanner shrugged. "We just beat you up here, I guess."

"You're on the 89th floor. That's not possible. Is there another entrance to your apartment or something?"

"Ah yes, that makes sense." Tanner nodded. "It was that one. I have many entrances to my apartment."

"Just tell them about the portal, Abuelo…"

"How about you go play knights with your friends, little man?" Tanner handed Jacob one of his sticks.

"Okay." Jacob jumped off the couch and ran over to Scarlett and Sophie who were sitting on the floor sipping juice boxes. He sat down between them and Scarlett handed him a juice box. The three of them did a cheers and all took sips.

It was the most adorable thing ever. Especially because Jacob was in a little suit and Scarlett and Sophie were both in frilly dresses.

"There you are," Rob said and walked over to us.

"Hey, man," Matt said.

Rob turned to him. "Oh, sorry, almost didn't see you there. Congrats again." Rob slapped him on the back and then turned to me. "A word, Brooklyn?"

"Ummm…" I really didn't want a private word with Rob, because I was terrified of what he was going to say.

"I'll go get us some drinks." Matt lowered his hand from my back. "Is some ginger ale okay?"

"That's perfect," I said. But I cringed when he left me alone with Rob.

"You all set on your end?" Rob asked.

"What are you talking about?"

He laughed. "What do you mean what am I talking about? The prank, Sanders."

"We're not doing a prank," I hissed.

"Yes we are. A classic Hunter Sanders mess around."

"Stop saying that. I'm a Miller."

"About to be a Caldwell, yadda yadda. I'm always calling you Sanders. This is going to be epic."

"What did you do?" I asked.

An evil smile slowly spread across Rob's face. "You'll see. We really did a good job this time."

"There is no *we* here!"

"Shhh, you don't want anyone to know what we're planning. Actually, wait, we need James to complete the original trio." Rob turned around and whistled. "Yo, James!"

"Don't you dare call James over here!" I hissed.

"Too late. He should be a part of it too. Like old times."

"No old times. Just new times. New times that don't involve inappropriate pranks. Do you not remember what happened last time?"

"You pretended to die because you were being overdramatic."

"I was kidnapped!"

"See…all about the drama."

"Robert Hunter, stop it."

"Stop what?"

"Everything!"

"Um...what's up?" James asked as he walked up to us. He looked back and forth between us. "Is everything okay, Brooklyn?"

I was about to tell him no and that his brother was insane, but Rob cut me off.

"We're golden." Rob slapped him on the back. "We're bringing back the pudding prank."

James lowered his eyebrows. "Excuse me?"

"You know...the pudding prank. From our last Thanksgiving with Sanders. And this time it's going to be even better." His evil smile stretched across his face again.

"I know what pudding prank you're referring to," James said. "But you can't be serious right now. It's their rehearsal dinner, Rob."

"Exactly." Rob nodded. "So epic. I can't wait to see Tanner's dumb face covered in pudding."

"Please make him stop," I said to James. "He won't listen to me. Maybe you can make him see reason."

James shook his head. "Rob, this is completely inappropriate, even for you."

"I don't know what you mean by that, but I think you meant this is genius, even for me." Rob smiled. "Just wait until you see the pudding."

I groaned.

Rob rubbed his hands again. "I feel young again. Hunters Sanders mess arounds always do that for me."

"Rob, I'm begging you. Not tonight. It's my rehearsal dinner. And it's my first Thanksgiving back with all you guys."

"Exactly. It'll be a night to remember. Thanks to all our hard planning." He elbowed me in the side.

"I didn't do anything."

"Sure." He winked at me.

What was he talking about? "I didn't. I'm not a part of this."

"Of course you're a part of this. Because you owed me that favor. And we decided this was how I was going to cash it in."

"What favor?" James asked.

"When she screamed my name," Rob said. "Did I never tell you about that?"

James shook his head. "I have no idea what you're talking about. When did she scream your name?"

"When she was beneath me, begging me for more." Rob raised his hand for a high five.

I shoved his arm back down. "False. That never happened. He pushed me into a dark room back in high school after betting me I wouldn't scream his name. Of course I screamed his name. He was holding the door shut and I was terrified."

Rob laughed. "I shoved her into a room with Matt. Definitely terrifying."

"That wasn't why. I didn't even know he was there. I was just scared."

"But you *do* owe me a favor. Facts are facts, Sanders."

I sighed. "Why tonight, Rob?"

"Because I figured it was better than tomorrow night."

Had he seriously considered doing this during my wedding instead? What the hell? "Don't favors have expiration dates? It's been 16 years, Rob."

"Expiration dates? It's not a gift card. It's a promise."

I pressed my lips together. I never liked breaking promises.

"This shit is really fucked up, Rob," James said. "Can't you just let this feud with Tanner go?"

"It's not about Tanner. It's so much bigger than that. You're just not getting it."

"Oh, I'm definitely not getting it," James said. "You're letting your beef with him ruin the rehearsal dinner of two of our best friends."

I smiled. It was sweet of him to refer to me as one of his best friends.

"Ruin it?" Rob shook his head. "I'm making it a night to remember. Rehearsal dinners are always overshadowed and forgotten. But no one's going to forget this shit." He giggled. "So. Much. Pudding."

"I still have nightmares from the last time," I said. "I don't want nightmares about my rehearsal dinner."

"But Matt's not going to be mad about this one. So it's cool."

"It's like you don't know Matt at all." I stared at him.

James laughed. "She's right. You know he has a terrible temper. And Tanner is one of his best friends."

"But not his best. That's me. This ends tonight."

"Rob..."

"Sanders." He put his hands on my shoulders. "We're all haunted by what happened 16 years ago. This will erase all that with a good memory. I'm doing this for you. For all of us."

It was sweet. In a weird way. "Wouldn't my rehearsal dinner just being a rehearsal dinner erase all that hurt?"

Rob shook his head. "Didn't you hear what I said about rehearsal dinners always being forgotten? This will make it unforgettable. Shit, Matt's coming back over. Everyone be cool!" He tapped James' chest with the back of his hand even though James was just standing there. "Not a word about this, Sanders. It has to be a surprise. And if you say anything, you'll just owe me another favor. And I'll cash in tomorrow instead."

Good God. The only thing worse than today was tomorrow. "I hate you."

"Love you too," Rob said.

James shook his head. "This is a really bad idea, Rob. Just call it off."

"It is a great idea, you're right."

Was Rob hard of hearing or something? Or did he just refuse to listen to reason?

"Here you go," Matt said and handed me my glass of ginger ale. "What were you guys talking about? It looked like a very heated discussion." He smiled, not at all aware that Rob was turning our rehearsal dinner into a shit show. Almost literally.

"Just reminiscing over the good old days," Rob said.

Definitely not. We were reminiscing over one of the worst days of my life. We were supposed to be erasing all that today and tomorrow. That was the reason we'd chosen the day after Thanksgiving for our wedding. And Rob was just bringing it all back up.

"You look a little pale, baby." Matt whispered. "Are you feeling alright?"

I felt like I was going to be sick to my stomach. But not because of morning sickness. I looked over at Rob.

He pretended to zip his mouth shut and then threw away the key. Which made no sense.

But I did believe his threat. If I didn't let him do this tonight, he'd just do it tomorrow. And Rob was not going to ruin my wedding day. And I honestly kind of understood where he was coming from. Emphasis on *kind of.* I wanted to erase all the hurt, just like he'd said. But did he really have to make me promise not to tell Matt? I didn't want to keep secrets from him. I'd learned my lesson the last time.

I cleared my throat. "Everything is great," I said.

Rob smiled. "Yeah it is. And about to be better."

"You know what I love?" I said. "Telling people stuff. Being open and honest. Best friends shouldn't have secrets."

"I agree," Rob said. But didn't offer any more information.

Robert Hunter was going to be the death of me.

A waiter walked up holding a tray of hors d'oeuvres.

I went to grab one.

"No thanks," Rob said and grabbed my hand and lowered it. "We're saving our appetite for the main course." He leaned over and whispered in my ear. "Remember last time when people started throwing up? It's better if our stomachs are empty so we don't embarrass ourselves."

Fuck me. I was already nauseous. This was going to be a disaster.

CHAPTER 32

Thursday

Matt

"What are you guys whispering about?" I asked as I stared at Rob and Brooklyn.

"Nothing important, man," Rob said. "Ugh, speaking of nothing important." He glared at Tanner getting up from the couch and joining us.

"Thank you for doing all this," Brooklyn said to Tanner. "These decorations are amazing."

Tanner smiled. "I'm glad you like them. Nigel really wanted live turkeys, and I'm usually an animal guy, but not when we're eating turkey for dinner."

Brooklyn laughed.

"The decorations are like mediocre at best," Rob said. "If you had let me throw your rehearsal dinner they would have been epic."

Brooklyn shook her head. "I don't think I like your idea of epic, Rob. But this is perfect, Tanner."

Rob's eyebrows lowered. "Perfect and Tanner don't really belong in the same sentence."

I sighed. "I know you have manners, Rob. Maybe try and use them?"

"I reserve my right to use manners for people who aren't liars."

I cleared my throat and hit him with a hard stare.

Rob just shrugged. "Fine. I will say…this is better than what we used to have to do as kids. My parents always made us go to the Pruitts' place on Thanksgiving. It was horrible."

"Was Richard not hospitable toward you?" Tanner asked.

"I mean…he was."

"Oh." Tanner tapped his index finger on his lips. "Was it perhaps possible that *you* were just a bad dinner guest? And increasingly rude to the host?"

Rob lowered his eyebrows again. "I'm a great guest. The best guest."

"Then maybe be kind to the host, Rob," Brooklyn said. "Like…really kind. Like don't do anything weird to his home."

Rob laughed. "You're hilarious, Sanders." He threw his arm around her shoulders and then whispered something in her ear again. "Actually, we're going to go circulate because someone can't be trusted alone right now," he said and pulled Brooklyn away from me.

What the hell was he doing? And who was he saying couldn't be trusted? Tanner?

Tanner shook his head. "Boys will be boys."

"He's older than you," I said.

Tanner laughed. "He certainly doesn't act like it."

"Fair."

I watched Rob and Brooklyn making the rounds, saying hi to everyone. It was like Rob was trying to commandeer my role here.

Penny walked over to us. "Hey, Tanner. Your home is amazing. I didn't think apartments in New York City could even be this big."

Tanner smiled. "Thank you. And this isn't even the main living area."

What was he talking about? I was pretty sure we were standing in his *living* room.

"I'm definitely going to need a tour after dinner," Penny said.

Tanner suddenly looked a little uncomfortable. Probably because he didn't like people poking around just as much as Nigel didn't. Something about snoopers getting burned. I really needed to ask him about that. But I wasn't sure Penny noticed his apprehension. She just smiled and turned to me.

"I got you something," she said. "It's just this small thing. Don't worry, we got you a real wedding present too." She handed me a velvet box.

"Are you proposing to me right now?" I asked with a smile.

She laughed. "Just open it, Matt."

I flipped open the lid. There was a set of plain silver cufflinks. "Thanks," I said. I looked back down at her.

"For James' wedding present to me, he got a tattoo of the date he met me."

"I remember," I said.

"And I was just thinking about that a lot over the last few weeks, with your wedding coming up and everything. And you're one of my best friends, Matt. You always made me feel so welcome here in New York. Even though you were struggling." She started blinking fast, holding back tears. "I feel so awful about how much pain you were in and you faced it all alone. I wish you had let me in sooner, but I understand why you didn't. I just…I want you to know how much I appreciate you. How much I love you. Like a brother," she quickly added with an awkward laugh. "I know it's something old, new, borrowed, and blue for the bride. But I figured it was okay for you to have something new with a memory of old. And I just thought that you should have these. To remember."

To remember what exactly? How much she loved me like a brother? I already knew that. And how was it new *and* old? I smiled at her. I didn't really understand the gift. But unlike Rob, I did have manners. "Well, thank you so much," I said. "These are great." I snapped the lid closed.

She laughed and grabbed the box from my hands. "You didn't even look at them." She opened the lid back up, pulled one of the cufflinks out, and turned it over to show me the inscription. It was dated from Black Friday 16 years ago.

"The day your life stopped." Penny dropped the cufflink in my hand and then pulled out the other. "And the day your life started again. When Brooklyn came back to you." She dropped the second cufflink in my hand.

I stared at the second inscription. The date of the homecoming football game. I swallowed hard.

"I just thought that you fell in love with Brooklyn as a teenager. And you re-fell in love with her now. And it was important to have that be a part of you tomorrow. That you're okay with both halves of your story. That you're at peace with the past. Because you love every side of her. You always have and always will."

"Thank you." My throat suddenly felt all clogged up. I leaned down and hugged her. "These are perfect." Penny had always been good at giving gifts. Even the silly tea kettle she gave me when I was single was great. Because Brooklyn loved tea. We used it almost every day now.

"I'm just so happy that you're so happy, Matt." She hugged me tight.

Tanner sniffed.

I pulled back and looked over at him.

He cleared his throat. "That's a really nice gift, Penny."

She smiled and then shook her head. "I didn't mean to make everyone emotional. I just wanted you to have those for tomorrow. Everyone smile."

I laughed and so did Tanner. But I pulled Penny into another hug. "Thank you, Penny. For always being there.

And this gift really does mean the world to me. I don't know what I would have done without you these past few years."

"Stop, you're going to make me cry."

The flash of a camera made me turn my head.

Kennedy had snapped a picture of Penny and I hugging, both practically in tears.

Penny laughed and released me from her embrace. "Wait, Kennedy, can we have another where we're smiling?"

"Of course," Kennedy said. "Say cheese."

Penny pulled Tanner into the frame, but he dodged out of it just as Kennedy snapped another photo.

Kennedy lowered her camera. "Tanner, I somehow missed you. Squeeze back in."

"No, I'm good," Tanner said and took a sip of his drink.

He was so weird about pictures.

Kennedy shrugged. "Matt, I've been trying to get one of you and Brooklyn together, but Rob keeps making me take pictures with him in them. Do you think maybe you could grab Brooklyn and pose in front of the tree?"

Seriously, what was Rob's deal right now? "Yeah, I'll go get her…" but my sentence was cut off when Nigel ran into the room.

"It's time, it's time!" Nigel declared. He lifted up an old-fashioned horn that looked like it was made from an actual animal horn. He blew it and the sound echoed around the room. Two waiters carried a huge platter overflowing with a strange variety of foods out of the kitchen. Followed by two more waiters with another huge platter. Followed by another set of waiters. They started placing the platters between the cornucopias and white pumpkins on the dining room table.

This was way too much food. And way too much seafood for Thanksgiving. But I was definitely curious about Nigel's world famous biscuits.

Nigel hooked his arm through Kennedy's and pulled her into the dining room with him. She started taking pictures of the tablescape.

I looked around for Brooklyn but she was already being escorted to the table by Rob. *Seriously, what the hell, Rob?* I started walking toward the dining room.

"Are you nervous for tomorrow?" my mom asked as she walked up beside me.

"Not even a little."

She smiled and grabbed my arm to stop me from entering the dining room. "You've always known exactly what you wanted. And gone for it. Your father and I couldn't be more proud of you, Matthew." She leaned forward and kissed my cheek. "And Brooklyn is absolutely glowing."

She was definitely right about that. I watched as Rob pulled out Brooklyn's chair for her and then sat down right next to her.

"Nana, Nana!" Jacob came running up to my mom.

I don't think I'd ever seen my mom smile that big before. I hadn't even realized she'd asked Jacob to call her that.

"Yes, my little prince?" she asked and crouched down in her expensive dress.

"Can I sit between you and my abuela?"

"Of course you can. Come with me." She put her hand out.

Jacob grabbed it. My mom gave me one last smile and then led Jacob over to where Mrs. Alcaraz was already seated.

"It's been 16 years since you showed up for Thanksgiving," Mason said as he stepped up next to me. "This is one hell of a way to bring the tradition back."

I smiled. "You know I'm fond of a grand gesture."

Mason laughed and slapped my back. "Please tell me you're not about to break out into song?"

"Definitely not."

"Are you excited for mom and dad's speech?"

"I didn't realize they were giving one." Mom had just given me a mini-speech already. Maybe she was testing out my reaction.

"Mhm," Mason said. "So Brooklyn's dad's a no-show, huh? Maybe he'll do that thing that James' parents did at James and Penny's rehearsal dinner. Just show up halfway very awkwardly."

"Honestly, I hope he does. Brooklyn really wants him here."

"Really?" Mason shrugged. "She has a bigger heart than the rest of us."

I nodded. Mason had been with me the day I'd been told that Brooklyn had passed away. He'd seen how little her father had seemed to care. It was hard to shake off that memory. It was hard to move forward. I looked down at the velvet box in my hand. But we were moving forward. I put the box in my pocket. "I'll be right back," I said.

"What? Dinner is about to start…"

I hurried out of the room and went down the hall to what had been my bedroom while I was living here. I closed the door behind me. All my stuff was still here because Nigel refused to help me move out. I sat down on the edge of my bed, pulled out my phone, and hit Mr. Pruitt's number.

I knew that Mr. Pruitt was out of cell phone reception or something. But if there was a small chance that he could get reception…I wanted him to hear from me too. The call went straight to voicemail.

I waited for the beep and took a deep breath. "Hi, Mr. Pruitt. It's Matt. Brooklyn really wants you at the wedding tomorrow. It would mean the world to her." I clenched my jaw. This was harder than I thought it would be. "And *I* really want you there." I clenched my jaw again. "I know we're not on the best terms. But I want to move forward. I know you were trying to protect Brooklyn 16 years ago. And even though I don't agree with what you did, I do understand wanting to protect her. I…" my voice trailed off.

I took another deep breath. "I do believe that you love Brooklyn. But you've been doing it in all the wrong ways. If you show up tomorrow though? You'll finally be doing something right. She wants you to walk her down the aisle. She wants her father there."

This was not coming out right. I wasn't trying to reprimand him. I was trying to convince him to show up for once in his fucking life. And if we were ever going to be a family, I knew what I needed to say. If Brooklyn was able to forgive her father, so could I. "I want to leave the past in the past. I want to move forward starting right now. So I just want you to know that I forgive you for the past 16 years, even though you put me through hell. I forgive you, Mr. Pruitt."

There. It was done. I exhaled slowly. Actually, that felt damn good. "Please come to the wedding tomorrow. We want you there." I tried to think of anything else I could say to him that would make him come. "Your daughter needs you." I ended the call.

"Dinner is ready."

I jumped. I hadn't seen Nigel walk in.

"Unless you need a pre-dinner bath?"

"I'm good," I said and stood up. "I'm excited about everything you prepared."

Nigel smiled. "Make sure to try the whole spread of wildfowl. I know how much you like your meats."

"Mhm."

"Everyone is already seated," he said as we made our way out into the hall. "But Robert didn't read the place cards and it's all awry. And the kids aren't at the kids' table. And you and I aren't even sitting at the head of the table together now. Should I reprimand Robert?"

"That's okay, Nigel," I said. "I need to sit with Brooklyn."

"Ah yes, of course. But there are no empty seats near Brooklyn either."

What the hell? I walked into the dining room. It didn't look like any couples were seated together. Nigel was right. This was absolute chaos.

"Actually, Nigel," I said. "Make everyone move."

Nigel pulled his horn out of his back pocket and blew it. "Ladies and gentlemen, dinner shall not be served until you are in your proper seats. Please make your way to your place cards." He blew his horn again.

And everyone actually got up and started moving around. The kids sat around the kids' table, and all the couples started to sit down next to each other. But Rob leaned over the table, swapped his place card with someone else's, and then sat back down next to Brooklyn.

I didn't know what he was up to, but at least there was still an empty seat on the other side of Brooklyn.

"Thanks, Nigel," I said.

Nigel nodded. "All in a day's work." He made his way over to the kids' table and sat down.

Why was he sitting… *Never mind.* Whatever made him happy. I sat down in the empty seat next to Brooklyn. "Hey, baby."

She smiled up at me, but it wasn't one of her normal carefree smiles. She looked nervous. "Hey." She pressed her lips together, like she was forcing herself not to say anything else.

"Is everything alright?"

"Everything is fine," Rob said and leaned forward so I could see him. "Brooklyn and I are having a marvelous evening."

"Why are you being so weird?" I asked.

"Why are *you* being so weird?" he said back.

"Everyone dig in!" Nigel yelled from the kids' table.

Mason laughed. "You don't have to tell me twice." He started to serve himself and then everyone else followed suit.

Brooklyn didn't put any food on her plate though.

"You were looking forward to turkey all day," I said. "Is your stomach bothering you again?"

"Mhm," Rob said and leaned forward. "She was just telling me that."

"Do you want more ginger ale?" I asked, ignoring Rob.

She shook her head, her face growing more pale.

I was getting worried that she was going to throw up on her plate. But she'd barely eaten anything today. I wasn't sure she had anything in her stomach to throw up.

"Do you think it's time?" Rob asked.

"No," Brooklyn hissed.

"Yeah…let's wait a bit."

"Time for what?" I asked.

"Nothing," Rob said and winked at me.

Why was he winking at me? What the hell was going on? "Baby, you really need to eat something." I served her some turkey and mashed potatoes. "Please. For me."

She lifted up her fork and Rob slapped the utensil out of her hand.

"What the hell are you doing?" I said. "She needs to eat."

"Psh. She doesn't need that."

I glared at him. "What the hell does that mean?" Was he calling Brooklyn fat or something? She was pregnant and she was hardly even showing yet. I was going to kill him.

"Sanders knows I think she's hot. Cut it out, Matt."

I needed to cut it out? I put my hand on Brooklyn's thigh and leaned in so I could whisper in her ear. "Blink twice if you're under duress."

She finally laughed and looked up at me, the worry momentarily gone from her eyes. "I love you so much."

"I love you too." I lowered my voice even more. "If Rob is bothering you…"

"He's not. I just… I mean he just…" she shook her head. "I honestly don't think anything could ruin this night, no matter how hard anyone tries."

Rob really did seem to be trying.

"You know, this is a first for me," Brooklyn said with a smile.

"Your first rehearsal dinner." I tucked a loose strand of hair behind her ear. "Hmm." I was starting to like the idea of being her last everything. Because she definitely wasn't going to be having another one of these.

"And I'm going to enjoy myself." Brooklyn took a bite of mashed potatoes and audibly sighed around her spoon.

Fuck. Now all I could picture were her lips wrapped around my cock instead.

"God, I was so hungry." She cut off a piece of turkey and put it in her mouth. She moaned around the meat.

She'd definitely be doing that around my cock later.

"I tried to warn you, Sanders," Rob said. "But I am kind of curious about this eel." He stabbed his fork into the slimy eel on one of the platters. But the fork didn't penetrate it and the eel rolled off the side of the platter.

"Don't make a mess, Rob," I said.

He chuckled. "Oh, I would hardly classify *this* as a mess. Just wait for it."

What the hell did he mean by that? But I had a sinking feeling in my stomach. Rob loved to say that. Right before he did something stupid. I took a deep breath. I was going to kill him if he messed up this dinner.

CHAPTER 33

Thursday

Brooklyn

Rob already had several opportunities to ruin this evening. And he hadn't taken one yet. So I was going to enjoy everything on the platter in front of me. At least everything that I recognized. My stomach was not in an adventurous mood.

"You sure everything is alright?" Matt asked me.

I glanced at Rob out of the corner of my eye. He was busy eating. Just like everyone else. When he'd paraded me around Tanner's living room, I'd jokingly told him the knives on the table looked sharp. Maybe he was actually scared that I'd cut him if he went through with the prank. I mean…it wasn't that far of a stretch. I was from a mobster family.

I would never actually hurt Rob though. And I hoped he'd never hurt me. He knew how I felt about the prank. And for all his teasing…I knew he loved me.

"Everything is great," I said and grabbed a biscuit off one of the trays. "Oh my God, this is so good. I'm going to need Nigel's recipe for these."

"He's pretty shady about his recipes," Matt said. "But these are really good." He took another bite of his biscuit too.

"So you really skipped Thanksgiving for 16 years?" I asked.

Matt took a slow sip of his champagne. "My mom always made the same things for Christmas too. I hardly missed anything."

I knew that wasn't true. He'd missed out on time with his family. Because he was busy missing me. Tonight righted a lot of wrongs.

I glanced down the table to see Jacob giggling with his new friends. I'd been a little worried about today. It was the first big holiday since Miller… I felt the tears immediately welling in the corners of my eyes. I blinked them away.

Today I promised myself I'd focus on the present. Because that was the only way forward. I looked around at all our friends and Matt's family. *My* family. No, my father wasn't here, but I loved everyone in this room. Matt had helped me see that I didn't always lose those I loved. Because I had a whole room full of people here who felt like family.

Someone clinked their knife against their glass. I turned to see Mr. and Mrs. Caldwell stand up.

They were both smiling at me.

"Our son already knows how proud we are of him," Mr. Caldwell said. "And his ego is big enough, so we have a few words for you, Brooklyn."

Matt laughed.

"We know your father couldn't be here," he said.

Couldn't? Didn't want to be? I wasn't sure anymore. I pressed my lips together.

"But we're your family, Brooklyn. We have been since you were a teenager."

The tears were back in my eyes again. I did my best to blink them away.

"And we're so thrilled that you made your way home to us." He could probably tell I was about to burst into tears because he quickly added, "And I feel like I've been waiting forever for grandchildren."

I glanced at Bee. Her cheeks had turned red. I wondered how much pressure she'd been getting from the Caldwells to pop out kids. If there's one thing I knew for sure, pressure did not help the situation. I'd thought about babies nonstop for the past few years. And it wasn't until I stopped thinking about it that I got pregnant again. I put my hand on my stomach.

Matt reached over and put his hand on top of mine.

My whole body felt warm and tingly.

"And now we finally have a grandson," Mr. Caldwell said and smiled at me.

I loved how quickly they'd accepted my son as their own grandson. How open their arms were. I remembered how vehemently Mr. Caldwell didn't want my father's bodyguards in his house. For some reason that made me smile. Miller would always be around now.

"And another on the way." Mr. Caldwell cleared his throat.

"We're both a mess," Mrs. Caldwell said with a laugh. "We love all you boys." She put her hand on James' shoulder. "And we love everyone you all chose to spend your lives with. We're just so…proud of each and every one of you." She put her hand on her heart. "And, Matt. My baby." Her lower lip wobbled as she tried to keep it together. "I feel like I finally have my son back. And I can't ever thank you enough for that, Brooklyn." Her voice cracked.

I couldn't stop the tears now. They started streaming down my cheeks. I grabbed a napkin and blotted my face as Matt put his arm around my shoulders and pulled me closer.

"We love you both," Mr. Caldwell said. "And we're so happy for you. Here's to the happy couple." He lifted his champagne glass.

Matt tapped his glass against my water glass.

I laughed and patted away the rest of my tears. But I knew they'd be back as soon as Mrs. Alcaraz stood up.

"Mi amor," she said. "I know you wish people who are not here could be. Your uncle would have had some words tonight in place of your mother. So I hope I find the right ones in place of both of them."

I was already crying.

"I know you are not my daughter, but you know I love you like my own. Both mis niñas mean the world to me."

I smiled at Kennedy. I smiled even more at the way Felix was staring at her. With stars in his eyes.

"When we lost you, we all broke," Mrs. Alcaraz said. "Everyone at this cena. And now we can heal. Together. And celebrate together. Matthew," she said and turned to him. "I thought you were trouble. Muy problema."

I laughed through my tears. Matt had been trouble in high school. But God I loved him.

Matt's parents found that line extra funny too.

"But I see your corazón." Mrs. Alcaraz tapped the center of her chest. "You're a good boy. A good man. And good for my Brooklyn. I wish you both a lifetime of happiness. Felicitaciones!" She raised her glass.

"Thank you, Mrs. Alcaraz," I said through my tears.

Matt leaned over and kissed my tearstained cheek, chasing away my tears.

"Do you think now is a good time?" Rob whispered beside me.

I ignored him.

"Pst. Brooklyn." He elbowed my side.

I wiped away the rest of my tears and stared at him. "No."

"I think it's a pretty good time." He made an exploding motion with his hand.

What was he going to make explode?! I'd tried to get more details from him, but he said he wanted it to be a surprise for me too. The only thing he'd said was that he had to pull a lot of strings. And now I was wondering if he meant a literal string. Was there a string somewhere that I could hide so that nothing bad would happen? Because if there was, I could stop this whole thing. Whatever this thing was. I pretended to knock my knife to the floor and then bent down to pick it up. My head disappeared beneath the tablecloth as I crawled onto the floor. I looked around for some kind of string dangling from beneath the table. But there was nothing down here. I was just about to look under Rob's chair when he slid under the table too, almost sitting on my face.

"Damn, Sanders. All you had to do was ask if you wanted to have the honor of sucking my dick for your wedding present."

I pushed on his thigh so the front of his pants would get away from my face. "That's not why I'm down here."

"Oh, right, the prank," Rob said as he crouched down next to me. "This way we can talk freely. So is it go time?"

"No. Rob, please don't do this. We're all having such a good evening."

"I mean…you were just crying. I think crying from laughter is always better. I like it when you smile, Sanders."

I smiled. Honestly, both ways of crying were good for the soul. But the last time he'd pulled a Thanksgiving pudding prank, a lot of people had cried for all the wrong reasons. And my life had taken a very traumatic turn. "For my wedding gift, I want you to call this off," I said.

"Too late. Daphne already picked something out for you guys. I'm still offering my cock if you want it though."

"You're ridiculous."

"I love words that have dick in the middle."

I sighed. "I don't know why you're hell bent on doing this prank tonight of all nights. Please don't ruin this for me."

"Please don't ruin it for *me*," Rob said. "I've been waiting 16 years for this moment, Brooklyn."

For a second I let my annoyance float away. That was actually really sweet of him to say. He'd wanted me to come back. He'd wanted me to marry his best friend. He'd been looking forward to our reunion for 16 years. "You've been waiting for tonight for 16 years too, huh?"

"Yeah." He smiled at me and then shook his head. "I can't believe you made me wait 16 years for this prank to come into fruition. Tonight is very important to me, Sanders."

And just like that, I was annoyed again. Of course he was just saying he'd waited 16 years for the favor. "I thought you were being sweet and saying you were excited for tonight because Matt and I are finally getting what we wanted since we were teenagers."

"I mean, of course that's great too. But this prank is going to be *epic*. I even made a playlist."

"What on earth do you need a playlist for?"

"You'll see. We really planned the perfect prank this time."

I sighed. There was no *we* here. I had no idea what the hell he had planned. But I knew I was going to hate it. "Maybe we can make a new deal," I said. I didn't know what else to do. A new deal would probably be awful. He'd probably ask for two favors instead of just one. And one was bad enough. But I was out of options.

Rob shook his head. "As much as I'd love to negotiate a new deal, the plan is already in motion. Nothing can stop it now."

Screw me.

"What the hell are you two doing down here?" Matt asked as he ducked his head under the table.

"Strategizing," Rob said.

Matt shook his head. "Strategizing what exactly?"

"Just wait for it."

"I'm going to need you to tell me what you're planning right now," Matt said.

"Nothing." Rob shrugged.

"I'm serious, Rob."

"So am I," Rob said. "I'm not *currently* planning anything."

Matt sighed. "I know when you say 'just wait for it' that you've done something awful. And I've heard you say that twice tonight. So whatever you're doing…just…don't."

"I'm not *currently* doing anything. But now that you're down here, it does probably look like we're having a threesome under this table, don't you think?" Rob winked at me. "Sanders really wants one last night of sin with her favorite Hunter brother."

"For fuck's sake," Matt said. "Stop talking to my fiancée like that the night before our wedding. And get back up here now," he said sternly to Rob. He pushed the tablecloth up and ducked back up.

"James is my favorite Hunter brother, not you," I said as I crawled back over to my seat.

"You liar. But James' dick is right there." Rob pointed to where James was seated across from us. "And I'm no cock blocker. Go have a taste before you get hitched."

I shoved Rob's arm.

And Rob slapped James' shin to get his attention.

James' chair scooted back and then he dipped his head under the table.

Shit.

"What are you two doing down here?" James asked.

"Talking about your dick," Rob said.

"We were not!" I felt my face turning red.

"We were too," Rob said. "Sanders was just telling me how much she wishes she could suck it before she says 'I do' tomorrow. She's always regretted not hooking up with us."

James laughed. "I'm sure it's the regret of her life."

I scoffed.

He chuckled. "But I know it's much more likely that you were actually down here talking about the prank. And I hope you've called it off."

"Never," Rob said. "The three of us planned a real winner this time."

James shook his head. "I only just found out about it."

"And yet you're down here whispering, looking like our number three."

"Shit." James quickly sat back up.

"You're so immature," I said to Rob.

"I do feel young again." He smiled. "God I love pranks. So about that blowjob…"

He was completely infuriating. "Daphne is going to murder you in your sleep one day."

"Nah, she's too busy riding me for us to ever get a proper night's sleep."

I slapped Rob's arm. "Rob, I'm on my hands and knees. Begging you. Call it off, seriously."

"You're acting like I'm not being serious. I've been so much more serious these last 16 years when you were gone. Now that you're back, I finally feel like me again. It feels like old times. You and me doing this together." Something in his eyes softened.

And the way he was looking at me made my chest ache.

"We were all broken without you. I couldn't even eat pudding for 16 years."

I swallowed hard. I understood that. But…

"I don't want to think about 16 years ago when I think of pudding. I want to remember a fun prank. Not losing you. This will undo all of it the only way I know how. A Hunter Sanders mess around to top the last one and erase it from our memories. I'm doing this for us. So we can move forward. I'm just trying to right my wrong." He had a little frown on his face and he was giving me puppy dog eyes.

Oh, Rob. He was going to make me cry. I hated how much I'd hurt all of them. And in Rob's weird way, this was how he could let all that pain go. I got it. I did. And I could tell by his determination that there was no changing his mind. He said he was doing this for us. I didn't need it. But he did. He needed it in order to move forward. And maybe it wouldn't be so bad.

"Okay," I said with a sigh.

His puppy dog eyes disappeared and he smiled. And it looked so freaking devious. "I knew you'd come around."

"But nothing as bad as last time, right?"

"Just wait for it."

"Promise me."

"Just wait for it," he said again.

I sighed and climbed back up into my seat.

Rob took his time coming back up.

Crap, was there actually a string down there that he was messing with?

When Rob finally reemerged he winked at me.

Tanner stood up and clinked his knife against his glass.

"No fucking way," Rob whispered. "I didn't know he was going to give a speech. This is better than I ever could have imagined. Game time, Sanders." He pulled a small remote out of his pocket.

What the fuck is that for?!

CHAPTER 34

Thursday

Matt

I put my hand on Brooklyn's thigh. I wasn't sure what was going on with Rob tonight, but I hoped he wasn't seriously hitting on Brooklyn.

Not that I didn't deserve it. I did. Karma or whatever. I'd constantly hit on Penny over the last several years. And Daphne and Bee a bit too. But that was different. I'd been a mess. Rob had his shit together. He had a very patient and understanding wife who somehow put up with his shit on a daily basis. He didn't need to be flirting with my fiancée.

Tanner cleared his throat. "I'm so happy to welcome you all into my home for such a special occasion. My best friend is getting married…"

"Oh please," Rob muttered under his breath but loud enough for at least me to hear.

"And I couldn't be happier for you, Matt," Tanner continued. He opened his mouth to continue his speech, but music started playing. Tanner looked around the room in confusion.

The music was playing pretty quietly. It sounded like it was coming from the floor for some reason. Were there speakers beneath the table? Probably a 'billionaire thing' as Tanner would say. I was pretty sure the music was *Dance of the Sugar Plum Fairy* from *The Nutcracker*.

Rob started giggling.

"Nigel, where is that music coming from?" Tanner asked and turned around to look at Nigel at the kids' table.

Nigel shrugged. "From the second story?" He looked up.

I was pretty sure it was coming from beneath us. Or maybe it was above? The music was very disorienting. Wait, there was no second story here…

Rob giggled even louder.

I turned to look at him.

"I got him so good," he whispered to Brooklyn.

Brooklyn just looked confused.

But Rob was barely controlling himself. It looked like he was seconds away from exploding with laughter. I breathed a sigh of relief. Rob loved pranks. But sometimes he went way too small. And this seemed like one of those instances. I'd hardly even classify this as a prank. The music was too quiet to interfere with Tanner's speech. And the music combined with the fairy lights crisscrossing above the table was actually quite magical.

Tanner shrugged. "Anyway, where was I? I am so glad the two of you found your way back to each other. I can't believe I almost made a terrible match for Matt which would have ruined both your lives in the process. Or I guess three lives?" He shrugged like he didn't care.

I was pretty sure that was a weird stab at Kennedy.

"No, four lives," Tanner said. He nodded to himself, like that was definitely the right number.

I guess that included Felix. I was glad that Tanner had been a little rude to Kennedy when we'd dated. She belonged with Felix. And I'd always belonged with Brooklyn.

"All four of you certainly made me work for it. Love was staring you all right in the face and you were all trying to run in the opposite direction or latching on to the wrong person." He shook his head and this time he did look at Kennedy.

Brooklyn and Kennedy both laughed.

Tanner turned his attention back to us. "I really can't remember meeting two people more perfect for each other with so many excuses on why they couldn't be together. But true love always prevails. That's why I started my club in the first place."

Where was he going with this? I wasn't sure this was the right time to talk about his sex club. My parents were here. I cleared my throat and stared at him.

"Right," Tanner said. "I give so many speeches in boardrooms, but not many like this. I've had a ton of best friends over the years, but none as great as Matt."

What other best friends? And why did he have so many?

Tanner smiled, but it looked sad. "I've experienced more love and loss in my life than anyone else here."

I wasn't sure he knew that for a fact…

"And I know moving forward isn't easy. But I am just so proud of you, Brooklyn. For embracing today. For being fearless. For believing that the love Matt has for you isn't replaceable. Because you're not replaceable. You're perfectly…you. And the two of you are a perfect match."

I looked over at Brooklyn. There were tears in her eyes again.

"Even if I can't verify it," Tanner said. "I know it. I've made enough matches over the years to know. This right here is true love in its most pure form. And it's worth waiting a hundred years for. Luckily the two of you didn't need to wait quite that long." He smiled. "And I just wanted to take a minute to congratulate my favorite couple. And to thank you for both being so wonderful to me. You are both so kind and…"

Suddenly the music changed. Tanner looked around again.

I definitely knew this song. It was *Russian Dance* from *The Nutcracker* this time. It started getting louder.

"Where is this coming from?" Tanner asked and looked around again. "I'm so confused."

Rob giggled even louder.

And then the volume increased again and the white pumpkin closest to Tanner exploded, sending brown goo in every direction. Some of it hit him right in the face, speckling his cheeks in brown.

Fuck, was that chocolate pudding?

Everyone near the pumpkin pushed their seats back, trying to get away from the mess.

Tanner wiped his hand across his face, smearing the chocolate pudding.

Rob burst out laughing.

Brooklyn threw her hand over her mouth in horror.

James groaned and shook his head.

Rob started pointing at the pumpkins as one by one they exploded down the length of the table. Each hard note of the violins caused another explosion. Rob kept pointing, acting like he was the conductor of this nightmare.

And I realized he definitely was. *What. The. Fuck. Rob!*

One of the cornucopias exploded, sending chocolate pudding and an assortment of zucchinis flying through the air. A zucchini hit the string lights, causing them to blink and sag down toward the table.

I pushed my seat back and pulled Brooklyn back too as mayhem broke loose.

The pumpkins down the center of the table exploded one after another as Rob kept pointing in rhythm to the music. And then the next cornucopia exploded. Everything in it was decimated this time, chunks of different colored gourds flying everywhere.

One slimy piece hit my cheek as more pudding flew through the air. I tried to block it from Brooklyn, but we both took it in the face.

I tried to wipe it out of my eyes.

"Rob, stop this!" Brooklyn screamed at the top of her lungs.

Rob just laughed. "But you said…"

Someone else screaming drowned out his words.

More lights fell and people started to get tangled up in them as they slipped in the chocolate pudding.

The lights connected to the Christmas tree. And it was only a matter of seconds before the huge tree started to fall. It smashed against the floor-to-ceiling windows in Tanner's living room. For a moment I thought I was going to break through, but it bounced off and slammed onto the couch instead. It knocked over a few candles on an end table in the process, and then the whole tree caught fire.

I instinctively put my hand over my junk, remembering my pants lighting up like a Christmas tree on that blind date from hell.

The blaze quickly spread to the couch. It was nowhere near me, but I still kept my hand in the front of my pants.

"Fire!" someone shouted.

The kids were far away from the mayhem, but they started screaming and running around. Tanner picked up Jacob to make sure he didn't get anywhere near the fire. Everyone else started running toward their kids, slipping in the pudding. I heard someone gagging, but I could barely see. I wiped more pudding out of my eyes.

"Robert Hunter!" Brooklyn yelled.

Nigel sprinted toward the fire with a fire extinguisher, blasting the spreading flames in white.

A crunching noise made me turn my head. Half the table started to fall through the floor. It tilted, sliding all the food, pudding, and any remaining decorations down into the apartment below Tanner's. The candles that teetered over immediately went out though, being snuffed by heaps of pudding. The table looked like the fucking Titanic, sinking into the ocean.

And then the rest of the floor started creaking.

I pulled Brooklyn farther away as the floor beneath the table collapsed, sending everything through with a deafening crash.

Bee almost slipped into the hole, but Mason grabbed her waist, pulling her to his chest as they both toppled backward into more lights. He reached behind him for purchase, and grabbed the corner of a cloth. He pulled downward and the cloth fell from the portrait, revealing Tanner in some kind of old-fashioned military uniform riding a horse.

The music stopped and everything was eerily quiet.

"My relics!" Nigel screamed, breaking the silence. He tossed the fire extinguisher to the side and ran to the edge of the broken floor. He stared down into the hole. I'd never seen Nigel so upset before.

I didn't know what to do. I blinked and looked around at the carnage. All the beautiful lights were flickering off and on. The fire was out, but the tree was still smoking. People were helping each other up off the slippery floor. Everyone was covered in pudding. And there was a fucking hole in the middle of Tanner's dining room floor.

"Good one, Sanders," Rob said.

Brooklyn shook her head.

There was no way Brooklyn had been a part of this...

"Rob, you didn't," Daphne said. She looked so disappointed in him.

"Yeah I did," Rob said. "Best prank ever. A classic Hunter Sanders mess around." He lifted his hand for Brooklyn to high five.

She pushed his hand out of the way. "I did not help with this! You could have killed someone!"

"James?" Rob held up his hand even though James was on the other side of the hole in the floor and couldn't possible high five him.

"You know perfectly well that I had nothing to do with this," he said. "We both tried to stop you."

Brooklyn turned around. "I'm so sorry." She looked back and forth between me and Tanner. "I did try to stop him. But he kept saying I owed him a favor from 16 years ago and he wouldn't listen to reason. And then he gave me puppy dog eyes."

What favor?

"And he said if I told you that he'd do the prank on our wedding day instead," Brooklyn said.

So Rob blackmailed Brooklyn the day before our wedding? Seriously? And did all…*this*? What the hell was wrong with him? I turned to look at Tanner. I was expecting him to freak out. But a smile slowly stretched across his face. And then he started laughing. Jacob looked up at him and started laughing too.

"What are you doing?" Rob asked. "You're not supposed to be laughing."

"It was a prank, was it not?" Tanner said.

"Yeah but…it was on you."

Tanner laughed louder. "Hilarious."

Rob just stared at him. He didn't seem to know what to do with Tanner's reaction. "But…" Rob's voice trailed off. "I set your Christmas tree on fire."

Tanner waved his hand through the air and laughed harder.

"And broke your couch. And blew up all your pumpkin decorations. And ruined your speech. And got chocolate pudding on everything and everyone."

Nigel started laughing too. "Close call. Someone moved all my valuables out of the way. Lucky day for me. Good one, Robert." He patted Rob's chest and then peered into the hole again.

Rob shook his head. "I mean, yeah. It was a good prank. But…" his voice trailed off again.

"Good one, Young Robert," Tanner agreed.

"I sent your dining room table through your floor, man," Rob said. "Into your weird storage room down there. It's complete chaos."

"But you moved all my things out of the way first," Nigel said. "Very respectful prank."

"Indeed." Tanner nodded. "And you didn't even ruin my favorite portrait." He pointed to the one of him on the horse. "Everything else is replaceable."

Rob stared at it and then turned back to Tanner. "I caused hundreds of thousands of dollars of damage, man."

Tanner laughed. "Who cares? It was funny."

Rob just gaped at him.

"That's like pennies to me, son."

And I couldn't help but laugh too. Tanner not caring about the carnage was more hilarious than the prank itself. And my laughing made Brooklyn laugh. And soon everyone was laughing as they wiped chocolate pudding off themselves. The news of it being pudding must have traveled quickly, since so many of us were there during that original chocolate pudding prank.

"You're seriously not mad?" Rob asked.

Tanner kept laughing.

"Au contraire," Nigel said and peered down the hole. "Master Tanner has been wanting to replace this table for years. And my schedule was very busy and I had no time to figure out how to get it out of here. You saved me some time. I'll leave it in the storage room. Thanks for the assistance."

Rob shook his head. "I don't believe this," he said. "You're not supposed to be thanking me. Look at your Christmas tree." He pointed into the living room.

"The foam actually looks a bit like snow," Tanner said.

Brooklyn laughed. "It really does." She turned to Rob. "Feel better now?" she asked.

Rob smiled and shrugged.

I wasn't sure what that was about, but Rob exhaled slowly and it looked like a weight had been lifted off his shoulders.

"Speaking of foam, we all need to clean off," Nigel said. "Let's go to the pool. I'll put bubbles in it. It'll be like a huge tub!" He looked so excited before he turned around and ran down the hall to their indoor pool.

This was the most ridiculous rehearsal dinner ever.

Brooklyn slid her hand into mine. "Race everyone to the big tub!" she yelled and started running, pulling me with her.

I couldn't help but laugh

"What favor was Rob referring to?" I asked as we ran down the hall. We'd gotten a good head start on everyone else.

"Remember that party at your house sophomore year? Rob bet me I would scream his name. I had no intention of ever doing that. But then he pushed me into your bedroom. Which was dark. And I didn't know you were there. I was scared and banged on the door, calling his name to let me out."

I shook my head. That was such a cheap bet by Rob. And to hang it over her head 16 years later? Actually…that sounded just like him. "And the asking him if he felt better thing?"

We ran in silence for a moment. "He wanted to undo his wrong 16 years ago. With another prank. To erase the prank 16 years ago from our memories." She smiled to herself. "It looked like it helped. I hope it did. Because we're not doing that again."

I laughed. Yeah, we were all trying to undo a lot of wrongs. But I did feel bad about all the damage to Tanner's place. It was a good thing he'd just thought it was funny. "It definitely looked like it helped him."

I pulled Brooklyn to a stop and opened the door to the pool. It was already overflowing with bubbles.

"This is so cool," Brooklyn said. She looked up at me. "I don't have a ton of great memories of you and pools. It seems fitting that we make that right tonight too."

"How can I right that wrong?" I asked. Tonight had suddenly turned into a time for healing old wounds. And it seemed fitting before the wedding to make amends. I wanted her to forget about whatever the hell she'd seen with Jen. It meant nothing. And I hated how something that meant so little had changed everything for us.

"Well, there was one thing I wish I'd done," Brooklyn said.

"Yeah?" I raised my eyebrow.

"Oh, yeah." She put her hands on my chest and then pushed me backward into the pool.

I laughed as I fell backward, splashing into the water. When I rose to the surface Brooklyn was jumping in. I pulled her into my arms as everyone else finally made it to the pool.

"Cannon ball!" Rob yelled and splashed into the water next to us. The water turned brown around him which made me laugh.

He came to the surface. "I'm free!" he yelled at the top of my lungs.

I thought I'd be mad at Rob. But I understood what he was trying to do. I understood that we all needed closure from 16 years ago in our own way. I should have known his way would be destructive. I hadn't realized it, but he'd been holding on to that pain for a long time. Especially since I'd forbid my friends from even talking about Brooklyn.

It was also easy not to be upset with him when Tanner was so cool with everything. And Brooklyn seemed happy too. Besides, ending tonight this way actually felt kind of perfect. I couldn't think of a more memorable rehearsal dinner.

Everyone started jumping in. Screaming and splashing water.

"Bath time!" Nigel yelled and belly flopped into the pool.

I shook my head. That man and his baths.

Brooklyn wrapped her legs around my waist. "We're getting married tomorrow!" she shouted over the noise.

I dropped my lips to her ear. "Just so you know…Tanner was right. I would have waited a hundred years to have you in my arms again."

Brooklyn's cheeks flushed.

The bubbles grew around us, blocking us from seeing anyone else. We were in our own little world. Just the two of us.

"Next time I do something wrong, push me in the pool right away," I said. "No reason to wait 16 years."

She laughed. "Now *that* I can promise. As long as you re-promise me something."

"Anything," I said.

"Don't break my heart, Matthew Caldwell."

CHAPTER 35

Friday

Brooklyn

I stared at Matt sleeping peacefully beside me. The light streaming in through the blinds made his hair look lighter. It made him look more like the boy I knew back in high school. My first love. My first kiss. My first time. The boy I promised all my firsts too. The boy whose heart I broke.

Tanner's words had been swirling around in my head all night. During his toast, he said the love Matt had for me wasn't replaceable. It was the second time he'd told me that. The first time was at the homecoming game when I saw Matt again for the first time since coming back to New York. I think Tanner brought it up last night because he wanted to remind me. He knew there were two sides to today. Joy and pain. He was probably worried I'd be a runaway bride or something.

But I wasn't really focused on his words from last night. My mind had settled on something else he'd said to me at the homecoming game. That I'd had a great love *twice*. That I was one of the lucky ones. And yes, I lost it. But only once. Matt never stopped loving me.

And I'd never stopped loving him.

My heart still had a hard time admitting that. But it was true. I'd never stopped loving Matthew Caldwell. As soon as I gave him my heart, it was done. He owned a piece of it.

And lying here in bed on the day of my wedding, I still loved Miller. Just like when I'd said 'I do' in the snow to Miller, I still loved Matt.

Apparently I was one of the lucky ones. Who knew that luck could feel so painful?

I took a deep breath and exhaled slowly.

But Matt knew my heart. He knew *me.* And he still wanted me just as much now as he did back in high school. I took another deep breath. I couldn't wait to marry him tonight.

He slowly opened his eyes and smiled when he saw me. "Were you watching me sleep?"

"Maybe," I said with a smile.

"I still think it's bad luck to sleep together the night before the wedding."

"No." I was lucky. Tanner said so. And I'd learned that Tanner was right about most things. "I don't think that sounds right."

He reached out and put his hand on my cheek as he stared at me. I loved when he looked at me like that. Like he adored me.

"I would have risked it either way," Matt said. "I don't ever want to wake up without you by my side ever again."

"I feel like I'm seconds away from crying or laughing. My emotions are haywire. Today is going to be crazy."

"Laugh. Cry. As long as you're happy."

"I'm very happy." I leaned forward and kissed the tip of his nose. "How could I not be? I'm marrying the most eligible bachelor in the city."

Matt laughed. "Hardly."

"I saw a tabloid with that exact headline the other day."

He shook his head.

"At least it didn't say most notorious playboy in the city."

Matt tickled my side.

I squealed as I tried to get away from him. But he caught my arms and pinned me against the bed beneath him.

For a few seconds we just stared at each other as we caught our breaths. And I wondered if he wanted to freeze time as badly as me. Because I always wanted to smile this hard.

"I was a little worried about this morning," he said slowly as his eyes searched mine.

"Why?"

"I thought you might be…sad."

I shook my head. "I'm so happy. Right here. Right now. With you."

He leaned down and kissed my forehead. "I have something for you."

"Is it another tickle attack?"

He laughed and shook his head. "No, I'll save that for later." He climbed off of me and grabbed a wrapped box out of his nightstand.

"What is this?" I asked.

"My wedding present for you." He placed the small box in my hands.

Wedding present? What was a wedding present? No one had told me about this. I didn't have a present for him. I couldn't believe I didn't know about this tradition. A million thoughts ran through my head at once. What the hell could I give him at the last minute? All I could think about was the fact that I was pregnant with our baby. That seemed like the best possible present, but he already knew about that…

"Open it," he said.

I slowly unwrapped the box. My mind was completely blank. Seriously, why didn't I know about wedding presents? I lifted the lid on the box.

It was the most beautiful necklace I'd ever seen. A huge teardrop blue sapphire was surrounded with diamonds. I don't think I'd ever even held something so expensive before.

"Old. New. Borrowed. Blue."

I looked up at him.

"The sapphire is new and blue," Matt said. "The chain is my mom's, so it's borrowed. Although I'm sure she wouldn't mind if you kept it. And the diamonds were on a bracelet I found in one of your mom's boxes. I had the jeweler be extra careful in case you want to put them back on the bracelet..."

"Matt," my voice cracked. "This is perfect. It's so beautiful." I lifted the necklace out of the box. I'd wanted a piece of my mom with me today, and he'd made sure I had it. "Thank you." God, he'd gotten me this perfect custom piece of jewelry and I'd gotten him...nothing.

"Let me." He lifted it from my hands.

I pushed my hair out of the way and he clasped it behind my neck. It fell right between my clavicle bones. It was going to look perfect with my dress. And my head was completely scrambled as I tried to figure out what I could give him.

"Beautiful," Matt whispered. But he wasn't even looking at the necklace. He was just staring at me.

"Close your eyes," I said.

"What?"

"Close your eyes," I said again.

He smiled and closed his eyes.

God, why had I asked him to do that? Now he was expecting something amazing for sure. And my mind was coming up empty. I grabbed my cell phone and ran out of the room. I closed the bedroom door behind me to make sure Matt couldn't hear me. And then I hit Tanner's number. One of Matt's best friends would surely have an idea.

"Hey," Tanner said. "Is everything okay?"

"No."

"What's wrong?" He sounded very concerned.

"Sorry, yes. Everything is fine. But Matt just got me the sweetest wedding present. And I didn't know wedding presents were a thing. And I..." my voice trailed off. "What should I do? I can't think of anything as amazing as the necklace he got me. I can't believe I didn't know people exchanged presents the morning of their wedding."

There was a long pause.

"Tanner? Are you still there?"

"I was just thinking," he said. "But I got it."

"Yeah?"

"Head."

"What?"

"Give him head."

I laughed. "Hilarious."

"I'm serious. Just give him head."

"You're not helping."

"That's all any man really wants anyway."

He was definitely not being helpful. But whatever. I had more people to ask. Maybe Rob was right and he really was still Matt's best friend, not Tanner. "Thanks, Tanner. Gotta go, bye." I hung up the phone and called Rob.

"Hey, Sanders. Get the rest of the chocolate pudding out of your hair?"

I ignored him. "I didn't get Matt a wedding present."

"Why?"

"Because I didn't know it was a thing!" I hissed. I looked over my shoulder to make sure the door was still closed. "What should I do? I need something last minute and he got me something so sentimental..."

"Easy," Rob said cutting me off. "Just give him head."

"What?" *Seriously?* How did Rob and Tanner not realize how similar they were?

"A blowjob."

"I know what head is," I said. "I need something sentimental."

"Give him really good head so he'll always remember it then."

"You're not helping."

"It's all he really wants, Sanders. It's all any guy wants as a gift. If you need to practice on someone first I could be over in a few minutes…"

"No thank you."

"Want me to call James to come give you some practice instead?"

"Of course not," I said.

"Well, I'm sure Mason would be up for it too. But I'd really recommend a Hunter brother for this since our cocks are bigger."

"You're the worst."

"You know you love me. Go give my boy a good memory. See you later." He hung up.

Gah, Rob. I would have called Mason, but I was worried he'd say the same thing. And I really didn't want to call James and talk about head on my wedding day. I sighed. Maybe Matt's friends were right. They did know him. And an idea was finally forming in my head.

I walked back to the bedroom and opened the door. "Eyes still closed?" I asked.

"Mhm," Matt said.

I opened the door the rest of the way. His eyes were closed and he was resting the back of his head against the headboard. I hurried over to one of his drawers and started rummaging through it. I opened another and another until I found what I was looking for.

I pulled off the old t-shirt I'd slept in and exchanged it for Matt's jersey. Then I slid into the blue high heels I was going to wear with my wedding dress tonight. I spun toward him and put my hand on my hip, doing my best to make this look sexy and planned.

"Open your eyes, handsome," I said.

He opened his eyes and groaned. His eyes trailed down my exposed thighs.

Tanner and Rob were right apparently. "Something old." I pressed the tips of my fingers against the front of jersey. "Something new." I gestured to my heels and then started walking toward him, making sure to sway my hips. "Something borrowed." I pointed to the jersey again. "And something blue." The jersey and the shoes were both blue.

Matt smiled. "You look so hot in my jersey, baby. Come here." He gestured toward the bed.

I shook my head. "No, you come here." I hooked my finger, calling him to me.

He pushed the covers off the bed and climbed off.

All he was wearing was a pair of boxer briefs. And I could already see the outline of his growing erection. He leaned down to kiss me, but I put my hand on his chest.

"I need to give you the rest of your present first," I said and dropped to my knees. I looked up at him as my fingers ran along the waistband of his boxers.

I wasn't sure I'd ever seen so much hunger in his eyes before. Hunger for me.

I pushed his boxers down. His erection sprung free, almost hitting me in the face. No, this wasn't a sentimental gift. But I was going to make it memorable. I licked my lips as I looked up at him.

His Adam's apple rose and then fell as he watched me on my knees. He had a way of always making me feel desired. And I wanted him to know I desired him just as much.

Normally I'd start slow. A few kisses and licks, teasing him. But this wasn't about teasing him. It was about giving him everything he wanted. So I lifted my lips to his tip, opened my mouth, and went all the way down.

"Fuck," he groaned and buried his fingers in my hair.

He usually guided me, setting the pace. But I knew what he liked. I moved up and down his shaft faster and faster. The gift he'd given me had been so sweet. What I was giving him wasn't. But I was going to make it unforgettable. I massaged his balls with one hand and gripped his ass with my other, trying to give myself more leverage.

Matt's fingers tangled in my hair and he pulled my head back. "Get on the bed. Now."

I knew what he was telling me to do. He wanted me to spread my legs so he could fuck me. But this wasn't about my pleasure. I shook my head.

He raised his eyebrow at me.

"You can have me tonight after we say 'I do.' But right now, I'm taking care of *you*." I pulled off his jersey and tossed it on the floor beside me. All I had on were my high heels now. "I want you to cum all over me." I kissed the side of his cock. "I want it dripping down my chin onto my tits. I want you to claim me everywhere." I wrapped my lips around him again.

"Brooklyn," he groaned. "Fuck, just like that."

I knew he was close. His breathing was growing more labored and he was gripping my hair even harder. I let him guide me now, letting him fuck my face just the way he liked.

His fingers tightened in my hair and he pulled me back as he wrapped his hand around his cock. "You want me to drench every inch of you, baby?"

I nodded up at him. I watched him stroking himself. God, I wanted him inside me so badly. I could feel myself dripping. But that would just make tonight even better. Waiting all day to have him. I was already desperate. Tonight was going to be explosive.

He stroked himself faster and his first shot landed right on my chin, dripping down onto my breasts like I'd requested. Shot after shot landing on my chest and stomach.

I didn't know I was supposed to get him a present. But it had worked out for the best, because he definitely seemed to like this. One last shot landed against my lips. I licked my bottom lip and he groaned.

"There is nothing hotter than you in my jersey, baby. Well, except your naked body covered in my cum." His eyes raked over me.

"Just wait until you see me in my wedding dress."

CHAPTER 36

Friday

Matt

Scarlett opened the door when I knocked. "Hi, Uncle Matt! Hi, Jacob!"

I sighed. "Kiddo, we've been over this. You really shouldn't be opening the door."

I set Jacob down on the ground. Luckily the building wasn't as many floors as Tanner's. But I was still a little out of breath.

Scarlett shrugged. "Okay, I won't."

But the shrug kind of contradicted her words.

"What do you want to play?" she asked. "Kickball?"

Jacob nodded.

Scarlett rarely offered to play anything but Barbie with me. She was much sweeter to Jacob. But we weren't here to play.

"Come on, guys," she said and turned to start running down the hall.

Penny walked out of the kitchen just in time to grab her. "Nope, no kickball in the house."

"Can we go to the park then?" Scarlett asked.

"Not today. We're on our way to Aunt Brooklyn's."

I smiled. It was the first time I'd heard anyone call Brooklyn that.

"But I want to play kickball with Jacob and Uncle Matt," Scarlett said.

"As fun as that sounds…" Penny smiled at me and then looked back down at Scarlett. "You get to get ready for the wedding with all girls and you finally get to wear your yellow dress."

Scarlett's eyes grew round. "Okay, Mommy, you have a deal."

She was terrible at negotiating. But I'd teach her more about making proper boardroom deals after the wedding.

"James!" Penny called over her shoulder. "We're heading out."

James walked into the hall in nothing but boxers. He was taking the skin on skin thing a little too seriously. But Liam was sleeping peacefully in his arms.

"See you in a few hours." He kissed Penny's cheek. "And be good, pumpkin," he said to Scarlett and kissed the top of her head.

"I'm always good," Scarlett said.

Eh. She'd literally just answered the door even though she knew it was against the rules.

But James didn't disagree with her.

Penny pushed a little hair off of Liam's forehead. "Have fun guys," she said. "If you need anything just call me." Which was code for: If Liam wakes up and starts crying, I'll come back to help.

But we had this.

Jacob watched the two of them walk out the door, his eyes trained on Scarlett the whole time.

She waved down at him and then blew him a kiss.

Jacob's cheeks turned rosy.

It was the cutest thing ever.

Jacob turned toward me after the door closed. "Can't I go with Scarlett? Pleeeeease?"

"Nope," James said. He didn't seem to think it was as cute as I did.

"You get to get ready with all the guys," I said. "I promise it'll be fun."

Jacob eyed James warily.

And so did I. "Where are your pants, man?" I asked him.

"I'll change into my tux in a few hours."

"Changing kind of requires an outfit *change*. Not just putting on clothes."

James laughed. "Liam burped up on my shirt earlier."

That still didn't explain his lack of pants. But it was his house. I just didn't want to give Jacob any ideas. He'd finally started wearing clothes thanks to Tanner's Odegaard line that I was pretty sure was exclusively for Jacob.

"Don't worry, Jacob," James said. "We're going to have fun."

"Are we playing football again?" Jacob asked.

Brooklyn would kill me if we played football right before the wedding. We were lucky James and Rob's faces were good at not swelling. Or Nigel's juice had just worked its wonders. Also, I was pretty sure Penny wouldn't love us breaking everything in her living room.

Rob walked in without knocking, holding RJ in his arms. RJ's eyes were closed and he was sniffling, like he'd been crying the whole way here. And I was grateful for the distraction. Maybe Jacob would forget about playing football for a few minutes.

"Coach." Jacob tugged on my hand. "Is Axel coming?"

Jacob did not seem that excited to hang out with a bunch of babies. Which I understood. Especially since they were both sleeping. "No," I said. "But he'll be at the wedding later. And your abuelo will be here any minute."

Jacob's eyes lit up.

"Why do you call Tanner your abuelo?" Rob asked.

"Because he's my abuelo," Jacob said.

"But like...why?"

Jacob shrugged. "Because he is."

"What about your actual grandfather? Mr. Pruitt?"

Jacob lowered his eyebrows. "Me and my daddy don't like him. If I see him again I'm going to have to hit him again."

Whoa, what? "Did you hit Mr. Pruitt?"

Jacob nodded. "Yeah. When I met him. I hit him like this." He threw his fist out toward me, but stopped an inch in front of my nuts. "Like my daddy taught me."

Holy hell. Jacob was a little boss.

Rob laughed. "Are you seriously telling me that you hit Mr. Pruitt in the nuts?"

Jacob looked confused.

"Right there," Rob said and pointed to my groin. "In the nuts."

Stop pointing at my dick, man. I pushed his arm away.

"Yessie," Jacob said. "I punched him right in the nuts."

"That's amazing." Rob laughed. "I think we've all wanted to do that in our lives."

James put his hand up for a high five and Jacob high fived him.

"Mommy hit him too," Jacob said. "She gave him a black eye."

I knew about that one. Honestly, it kind of made sense that Mr. Pruitt had skipped town. He was probably sick of being hit by his family members. I probably should have told Jacob not to hit his grandfather. We were trying to move forward with Mr. Pruitt. But it wasn't really my place. If his father had told him to do it, I was going to respect Miller's wishes.

James smiled. "You're a good kid, Jacob. Come on, let's go hang out in the family room." Everyone started walking out of the hall. A few minutes ago he didn't like the way Jacob was looking at his daughter. But now he seemed thrilled with Jacob. He probably thought Jacob would be a little bodyguard for Scarlett.

I knew James hated the way Axel seemed smitten with his daughter. They were just kids, but James was reading this wrong. Jacob looked at Scarlett with stars in his eyes. The same way Axel looked at Scarlett. Scarlett was going to be trouble when she grew up if she already had two boys obsessed with her. James was probably going to try to lock her at the top of a tower when she turned 13.

I sat down on the couch and Rob plopped down beside me and handed me RJ.

RJ was sound asleep now, his sniffling done.

"It's weird how much like you he is," Rob said.

I looked up from RJ. "I swear I didn't have sex with Daphne."

Rob laughed. "I meant Jacob, not RJ. But good to know."

I looked over at Jacob who was tossing a football up and down. I smiled. Yeah. He was a little piece of me.

The bell rang and James went to go answer the door.

"Did you have a good morning?" Rob waggled his eyebrows at me.

"Um…yes? What are you doing with your face?"

Rob laughed. "I've just always wondered how good Brooklyn was at giving head. I mean, probably better now than she was in high school. A lot more practice and what not."

I didn't love thinking about that.

"On a scale of one to ten," Rob said. "Hit me."

"Are you watching our security feed or something?"

"Nah," was all he offered.

I'd change the password, but only Nigel had access to it. I'd have to talk to him about that. "A ten," I said. God, she was so fucking sexy with her lips wrapped around my cock.

"Knew it."

"Knew what?" Mason asked. He and Tanner had both walked into the room.

"I was just asking about how good Brooklyn is at giving head," Rob said.

Tanner smiled. "I'm guessing you had a good morning, Matt?" He winked at me.

"Why does everyone know I got head this morning?"

"Because Brooklyn called me," Rob said.

At the same time, Tanner said: "Because Brooklyn called me for some advice."

They glared at each other.

"She called *you*?" Rob said and stood up.

"Probably first," Tanner said.

"Lies," Rob said. "I'm Matt's best friend so she called *me* about giving him head."

Why was Brooklyn calling any of them about this?

Tanner shook his head. "If she called you about giving him head it was because I already suggested it to her..."

Mason laughed. "All this best friend talk. While I'm sitting here as the best man." He sat down next to me, stealing Rob's seat.

"I'm sorry, why was Brooklyn talking to you two about blowjobs?" I asked.

Rob and Tanner looked at each other.

Rob sighed. "She wanted to know what to get you for a wedding present because she didn't know they were a thing. And needed something last minute."

I opened my mouth and closed it. So that's why she left the bedroom for a while this morning. She didn't need to get me anything. Her marrying me was the best gift possible. But I did really love this morning.

"Young Robert, I never took you for a snitch." Tanner looked very disappointed in him.

"I'm not a snitch. But I'm not going to lie to my friend."

"Brooklyn is our friend too."

"I don't like the *our* in your sentence."

Tanner shrugged.

"Which one of you told her I'd get off if she wore my jersey?" I asked. Because honestly, whoever gave her that advice *was* my best friend.

Mason laughed. "Damn that's hot."

"Sexy," Rob said. "But I didn't tell her that."

Tanner shook his head. "Me neither. I would have told her to wear a football jersey."

I knew he meant soccer by that. But that meant that no one had told her to dress up. They'd just told her to give me head. I smiled. I said whoever told her to wear my jersey was my best friend. It made sense that Brooklyn had come up with it all by herself. She knew me best.

***

I never thought this day would come. It's what I'd always wanted. But for 16 years I'd given up on it. I'd given up on living.

There was a knock on the door. "It's almost time," Mason said from the other side. "You ready?"

"Yeah, one second." I finished putting on my tie and then opened the door. Mason was dressed just like I was. In a navy tux with a yellow tie. The tie matched the yellow bridesmaid dresses. "Could you help me with these?" I handed him the box of cufflinks that Penny had given me as I finished buttoning my vest.

Mason popped open the lid and pulled one of the cufflinks out. He stared at the inscription but didn't say anything. He put one on and then the next, not saying anything about the second inscription either.

I slid my tuxedo jacket on and straightened my lapels.

"Were those from Brooklyn?" Mason asked.

I shook my head. "No. Penny."

He smiled. "Figures."

"The day my life stopped. And the day my life started again." But today felt the most momentous to me. Everything had led me to this point.

Mason folded his arms and leaned back against the vanity. "I was worried about that for a while."

"Worried about what?"

"Penny."

Yeah, all my friends had been worried about that.

"You put me in a very awkward position," Mason said. "And I think I would have had to beat the shit out of you if you ever tried to pull something on her."

I laughed. I'd certainly thought about it. I'd tried to fill this hole in my heart with anything I possibly could. My crush on Penny was probably the most destructive though. Because it would have hurt all my friends. Penny included. And James and I had been through enough fighting for one lifetime.

"But it was hard to be mad at you when you were walking around like your life was over," Mason said. "I'm so glad Brooklyn came back."

"Me too." I think I'd always have a hard time thinking about the time she'd chosen to stay away. But the important thing was that she'd come back to me. And that was all that fucking mattered.

Mason cleared his throat. "And here you are saying that you're ready, and your tie isn't even straight." He adjusted my tie for me. "There. Let's do this thing." He cleared his throat again.

My brother was not an emotional guy. But I could tell he felt it today. I'd put him through hell the past 16 years. I think I'd worried him the most because he saw me the most. "Thank you, man."

He nodded. Like he knew I was thanking him for more than straightening my tie.

We walked out of the bathroom, down the hall, and into James' living room. My father and all my friends were all dressed, standing around talking. Except for Nigel.

"Where is Nigel?" I asked. He'd been popping in and out all afternoon, but he promised he'd be ready on time. I had no idea where he'd been running off to all day.

James turned around in a circle. "I swear he was just here. Liam was crying and he quieted him down."

"He was definitely here a minute ago," Rob agreed.

"I think he may have said to just meet him at the venue," Tanner said. He snapped his fingers. "That was definitely it. He's just helping out with last minute stuff, I'm sure."

"Should we leave him a note just in case?" I asked.

"The door will be locked," James said.

"A note on the door then."

"Sure, I guess," Tanner said. He pulled a pad of sticky notes out of his pants' pocket and grabbed a pen from his breast pocket. He quickly scrawled something across the note. "There. That'll do."

I could only see the note out of the corner of my eye, but I swear it said: "Stop it right now before they pull out the binoculars!"

Who the hell would be bringing binoculars to the wedding? Nigel was so strange sometimes.

"Looking dapper, Matt," Tanner said as he walked toward the door to hang his note.

I laughed since we were all dressed exactly the same. Jacob was in a miniature version of the same tux too.

"You ready, son?" my dad asked and put his hand on my shoulder.

I nodded and looked down at Jacob. "You ready?" I asked him.

He nodded. "Ready, Coach."

CHAPTER 37

Friday

Brooklyn

"Brooklyn." Kennedy's voice cracked. "You look so beautiful."

I had dreamt so much of today. Both recently and 16 years ago right around this time. And here I was. Standing in the same wedding dress I'd picked out all those years ago. I stared at the new deep V of the neckline. Justin had been right. The tulle material made it classy. It also made it very easy to see my old wedding ring and engagement ring. They were dangling from the gold chain Matt had bought me to hold them. I blinked fast, trying my best not to ruin the makeup Justin had expertly put on me.

I felt whole.

I felt broken.

I had no idea how I could feel both at the same time. My fingers dropped to the center of my chest. The gold chain holding my rings clashed with the necklace Matt had given me this morning. I would miss Miller every day for the rest of my life. He would be with me every day. I clasped the rings in my fist.

But I couldn't think about Miller today. If I did, I was worried I wouldn't be able to walk down the aisle to Matt. And as much as it killed me, I needed to focus on the present. It's what Miller wanted. I felt my bottom lip trembling.

"Can you unclasp this chain?" I asked.

Kennedy put her hand on top of my fist. "You don't have to."

I took a deep breath. Actually, I did. Matt knew I'd never stop loving Miller. He didn't need that reminder today though. Today was about us. "Please."

Kennedy didn't say anything else. Her hand dropped from mine and she slowly unclasped the chain. She placed the rings and chain in my hand.

I'd put it back on tomorrow. I tucked the rings into a drawer and turned back to Kennedy.

"Are you okay?" she asked.

I nodded. "Could I actually have a minute alone?"

"Of course." She hugged me tight and then closed my bedroom door behind me.

I opened the drawer I'd just put my ring in and pulled out the letter Miller had written me. I needed to remember his words. Exactly how he'd said them.

Hey Kid,

Fuck. I stopped reading. I couldn't read the whole letter. My tears were already threatening to fall after that one line. I just needed to find the part about Matt. I scanned down the letter.

I'll always love you. And I know you loved me too. I know that. Don't ever doubt that. I knew.

But you have to do what your mom told you. You have to keep living. I've given this a lot of thought. And I need you to hear me say this. I know there was someone before me. I know you still think about him sometimes. I just want you to be happy. And safe. And I want the same for Jacob. This isn't easy for me to say, but I need you to know that I'm okay if you choose him now. Because I never want you to stop smiling.

The tears were streaming down my face now. Justin was going to kill me. But I skipped down to the end of the letter and kept reading anyway.

And when you miss me, just look up at the stars. Because we were always written in them.

Yes, we promised each other forever. But we both know forevers are sometimes cut short. So you need to forget about all those promises. The only thing I want you to do is keep living. Embrace life. Be happy. Be so blissfully happy every day that you have. Don't waste another second of your time on this earth. Will you promise me that? Do this one last thing for me?

Keep living, kid.

Love always,

-Miller

"I promise," I whispered out loud through my tears. I let my face fall into my hand as I kept crying. I pictured dancing with Miller in the kitchen. And swimming with him in the lake. And staring up at the stars together in our garden. It was almost like I could feel his arms around me if I closed my eyes tight enough. Like he was right here with me. Snuggling in front of a warm fire. "I promise I'll keep living, Miller." I opened my eyes and the image of him beside me vanished.

There was a knock on the door.

I quickly put the letter back in the drawer and closed it.

Justin walked in. "Kennedy said you might need me…" his voice trailed off. "Oh no."

I waited for him to scold me.

Instead he opened up his arms. "Come here, gorgeous."

I closed the distance between us and hugged him.

He held me for a minute, rubbing his hand up and down my back. "I actually have someone on the phone for you," Justin said.

"What?" I pulled back.

He was holding his cell phone in one hand. I'd been too busy crying to notice. He placed it in my hand. "Talk to him while I fix your face. No more crying, deal?"

I nodded. God, Matt always knew when I needed him. "Hey, Matt, I…"

Justin smiled at me as he wiped beneath my eyes with a wet cloth.

And the person on the other end of the line cleared their throat. "Brooklyn," said Tanner. "I can get Matt if you want but I was hoping I could talk to you first."

I smiled. I should have known it was him. He was the first person I really opened up to when I came back to New York. And he had a really good habit of showing up exactly when I needed him.

"I just had a feeling you might need to talk before the ceremony."

"Thank you, Tanner. I was just reading the letter…"

"Miller's letter?"

I exhaled slowly. "Yeah."

"Oh, Brooklyn." He sounded so sympathetic, even through the phone. "Are you okay?"

"I just wanted to read the part about Matt. Miller was giving me his blessing. He wanted me to keep living. And I just needed to remember that. I need to remember that most days," I said with a sad laugh.

"Of course that's what Miller wanted. Humans have such a bad habit of wasting time, even though their time on this earth is so fleeting."

I laughed. He always said stuff like that. As if he wasn't one of us mere mortals. "Does Matt seem nervous?"

"No," Tanner said firmly. "He's wanted you and only you since he was 16 years old."

His words eased the ache in my chest. "I know."

Justin started fidgeting with a few strands of my hair even though I was pretty sure I hadn't messed it up. I'd left it down and Justin had put some loose curls in it. It was the same way I'd worn it back in high school. Only a million times better with Justin's help.

"Remember what I told you?" Tanner asked. "That you're one of the…"

"One of the lucky ones," I said. "Yes. Because I got to experience a great love *twice*."

"Exactly. And it's okay to love both of them equally. I think I may have forgotten to mention that bit before. It's okay that you loved Matt when you were married to Miller. And it's okay that you will continue to love Miller when you're married to Matt. It's okay, Brooklyn. No one is asking you to forget. No one wants you to erase your past with Miller. Matt loves you exactly the way you are right now in this moment."

I nodded and Justin grabbed both sides of my face so I'd stop moving. I smiled at him.

He tsked me and grabbed a makeup brush.

"Thank you, Tanner," I said. Tanner had told me exactly what I'd needed to hear.

"So you're not getting cold feet?" he asked.

I laughed. "Definitely not."

"Good, good. Because I'm not sure I could pick up the pieces a second time. Matt needs you."

"And I need him." I smiled and put my hand on my stomach. We both needed him. And Jacob too. *The four of us against the world.* I smiled, thinking of my mom.

"And Brooklyn?"

"Yes?"

"Is Nigel with you? Matt is getting nervous about where he keeps running off to. And I'm assuming he's with you."

I laughed. "He is. I'll tell him to head back to you guys." Nigel had been so wonderful all day. Popping in and out to make sure I didn't need anything. Even though he was a groomsman and should have been focusing on Matt.

"I will let your ladies take it from here. I'll see you soon."

"Thanks, Tanner. For…everything."

"Anything, for my best friend's friend," he said.

I laughed, remembering when he was pretending to be Kennedy's best friend. I had no idea how Tanner had gotten Matt and I back together, but I knew he'd had a lot to do with it.

"Or in this case my best friend's wife. In a few hours, anyway. Call me if you need anything, okay?"

"I will."

We both hung up and now I couldn't wipe the smile off my face.

Justin smiled and stepped back. "Perfect."

"But you barely did anything." I'd only seen him with one makeup brush. I touched my cheek and he swatted my hand away.

"Because I put waterproof everything on you. You're not my first shotgun wedding. Pregnant women always cry the most."

I'd hardly call my wedding to Matt a shotgun wedding. Yes, we'd quickly planned it when we found out I was pregnant. But it was 16 years in the making. *We* were 16 years in the making. I took another deep breath.

"You're all ready," Justin said.

I nodded. I was. I lifted up the skirt of my dress. "Let's go get married."

Justin laughed and put his arm through mine. "Don't tempt me. You know I'd run off with you in a heartbeat."

I laughed. "Are you excited to see Donnelley?"

"*He* should be excited to see *me*. I'm the one in the amazing yellow tux." He gestured to his tux that absolutely was amazing. I had no idea how he's gotten one to match the bridesmaid dresses perfectly. And his navy blue bowtie brought the whole thing together.

Justin escorted me down the stairs.

Mrs. Caldwell put her hand to her chest and tears pooled in the corners of her eyes.

God, she was going to make me cry again.

Kennedy hurried over to me. "Everything good?" she asked.

I nodded. "Everything's perfect."

Mrs. Alcaraz hugged me and then grabbed both sides of my face. "Bonita."

"You look so beautiful," Mrs. Caldwell agreed and squeezed my arm.

"Is there anything else at all that you need?" Penny asked.

"No, I'm ready."

Bee grabbed my hand. "I can't believe we're going to be sisters."

"All of us," Daphne said with a smile.

These girls really did want to make me cry again.

"I have all the bouquets..." Nigel's voice trailed off when he saw me. "Belle."

"Who me?" Justin asked.

"What?" Nigel looked confused.

"My last name is Belle," Justin said. "I often go by Mr. Belle." He winked at Nigel.

Nigel shook his head. "No, I was talking about Brooklyn." He turned back to me. "Belle femme. You are the most beautiful bride."

"Thank you, Nigel. But you need to get back to the groomsmen. Matt is wondering where you are."

"He requested my services?" Nigel asked.

That was a weird way to put it, but kind of. "Mhm."

"I must be going then." He quickly handed us all our bouquets. The flowers were a combination of white and yellow roses and some baby's-breath arranged throughout. "But please telephone me if you need anything, mademoiselle. Or fax if you're in a hurry. Wait, unless you want me to drive the limo?"

I quickly shook my head. I'd driven with him before and once was definitely enough. He was the sweetest guy, but a complete madman on the road. Especially in his Hummer.

"See you all soon." He took a turn kissing the back of each of the bridesmaid's hands. Only skipping Justin.

They all blushed and giggled.

Nigel really was such a ladies' man.

He did the same with Mrs. Caldwell, Mrs. Alcaraz, and Scarlett and Sophie. The two little girls were both in frilly yellow dresses. They made the most adorable flower girls.

"Au revoir," Nigel said. Then he ran through the door that connected our houses and quickly closed it behind him.

Justin looped his arm back through mine and then started snapping instructions at everyone.

"Do you need me to grab anything?" I asked as he guided me out of the house.

"You don't need to lift a finger. I'm handling it all. I just got a text saying everything is ready at the venue. And the men are en route."

A chauffeur opened the limo door for us.

"Thank you," I said.

He nodded and smiled at me as Justin and I climbed in. Justin's phone buzzed again. He started texting furiously.

As everyone else climbed into the limo, I noticed that there was a little envelope sticking out the top of my bouquet. I pulled it out and opened it. I thought it was a thank you note from the florist, but instead there was a polaroid inside. A picture of me and Matt on the field of Empire High 16 years ago. He'd just won a game and he was twirling me around in his arms. My heart felt all warm and fuzzy. He was smiling so big in the picture. I remembered falling in love with that smile. Dreaming of that smile. Promising forever to that smile.

I turned the picture over. Written on the back in Matt's handwriting was: "It's always been you, baby. Always and forever."

I smiled and slid the picture back into the bouquet. It didn't hurt to have one more old thing for good luck. *Always and forever, Matt.*

CHAPTER 38

Friday

Matt

I was standing in front of the bridge in Central Park where I'd asked Brooklyn to be my girlfriend. *Our bridge.* She'd thought I was about to pull out a ring, but instead I'd given her a hotdog. God, it felt like a lifetime ago. But just thinking about it made me smile. I'd already known I wanted to spend my whole life with her. I just didn't realize that I'd have to wait 16 years to truly start living.

The bridge was sectioned off behind us so that no one could disrupt the ceremony. Christmas garland and twinkle lights with gold leaves were wrapped around the railings of the bridge and around the arch I was standing in front of. And the aisle leading up to me had a row of white pumpkins. It was all decorated similarly to Tanner's apartment last night. And I knew he and Nigel had helped more with the arrangements than I even realized.

There were only several rows of seats in front of me. We'd agreed to keep the ceremony small. My parents and Mrs. Alcaraz were in the front row. There were a couple of old friends from Empire High, including Felix and some of my teammates. A dozen friends from Harvard were here as well. And some of the people I worked with. My receptionist, Mary, smiled at me. Hailey and Tyler were there too with Axel perched on Tyler's knee. But there was one noticeably empty seat in the front row. *Mr. Pruitt's.*

Mason leaned forward. "Do you want me to go check on them?"

I shook my head.

"What if she's getting cold feet?" Rob whispered.

"She's not," I said. But she would be thinking about the people who weren't here. Her mom. Her uncle. Her father. I pressed my lips together.

"I'm getting cold feet," James said. "And hands." He rubbed his hands together to warm them.

It was cooler today than the original forecast had predicted. And we'd been standing up here for a good 15 minutes.

"Maybe I should go talk to her," Tanner said. "I know she was upset about her dad. I feel like this is my fault."

I leaned forward to see him. "You did everything you could."

Tanner nodded, but he didn't look appeased by my words. He was staring at the restaurant doors where Brooklyn was supposed to walk out.

I stared at the door too. I knew it wasn't just Brooklyn's mom, uncle, and father that might be upsetting her today. If Brooklyn wasn't coming out it wasn't because of them. It was because of Miller. I swallowed hard.

The photographer snapped a picture of us standing there. That definitely wouldn't be a good one. We all just looked cold and worried.

I knew Brooklyn wanted to marry me. But I also knew how hard it was for her to break a promise. She probably felt like she was breaking a promise to Miller today. And I understood that better than anyone. I cleared my throat. "I'll be right back." I walked toward the restaurant before any of my friends could stop me. The blast of warm air when I opened the door didn't feel like a relief. I needed to know that Brooklyn was okay.

I made my way through the empty restaurant to the back room where I knew she'd be. "Brooklyn?" I knocked on the door.

Kennedy opened it. "Thank God you're here. We don't know what to do. She won't come out of the restroom and she won't tell us why." Kennedy grabbed my arm and pulled me toward the closed door.

"Can you give us a moment?" I asked.

She nodded and got all the bridesmaids and the kids to leave the room.

"Brooklyn?" I tried to open the door but it was locked. "Baby." I pressed my palm against the door. "Let me in."

"You can't see me in my dress. It's bad luck."

"Don't make me knock the door down again."

She laughed.

That seemed like a good sign. "I swear I'll do it."

"It's bad luck," she said again.

Is that what this was about? Luck? "Remember what I told you when I proposed? I'm not scared of bad luck. The only thing that scares me is living one more second without you."

"I know." She didn't sound upset. She sounded sure of herself.

I was so confused about what was wrong. Because from her voice, it didn't seem like anything was. "Baby, tell me what's going through that head of yours." *Even if it hurts me.* Because this had to be about Miller. I rested my forehead against the door. I just wanted her in my arms. But this was as close as I could get.

"I just want to wait a few more minutes. And everyone is rushing me."

"I'm not trying to rush you. But it's kind of cold outside."

She laughed again.

The sound made me smile. "Tell me why you want to wait. Because I've been waiting for 16 years. I don't mind waiting a little longer. But I want to understand why."

"It's not about that."

"Then what is it about?"

She sighed and I could tell she was right next to the door. Maybe she'd pressed her hand against the wood to get closer to me too. "I am one thousand percent in," she said. "I love you with all my heart, Matt."

"And I love you." If she wasn't thinking about Miller then…

"I just need to wait a few more minutes."

"Okay," I said. I didn't understand, but maybe I didn't need to. Maybe she just needed me here beside her. "Then I'll wait with you."

Silence stretched between us.

I so badly wanted to break down the door. But I didn't want her to ever think she was bad luck.

"I just thought…" her voice trailed off.

I didn't respond. I just waited for her to keep going.

"That maybe if I waited just a few more minutes my father would show up. I wanted today to be a fresh start. A clean slate. I know I don't need him. I can walk down the aisle to you all by myself. But I wanted him here." Her voice cracked.

Oh, baby.

"I wanted answers. I wanted to move forward. I just…wanted him to show up for me. Just for me for once. Not showing up in some twisted reason for his own gain. But showing up because he loves me." She sniffed. "Because he wants a relationship not full of secrets and lies. I just want him to be…my dad."

"He does love you, Brooklyn. He just didn't get the messages."

She sniffed again. "Maybe just a few more minutes?"

"We can wait as long as you want, baby."

"I know it's silly," she said. "I have all the letters. I know he wanted me. I know he loves me. I just wanted to talk to him before I walked down the aisle today. I don't want to hold on to all this hurt anymore. I just want to be free."

"It's not silly." I wanted today to be everything she'd dreamed of. She wanted a fresh start with her father though, and it was the one thing I couldn't give her. And I understood wanting to be free from the pain of our pasts. "But even though you can't talk to him today, it doesn't mean you won't be able to soon. He loves you, Brooklyn. I know he does."

Someone cleared their throat behind me.

I lifted my forehead from the door and turned around.

Mr. Pruitt was standing there. With a smile on his face. He put his hand on my shoulder. "I think I can take it from here, Matthew."

Fuck, he actually came. I did the first thing that popped into my head and hugged him.

For a second he went completely stiff. But then his arms wrapped around me and he hugged me back.

"Thank you for your message," he said. "And your friend Tanner is relentless. But I'm glad he was. Or I would have missed today."

I pulled back from our hug. "I'm going to give you two a moment. I'll be outside waiting when you're both ready."

Mr. Pruitt nodded.

I started to walk out the door.

"And Matthew?" Mr. Pruitt said.

I turned to look at him.

"I know I already apologized for everything."

I just shrugged. He had. *Kind of.* He said he wasn't sorry for faking Brooklyn's death though. Which was fucked if you asked me. But I knew he was trying to protect her. And he'd apologized for all the shit leading up to it. This wasn't really about him and me though. This was about Brooklyn.

"But I do appreciate you saying you forgive me. Your message meant a lot to me."

I didn't think Mr. Pruitt was capable of empathy. But he looked sincere when he was talking. I nodded. "Thanks for coming." With that I walked out of the room.

Donnelley was standing outside the door, guarding it.

"I can trust you to not kidnap her, right?"

Donnelley smiled. "I'm not one to advise Mr. Pruitt, but I can tell you that he has no intention of doing that. He just wants her to be happy. And so do I."

"Thanks, Donnelley."

"How is Jacob doing with everything?"

"Good. Let me go get him so you can say hi." It didn't take long to find Jacob even though he was playing hide-and-seek with Scarlett and Sophie. Jacob was not great at hiding. His shoes were poking out from underneath a table.

I lifted the tablecloth and ducked down. "Hey, kiddo. Remember your mom's friend Donnelley?"

"My daddy's friend?"

I nodded. "You want to come say hi?"

"Yessie." He slid out from underneath the table and followed me down the hall. "Hi, Mr. Donnelley!"

Donnelley leaned down and hugged him. "Hey, little man."

"Do you want to play hide-and-seek with us?"

"Oh, um…" Donnelley looked up at me.

I nodded. "It's okay. I can keep a look out." It honestly put me at ease to keep an eye on Mr. Pruitt. I wanted to trust him. I just wasn't totally convinced yet.

Donnelley followed Jacob into the main room and I could hear him counting.

"Go on outside with your groomsmen," Kennedy said as she walked up to me. "I won't let anything happen to Brooklyn. Besides, James' bodyguards are patrolling the place. No one is coming in or leaving without them knowing. Plus Penny is on high alert because of what happened at her wedding. Trust me, we've all got this." She leaned against the wall beside me and folded her arms across her chest, looking very much the part of a bodyguard.

I laughed. "You look very intimidating."

"My pepper spray is even more intimidating." She smiled up at me. "It's strange isn't it? For everything in the world to suddenly feel right again?"

I smiled down at her. "It really does."

"Now go." She waved her arms through the air. "Brooklyn will kill me if I let you see her dress before she walks down the aisle."

"Thanks, Kennedy." I went back out into the cold. My friends had abandoned their line and were standing in a circle talking. I jogged down the aisle and joined them.

"He came," I said.

Rob scrunched up his nose. "Who came? And where? And why were you watching?"

"That's not what I meant. I'm talking about Mr. Pruitt."

"You watched Mr. Pruitt cum? Gross man."

I hit Rob in the back of the head.

"Fuck yes," Tanner said. "I knew I'd finally get through to him. I saved the day!"

I smiled. "You really did. Thanks, man."

"I mean…I kind of saved the day too," Rob said. "Well, Daphne did. She got these little hand warmers." He tossed me one. It was already warm. "Thanks, Rob," I said.

"Totally saved the day too," he said.

"Not." Tanner faked coughed. "As." Cough. "Much." Cough. "As." Cough. "Me."

I laughed. Tanner was actually correct. But I wasn't going to take sides. And this hand warmer really was nice. I'd have to thank Daphne.

"So are they coming out soon?" Nigel asked. "Or should I go serve them refreshments? If you want I can be Francois again and…"

"That's okay, they'll be out soon." We did not need handsy Francois in attendance today.

Nigel started jumping up and down to stay warm. "I'm so excited about our wedding."

"Our?" I stared at him.

"Yes. Since we basically live in the same house, it's our wedding." He winked at me.

"You don't live in my house."

"But I'm the only one with a key."

I frowned. That was true.

"It's okay, I'm a grower."

Rob laughed. "What the fuck? Where did that come from?"

"The more you get to know me, the more I grow on you," Nigel said.

"Wow." Rob shook his head. "Not what being a grower means, man."

James laughed.

"I'm a grower in that way too," Nigel said. "It's a menace."

He wasn't kidding. Boy had trunk. And he kind of was a menace to society wielding that thing. I shook my head.

Why the hell were we talking about Nigel's penis right now? "Any last minute advice for me, guys?"

"About marriage?" James asked.

I nodded.

"Role playing," Mason said.

James tilted his head to the side as he thought it over. "Yeah, that's not bad advice. Or like…reenacting stuff from your past."

I laughed. "You mean professor student stuff?" He did have a point. I liked reenacting things with Brooklyn. And her wearing my jersey this morning? Sexy as hell.

"Oh, Professor Hunter, harder," Rob said in a high-pitched voice, mimicking Penny.

James elbowed him in the side.

"What? I've definitely overheard the two of you. It's solid advice though. Also, if she secretly reads romance novels you're a lucky man. Daphne is kinky as hell. I love bookworms. I'll get Brooklyn a spicy romance book for Christmas."

Okay then. These guys had the best marriages I knew of. Maybe role playing and spicy novels were the key to everything. Hell, Penny even wrote steamy books. Not that I was asking about how to keep the spark alive in the bedroom. We didn't have any problems with that. I was asking for advice on how to have a great marriage. But I guess sex was a part of that. Figures my friends would just offer advice on that.

"It's true love," Tanner said. "You have nothing to worry about."

Rob rolled his eyes. Probably just because Tanner said it. Hopefully not about the true love thing, because I happened to agree with Tanner on that.

"Thanks, Tanner."

"We're 99 percent sure of it," Nigel clarified.

Well, I was 100 percent sure.

CHAPTER 39

Friday

Brooklyn

Matt knocked on the door again.

"Just one more minute," I said. I knew it didn't make any sense. My fresh start with my dad could begin any day. I just had this hope in my chest that it would be today. A clean slate. A new beginning. Today was the start of my future. Of my new forever.

He knocked again.

I knew I was making people wait out in the cold. I took a deep breath. I'd waited long enough. I pressed my lips together. My father wasn't coming.

"Angel," said a voice that was definitely not Matt.

My heart started racing. I quickly unlocked the door and opened it. My dad was standing there, smiling down at me.

"Dad?" My voice cracked.

He closed the distance between us and wrapped his arms around me. "You didn't think I'd miss your wedding, did you?"

I laughed and pulled back. "Actually I did." I hugged him again. "I'm so glad you're here."

He kissed the top of my head. "I didn't think you wanted me here. That's why I left. But then I got all your texts and voicemails. And a ton from Tanner. And one from Matt."

"Matt left you a voicemail?"

"He did. Saying he forgave me."

Oh, Matt. I knew how hard that must have been for him to do. Every day he surprised me more and more. I looked up at my dad. "I found the letters. That you wrote to my mom."

He raised his eyebrows.

"Why didn't you tell me that you changed your mind about wanting me?"

He didn't say anything.

"I read all the letters that were in that box in mom's apartment," I said. "She never saw them. But I did. You regretted telling my mom to get rid of me. You wanted the three of us to become a family. Why didn't you tell me?"

He exhaled slowly. "Because it was too late."

"It wasn't too late. I'm right here."

"It didn't make a difference…"

"It makes *all* the difference," I said and hugged him again. "To *me*."

He rested his chin on the top of my head and sighed. "I thought she'd gone through with it. I thought I was too late. And your mother wanted nothing to do with me. She returned every letter unopened."

I hugged him tighter. I wondered how different my life would have been if my mom had opened one of the letters. If she'd forgiven him. Maybe, just maybe, she'd still be alive.

But there was no going back. No rewinding time, no matter how much we wished we could. I took a deep breath. "It just felt nice to know that I was wanted."

"Of course I wanted you," my dad said. "I loved your mom, more than I ever loved anyone. I didn't even know what love was until I met her. All I wanted was to run away with her. I just…" his voice trailed off. "It took losing her to make me realize I couldn't live without her. And then it was too late. I didn't know you were alive. If I had,

I would have come, Brooklyn. I would have done anything to be part of your lives."

It was too late for him and my mom. But it wasn't too late for us. He'd wanted me. And he'd shown up today simply because I needed him. It was the first time it felt like he had no ulterior motives. This was just…love. I pulled back again. "You didn't need to make me think you were a monster, Dad."

He shook his head. "When I married into the Cannavaro family, I was young and foolish. What I thought I wanted…" his voice trailed off. "I was a poor kid, from the wrong side of the tracks. I wanted power. And wealth." He shook his head again. "But I was wrong. About all of it. I didn't want this life."

I didn't realize he'd grown up poor. Like me. But I'd never wanted power or wealth because I'd been surrounded by love. My mom's. My uncle's. Miller's. Matt's. My father had gotten stuck in a terrible position because he'd never known love until he met my mom. And then it truly was too late.

"I just wanted your mom. And you." There were tears in his eyes. "And I missed out on everything."

"Not everything. You're here to walk me down the aisle."

He sniffed and smiled down at me. "You want me to walk you down the aisle?"

"That's what dads do."

He smiled. "I am so sorry, Brooklyn. I should have told you all this sooner. I'm not used to being…" his voice trailed off.

"Honest?"

He laughed. "Hmm. Maybe so. I need people to see me a certain way in this business. Well, not anymore I guess."

"It really is done? You're 100 percent out?"

"I am. I'm not letting the business ruin the rest of my life too. I don't want to miss out on anything else."

My father had done terrible things. Awful things. He was a murderer. I'd seen it with my own eyes. He'd done awful things to me, even if he was trying to protect me.

But I was done holding on to all that pain.

What mattered was that my father loved me. He was the only family I had left. And he'd given up his business, which was essentially his whole life, hoping that I'd let him be a part of mine.

I always thought at some point, my heart would be too broken to ever heal again. But it never happened. And my heart was big enough to forgive him. It was big enough to leave the past in the past. "No more lies. Or betrayals. Or secrets."

He nodded. "I promise."

"On that note. I do have some news." I was pretty sure everyone outside already knew. And I didn't want my father to find out from someone else. "I'm pregnant."

His eyes grew round and they fell to my stomach.

I laughed. "I'm not really showing. Yet." I placed my hand on my stomach. "I mean, maybe a little…"

"You look beautiful, angel."

I smiled.

"Do you know if it's a boy or a girl?"

I shook my head. "No, not yet." I wasn't sure I wanted to know. This baby was a surprise. And I kind of liked the idea of keeping the sex a surprise too. "But I'm excited for you to meet him or her."

"So you're saying no more paying someone to take photos of my grandkid from a distance?"

I shook my head. “Definitely not.” I wanted him to be a part of our lives. He was right, he’d already missed out on so much.

“Well good,” he said.

“Good,” I agreed and nodded. I had no idea how long we’d been standing here, holding everything up. I looked over at the closed door.

“We should probably get out there. I know there’s someone who’s been waiting a very long time to marry you.”

I nodded.

My father put his arm through mine and walked us over to the door.

But I put my hand on the door before he could open it. “Wait.”

“Second thoughts?” he asked.

“Definitely not. But there is one more thing I need to know. Those contracts I signed when I was a teenager. What else was in them?”

“Just the usual stuff.”

“There was nothing usual about them. Was there anything else I should know of?”

“They were designed to keep my family safe. *You* safe.”

“And the relationship agreement?”

“Extended the courtesy to your significant other. I never terminated the one you had with Matthew. And I fulfilled my end of the bargain. I kept Matthew safe.”

Had he really? Because Matt kind of thought otherwise. “Matt mentioned you recently hired a hitman or something…”

My dad laughed. “I have many wet workers on my payroll. *Had,* I mean. Past tense. And I never hired anyone to hurt Matthew. Recently I hired a someone to follow him around to make sure he was safe after the Locatelli…incident. But he's been dismissed now of course."

Oh. My father thought I may have died in that car bomb. But he'd still protected Matt. I was thankful for that.

"Like I said, I kept Matthew safe all these years, despite any threats. I probably did things he didn't even realize to ensure he was safe. Because I knew you would have wanted that."

I honestly had no idea what he was referring to. And maybe it was best that I didn't. If he'd done something in my absence to protect Matt, I was grateful. But I wasn't done talking about those contracts. "We agreed to no more surprises. I want you to destroy the contracts."

"Or you could just read them."

I shook my head. "I don't want a contract with you. I just want a normal father-daughter relationship."

"It's my duty to keep you safe…"

"Without a contract," I said firmly.

He sighed. "Without a contract," he agreed. "But you do have a prenup with Matthew, right?"

Was he serious? "Dad, no."

"I really think…"

"No."

He sighed. "Okay. Fine. No more contracts."

"Thank you." I'd never known my dad to be agreeable. But he seemed…different today. Definitely more relaxed. It was good that he'd stepped down. I was pretty sure that job was slowly killing him. And I'd only just gotten him back.

I took a deep breath. "Okay. Let's do this thing. I've made Matt wait long enough."

My dad opened the door.

The kids were running around the restaurant, but it didn't take long for Justin to corral everyone by the doors.

"You look beautiful, Mommy," Jacob said.

I crouched down in front of him. "Thank you."

"Will you save a dance for me?"

Who had taught him to ask me that? I couldn't stop smiling. "Of course. Are you ready? You have a very important job, sweet boy." I gestured to the rings tied to the little pillow in his hand.

"Yessie."

I kissed his cheek.

And then he turned to my dad. "I think I'm supposed to hit you again."

My dad immediately put his hands over his junk.

I stifled a laugh. "We're all going to start over and be friends."

Jacob stared at my dad skeptically.

"A new beginning," I said. "Everyone deserves a second chance. Especially family."

Jacob scrunched his mouth to the side. "I already have an abuelo."

"Maxwell?" my dad asked.

"I don't know who that is," Jacob said.

I smiled. Max was Mason's dad. Jacob just knew him as Grandpa. Jacob was referring to Tanner when he mentioned his abuelo. Which felt like a long, confusing conversation for this moment.

"Well, how about you call me Nonno?" my dad said.

"Nooooooo nooooo," Jacob said, drawing the no's out in the adorable way I loved. "Okay. I'll call you that. And be good so I don't have to punch you."

"Deal," my dad said.

Justin whistled. "It's starting!" he shrieked at the top of his lungs. He downed the entire contents of a mug of coffee and slammed it on a table. I was surprised the mug didn't shatter.

He'd had way too much caffeine. But he had pulled everything off. I knew he'd be able to do it. I'd always known he was the best.

I squeezed Jacob's shoulder and stood back up.

Justin opened the door. All the groomsmen had assembled right outside to escort the bridesmaids down the aisle. Kennedy walked out first and Mason looped his arm through hers. The door closed for a moment before Bee stepped out to walk with Rob.

I pulled the curtain a bit to the side to watch. The bridge, altar, and path up to it were beautiful. Everything was decorated similarly to Tanner's apartment last night. White pumpkins, gold fall leaves, garland, and twinkle lights. Matt was standing at the altar, fidgeting with his cufflinks. He looked so nervous, but so sure at the same time. I let the curtain fall back into place.

James grabbed Penny's hand as she walked out the door. But before it closed, Tanner stepped in.

"Just wanted to make sure everything was good..." his voice trailed off when he saw me. "Wow. Brooklyn."

I smiled. "Everything is good."

"You look exquisite."

"Thank you, Tanner. Thank you for...everything." I'd seen the decorations outside. They matched the ones in his apartment. And I knew he'd helped Justin pull all this off.

Tanner nodded and turned to my dad. "Thank you for coming, Richard. It means the world to me and my friends."

"I wouldn't have missed it. But thank you for alerting me so...obsessively."

Tanner laughed. "I couldn't let you miss it." He clapped my dad on the back.

"It's your turn, you big hunk of man meat," Justin said.

Tanner grabbed Daphne's hand. Everyone else that wasn't in a couple had done the signature arm loop. I was pretty sure Tanner did it just to piss Rob off. Tanner escorted Daphne outside.

"Okay that's our cue," Justin said to Nigel and put his hand out for Nigel.

Nigel sighed. "No holding hands. We'll just walk adjacent. And doesn't that big stranger need to get outside?" He pointed to Donnelley who was just standing there with his arms folded across his chest.

Justin's eyes grew round. "You! Get that gorgeous ass outside immediately. You're ruining everything." He slapped Donnelley's butt.

Donnelley laughed.

And I couldn't help but smile. I wondered if this was the first time they'd talked. It wasn't a bad re-introduction after 16 years.

Donnelley looked at my father.

"It's okay," Mr. Pruitt said. "Go on out." He nodded towards the door.

Donnelley winked at Justin and then walked out the doors.

As soon as the doors closed Justin squealed and spun toward me. "Did you see that?! He winked at me! What does it mean?! Does he remember me?" He started fanning himself. "I think he remembers. We did so much stuff in the closet. Not the figurative closet, I was way out, even though he was way in. The actual literal closet. We used to hook up in closets is what I'm trying to say..."

"I think he remembers," I said.

Justin shrieked again. "He is the hottest man I've ever been with. Should I go talk to him? I think I should go talk to him…"

"Justin?"

"Yes?"

"I think it's your turn to walk down the aisle."

"Oh my God. You're right. It's such a tease move. He won't be able to keep his eyes off me." He spun toward Nigel. "Please, Nigel. Hold my hand. I want Donnelley as jealous as possible." He put his hand out for Nigel.

Nigel sighed. "Put your arm though mine. Final offer."

"Deal." Justin slid his arm through Nigel's and Nigel escorted him to the doors.

"And Brooklyn?" Justin said over his shoulder. "In exactly 30 seconds, the music will change. Send the ring bearer and flower girls out at 35. And you start walking 30 seconds after that. Or really just whenever they make it to the altar. So that all eyes are on you instead of on the adorable kids." He patted Jacob's head. "Okay?"

I nodded and then the door closed. I started counting but then my father pushed up his sleeve to look at his watch. My father had this covered, so I pushed the curtains aside again. Everyone seemed to be laughing at Nigel and Justin walking down the aisle. But I saw Donnelley staring. I smiled and looked back at Matt. He was laughing too.

I couldn't help but smile.

"That's 30 seconds," my dad said. "Jacob, you and the girls are almost up."

"Come on, Scarlett, come on, Sophie." Jacob waved them over to the door.

The girls looked so cute in their frilly little dresses. They each had a basket filled with yellow rose petals.

And even though they'd practiced walking separately, Jacob put his arms out like he'd seen the other men do. Each girl linked an arm with Jacob. He looked like such a little stud between them.

"And 35," my dad said and opened the door. "You're on."

Jacob escorted them both out the door. I could hear all the "aws" before the doors closed.

In 30 seconds I'd be walking down the aisle to Matt. It was weird. I thought I'd be nervous. But I'd never been more sure of anything in my life. I was about to marry Matthew Caldwell. I was going to be Brooklyn Caldwell. I'd remembered doodling that in my notebooks back at Empire High. I felt tears welling in my eyes. In a thousand years, I never thought today would come. But here we were. Together after everything in the world had tried to keep us apart. It felt like fate. Twisted and cruel fate, but fate nonetheless.

My dad peeked out the door. "They're just about there." He glanced at his watch. "Perfect timing too." He put his arm out for me. "It's time."

I wasn't sure how I was going to hold it together. I was already blinking fast to keep my tears at bay. But putting my arm though my dad's calmed me down.

He opened the door and we stepped out.

I heard a few gasps. I wasn't sure if it was because of my dress or because of my dad's presence. I was too focused on the song that was playing. I recognized it right away. It was an instrumental string version of *My Dirty Little Secret.* Yeah, I was definitely not going to get through this without crying. Matt and I had been so busy, we didn't have much time to think about music. But Tanner had mentioned something about handling it. He'd done this.

Honestly, I wasn't even sure a string version had existed before. He really could make anything happen.

The chairs were full of people, but I didn't truly see any of them. My eyes were focused on Matt. He rubbed the tip of his nose with his index finger.

Our signal. I was smiling so hard it hurt.

Walking up to him right now, I couldn't believe I'd stayed away for 16 years. I couldn't believe all the pain I'd caused him. I'd spend the rest of my life making it up to him.

When I got closer, I realized there were tears in Matt's eyes.

God, he was going to make me cry.

But I loved the way he was staring at me. Not like he was picturing me 16 years ago. But like he loved me right now. In this moment.

My dad and I stopped right in front of the altar. "Congratulations, angel." He leaned down and hugged me.

Matt put his hand out for him.

My dad shook it. "Take care of my girl."

"Always," Matt said and then put his hand out for me.

I slid my hand into his and joined him in front of the altar. He cradled both my hands in his as he stared down at me.

"You look so beautiful," he said.

"Matt, stop," I whispered. "You're going to make me cry."

He blinked fast and cleared his throat. "I'm going to be promising the world to you, but I can't promise not to cry."

I laughed and squeezed his hands.

"Are the two of you ready?" the pastor whispered with a kind smile.

We both nodded. I'd only met him just a few weeks ago. But he'd married Matt's parents. I couldn't think of anyone better for this occasion.

"We're gathered here today to witness the sacred union of Matthew and Brooklyn." He kept going, but I barely registered his words.

I just kept staring at the man in front of me. I'd fallen in love with a boy. We'd both grown and changed so much. But we'd still found our way back to each other. And Matthew Caldwell was all man now.

"You're shaking," Matt whispered and inched a little closer to me.

"I'm just cold."

He tried to release my hands so he could give me his jacket.

I held his hands tight. "Nope. We did not spend a fortune altering this dress just for me to cover it up."

"But…"

"Don't even think about it."

He smiled.

The pastor cleared his throat.

We both turned to him.

"You have agreed to read your own vows, right?" he asked.

The crowd chuckled.

I was pretty sure this wasn't the first time he'd asked us.

"Yes," Matt said. He let go of my hands and grabbed a piece of paper from his jacket pocket. He slowly unfolded it and looked at me.

And I already knew he was going to make me cry.

CHAPTER 40

Friday

Matt

God was Brooklyn beautiful. For a second I just stood there staring at her. I really couldn't believe this was happening. I didn't bother to look down at the paper in my hand. I knew what I wanted to say.

"I feel like I'm dreaming, and any moment I'm going to wake up."

Brooklyn nodded. "Me too," she whispered.

"For 16 years, I've been lying to myself. Lying to my friends." I looked behind me. "My family." I looked at my parents sitting in the crowd and then back at Brooklyn. "I told myself I didn't want to get married. That I didn't want kids. That I didn't want a wife. But I did. I just only ever wanted it with you. It's only ever been you, Brooklyn. And it'll only ever be you."

Fuck, I really am going to start crying.

"I'm a mess without you, baby. Each day after I thought you passed away, I died a little more inside. I felt like a ghost walking around the city. And I could only ever breathe when I thought I saw you on a crowded sidewalk or in the stands of Empire High." I closed my eyes for a moment. "Or when I smelled fall leaves. God, the falls were the hardest." I opened my eyes again and stared at the tears in hers. "But the falls were also the best because I never wanted the memory of you to disappear. Because I don't know how to live without you."

"I love you," Brooklyn mouthed silently at me.

"I wrote my vows to you 16 years ago. And I still have them." I held up the paper in my hand. "I read part of them once, on one of the worst days of my life. When we buried you." It took all my self-control to not start crying. Especially when I saw a tear fall down Brooklyn's cheek.

I reached out and wiped the tears from beneath Brooklyn's eyes with my thumbs.

"And I want to make the world right again. I never should have read these at your funeral. Because they were always meant for today. I know I'm not 16 years old anymore. And I love you even more now. But I was a pretty good writer back then."

Brooklyn laughed through her tears.

"So let's try this again. Today. The day I was always meant to read them." I cleared my throat and looked down at the paper. "Brooklyn. When I first met you, you thought you were invisible. But I always saw you. The first thing I loved about you was how your eyes lit up whenever you saw me. Like I was the only one that could make you happy."

I looked up from the paper and smiled at her. This felt wrong to read these when I could so easily picture reading them at her funeral. But I wanted to make this right. Fix that wrong. I remembered standing up there in the church, thinking that the words were lies. That I hadn't made her happy. That I'd fucking destroyed her. But that wasn't true. Because she was standing right here. With me.

"But you were the one making me happy. You were a breath of fresh air in this city. I was infatuated with you before we ever spoke. And I fell harder for you every single day since you first let me in. And I know that I'll keep falling harder every day from here." I looked up at her again. "That ended up being very true."

She laughed again.

"I know you're scared of time. But I'm giving you all of mine. Every second. I'll cherish you, Brooklyn. I'll keep you safe," my voice cracked.

"Matt," she whispered and grabbed my wrist. "You don't have to keep going."

I shook my head. I really did. "I know that we're young. But you've taught me that the one thing in this life we can't waste is time." I shook my head. "Baby, I can't imagine my life without you. I'd be lost if we weren't together. I'm only happy when I know that you're happy too. And it took me being an idiot, but I know for a fact that I'm only really living when we're together. And I don't want to go another day without you by my side." All of this was still true. Except I'd been an idiot a second time without even knowing it. In that pool with Jen. I was such a fucking fool.

"I promised to be all your firsts. First kiss. First love. First husband." Well, I felt like an idiot again right now. I'd forgotten it had said that. It was an inside joke back then. If I'd read it 16 years ago, she would have laughed. Instead of looking up at me with a sad, knowing smile. I wasn't trying to make her feel bad. The next lines were about more first we'd experience together. Like our first child. We were going to have one soon, but it wasn't Brooklyn's first. And I didn't want her to ever think I didn't think of Jacob as a son.

I cleared my throat. "Some of this no longer applies."

The crowd laughed but Brooklyn looked like she was going to cry again.

"Which is fine," I quickly added. "Because I don't care about firsts anymore. I'm standing here, asking you if you'd do me the honors of being all my lasts."

The smile was back on her face. "I think that can be arranged," she said.

"But I do want to take a second to let you know I'm not upset about the time we were apart. It feels like this was always meant to be. Right now. Right here. And I am so thankful to Miller for taking care of you when I couldn't…"

"Matt…" her voice cracked.

"I know a piece of your heart will always belong to him. And that's okay. I know it doesn't mean you love me less. And I will do my best to make sure his memory lives on for you and Jacob. I promise." I wiped away her tears again and looked back down at the paper in my hand. "All I've ever wanted was to make a family with you. And you came back to me, giving me my dream. With Jacob. And with this baby." I pressed my palm on her stomach. God I was so excited about this baby.

I looked back down at the paper. "Brooklyn Sanders. Or Pruitt. Or Miller," I added. "It doesn't matter what your last name was. Because you're a Caldwell now. My wife." I tried to steady my voice, but it was impossible. "My home. My heart. My best friend. And the love of my life. I promised you that I've only ever loved you. And that I will only ever love you. And I'm standing here today, doubling down on that promise, baby. Because I will love you and only you until the day I die."

This time Brooklyn reached out and wiped away my tears.

"I promise," I said again, knowing that she couldn't say it back. Because she did love someone else. She'd lived a whole life with Miller. She still woke up in the middle of the night crying, missing him. But it didn't change how I felt.

"I love you," I said. "I wasn't living without you. I…need you. You're everything to me. And you're worth fighting for." I knew some of her uncle's last words to her were, 'You're worth fighting for.' I was so lucky to have met him. And he was so damn right. Brooklyn was worth fighting for.

She stood on her tiptoes and kissed me.

I grabbed her waist, pulling her in closer.

The pastor cleared his throat.

Brooklyn pulled back and her cheeks flushed. I loved how she kissed me the same, even when we were in front of a crowd of people.

And was it just me, or were her breasts bigger than usual? Fuck me, how was I supposed to go through this whole ceremony and reception when all I wanted to do was take her right on the bridge?

I felt the pastor staring at me, like he could read my sinful thoughts.

Mason stepped forward and handed me the rings. I had honestly completely forgotten what I was supposed to do next. I was too busy staring at my bride. I grabbed Brooklyn's hand and slid the ring onto her finger. I'd been waiting a lifetime to do that.

For a few seconds we just stared at each other.

I put my hand on the side of Brooklyn's face, hiding her rosy cheek. "I think it's your turn." I dropped my hand from her cheek and placed my ring in her palm.

"Matt, I…" her gazed dropped to the ring in her hand. "I…can't."

CHAPTER 41

Friday

Brooklyn

It looked like Matt was going to drown in his pain. I saw it flash across his face, if only for a moment. And he was misunderstanding what I was about to say.

He already knew I couldn't say all that back to him. I'd fallen in love with someone else. Had a life with someone else. Had a baby with someone else. I couldn't tell him that I loved him and only him. But I could tell him exactly how I felt.

"I can't..." I smiled. "...possibly put this as eloquently as you did."

Our family and friends laughed.

"Really not funny," Matt said.

"A little funny." I smiled up at him. "Did you seriously think I was about to run from the altar?"

"It wouldn't be the first time I had to chase you. But like I said...you're worth fighting for, Brooklyn."

His words made my heart beat funny in my chest. My uncle had told me that exact same thing. And I couldn't believe that Matt remembered how much that meant to me. After all these years, Matt truly did remember everything about our time together. And it felt like fate. Because that was exactly how I was planning on ending my vows to him. It was the sweetest thing anyone had ever said to me. And I wanted him to know that's how I felt about him.

Matt was so full of surprises. And he was making me like surprises again. For so long I was scared. But I was done running.

"I'm in love with you," I said.

"Good, I'm in love with you too." He smiled down at me.

"You're not supposed to respond to everything I say. Let me get this out."

The crowd laughed and Matt nodded silently.

I stared up into Matt's eyes. "I'm serious. I can't top what you just said." Seriously, why had I let him go first? "But you're right about all of it. When I first met you, I felt invisible. I used to stare at you because you looked so…happy. And I was so sad. I thought maybe, if I was lucky, that some of your joy would rub off on me. And that maybe I'd learn how to smile again. *You* were the breath of fresh air in a city that didn't feel like my home.

"I have this whole thing with home. Because I kept losing mine. But I always had you. Even when I thought I didn't. Even when I stayed away for 16 years, you were still there. Waiting. Perpetually waiting. Fixing up homes that we were always meant to share together. Because you are home to me, Matt. You've always been home to me.

"I can't stand here and say I regret anything that's happened. But I can say that I'm sorry. I'm sorry I didn't talk to you 15 years ago when I escaped. I'm sorry I ran away from you when I promised I'd never run away. We promised that we'd always talk things through…"

"Baby." Matt grabbed my hand. "It's okay. It's…"

I shook my head. It wasn't. I'd hurt him. And I couldn't undo that pain. "I will spend the rest of my life making up for that hurt. By loving you. By choosing you. By being Mrs. Matthew Caldwell."

He smiled.

"Because I never forgot you, Matt. I baked so I could smell cinnamon in the air. Watching football reminded me of you. Crisp fall air reminded me of you. Certain songs reminded me of you. I put all my hopes and dreams on you for so long. And that doesn't just go away. Not even in 16 years.

"No, you're not the same boy I fell in love with. And I'm not the same girl that you fell in love with. But you still are and always will be the boy I stare at when I think no one's looking." Tears started streaming down my cheeks. "I still want your joy to rub off on me. And I still dream of being your wife. Today it feels like all my dreams are coming true."

Matt reached out and wiped my tears away with his thumbs.

"You were my first love. And my last love. And I will love you until the day I die, Matt. Always and forever. I promise to never run away from what we have ever again. Because you're worth fighting for too." I went to slide the ring on his finger, but he pulled me into a searing kiss instead.

God I'd never grow tired of Matt's kisses.

I heard Rob whistle.

And the pastor cleared his throat.

I put my hand on Matt's chest.

He slowly pulled back.

The pastor looked down at the ring in my hand.

Oh, I'd almost forgotten. I grabbed Matt's hand and slid the ring onto his finger. I smiled up at him. That felt like a long time coming. I was so lucky that he'd waited for me. And I meant what I'd said. I'd spend my whole life making up for all the time we'd spent apart. We were finally allowed to be happy. We were finally free.

"Matthew Caldwell," the pastor said. "Do you take Brooklyn to be your lawfully wedded wife? To have and to hold until death do you part?"

Matt smiled down at me. The kind of smile he used to have back at Empire High. Like everything was right in the world. "I do."

"Brooklyn, do you take Matthew Caldwell to be your lawfully wedded husband? To have and to hold until death do you part?"

A thousand percent yes. "I do."

"Then by the power vested in me by the state of New York, I now pronounce you husband and wife. Go ahead and kiss your bride *again*," he said with a smile.

I laughed.

Matt leaned down and kissed me as cheers erupted from all our friends and family.

Our first kiss as husband and wife.

Sixteen years in the making.

And I was going to make it count. I grabbed the lapels of his jacket to deepen our kiss.

His hands slid to my ass.

And I didn't even care. I didn't care who was watching. Or silently judging us. All that mattered in that moment was him and me. The kiss was somehow sweet and sinful, and salty from my tears. And I never wanted this moment to end.

But then I felt something land on the tip of my nose.

I pulled back and stared up at the light snow that had started to fall. Today had been much colder than the original forecast had predicted. And no one had predicted snow.

I smiled. I knew in my heart that this was Miller's doing.

I lifted my hand and watched a snowflake land on my palm and melt away. I closed my hand in a fist and looked back up at the falling snow. Each flake that landed on me felt like a kiss from Miller.

Miller and I had gotten married in the snow on Christmas day. Just the two of us. The only witness the silent falling snow.

Yes, this was definitely him. His blessing. He'd meant what he'd written in that letter. He wanted me to keep living. To keep loving. To never take a single day for granted. Another snowflake landed on the tip of my nose and I smiled at Matt. "It's snowing."

"That's all you have to say?" Matt said. "We're married!" He lifted me into his arms and spun me around.

"We're married!" I yelled and lifted my hands in the air.

"You're supposed to start walking," Mason said. "Everyone's freezing their asses off."

I laughed and Matt lowered me to my feet.

"We're married," he said again, this time like he couldn't believe it. Like he really did think he was dreaming.

"You're my husband."

"You're my wife."

Hearing him say that made tears pool in the corners of my eyes.

Sixteen years ago we'd dreamed of a future where we'd be married. Our future was finally here. Our happily ever after.

I grabbed his hand and lifted it in the air.

Everyone cheered again.

And then we ran through the falling snow toward the restaurant.

For some reason I kept laughing. Like I'd been holding on to all this joy in my chest and it finally wanted out.

From this day on I was choosing to be happy.

From this day on I was Brooklyn freaking Caldwell.

It was a blur of pictures and congratulations. We took a lot of pictures inside but ventured outside in the falling snow for a few in front of our bridge.

Rob almost pushed Tanner into the freezing cold water, but luckily Tanner had excellent balance.

But I was barely paying attention.

I kept waiting for someone to pinch me.

Because for a while there, I was so scared I'd never smile again. And now I couldn't seem to stop.

"So this was the dress you picked out in high school?" Matt whispered when we were supposed to be posing.

"With a few alterations." I put my fingers on the tulle between my breasts.

Matt groaned. "Who knew that 16 years would make you such a tease."

I laughed and pushed on his arm.

"But seriously, baby. You are the most beautiful bride." He intertwined his fingers with mine. "And I am the luckiest man alive."

For so long I'd felt like bad luck. But it was easy to believe my luck had changed when I was standing here in my wedding dress. "I feel pretty lucky myself." I squeezed his hand.

"This is the best day of my life."

"You might feel differently in several months." I put my free hand on my stomach. He didn't know the joy of holding his child for the first time.

He dropped his forehead to mine. "I'm scared for someone to pinch me."

I smiled. I'd just been thinking the same thing. "Oh, this is very much real." I reached out and pinched him.

He laughed.

"Pinch me back."

He lightly pinched my elbow.

I smiled. "Guess we're not dreaming."

"Mommy, Mommy!" Jacob ran up to us through the snow. "Snowball fight!" He threw a very tiny snowball right at Nigel.

"Oh, it's on, Mr. Jacob." Nigel leaned down and started to make a much bigger snowball.

"Nope," Matt said sternly to Nigel. And then Matt turned back to Jacob. "We'll do that later, kiddo. But right now I need you to smile for the cameras."

Jacob reached up to him, the way he did when he wanted to be lifted up.

Matt immediately picked him up.

They already understood each other. We were already a family. And I couldn't wait for it to grow even bigger.

The photographer kept snapping pictures.

Tanner and Nigel started moving farther and farther away from everyone. I tried to wave them back over. But it was pretty clear that they both hated being photographed. And I couldn't force them.

Soon Nigel was just standing by the photographer, helping organize everyone for photos.

And Tanner kept telling me how to pose.

"Tanner, this doesn't feel right," I said as I awkwardly arched my back. No one stood this way.

He grabbed the camera from the photographer, turned it around, and let me see the photo.

Oh my God. I'd never looked so good in a picture before. All the awkward angles actually looked so normal in the photographs. I looked up at him. "How do you know all this stuff?"

"I'm the founder of Odegaard, remember? I know my way around a fashion show. And certainly around the perfect photo."

I shook my head. He *had* said that to me before. But it made no sense then and it made no sense now. Because Odegaard was older than he was. And he was a venture capitalist, not a photographer on a runway. "You mean you *own* Odegaard?"

"Isn't that what I said?" He shrugged.

No, it wasn't. "Tanner, please get in some of the pictures."

He cleared his throat. "Um…I can't."

I just stared at him.

"It's a billionaire thing. Matt wouldn't understand."

Matt laughed. "Dude. James and Penny are in the pictures."

"Old wealth versus new wealth me thinks."

Me thinks?

"They do have old wealth," Matt said. "Ish."

The Hunter family was very wealthy. But I knew James had made his own personal fortune as well.

"Ish," Tanner said. "The ish is the difference."

"Between paupers and princes," Nigel said.

"That's not what I said." Tanner stared at him.

Nigel shrugged. "But it's what you meant."

"I wasn't calling our friends paupers," Tanner said.

"But you're saying they're all destitute."

"No," Tanner said firmly. "I didn't mean that."

"But you said…"

"Hush, child," Tanner said. "Let's help the photographer more." He walked away before I could question him or pester him to be in the pictures again.

I couldn't help but laugh. Why had Tanner called Nigel a child? Nigel was a grown man. Well, mostly. He did look awfully young actually. "How old is Nigel?" I asked Matt.

"I have no idea," he said. "A little younger than Tanner?"

"Huh." The more I looked at him, the more I thought he could pass for a teenager. He just had this young suave look about him.

Tanner kept giving us instructions, the photographer snapping away.

Soon my cheeks actually hurt from smiling so hard. And I started to shiver.

This time I didn't protest when Matt took off his jacket and wrapped it around my shoulders.

"Do you think that's enough pictures?" Matt asked me.

I knew he wanted this to be perfect for me. But honestly, all I wanted to do was kick off my heels and curl up in front of a warm fire with him. And there was a fireplace in the restaurant…

"I think that's plenty."

"Thank fuck," Rob said. "I'm freezing." He looped his arm through mine and pulled me away from Matt.

"What are you doing?" I asked. I tried to look at Matt over my shoulder, but Rob kept guiding me farther away.

"Escorting you inside. And taking a moment to congratulate you."

"Well, thank you."

"And Daphne said I need to apologize for last night. I didn't know anything would be set on fire. So I am sorry it got a little dangerous. But the rest worked, right? You'll always remember that prank and forget about the one from 16 years ago?"

I smiled up at him. "Yes, Rob. I'll always remember last night instead."

"Good. So I thought now might be a good time to talk about our next prank…"

"Rob," I groaned.

"I like when you say my name like that."

I slapped his arm.

"I like that too, Sanders."

I gave him a hard stare. "Caldwell."

"No fucking way. That's what I call Matt or Mason when they're being dicks. You'll always be Sanders to me."

I smiled. I actually loved that nickname.

"And don't worry, I'm not planning another prank. Yet. That's my wedding gift to you. No more pranks for…a year."

"A year?"

"Yup. Scouts honor."

"Were you even in boy scouts?"

Rob shrugged. "Never heard of it."

I laughed. "You're ridiculous."

"Just wait until my speech."

"You're not giving a speech. Only Kennedy and Mason are."

"Psh." Rob dropped my arm and opened the doors to the restaurant for me. "It's like you don't know me at all. Of course I'm giving a speech. Matt's my best friend. Just because I'm not his best man doesn't mean I'm letting this day pass without making fun of him publicly. Besides, it's going to be epic."

Oh no. That's exactly what he'd said about the pudding prank last night. "Why exactly is it going to be epic?" We walked over to the fireplace to warm our hands. *Please don't set anything on fire.*

He smiled. "Because it's going to make you blush."

"Robert Hunter, stop flirting with me. I'm a married woman." I waved my hand in his face, showing off my new ring.

"Eh. It's never stopped me before. Flirting with off-limits women is kind of my thing. Specifically my friends' spouses. Just ask Penny."

I hadn't heard Matt approaching, but he put his arm protectively around my shoulders.

"Is this strange man bothering you?" Matt asked.

I laughed.

"You're married!" Rob yelled and jumped into Matt's arms.

I laughed even harder as Matt almost fell over from the impact.

A flash made me turn my head. The photographer hadn't captured the moment, but luckily Kennedy had.

"Congratulations," she said and put her arm around me. She rested her head on my shoulder. "I'm so happy for you. Who ever thought that when we were having sleepovers in your old apartment that one day we'd be here?"

"I never could have predicted any of this."

"Maybe we could have predicted it a bit," Felix said as he walked up to us. "Congratulations, Newb." He leaned down and hugged me.

"Thank you." And he was right. I could have predicted it a little. I'd wanted Matt back then. And I'd always thought Felix was a good fit for Kennedy.

"Is everything good with your dad?" Kennedy asked as I pulled back from the hug.

I looked over at my father. He was talking to Mrs. Alcaraz. "Yeah. I think it really is."

"You should get a picture of that," Tanner said as he joined us.

"Hm?" I looked up at him.

"Richard and Kennedy's mom." He pointed back at them talking.

"Why?" Kennedy asked.

"Because I have a feeling they could be a perfect match."

Kennedy scrunched up her nose. And then immediately said: "Sorry. I just…it's your dad."

I laughed. Trust me, I got it. Trusting him was going to be an adjustment for everyone. But as I saw Mrs. Alcaraz laugh, I wasn't sure if Tanner was that far off. And he'd mentioned something about my dad and Kennedy's mom before. I turned back to Tanner. "A perfect match, huh?" I asked.

"Almost as perfect as you and Matt."

I looked over at my husband. *My husband.* I wasn't sure I'd ever be able to think that without smiling. James was giving him a big hug.

"But they met 16 years ago," Tanner said with a sigh. "Why has everyone always met before I introduce them? I never get any credit."

"Credit for what?"

"The match."

"I promise I'll give you credit if our parents get together." I looked at Kennedy and she laughed.

But Tanner just sighed again. "If only."

I didn't get a chance to ask him what he meant because Justin hurried over to us. Without saying a word, he grabbed my hand, pulling me away from my Kennedy and Tanner. And then he did the same with Matt, pulling him away from James and Rob.

Justin walked us into the middle of the restaurant where all the tables had been moved for a temporary dance floor.

"You two are very hard to corral." He pushed me and Matt together. "I know you've rented out the restaurant for the whole night, but there's still a schedule to keep. And it's time for your first dance as husband and wife."

"For the first time ever, may I present, Mr. and Mrs. Matthew Caldwell!" the D.J. said from behind me.

Our song came back on. The original version this time.

"Now dance, you two." Justin slapped my butt before walking off the dance floor.

I laughed as Matt pulled me in close.

"I really hate the way everyone keeps inappropriately touching my wife."

I just stared up at him with stars in my eyes. I'd never grow tired of hearing him call me his wife.

His fingers sunk into my hair. "I thought I'd go through my whole life thinking about what could have been."

I ran my hand down the back of his neck. I thought about Matt all alone for a decade and a half, thinking about our time together as teenagers. In his head about all of it. "This is our fresh start. Our new beginning."

"Hm. I like the sound of that."

It felt like the world around us hushed. It was just the two of us. In our own little bubble.

I took a deep breath, the smell of cinnamon swirling around me. "You know...dancing with you will always remind me of you being super drunk at homecoming."

He laughed. "I was hoping it would remind you of prom now. And me proposing."

I smiled. "Nope, still thinking about drunk Matt."

He twirled me around. "Well now you'll think about our wedding whenever we dance."

"It's going to be *really* hard to top homecoming."

"What about all our dancing in the kitchen?"

I smiled. I loved dancing with him in the kitchen. And I loved this moment too.

He spun me around again. "I know how to make it memorable." He let go of me for a moment and shimmied his shoulders.

I laughed and he pulled me back in close. What I loved so much about dancing with him at homecoming was that he'd been so honest with me. I'd gotten to really see…him. But he was always honest with me now. And tonight was unforgettable. "Okay, fine. Maybe this beats dancing with you at homecoming."

He leaned closer and his lips brushed against my ear. "This definitely beats homecoming. Because you're finally, officially mine, Brooklyn Caldwell."

"I've always been yours." A piece of me. I knew it was true. And I was done feeling guilty about everything. I was ready to live in the moment.

He kissed the spot right behind my ear.

I swallowed hard. I didn't think anyone had ever kissed me there before. And I felt so…loved.

He dipped me low as everyone clapped. When the last note of the song played, he pulled me back up to his chest. "I can't wait to rip this dress off of you."

I laughed. "I want to keep it though. In case our daughter wants to wear it one day."

Matt's eyes grew round and his gaze fell to my stomach.

CHAPTER 42

Friday

Matt

It's a girl? I stared at her stomach. "We're having a girl? When did you find out?"

Brooklyn opened her mouth and then closed it. "No. Yes. Maybe? I'm so sorry, I don't know. I just..." her voice trailed off. "I feel like it might be."

I smiled. She was so adorable.

"And if it is, I'd like her to have the option of wearing this dress. So please don't rip it into pieces."

"I'm not a wild animal. I was probably just going to pop a few buttons." Although the tulle between her breasts was just begging for me to rip it with my teeth.

She raised her eyebrow at me.

"But I promise I won't." My eyes trailed down between her breasts to her stomach. "A girl." I smiled. "I was thinking it was probably a boy. But I could picture us having a little girl. A little *you.* I want to fill our house with little Brooklyns."

"I feel like if I smile any more my cheeks are going to freeze like this."

I leaned down and kissed one of her cheeks. "I hope they do. I love it when you smile."

Her smile just grew even more. "This is so much better than Black Friday 16 years ago. And now we can always remember this instead."

I thought I wanted to completely erase that memory. Set the world right. But I was grateful for every moment we'd had rekindling our relationship. I was happy right here, in this moment. And so was Brooklyn. That's all that really mattered.

Someone tapped their silverware against the side of their champagne flute. I turned to see Mr. Pruitt stand up. "A toast," he said. "To the happy couple."

The D.J. handed him the microphone.

"I didn't know the father of the bride was going to make a toast!" Justin said from behind us. "Brooklyn, why didn't you tell me?!"

Brooklyn laughed. "Justin, I didn't even know he was coming. How could I have possibly told you he was making a toast?"

"You two need to go sit down! The toasts have been commandeered! This is an emergency!"

"Justin," Brooklyn said and put her hands on his shoulders. "Kennedy and Mason's toasts were planned for right now anyway. It's fine. But because this seems like a big deal to you…I should probably warn you that Rob is planning a toast too."

I laughed. Of course he was. Rob would never miss an opportunity to upstage my best man.

"Damn that hilarious hunk of man meat! Sit, sit," he shooed us toward our table.

I put my hand on Brooklyn's lower back and guided her to our table. The curtains on the windows had been opened, and the snow was falling harder now. I always loved when it snowed in New York. It was the only time the city ever felt quiet. I pulled Brooklyn's chair out for her and we both sat down.

It felt so surreal to be seated here with Brooklyn, staring out at all our family and friends. I knew Brooklyn had already pinched me, but I kept thinking I was about to wake up.

"Angel," Mr. Pruitt said and lifted his glass. "I know we've had our ups and downs."

I stared at Brooklyn and then back at him. That was the understatement of the century.

"Even the name angel…" he shook his head. "But you are my angel. You saved my life."

I clenched my hand into a fist under the table.

Brooklyn reached over and put her hand on top of my fist.

I turned to look at her.

"A new beginning, remember?" she whispered.

I unclenched my fist. My wife was the most understanding person in history. I took a deep, steadying breath.

"I wouldn't be standing here today if it wasn't for you," Mr. Pruitt said. "And for more than just the obvious reason. You gave me a new purpose, Brooklyn. You are so much like your mother. You reminded me of who I wanted to be. Who I still could be. For you."

I stared at the tears welling in Brooklyn's eyes.

"And Matthew."

I turned to look at him.

"You weren't my first choice, as you know. It's no secret that I tried to push Brooklyn toward your brother back in high school."

Asshole. We'd had a nice moment before the wedding. Why was he bringing that shit up?

Mason chuckled.

Mr. Pruitt shook his head. "Matthew, you were basically a gnat that wouldn't go away."

Someone's fork clanged onto the floor and another person coughed.

"Dad," Brooklyn said.

"I'll get to the point," Mr. Pruitt said. "It turns out you were the good kind of gnat."

What the hell was a good gnat?

"And you surprised us all by taking over MAC International. A proper heir. And as it turns out…the right choice for my daughter."

I looked at Mason. He wasn't chuckling anymore. He folded his arms across his chest and glared at Mr. Pruitt. Bee whispered something in his ear and he smiled. I wondered if she'd told him he was allowed to punch him or something. I wasn't completely opposed to that.

Justin slowly clapped and walked up to Mr. Pruitt. "Excellent speech, sir. Maybe the best man would like to pick it up from here…" He tried to reach for the microphone but Mr. Pruitt sidestepped him.

"I'm almost done," Mr. Pruitt said. "Where was I? Ah, yes. Heirs. For the longest time, you were my only living heir, Brooklyn. And now I am so lucky to have a grandson, and another heir on the way. I can't wait to get to know both of them."

Well, that was sweet. But I didn't love the way he kept referring to our kids as heirs. Calling them his grandchildren was preferable.

"Our family will persevere despite all the attempts at our lives. And hopefully those will stop now that I've stepped down from my…job."

"Was he in the mafia or something?" I heard one of my friends from college try and fail to whisper.

I never took Mr. Pruitt for being bad at speeches. But this was not great. Or maybe it was exactly what he wanted it to be. He always had liked putting me down. He had a minute to wrap this up or I'd be the one hitting him instead of Mason.

"I am so thrilled that you came back to the city, Brooklyn. And that you found your way back to Matthew. Because I do see it now. He looks at you the way I used to look at your mother. And the way your mother used to look at me." He cleared his throat.

Okay, that was actually kinda sweet.

"And now that he's a grown up, I do believe he can protect you."

I sighed. Another jab from the past. I didn't remember Mr. Pruitt being so sassy.

"I didn't have time to pick up a gift because I was informed fairly last minute of this wedding," he said. "So as my gift to you, I'll of course be paying for all this." He gestured around the room.

"That's really not necessary..." I started.

"I insist," Mr. Pruitt said. "And I wish you both a lifetime of happiness. And here's to many more heirs to come. Our legacy shall live on."

Rob started clapping.

Daphne elbowed him in the side.

And I just laughed. We'd have time to work on the whole heir and legacy thing. Because my family was not going to be anything like his. "Thanks," I said.

Brooklyn lifted her water glass. "Thanks, Dad."

Her father finally sat back down.

"That was a lot," Brooklyn whispered to me out of the corner of her mouth. "I'm so sorry." But she actually looked...pleased. Brooklyn didn't have a father growing up. She didn't know what it was like to be embarrassed by him in public. And I think it tickled her.

"Well, he was right about a few things. I will protect you. We're going to make lots of *heirs* for him. And I am the better Caldwell brother."

Brooklyn laughed.

"Mhm," Mason said and stood up from the table right next to ours. "I heard that."

"I was just kidding," I said.

"Sure you were." He tapped on the microphone and lifted up his glass. "To my annoying little brother."

Everyone laughed.

He smiled and turned toward me. "I don't really mean that. Weirdly enough, we've always gotten along. All four of us." He nodded at Rob and James. "But that doesn't mean I'm not about to embarrass the shit out of you."

Oh no, what are you about to say?

Brooklyn laughed.

Mason smiled at her. "There's something you should know about the man you just married. He's been head over heels in love with you since the moment you stepped foot in Empire High."

Well, he wasn't wrong about that. And I wasn't embarrassed.

"When we were teenagers, I used to joke around with him about it. But I've always respected him for knowing what he wanted. And not settling for less. He wanted the kind of love my parents have for each other. The kind of love we grew up around. And he found that with you. I think he taught all of us that we could be happy if we found the right person."

James nodded. Rob too.

"And when we lost you?" Mason took a few seconds, and I knew he needed to try to steady his breathing. "Sis."

Brooklyn sniffled beside me.

I put my arm around her shoulders and squeezed her tight.

"Your disappearance brought the whole world down with you. Nothing was ever the same again. You broke my brother. Hell, you broke all of us." He took a deep breath. "But when you came back? I see him again now. You gave me my brother back. The little lovesick puppy that he is."

I laughed even though I was biting back tears myself.

"And Rob is probably going to kill me, but I think we all need to take a second to thank Tanner for getting the two of you back together. Because I've never met two such stubborn people in my life. And without Tanner's meddling, I don't know if we'd be sitting here today, exactly 16 years after one of the worst days of our lives."

Rob groaned.

I nodded at Tanner. "Thank you, man."

He smiled. "It was easy. All in a day's work."

I knew that wasn't true. Mason was right. Brooklyn and I were both stubborn and we'd both held on to so much anger. Tanner had given us the push we needed to keep running into each other and sorting our shit out. We were here today because of him.

Mason cleared his throat. "I would also like to add that as your best friend and best man…"

Rob groaned again.

"Sorry, I have nothing to say about that really. Just wanted to rub it in Rob's face."

"This is such bullshit," Rob said.

Mason ignored him. "So, sis." He lifted his glass. "To the OG girl in the Untouchables."

Brooklyn sniffed again.

"The world crumbles without you in it. So please stick around because my brother is worthless without you."

I wouldn't necessarily say I was *worthless*, but…he had a really good point. My life was certainly worthless without Brooklyn in it.

"I love you both. And I wish you a lifetime of happiness. To the new Mr. and Mrs. Caldwell. Welcome to the club." He put his hand on Bee's shoulder.

I pulled Brooklyn even closer and looked down at her. "What happened to smiling so hard that your cheeks would get stuck that way?"

She blinked her tears away. "Happiness has a lot of different faces."

I leaned down and kissed her. I forgot we were in a crowded room until a few people whistled.

Brooklyn laughed and pulled back.

"I don't know how I'm going to top that," Kennedy said and slowly stood up. She took the microphone from Mason. "I remember trying to think of what to say 16 years ago for your wedding. Back then everything seemed so much simpler. It was just…my best friend in the whole world getting married. But now?"

Kennedy shook her head. "I've made so many mistakes. And I am so *so* sorry that I haven't always been the best friend I should have been. Back then. *And* more recently." She cringed.

This was a little awkward…

"For years, I thought I lost my best friend. I felt so stuck in the past. I missed you so damn much, Brooklyn." Kennedy started blinking fast. "I think the only person that missed you more was Matt. He never stopped missing you. Never stopped loving you. There's always been a hole in his heart, waiting for you to come back and fill it. And everything finally feels right in the world now that you're back."

I turned to look at Brooklyn.

"Thank you," she mouthed silently at Kennedy.

"It finally feels like we all get to live happily ever after. No more dark clouds. And no more bad luck," she said firmly to Brooklyn. "Nunca."

"Nunca," Brooklyn said and lifted her glass.

Kennedy laughed. "Here's to the happy couple. I wish you both a lifetime of happiness and laughter and joy. I've said it once and I'll say it again, no one deserves that more than you, Brooklyn. I love you. And I'm so so freaking happy for you both."

"I love you too," Brooklyn said.

Everyone clapped as Kennedy sat back down.

That speech could have been the most awkward thing ever, but she'd ended up pulling it off. I still couldn't believe that I asked Brooklyn for a sign and then Kennedy had shown up. I really *really* read into that too much. And at such a terrible time, right when Brooklyn came back. But Kennedy was right. Everything had worked out exactly how it was meant to. I was back with Brooklyn, where I belonged. And she was with Felix, who I apparently cock blocked like crazy in high school. I still felt really bad about that.

But this was a new beginning. A fresh start, just like Brooklyn had said. And I knew the four of us would always be friends.

The microphone made a screeching noise as Rob grabbed it from Kennedy.

Speaking of my friends…

"Great speeches, guys," he said with a chuckle. "Bravo. But I feel like we didn't embarrass anyone enough."

Ah, fuck me.

"As Matt's best friend…"

Tanner cleared his throat.

"Suck it, Tanner."

Tanner rolled his eyes.

"As I was saying. As Matt's best friend, I think it's very appropriate to mention the fact that he almost didn't get to win Brooklyn over. Because she almost got engaged to James."

Not true, man.

Brooklyn laughed.

"And actually, Mr. Pruitt has a point too. Mason is clearly the better brother. He's more...Masony."

What the fuck does that even mean?

"Word," Mason said.

"And Brooklyn's certainly screamed my name before." He winked at her.

Brooklyn's cheeks turned red.

"But alas, she chose you or whatever. And you already knocked her up." He laughed. "I'd call it a record, but I'm pretty sure Daphne *and* Penny were farther along when they walked down the aisle. The Hunters win." He put his hand up to high five James.

I was surprised that James actually high fived him.

"I think that finally closes the case. The Hunters have bigger dicks. Enough said."

"Shotgun weddings are not proof of dick size," Mason said.

"Said the only one of us who didn't knock up his wife before the vows were exchanged." Rob raised his eyebrows at him. "This has been a long standing debate for anyone who doesn't know what we're talking about."

"I don't understand where this is going..." Brooklyn said.

"Everywhere," Rob said. "Also, I just think it's important for the best friend of the groom to speak. Because that's why we're here. And that's what we are. Right, Matt? I'm your best friend? I want you to say it. So everyone can hear."

This wasn't supposed to be a moment for my vows to him. What was he doing? "You know I love all my groomsmen equally."

"I knew it!" Nigel yelled. "Matt loves me! He said so. All that bath time we spent together really paid off."

Umm...

"What is happening?" Brooklyn asked.

She'd figure out soon enough that I'd become a bit of a bath man.

"Chill, Nigel," Rob said. "This isn't about you. And I didn't want it to come to this, Matt," Rob said. "But you leave me no choice. Check this out." He pulled out his phone and hit a button.

My voice filled the room with a recording: "Rob is my best friend. I like him the most of all my friends."

Fuck. I'd forgotten about that.

Rob had somehow synced up to the D.J.'s speakers.

"Son of a bitch," Tanner said.

"Let me play it again in case you didn't hear." Rob hit the button again. "Rob is my best friend. I like him the most of all my friends."

Tanner glared at me.

"You were messing with my life," I said. "I was pissed at you." It had actually been because he kept trying to set Kennedy up with Felix. But I was not about to say that out loud right fucking now. *What the hell, Rob?!* He said he was going to save this recording for Tanner's wedding one day. He'd never said anything about playing it at mine.

"But I was right about everything," Tanner said. "Clearly." He pointed to Brooklyn. "She's always been your perfect match. It's true love."

"Well…yeah." What else was I supposed to say? In the moment, I'd hated Tanner for interfering. But yes, I was obviously very fucking grateful. And I was not going to talk about that little hiccup with Kennedy on my fucking wedding day.

"So take it back," Tanner said.

"Of course I take it back."

"You can't take it back," Rob said. "Listen: 'Rob is my best friend. I like him the most of all my friends.' "

"Stop playing that," I said.

"No taksie backsies!" Rob yelled.

"Young Robert, we're supposed to be celebrating the happy couple. Not…whatever it is you're doing. Sit down, son." Tanner tried to reach for the microphone, but Rob pulled it away with a deafening screech.

"Did you just call me son?" Rob looked deeply offended. "Why I oughta…"

"Enough," James said and tried to pull Rob down into his chair.

But Rob shook him off. "Face havin'," Rob said and put his hand in front of Tanner's face.

"What does that even mean? Of course I have a face." Tanner pushed his hand away.

"Based on the delivery and context, it seems as though Rob just directed a horrible insult at you," Nigel said. "You should be devastated right now, Master Tanner."

"You should be so devastated!" Rob said. "The most devastated. Ha!" He pointed at Tanner's face.

But Tanner didn't look devastated. He just looked confused and slightly entertained.

James successfully wrangled Rob into his chair.

"Congrats to the happy couple!" Rob yelled. "And my best friend!" Rob dropped the microphone and it screeched again.

"Um…thanks?" Brooklyn said.

"You're welcome." Rob winked at her.

I just shook my head. Although, that had been wildly entertaining. I expected nothing less from Rob commandeering a speech. I was pretty sure he was also already drunk.

Brooklyn looked up at me. "Interesting friends you got there."

I laughed. "They're your friends too."

"Touché. But are you seriously never going to tell them who your best friend is?"

"No, I think they'd be too jealous when they found out it was you."

She smiled up at me.

I ran my thumb along the tulle of her dress, tracing her clavicle bone.

Her throat made an adorable squeaking noise as she stared up at me.

Seriously, how much longer was she going to make me wait to get her out of her wedding dress?

CHAPTER 43

Friday

Brooklyn

Matt had loosened his tie and abandoned his jacket somewhere. The combination of his shirt sleeves rolled up and his vest did something to me. And that smile. God I loved when he smiled at me like that. He had this way of making time stand still. And for someone who was always worried about running out of it, his smile calmed me.

He pulled me back in close. "Today has been perfect," he said.

"So perfect." I reached up and wiped a little icing off the side of his jawline. I wasn't even sure how I'd gotten it there. I'd done my best to smash the cake right against his mouth.

We started dancing slowly even though the song was fast.

I looked around at everyone else dancing. Pretty much all our friends were very drunk. It actually reminded me a lot of homecoming. I smiled, the old memories swirling with the new ones as my hips swayed to the song.

Matt had wanted to right some wrongs from our past today by reading me his original vows. And there was something I'd always wanted to make right too. I should have run to him when I'd gotten in trouble after homecoming 16 years ago instead of running to James. I'd spend the rest of my life running into Matt's arms. Or maybe just not leaving them at all.

Starting tonight. "Truly magical," I said.

"Mhm," Matt said with a smile. "Enchanting."

"Fantastical."

He laughed. "I'll come up with synonyms for how perfect tonight is all you want. But I feel like maybe something else is on your mind?"

I bit my lip and looked up at him. "I just wanted you to know how much I loved today. But do you maybe want to get out of here?"

His smile grew even bigger. "I thought you'd never ask."

I tried to pull him off the dance floor, but he didn't budge. I looked up at him.

"There's just one small problem," he said.

I looked down at the front of his pants.

"What?" He laughed. "No. As fun as grinding all night with you has been…"

I hit his arm.

"…I wouldn't refer to that as a *small* problem."

"Fair," I said with a laugh.

"The problem is that I don't think we can go to the beach tonight."

James and Penny had been kind enough to offer us their beach house for the weekend. I hadn't been to Rehoboth since I was a kid. We were going to take a limo down and spend tonight and all day there together tomorrow. And then all our friends were going to join us on Sunday. Jacob had been so excited about getting to have a sleepover with Scarlett before joining us there.

"Why?" I asked. I'd kind of been thinking about limo sex for the last few hours.

"I don't know if you've looked outside recently, but the snow never stopped. It's a mess out there."

I smiled. "Snow is never a mess. It's one of my favorite things."

"I know. Nevertheless, it's not safe to drive all the way to Delaware tonight. I-95 is definitely a mess, even if the snow isn't."

I looked out the window. It was really coming down. "So should we just go home?"

He slowly shook his head. "I have a better plan. Do you trust me?"

"With my whole heart."

He smiled. "Give me one second. I need to go talk to Nigel."

Before I could protest, Matt dropped my hands and disappeared off the dance floor. I wasn't sure what our evening had to do with Nigel...

"May I have this dance?" Tanner asked, stepping into where Matt had been standing.

"Yes you may." I laughed as he pulled me in a little closer. He put one of my hands on his shoulder and grabbed the other before guiding me around the room.

Dancing with him felt like I was in a Disney princess movie. I loved dancing, but I didn't know any fancy dances. But it was like I did when I was dancing with him.

"He's going to love you for a thousand years," Tanner said.

"A thousand?" I laughed. "More like...sixty." I pressed my lips together. I didn't ever want to think about losing him.

Tanner cleared his throat. "Right. Hopefully longer than that though."

"Hopefully."

He spun us around the dance floor. "I just want you to know that I'm always here if you need a shoulder to cry on."

"I know, Tanner."

"When you first came to the city, I know you flirted with me quite a bit but…"

I laughed. "I never flirted with you."

"You asked me out on several dates, Brooklyn."

"I did not…"

"You asked me to go to a high school homecoming game with you. If that's not a date…"

"*You* asked *me*." It had been a ploy to get Matt and I back together. He was remembering it all wrong. "You're ridiculous."

He smiled. "I try. But seriously, I'll always be here as your friend. Forever. A thousand years," he added with a laugh.

"Thanks, Tanner. Honestly if Matt hadn't asked you to be a groomsman, I certainly would have asked you to be a bridesman."

He smiled. "Even though I brought the two of you together and it's not technically my match, I feel like a billion bucks tonight."

"I think the saying is a million bucks."

"For commoners, maybe."

I laughed. "You are definitely not a commoner."

"No. I'm ridiculous." He winked at me and spun me around again. "I know the two of you are heading to the beach, but my offer still stands. I can have a private jet ready for you to go to my private island in just a few minutes if you want."

It was very sweet of him to offer. But I'd been looking forward to a simple trip to Rehoboth. Although I doubted that James' beach house was simple. It didn't matter now anyway though. "It's snowing too much for us to leave the city."

Tanner looked out the window. "Oh no."

"Matt said he had an idea…" I felt a tug on my dress and looked down at Jacob.

"May I have this dance, Mommy?" Jacob bowed.

And I realized where he'd learned that from. It was 100% a Tanner move. "Yes you can, sweet boy."

"I'll leave you in my grandson's care," Tanner said. "I should go help Matt with the arrangements. Congratulations, Brooklyn. Thank you for coming back. Thank you for making my friend smile again." He kissed my cheek and then placed my hands in Jacob's.

I blinked away the tears in my eyes and smiled down at Jacob. "You've been dancing quite a bit tonight."

He shrugged. "Scarlett likes to dance."

"And so do you."

"But even if I didn't, I'd dance with her."

God, he was the sweetest boy. I lifted his hands into the air and we both shook our hips.

"Jacob, Jacob!" Scarlett said and ran over to us. "Can you dance with me again? Sophie stole Axel. And I like this song too."

I looked over at Sophie and Axel hopping around the dance floor. It actually looked like Axel did not want to be dancing. But Sophie kept pulling him back onto the dance floor. They were so cute.

"Duty calls, Mommy." Jacob dropped my hands and practically sprinted off.

I laughed. He was so smitten with her.

"So I took into account that you love snow," Matt said.

I spun around and looked up at him.

"Close your eyes, baby."

I shook my head, but closed my eyes anyway. He guided me off the dance floor and helped me into a chair.

His hand fell from mine and then I felt his fingers slide down my ankle.

"Matt." I opened my eyes to see him kneeling in front of me right off the dance floor.

"You said you trusted me."

"I do."

"Then keep your eyes closed."

I smiled and closed my eyes again. My breath caught as he undid one of my high heels and then the other. And then I felt the most comfortable slippers replace my heels. I sighed. So much better.

"Okay, open your eyes."

I opened them. Matt was still kneeling in front of me. But he hadn't put slippers on my feet. I was wearing snow boots. My eyes met his.

"We are going to go for a snowy walk to a very nice hotel that overlooks Central Park. If that's okay with you."

"How on earth did you get snow boots here that fit me so well?" I stared at the pile of jackets on the table next to me. "And where did all those jackets come from?"

He shrugged. "Nigel sorted out the logistics."

"We helped too," Mason said as he joined us. He and Bee were already in winter coats and snow boots too. "You're staying with us tonight."

"Oh." *Umm.* I loved Mason and Bee, but I didn't exactly want to spend my wedding night with them. I was thrilled that all of our friends were going to join us at the beach on *Sunday*. But I wanted some alone time with Matt right now.

Bee laughed. "Not *with* us. He meant at the hotel we live in. A separate hotel room. The honeymoon suite, actually. The owner owed us a favor after he took a week to fix…never mind. Not important. Are you guys ready?"

"Absolutely," Matt said and kicked off his dress shoes. He pulled on a pair of snow boots too.

"This is going to be fun," Rob said and walked over in a big puffy jacket.

"You're coming too?" I asked.

"Not yet." He winked at me. "But I'm sure Daphne will have me cumming soon enough." He slapped her butt.

She looked truly horrified for a second and then laughed. "I have had too much to drink. And I get very handsy when I'm drunk. Wait, where did Sophie go? She was right here a second ago…"

"Don't worry," Penny said as she grabbed one of the jackets off the table. "We're still on kid watching duty. But we figured it was safer to stay at the hotel than drive…crap, you're right. Where did Sophie go?"

"Got her," James said and pulled out her chair. Sophie had been sitting there pushing icing off her cake. She grabbed the cake in her hand as James picked her up.

It was like a big sleepover. But in separate rooms. And I could definitely get down with that.

"Is this okay?" Matt asked as he pulled me into his arms.

"It's perfect."

"Magical," he said.

"Enchanting."

He laughed. "Fantastical. Let's find you and Jacob jackets that fit."

It didn't take long for us to all get bundled up. Nigel had even gotten us handmade mittens somehow. They were so warm and cozy.

"Wait," Matt said. "We almost forgot something very important."

He dropped to his knees again in front of me and started to lift up my skirt.

"What are you doing?" I tried to put my hands on his shoulders, but his head disappeared beneath my dress.

And then I felt his kiss on the inside of my thigh.

Jesus.

He grabbed my garter with his teeth and slowly pulled it down my leg.

Rob whistled as Matt's head reemerged.

Matt winked at me and then turned around. He shot the garter into the air and even though Tanner tried to sidestep it, there was no room for him to move. It landed against his chest. He grabbed it, shook his head, and then handed it off to Rob.

"Dude, I'm married," Rob said with a laugh and tried to hand it back.

"I am most certainly not the next man here to be married. Here." Tanner grabbed the garter and handed it to my dad.

My dad looked equally bewildered.

I couldn't help but laugh.

"Your turn," Matt said and picked my bouquet off the table.

I looked around for Kennedy. I really wanted to aim it at her, but I didn't see her or Felix anywhere. I smiled. They must have snuck off somewhere. I didn't see Justin anywhere either. Or he definitely would have reminded us to do this before we left. I turned around, took a deep breath, and tossed the bouquet over my shoulder. I spun back around just in time to see it land in Scarlett's outstretched hands.

"I'm getting married! I'm getting married!" Scarlett yelled. The smile on her face was so big. "Daddy, look!"

And now James was the one that looked bewildered.

"Sorry," I mouthed silently at him.

He shook his head. The scowl he used to wear so frequently back in high school was etched across his face.

I smiled when Scarlett took turns holding the bouquet with Jacob and Axel for pictures. She was going to be so much trouble when she was older.

We said our goodbyes to our parents and other friends and headed outside into the snow. The whole city was hushed in a white blanket. I had a feeling I was really going to love winters here. I smiled and looked up at the sky, remembering dancing in the snow with Miller.

Matt wrapped his arm around my shoulders and guided us toward the hotel.

I smiled when I saw Justin and Donnelley chatting by the bridge. As we walked closer, Justin gave me two thumbs up.

Even though it was cold, I felt warm with all the laughter around us.

We made it across the bridge before the first snowball flew through the air. It hit Nigel in the back of the head. I spun around to see Jacob laughing.

"Snowball fight!" Nigel yelled and then immediately got hit in the face with another snowball from someone else. He dove behind a big rock as the kids started pelting him.

I laughed and then screamed when a snowball hit my back. I spun around to see James laughing.

"Oh, it's so on." I leaned down and started to make a snowball. But I got pelted with two more before I stood back up. I tossed one at Rob and he used Daphne as a human shield.

"Hey!" Daphne tackled him into the snow in a fit of laughter.

Matt started throwing snowballs at Tanner.

Tanner looked completely shocked.

"Don't tell me they didn't do this overseas either?" Matt asked.

"No, they did." He brushed the snow off his jacket. "I just didn't think anyone was silly enough to start a war with me." He made a snowball at record speed and started chucking them at Matt.

It took five seconds before the silent night descended into chaos.

"What the fuck?" Matt said and tried to block them from hitting his face.

I threw one at Tanner to help out Matt.

But Tanner didn't seem at all phased by the cold snow. He was like a snowball machine.

And then the most shocking thing happened. Rob joined him and started pelting us.

They were working as a team. Finally. But in the worst way possibly for me and Matt.

Matt tried his best to shelter me from the flying snowballs. But they were coming from every direction now.

I tossed one at James.

He tossed three back at me at record speed.

Justin and Donnelley ran across the bridge and joined in too.

All you could hear was our laughter in the swirling snow.

Penny laughed as James took a snowball right in the face.

And Bee kept screaming and trying to hide behind Mason.

"Help me!" Mason said. But then he realized that Bee didn't have any gloves.

Penny didn't have any either, but that wasn't slowing her down. She was throwing them even faster than James.

The kids had started making snow angels, already bored of the snowball fight. But the adults were very much enjoying attacking each other.

I tried to dodge a snowball from Mason and started to slip.

Matt caught me around the waist and somehow we both toppled into the snow.

He moved on top of me to cover me from the onslaught of snowballs.

I couldn't stop laughing. But Matt silenced me with a kiss. God, I'd been dying to be alone with him all night. And even though it felt like just the two of us in that moment, I knew we were surrounded by people. And snow. So much snow. It fell around us and I couldn't really describe the feeling in my chest. I felt at home whenever I was with Matt. But I felt it so much in that moment. It was like a piece of the lake house was back here in the city with me.

The tip of Matt's nose was red. And his cheeks were rosy. And even with all the planning and craziness leading up to this day, I was pretty sure this was what I'd remember most. The snowball fight with our friends.

His lips fell from mine and moved to my ear. "So much for not ruining your dress."

I groaned. I could already feel the chill seeping through the thin material. "At least it's just snow. But you do have a good point. Are you thinking what I'm thinking?"

"That we should get you and the baby out of the snow?"

I laughed. "Not exactly." That was another good point though. I bit my lip, hoping he'd get the message that my thoughts were much more sinful.

He smiled. "Then you're probably thinking we need to get you out of this wet dress and hang it up to dry. Immediately. So it doesn't get ruined. Right?" He smiled.

I doubted he really cared about the state of my dress. He was staring at me like he was just excited to get me out of it. "Yes, please."

He pulled me to my feet.

I took one last look at all our friends playing in the snow. When I was around Matt, I truly did feel like a teenager again. This was honestly madness. And the best wedding ever.

"Ready?" Matt asked.

I squeezed his hands. "I've been waiting for this moment all night."

CHAPTER 44

Friday

Matt

We said goodnight to Jacob and goodbye to all our friends. They responded by throwing more snowballs at us. Getting pelted by snowballs for our departure wasn't exactly what I'd pictured. Weren't you supposed to throw seeds or have sparklers or something?

Part of me wanted to stay and win this fight. But a much bigger part of me wanted to be alone with my wife.

Brooklyn and I ran hand in hand through the snow falling in Central Park.

Her laughter was the only thing I could hear in the snowy night. Walking in Central Park with her had always been one of my favorite things. But running with her through the snow in her wedding dress? Nothing was ever going to top this.

When we reached the hotel, she pulled me to a stop.

I put my hands on her hips as she put hers behind my neck. Her mittens were cold from the snow, but I barely felt it.

We just stood there, staring at each other.

"Here's to forever," I said and leaned down, stopping a fraction of an inch from her lips.

She stood on her tiptoes, closing the distance, and kissed me.

I pulled her hips, pressing her against me.

"Here's to never growing up," she said with a smile. "I think snowball fights on our anniversary should be a new tradition."

"Then I promise to take you somewhere it's snowing every year on our anniversary. But there's something else that needs to be a tradition too."

"And what is that?"

"Ravishing your body."

She squealed as I lifted her into my arms. "What are you doing?!"

"Carrying you through the threshold." I walked up the steps to the hotel.

The doorman opened the door and we ducked inside. The heat was on full blast and I could almost feel my nose again.

"I think that's for *our* door, not the hotel door," Brooklyn said.

"Eh, I wasn't sure. Just wanted to be on the safe side."

"You can put me down." She looked up at me.

"Not a chance."

She laughed the whole way to the check-in counter. And as I managed to balance her in my arms and grab the keycard.

I carried her to the elevator. The instrumental music seemed endless as the elevator climbed to the top floor. Brooklyn looked amazing in her dress. But I'd been waiting all day to get her out of it. The doors finally dinged and parted. I carried her to our door and swiped the keycard against the lock.

The suite was exactly what Nigel promised. The fireplace even had a roaring fire already going. I carried Brooklyn over to it and put her down on her feet. I leaned down to kiss her, but she'd already spun around.

"Oh my God." She looked out the window at the snow falling slowly over Central Park. She turned back to me with a smile. "So this is how the other half lives, huh?"

"Baby, *you're* the other half now. Better get used to it."

She laughed and turned back to look out at the snow.

I pulled off my mittens and jacket and tossed them on the couch.

"You can see the twinkle lights on the bridge, even from all the way up here." She pointed to our bridge in the distance.

I walked up behind her and wrapped my arms around her.

"Oh my God, I think I can see our friends too! Look! They're still having a snowball fight." She laughed.

I didn't need to see our friends throwing snowballs right now. All I wanted was her. I slowly unzipped her jacket.

Her laughter died in her throat as I pushed her jacket off her shoulders.

I kissed the side of her neck. Her skin pebbled under my lips, but I wasn't sure if it was because of me or the cold. "Let's get you warmed up," I said and pulled her in front of the fire. I peeled off her wet mittens and tossed them onto the ground.

The shadows from the fire danced across her face.

And for some reason, I felt like a teenager again. Staring at her for the first time. Desperate to make her mine. Sixteen years ago, I'd stolen her first kiss. I didn't want to steal anything from her ever again. I wanted her to give me everything willingly. I wanted her to beg me for it.

"Tell me what you're thinking," I said.

"That I've never seen you look so handsome before."

I reached out and trailed my fingers down the fabric between her breasts. She wasn't wearing the rings Miller gave her tonight. She was only wearing the ones from me. I knew how hard that must have been for her. Tonight she was mine, and only mine.

"What are you thinking?" she asked.

"All I've been thinking about all night is how much I want to get you out of that dress. But now that we're standing here, I kind of want you to keep it on."

She smiled. "So you just want to stand here staring at me in my wedding dress?"

I shook my head. "No, I want my head beneath your skirt and you screaming my name."

Her cheeks flushed. But I knew it wasn't from the fire.

I ran my fingers lightly across one of her rosy cheeks and brushed my thumb along her lower lip.

She bit down on my thumb.

Fuck me. I pulled my thumb out of her mouth. "God I love you." I grabbed her ass and lifted her up.

She wrapped her thighs around my waist as my teeth sunk into her lower lip. I loved when she bit me. But I liked biting her even more.

She moaned.

I kissed her hard as I moved to my knees. I did my best not to slam her back against the carpet as I set her down in front of the fire. All I wanted to do was fuck her senseless. I knew how much she loved when I was rough with her. But I was very aware of my baby growing inside of her. And tonight wasn't about any of that. It was about savoring every inch of her.

She tried and failed to unbutton the buttons on my vest, her fingers frantic. And I knew her thoughts had been just as sinful as mine all day.

I bunched up her skirt in my fist, pushing it up her thighs. This was way too much material. Especially when I preferred her in nothing at all.

She laughed as the fabric started to fall back into place.

Well, I did say I wanted my head beneath her skirt. I ignored the fabric and pulled off her snow boots. And then I leaned down and kissed the inside of her ankle. I kissed and nipped at the skin along her shin.

"Matt," she moaned.

But I was taking my damn time. I left a trail of kisses up the inside of her knee and thigh. I stopped right at the top of her thigh and then moved to her other ankle to repeat the whole thing over again.

She groaned in frustration.

"You know what I want," I said and kissed her calf. "I want my wife to beg me."

"Matthew Caldwell, fuck me right now."

I chuckled against her skin. That was not at all what was about to happen. Maybe after I made her come with my tongue and made slow love to her in front of the fire. Yeah, definitely after those two things. I kept kissing up her thigh.

She put her hands on my shoulders, trying to pull me up.

But I wasn't hurrying the moment. I'd already told her what I was going to do. And I always made good on a promise. I'd have her screaming my name with my head beneath her skirt soon enough.

She gave up and grabbed the sides of her white silk thong to lower it.

But I pressed my fingers along the front of it to stop her. "I like this."

"Matt!"

She'd be saying my name a lot differently in a few minutes. I bit the top of her thong and pulled it down with my teeth. After removing her garter earlier, all I wanted to do was remove all her clothes like that. I pulled it down her thighs.

She kicked it off and then put her bare foot on my chest. "Now fuck me."

I shook my head.

"Matt!"

"Not until I taste you." I bunched her skirt up her waist, leaned down, and placed a long stroke along her wetness.

Her hips rose to meet my face and her fingers tangled in my hair to hold me in place. But I wasn't going anywhere.

I slid my tongue deeper, pressing my nose against her clit.

She moaned.

I knew I'd have her in less than a minute. I knew her body like the back of my hand. I knew everything she liked. Everything she needed.

I swirled my tongue around her and her thighs gripped the sides of my head.

She was always so worried that I'd pull away. But I loved when she finished on my face. I moved my hands to her ass and lifted her up so I could feast on her sweetness.

Each squirm and moan made me know I was close.

Her fingers tightened in my hair.

I moved my mouth to her clit and slid two fingers inside of her. She was so fucking wet for me. So ready to grip my cock. I sucked on her clit as I slowly slid my fingers in and out of her. *Come for me, baby. Scream my name, just the way I like.*

I lightly bit down on her clit and her pussy started pulsing around my fingers.

I moved my fingers and thrust my tongue back inside of her. I loved the way her coming felt against my tongue. I traced slow circles on her clit with my thumb as her hips rose again.

"Matt," she moaned exactly the way I liked. Her fingers dug into my back, trying to rip off my shirt.

I just thrust my tongue deeper, lapping up her juices as her first orgasm subsided. Yes, her first. Because I wasn't going to be able to keep my hands off of her tonight.

I slowly lifted my head and wiped my mouth with the back of my hand. "Delicious."

She grabbed my tie and pulled my lips to hers. I knew that she could taste her own sweetness on my tongue. And it was so fucking hot that she didn't care.

She reached down and palmed my erection through my tuxedo pants.

I groaned as my tongue swirled around hers.

Unlike her attempt on my vest, she managed to undo the buttons and zipper on my pants. She pushed them and my boxers down my hips and grabbed my cock.

Fuck.

She guided my tip to her wetness.

She was trying so hard to be fucked right now.

But I wasn't doing that. I pressed just my tip into her wetness.

Brooklyn groaned in frustration.

"Baby, it's our wedding night." I slowly slid in another inch. "Let me cherish you."

She wrapped her legs around my waist and used the leverage to make me thrust my length into her hard. All the way to the hilt.

I groaned. What was she trying to do to me? "I love you." I buried my face in the side of her neck, biting down on her flesh, trying my best to keep my pace slow.

"Harder." She tried to match my slow thrusts with her hips.

She was driving me crazy with her requests. Suddenly all I could think about was tying her up. Teasing her. Fucking her senseless. I was trying so hard to remain in control.

But even the heat from the fire seemed to be spurring me on.

I reached up and pulled the front of her dress down. I heard something pop.

"Matt! There's buttons!"

I knew she'd specifically asked me not to ruin her dress, but she was driving me fucking crazy. "We can get it fixed."

"Screw it." She grabbed the sides of my face and pulled my lips back to hers.

I undid a few of the buttons on the back of her dress as she pushed off her sleeves.

I pulled down the front of her dress without any resistance this time. I kissed between her breasts.

"Harder," she said again.

I bit down on one of her nipples and she moaned. But I didn't increase my pace. I slid in and out of her slowly. She gripped me tight, like she was trying to make me lose control.

"Harder," she repeated.

I chuckled against her skin. "Baby, do you seriously want to remember our wedding night with…you on your knees and me fucking you from behind?"

"Yes, that! Good idea." She pushed on my chest and slid away from me. And then she got on all fours. She hiked her skirt up out of the way.

I was really loving what being pregnant was doing to her. I leaned forward and kissed one of her exposed ass cheeks.

"Matt," she said. "Fuck me so hard that I can't walk for days."

If that's what she wanted, I'd give her what she liked. I'd wanted this to be the perfect romantic night. But it didn't matter, we'd always remember tonight as being romantic. And I had an idea. "Be a good girl and go put your hands against the glass."

She looked over her shoulder at me.

I nodded toward the windows and then spanked her ass.

She moaned.

I stared down at the wedding band on my finger. The red mark left on her ass was the same, but the ring made it feel different. And I could definitely get used to the sight of that. I massaged where I spanked. "You know I hate repeating myself. Hands on the glass. Now."

Brooklyn stood up, lifted her skirt, and walked over to the window. She let her skirt fall back in place. And she didn't seem to care at all that the front of her dress was pulled down. I could see the reflection of her tits in the glass.

She was so fucking gorgeous.

I watched her place her hands on the glass and arch her back.

I stood up and pulled my pants back up. My erection strained against the zipper. I slowly approached her. I was completely transfixed by the shadows dancing across her skin.

I'd wanted to make love to her.

To take our time.

But I could make this memorable too. I glanced out at the view of Central Park and the city in the distance. She was about to give me another first.

CHAPTER 45

Friday

Brooklyn

I could feel his eyes on me. His gaze sent goosebumps chasing across my skin. All I could think about was *more*. I wanted him in every way possible.

But this? I stared at his reflection stalking closer in the glass. I don't think I'd ever wanted him so desperately. He stopped right behind me.

The top of my dress was pushed down and my hair was everywhere. But Matt was still completely dressed and composed. The sleeves of his dress shirt were rolled up, just like they had been when he'd restrained me at Club Onyx. This was the kind of thing he liked. He was in his element. And I really liked it too.

He put his hand on my lower back, making me arch more. "Spread your legs." His voice was low and gruff. The way it was when he'd tied me up. Like something had shifted inside of him.

I swallowed hard and spread my legs wider.

"I will spend the rest of my life cherishing you. But right now? I'm going to make you scream. Because you asked. And I like giving my wife what she wants."

Jesus. Every time he said "my wife," I swear it made me even more desperate for his cock. I was Matthew Caldwell's wife. I was his and he was mine. And by the tone of his voice, he was definitely about to make this a night to remember.

"Remember our first kiss in the auditorium?" His fingers gently traced down my spine.

I shivered from his touch. "You mean the one you stole?" I tried to hide my smile.

His fingers ran over the fabric of my dress. "Baby, you gave it to me willingly."

I swallowed hard. We both knew he was right.

"I missed out on a lot of firsts." He pushed my skirt up. "But I have a feeling you've never had sex when the whole city could be watching."

I stared out at Central Park. *Oh my God.* I hadn't even thought about someone seeing us. We were really high up, but it was dark outside. The snowstorm probably helped obscure us from view too. *But...* My eyes refocused on the reflection of us. My breasts exposed and my skirt hiked up. "Do you really think someone could see us?"

"I hope so." His fingers dug into my hips. "I want everyone to know that you're mine." He thrust into me hard.

Fuck. I pressed harder against the glass. The new angle felt amazing. Or maybe it wasn't the angle. Maybe it was the thought of having the whole city watching.

Matt slid in and out, faster and faster.

Anyone could look up and see us. My wedding dress scrunched around my waist and my husband fucking me hard from behind.

"After that kiss, all I wanted to do was bend you over one of the auditorium seats and fuck you so hard." His fingers dug into my hips. "For teasing me." *Thrust.* "Torturing me." *Thrust.* "And for saying that I stole that kiss when you were pulling me closer."

God. "You didn't steal it. I wanted you. Desperately."

He slammed into me again.

I thought back to the homecoming game, when we ran into each other in the auditorium. When I arrived back in the city. He'd reclaimed me in that auditorium. I didn't know that he'd been fantasizing about that ever since our first kiss.

"I always knew it," Matt said.

"Of course I wanted you to kiss me." I could barely keep my eyes off him at Empire High. There wasn't a chance in hell that I'd be able to keep my lips off him either.

"Not just that."

I stared at his reflection in the window. It made it look like the snow was falling around us, even though we were safely inside with a fire warming us.

"I knew one day I'd make you my wife." He groaned as I matched his thrust by pushing back on the glass.

He had known. He'd always known. And Matt always got what he wanted. I knew it back then. And nothing had changed. He'd wanted me. He'd wanted a family. And together we were making it all come true. With the whole fucking city watching.

"I was made for loving you," Matt said.

I felt tears welling in my eyes. Matthew Caldwell had owned my heart since I was 16. Time and distance changed nothing. I still thought of him over the years. It was like he was in my veins ever since I first saw him in the halls of Empire High. "I was made for loving you too, Matt."

Normally saying something like that would make guilt grip my heart. But I knew how big my heart was. How much love it was capable of giving. And I loved Matt. Fiercely. I always had. And I always would.

"You are so gorgeous," Matt said.

My eyes met his in our reflection. The crackling fire sent shadows dancing across his features. And I saw it all. Our whole story staring back at me. I saw him washing my cut in the bathroom at that stupid party I was catering. I saw him sitting down next to me in the cafeteria. Him turning around and talking to me in class. Him demanding I take off Felix's jacket. Him dancing on the homecoming float. Him holding me when I cried every night, missing my uncle. Him proposing. Twice. Him fighting to win me back after 16 years. Him continuously showing up and learning to love the new me. Him sending me 16 years' worth of yellow roses to make up for our time apart. Him treating my son like his own. Such small moments that would last forever in my heart.

I felt tears streaming down my cheeks.

"Baby." He slowly pulled out of me. "Did I hurt…"

"No." I turned around and looked up at him. "You healed me." Just like Tanner had said he would. If I let him in again.

Matt dropped his forehead to mine. "You healed me. By coming back to me."

I tried to blink away my tears. "You were right." I took a deep breath. "I want to cherish this moment." I slowly unbuttoned his vest as he tilted my chin up so he could kiss me.

Not a rushed kiss like 16 years ago in the auditorium. A slow one. Like we had all the time in the world. And God, I hoped we did. I hoped my curse didn't extend to him. Because I knew I couldn't live without him.

He'd always been there. Even when I tried to ignore his existence.

He was my rock.

He was my shoulder to cry on.

He was my home.

He was everything to me.

I pushed his vest off his broad shoulders and undid his tie as his tongue swirled around mine. I unbuttoned his shirt next and pushed it off too. My fingers ran down his six-pack as he somehow managed to undo the rest of the buttons on my dress. I felt it pool around my ankles at the same time I pushed down his tuxedo pants and boxers.

I pulled back from our kiss and looked up at him. I was still getting used to this version of him. For so long, he'd been frozen at 16 in my mind. "I can't believe we found our way back to each other."

"It's fate," he whispered against my lips.

"But you never deserved to be in pain for 16 years, Matt." I hated that he thought that. That he'd *lived* that.

"Maybe I just needed 16 years to grow up to be worthy of you."

I reached up and ran my fingers through his hair. "I was always the one reaching. You were way out of my league."

He smiled down at me. "Not a chance in hell, Brooklyn." He took a step forward, caging me in against the glass. "I'm the luckiest man on earth because you chose me." He ran his thumb along the scar on my stomach. "Twice."

"I'm the lucky one." I stood on my tiptoes and kissed him again. "And I want to make love to my husband." *My husband.* I felt a lump in my throat. But I refused to think about the pain right now. I just wanted to focus on him. Because I needed him to know he was wrong. He'd always been worthy of me. When we'd first fallen in love, we were so young. And foolish. We'd both made mistakes. But what mattered was that we were here right now. Together. Forever.

I left my heartache behind as he lifted me back into his arms.

He laid me down in front of the fire again.

"Now, where were we?" He leaned down and kissed my ankle.

I groaned. "Not again."

He laughed against my skin and sat back. "Then how about you show me exactly what you want." He grabbed my wrist and pulled me on top of him as he lay down.

I straddled his waist and slowly lowered my hips, letting him sink inside of me. *God yes.* I put my hands on his shoulders to steady myself as I moved my hips up and down.

At first he let me set the pace. He ran his index finger along the necklace he gave me, and then his fingers trailed down my bicep and forearm, until stopping at my hand. He lifted my hand and kissed where my rings sat. The rings he'd given me.

I shifted my hips and he groaned and dropped my hand. I leaned forward, pressing my breasts in his face.

He mumbled something unintelligible against my chest. It sounded a whole lot like "perfection." And I couldn't stop smiling.

His tongue swirled around one of my nipples as his free hand squeezed my other breast.

I started grinding against him, his cock stretching me, claiming me. The heat from the fire made sweat drip down my back.

Matt groaned again. His fingers tightened on my waist and he started guiding me.

Fuck. I tilted my head back. He knew my body so much better than I did.

He moved one of his hands off my hip and his thumb brushed against my clit.

He sat back up, capturing my lips in a searing kiss. And somehow managed to roll us over so that I was on my back now. He thrust into me deeper. Harder. Exactly how I wanted.

My fingers dug into his back as I started to clench around him. "Matt," I moaned. "Yes! Yes, God!"

He groaned and thrust forward, again and again, emptying himself in me as I gripped him.

Our chests rose and fell as we stared at each other.

I reached up and ran my hand along the scruff on his jawline.

Matthew Caldwell was all mine.

CHAPTER 46

Saturday – One Week Later

Matt

I kept waiting for someone to pinch me. It felt like I was in a dream. A perfect dream where I had everything in the world I'd ever wanted. I was used to living in hell for the past 16 years.

The wind blew and I closed my eyes. The snow had melted pretty quickly and the weather was unseasonably warm. It felt like fall. And it smelled like fall. It smelled like her.

A chill ran down my spine. I opened my eyes and looked up into the stands of Empire High, expecting to be searching for a ghost.

But Brooklyn wasn't a ghost.

She was standing there very much alive. Cheering for me in my old jersey.

I blinked and she was still there. All my friends were there too. I was still getting used to seeing them here. They'd avoided Empire High like the plague since graduation. I was the only one that refused to try to move on. And I was so glad I hadn't.

Jacob was standing on the bleachers cheering like crazy. Even Mr. Pruitt was up there. His crisp suit looked very out of place, but he was cheering along with everyone else.

I waved up to them.

Jacob waved back and Brooklyn blew me a kiss.

I smiled and turned back to the field. I needed to get my head in the game. Because the score was tied and our defense was looking sluggish. If this went to overtime, we'd be screwed. And we hadn't been winning all season just to lose the championship game.

It was fourth down and we were only two yards away from a touchdown.

"What do you think?" Kennedy asked. "I don't think we'll win if it goes to overtime. Our D is depleted."

"Exactly what I was thinking."

"Same," Nigel said and handed me a champagne flute full of water.

I shook my head. Always with the glassware on the field. It was probably a hazard. But the coach across the field looked very perplexed by it. I had a feeling that Nigel was secretly just very good at psychological warfare.

"We need to blitz," Nigel said. "And huddle. Probably a safety or two. Oh, what about a squib kick?"

I laughed. Yes, Nigel was good at psyching out the opposing team's coach, but he still did not understand American football. "Good thinking, Nigel." I looked at the clock and let it tick down to three seconds. And then I blew my whistle for a time out.

"We're doing the squib kick?! Yes!"

No, we weren't going to kick the ball away in a weird way when we were about to score. But we were going to kick it. "Sure." I slapped his back.

"I knew it!" he yelled.

Kennedy laughed.

Everyone ran off the field toward us.

"We could run it," Kennedy said. "They'll be expecting a throw."

"We could do that…" my voice trailed off as the quarterback, Smith reached us.

"I can do it," Smith said. "And if no one's open, I'll just run it in."

I shook my head.

"But, Coach..."

"We're kicking it." I looked over at Jefferson who was still sitting on the bench.

He hadn't even joined the huddle. It looked like he was about to shit himself.

"Jefferson's got this. Right?" I asked him.

"Oh. Um. I..." His cheeks puffed up like he was going to vomit. He was gripping the sides of the bench so tightly that his knuckles were turning white.

I expected Smith to argue. Or throw his helmet. What I didn't expect was for him to nod his head.

This was his last game at Empire High. It could be the last game he ever played anywhere. I knew he wanted the glory.

"You're right, Coach," Smith said. "Jefferson's got this."

"I do?" Jefferson asked.

"Of course you do," Kennedy said. She grabbed him by his elbow and pulled him to his feet.

Jefferson looked uneasily up at me.

I put my hands on his shoulders. "Just remember everything Coach Alcaraz has taught you."

He slowly nodded.

I'd set out to help him fit in. He'd made most of the field goals and extra points the second half of the season. He'd been practicing late most days. He'd improved so much since the beginning of the season when he kept setting off car alarms.

And I knew he was scared. But I also knew that no matter how scared you were of something, it was always worth it to take your shot. No matter how insurmountable the thing felt. Or how hard it would be. I looked over my shoulder at Brooklyn in the stands. Yeah, it was always worth it.

The ref blew his whistle, signaling the end of our time out.

"Go Eagles on three," I said and put my hand out.

The team threw their hands in too.

"One, two, three…Go Eagles!" we all yelled at the top of our lungs.

The team sprinted out onto the field, minus Jefferson.

Jefferson just stood there, his eyes like saucers.

"Go get 'em," I said.

He gulped.

"You've got this."

He slowly nodded, took a deep breath, and jogged out onto the field.

I heard a few gasps from the stands.

But Jefferson had this. I knew it. I pictured Brooklyn singing to her tomato plants. All those little Henrys. She'd made them thrive. And it felt like Henry Jefferson had tied us together somehow. Through the distance and time. And I was putting all my chips on him. He had to thrive too.

"Go Henry!" Kennedy yelled from the sidelines. And then she whispered to me: "It looks like he's going to faint."

"He's got this," I said firmly.

I held my breath as the ball was snapped. Smith caught the ball and placed it on the ground for Jefferson.

Jefferson's foot collided with the ball.

The whole crowd hushed as the ball took off from the ground. It flew over the heads of everyone on the line. Above a defender's hand who jumped to try and block it. Up, up, and right through the center of the goal posts as the clock ticked down to zero. The buzzer sounded, signaling the end of regulation time.

For just a second, everyone in the stadium was silent.

And then the cheers erupted louder than ever before.

The whole crowd was chanting: "Jeff-er-son! Jeff-er-son! Jeff-er-son!"

"Victory is ours!" Nigel yelled.

The team lifted Jefferson up on their shoulders and joined in on the chanting.

I breathed a sigh of relief and a smile spread across my face. *Fuck yes!*

Coaching this team had been the only thing holding me together for the past several years. They'd needed me. They'd relied on me. And normally I'd be out on that field screaming with them.

But I knew that focusing on coaching was just my attempt at filling a void. Because all I'd ever wanted was Brooklyn. To need me. To rely on me. To love me. She was all I'd ever needed. All I'd ever wanted.

I turned to look at the stands. Brooklyn was pushing her way through the crowd that was flooding the field. But the stadium was packed. She was barely halfway down the stands.

So I started running toward her.

Game days had always been the days I missed her most. Seeing flashes of her in the stands. I used to visit her grave a lot on those days to talk to the old her. When I first realized she was alive, I'd wanted to keep talking to the old her. But I was so glad we weren't the old us. Because I loved this version of her even more. She was finally wearing a wedding band I'd given her. She was finally Brooklyn Caldwell. She had my baby in her stomach. Yeah, I loved the new her.

I pushed through the crowd. I could just make her out in the sea of people. All I wanted was her in my arms. To celebrate with a kiss. Just the way we used to when I was the one playing.

Even though we'd gone through so much pain to get here, I knew I was lucky. Lucky to get to fall in love with her all over again. Maybe the first time wasn't meant to last. But this time? This was forever.

CHAPTER 47

Saturday

Brooklyn

I tried to run down the bleachers, but there were too many people in my path. It felt like I was in high school again, watching Matt play. Everyone cheering his name, but knowing he only cared that I was cheering for him.

I no longer saw him out on the field. He'd disappeared in the sea of people rushing the field to celebrate with the team. I ducked under someone's arm and sidestepped someone else. I was barely halfway down the bleachers.

I turned around to make sure Jacob had stayed where he'd promised. I laughed when I saw him perched on Tanner's shoulders so he could see better. They were both cheering like crazy. And so were the rest of our friends. The Hunters and Caldwells all back together again. New friends and old. I felt tears welling in my eyes.

For so long, I thought everyone was better off with me gone. But I was wrong. About all of it. I'd needed them in my life again. And they'd needed me too.

And for just a second, I saw a flash of brown hair behind them. Matt had told me that if he looked into the crowd and squinted, he could almost see me. That it almost felt like I was there when he thought I was dead.

I squinted at the crowd, picturing Miller.

I smiled. Matt was right. It was easy to picture ghosts when you wanted to. Especially here where everything all began. I touched the ring that was once again hanging from my neck.

Miller would always be here.

He'd always be in my heart.

I turned back around to search for Matt.

And suddenly he appeared in front of me, one step below me. I leaned down and kissed him as he pulled me into his arms and spun me around.

I laughed against his lips. It felt like we were in high school again. Me cheering for him and then jumping into his arms. I felt carefree. And young. And safe in his arms.

I kept thinking to myself that I couldn't possibly be any happier. And then another moment would come where I couldn't stop smiling.

Matt had always been good at making me smile. Even though he said he remembered making me cry more than laugh. That wasn't true. He'd been the reason my heart kept beating after my mom died. And my uncle.

There had always been so many reasons why Matt and I wouldn't work. He was New York City's elite. And I was just a poor girl from the wrong side of the tracks.

But we'd defied all the odds.

"We won," Matt whispered against my lips.

And I wasn't even sure if he was referring to the game. Or us.

"I love you, Matthew Caldwell," I said. I wasn't sure he heard me through all the cheers.

But then he whispered: "I love you, Brooklyn Caldwell."

I laughed and he kissed me again.

I was pretty sure I fell in love with him the first time I saw him laughing in the halls of Empire High. I'd loved him. Then hated him. Then loved him even more. And then hated him a ton. And now I loved him even more than I thought possible.

It reminded me of a silly game I used to play with my mom. We'd pick flowers in our backyard and then sit in the grass. We'd pick off a petal and say: "He loves me." And then pick off the next petal and say: "He loves me not." We'd say he loves me, he loves me not until all the petals were gone. And whichever saying was accompanied by the last petal was what was true.

I wondered if she'd been thinking of my father as she picked petals. Wondering what could have been.

I hadn't really been thinking of anyone at all when I'd played. I'd just been happy sitting with my mom. Because I hadn't met Matt yet. My first love. And my last love.

I no longer needed to pick a petal and leave it to chance.

Matthew Caldwell loved me.

And I loved him.

Forever this time. I was meant to be right here in his arms. At Empire High where it all began. And I'd never stop loving him. Never.

I smiled.

No.

Never.

Nunca.

WHAT'S NEXT?

How will James and Penny's daughter react to Jacob when they're at Empire High together? Spoiler Alert – she's going to think he's hot.

See it all happen in *Scarlett and the Kiss Thief*, coming soon.

While you wait, see what Matt was thinking when he first met Brooklyn back in high school.

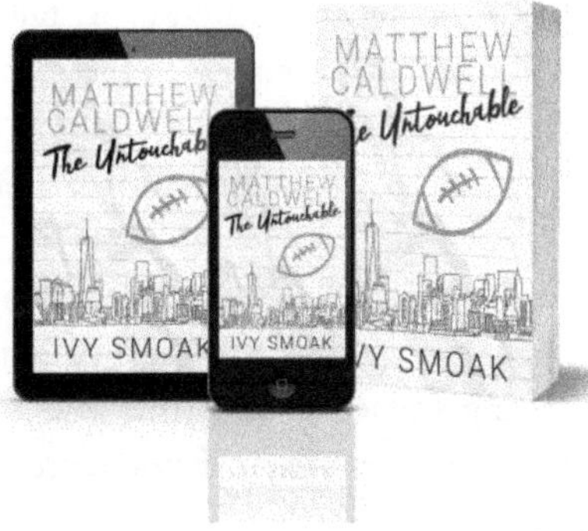

To get your free copy of Matt's point-of-view, go to:

www.ivysmoak.com/eh8-pb

A NOTE FROM IVY

The End. I can't believe this journey is over. I fell in love with these characters while writing The Hunted Series. And after writing Empire High, I love them all even more. I am so grateful to each and every one of you for understanding my heart. And for going on this crazy journey with me.

This series broke me and put me back together. I always knew how I wanted the story to end. But it was such a roller coaster getting there. Not just in the pages. But outside of them too. I debated whether to talk about this next bit. But I think it's important, even if it is hard.

When I was writing book one, I wanted to put a piece of me into this story that I hadn't shown before. I was bullied when I was younger. I wanted to show people that there is no reason to be cruel. To always choose kindness.

I had no idea that putting my heart into these pages would lead to being bullied again. And that the message was so missed by some readers. If you're reading this, I think you know and connect to Brooklyn and me. You know that there are consequences to bullying. Even if you don't see them. They can be carried around like invisible scars.

I wrote this series to release that pain. And instead? I just endured it all over again. The emails and private messages sent just to hurt my heart. The Facebook groups made to spew hate toward my books and me as a human. The posts I was tagged in to make sure I didn't miss anyone's vitriol. I heard you. I saw you. And I'm so sorry for you. Because you didn't silence me. I almost let hate and cruelty win. But that's the thing – broken hearts keep beating. As Brooklyn knows best.

And I wrote "The End" to this book as a stronger person. On the other side of Empire High I've learned to guard my heart. And to find the good even in the bad. The joy in the pain. To celebrate the readers like you who joined me on this whole journey. And to keep writing from my heart. Always.

Goodbyes are hard. I cried saying goodbye to Brooklyn and Matt. I wrote this last book slowly, because that's what my heart needed. I wanted to take my time because it would be the last time I ever wrote from their perspectives. But I know it's not really goodbye. You will see glimpses of all these characters in my new series, Scarlett. A next generation story that takes place at Empire High where it all began.

Thank you for going on this journey with me. Thank you for being a good human. And thank you for always taking a chance on the next story I write.

Ivy Smoak

Ivy Smoak
Wilmington, DE
www.ivysmoak.com

ABOUT THE AUTHOR

Ivy Smoak is the USA Today and Wall Street Journal best-selling author of *The Hunted Series*. Her books have sold over 3 million copies worldwide.

When she's not writing, you can find Ivy binge watching too many TV shows, taking long walks, playing outside, and generally refusing to act like an adult. She lives with her husband in Delaware.

TikTok: @IvySmoak
Facebook: IvySmoakAuthor
Instagram: @IvySmoakAuthor
Goodreads: IvySmoak

Recommend *Forever* for your next book club!

Book club questions available at:
www.ivysmoak.com/bookclub